FORBIDDEN DESIRE

"But it's wrong, don't you see? If we want each other so much, we should—we should be married first."

"Married?" he repeated, aghast.

She let her hands fall to her sides. "Is that so outrageous?"

He sneered at her. "Your husband is dead less than three months, and you're already proposing marriage to another man."

"I didn't propose!" she insisted. "I merely stated that if we want to bed each other so badly, we should be married. That is, after all, what's known as the act of marriage."

"My, my," he said. "I didn't know you were such a prude."

"That's not prudish! It's proper."

"Proper! For a man to marry his stepmother?"

Other Leisure books by Maureen Kurr:

NORTHWARD THE HEART
SWORD OF THE HEART

Maureen Kurr

Book Margins, Inc.

A BMI Edition

Published by special arrangement with Dorchester Publishing

Printed in the United States of America.

This is dedicated to my daughter Torie,
with affection for the friend you already are,
with pride because it's clear you're such a special person,
with gratitude for letting me work while you entertained
yourself so well, and most of all with love,
because you deserve it.

1

1705

"Damnation! What is he doing here?"

Anne Thornton scowled at the sight of her father's large figure upon the huge, black horse in the distance. Though he was still far off, she had little trouble seeing Jarvis Melbourne across the treeless expanse of rock and brier that covered the unwelcoming pathway to the Thornton seaside cottage. She turned from the sight, letting the heavy brocade drape fall back to cover the window, then turned to the other two women in the large sitting room behind her. Her scowl turned to a worried frown as her gaze fell upon her mother. Damn her father, he wasn't supposed to come here, not here to the country home that was their refuge.

"Pel, take Mother upstairs to her room."

While the dark-haired girl in servant's clothing hurried to do Anne's bidding, Anne herself took up the delicate crystal decanter filled with wine and locked it in the intricately carved cabinet on the far side of the room. She dropped the key in one of the deep pockets of her rather plain linen apron then turned around, dismayed to see her mother still seated within the room.

"Come with me, Mistress Melbourne," Pel was saying coaxingly, but the older woman simply would not budge. She stared ahead in that vacant way, as if her mind were somewhere far distant from her body. The look Jarvis Melbourne had put there through the years. The hollow look that Anne hated, pitied, and sometimes envied.

Hurrying opposite Pel, Anne bent to lift her mother

while the servant did likewise on the other side. "Come, my darling," Anne whispered, hoping the urgency she felt within wasn't revealed in her voice. "We'll all go upstairs, all right?"

Elsbeth Melbourne made no sound, no movement to show she either understood or recognized any distress in her daughter. Yet, as always, she followed Anne's wishes, letting Anne and Pel lift her from the cane chair and lead her out of the sitting room and through the hallway to the stairs.

But they'd gotten no further than halfway up when the bold knock sounded at the door.

"Should I answer it?" Pel asked, a look of pure dread on her face. It was obvious she'd guessed already who was knocking.

"Help me with Mother; I'll see what he wants once she's in her room."

Pel's relief registered immediately on her face. Anne didn't blame her. Cowardice had never been one of Anne's traits, yet there were times she wished she could ask someone else to deal with her father. Although this was definitely one of them, there was not a single male servant within calling distance. Even Anne's aged and sickly husband would have been defense enough; Anne's father knew not to stir the wrath of Selwyn Thornton—not while he still possessed the greatest wealth in their county. But even Selwyn was nowhere around; he was at the manor house, knowing the seaside cottage was a special retreat even he was not welcome to intrude upon.

It seemed an eternity before Elsbeth was safely ensconced in her room. Now seated in her favorite cushioned chair near the fireplace, Elsbeth accepted the small hoop of stitchery from Anne's outstretched hand. Then, kissing her briefly, Anne whispered in her mother's ear.

"I'll be back in a few minutes, Mother." She started to rise, then knelt once again. Was it only stubbornness that made her believe her mother knew more than it appeared? Was she irrational to deny that her beloved mother's mind had so totally snapped? Whatever the truth, she leaned closer and said, "You know who's here, I know you do, but do not worry. Pel will stay with you.''

Then Anne stood straight, paused a moment as if to fortify herself for the coming visitor, glanced once at Pel in silent entreaty to be calm for her mother's sake, then left the room.

By the time Anne approached the heavy wooden door, her father's pounding was so fierce Anne feared the small, leaded glass mounted in the door's center might shatter. After one last pause and a deep breath of air, Anne unbolted and opened the door, forcing a smile to her lips.

"What in blazes took so long!" said Jarvis Melbourne as he stepped past his daughter before she'd even had a chance to stand aside. Anne leaned hurriedly against the open door to avoid a collision. "Where's that servant, anyway? I told you long ago it was a poor idea, taking one of those Escott girls. They're all lazy, every last one of them. You should've known that from living so close to them when you were home.''

Although Anne would hardly describe her father's small manor house as a home—the kind of home Pel had had, the kind Selwyn had once hoped to provide for Anne—she did indeed remember sharing the same roof as Jarvis Melbourne. During the first sixteen years of her life, Anne had spent most of her time dreaming of escaping that house. Ultimately, she'd remained there only for her mother's sake.

Anne followed her father into the sitting room. It was a good-sized room, especially when compared to Anne's memory of the cottage Jarvis still occupied. The entire Melbourne manor house would probably fit comfortably within this country cottage, she thought. Anne watched her father take in the surroundings; she knew what he was looking at. But when she entered, he eyed her appearance and scowled anew.

"Is that any way for a countess to dress? Look at you! You look more like a village brat than the mother of the next earl of Highcrest.''

Anne squared her shoulders. She always dressed as she pleased when within these walls, liking the feel of a loose bodice and a linsey-woolsey petticoat skirt. So far, she'd had to explain herself to no one. She wished she didn't have to now.

"As you so often remind me, Father," she said with an even, controlled voice, "I am *not* a mother yet, so if I care to dress as a peasant in the privacy of this home, it is my own business."

He scoffed. "This place." He looked around again. "Why do you continue to come here? It's bloody hell to reach."

Anne said nothing as she considered the route she and her mother and Pel always traveled, the road Selwyn ordered frequently repaired. It was a far smoother pathway than the rocky one Jarvis had traveled, though not nearly so direct. He'd have noticed it himself at the base of the cliff had he been more observant.

Jarvis appeared quite observant at the moment, however, his heavy-lidded, dark eyes continuing to scan the room. "You never did know how to make a father feel welcome. Where is it?"

Trying to keep her smile firmly in place, she asked in the sweetest voice she possessed, "Where is what, Father?"

"Are you going to get me something to drink, or do I have to shout for that worthless servant of yours? Or perhaps for your mother?"

Anne hesitated only a moment longer; she knew he'd do exactly as he said, and she would not allow her mother to be disturbed—most especially by him. However, the decanter of wine she'd hidden was nearly full, and she hardly wanted to supply him with that. It would only extend his visit until the very last drop was gone. She remembered the bottle in the kitchen which Pel used for cooking. That one was nearly empty and, she noted to herself with some satisfaction, not quite the same quality as that provided for visitors who were welcome.

"I'll get something for you, Father," she said quietly, then disappeared into the kitchen.

When she reentered the sitting room, her father was looking through the drawers of the very cabinet in which she'd hidden the wine. He could not open the top section, she knew, although he was more than likely searching for a key. All he found in the lower drawers was Elsbeth's old spectacles, a volume on etiquette given to Anne by her husband, and the servant's mobcap that had come with the gown Pel now wore. The drawer squeaked shut as Jarvis pushed it back in place.

Anne held up the single glass and poured Jarvis a liberal amount of the wine. Handing it to him, she asked, "This is a fair journey from town, Father. What brings you here?"

After a long swig from the glass, Jarvis swiped at his wet mouth, apparently not noticing the poor quality of the drink he'd been given. The fact that he did not sit down was a good sign; Anne was sure he would have if she'd offered a full bottle, no matter what taste the alcohol boasted.

"I'm to meet another shipment tonight, not far from here," he said, then took another long gulp. Surprisingly, his mouth twisted in disgust after the second swallow. "Gad, it better bring finer wine than this. Selwyn surely didn't buy this wine through me."

"It's been left open on the shelf awhile," Anne admitted. "You know Mother and I never partake; we hardly care what quality Selwyn keeps out here."

"You'd think he'd have something fit to drink for visitors, at least," Jarvis complained, but he finished off the last of it nonetheless.

"We have few visitors here," she reminded him. "As you say, it is difficult to reach." Thank God Jarvis believed that. Perhaps it would keep him from visiting again. And thank God for Selwyn's generosity, for he'd given her this home. "I remember the shipments arriving much closer to home," Anne said after a moment. She knew full well her father frequently met smugglers on the channel coast, buying ill-gotten goods from France. With strife seemingly endless between the two countries, it was easy to buy such goods since the recent round of English supremacy in the latest war over the Spanish crown. The war, however, did not make her father's smuggling practices any easier to tolerate. Besides depriving their Queen and country of their lawful duties, Jarvis bought the illicit goods with money received from

Selwyn. Certainly it was true that Selwyn had no knowledge of how Jarvis spent the money issued him; those details were not part of the lucrative marriage settlement Jarvis had cleverly arranged.

"Oh, this is a new band of men I'll be working with," Jarvis said. He seemed to puff up before her eyes, and Anne recognized the prelude to her father's boasting. His chest expanded, he got somewhat taller than his medium height, and his pale blue eyes seemed to get a bit lighter. "They do twice the business the last group did, and I get first choice at their goods before they go on to London. Aye, I'll be making a fortune to match Selwyn's one day."

Anne sincerely doubted that, yet she said nothing. Perhaps Jarvis did not know the extent of Selwyn's wealth, although she suspected he knew more about the Thornton money than Anne herself since he was far more interested in it. But to make a fortune to match Selwyn's, Jarvis Melbourne would need a good deal more than stolen French wine—even Anne knew that.

"The sun will be setting soon," Anne commented, unable to keep the eagerness from her voice. "You'll be leaving for the coastline after that?"

"There's no hurry for me," he told her. "A boy will come for me when they've landed, and until then—more likely hours from now—I can relax in the comfort of my only child's country cottage. Ah, what a lucky man I am. I'll want to be taking a nap before long, but first fetch me a bit of food, and more wine."

"That was the last of it," she lied smoothly. Her father had been congenial enough so far, but that could change all too quickly if he had any more to drink.

Anne brought her father a tall glass of cool cider to accompany the meat pie, warm bread and thick onion soup which Pel had prepared for their own supper. He ate it all without saying a word, soaking up the last of the soup with a hefty chunk of bread.

At last he sat back in his chair, eyed Anne closely, belched loudly and said, "The only sane reason I can see for coming out here is confinement for mourning or birthing.

And since you're obviously not carrying . . . You're not taking after your mother's ways, are you? Given to mind fevers and the like?"

"There is nothing wrong with Mother's mind," she immediately defended her. "Nor mine."

Selwyn laughed. "Your mother is mad, everyone knows. If you didn't keep her hidden away, the villagers themselves would petition me to see her kind locked up. They say her tongue has been bewitched. And as for you, I'm beginning to wonder, the way you keep coming out here by yourself. You should be with Selwyn, wherever he chooses to be. In his bed, child, that's the only place for you until you've begotten his heir."

This was her father's favorite subject with her; such comments and questions had begun a few short months after she'd wed Sewlyn, and continued with increasing frequency. She'd been married to Selwyn for well over a year, and while she and Selwyn knew the real reason behind their lack of children, she was not about to share the truth with her father.

"God will decide," she said lightly, reaching to take away the empty tray.

But Jarvis grabbed one of her wrists, none too gently. "They're saying in the village that you're barren," he said through tight lips.

Her father's sudden change in mood didn't take Anne by surprise; he could often be subdued one moment and irate the next. It was one of the many reasons for Elsbeth's confused state. But Anne had learned long ago to expect this from him, and she knew the best course of action was to completely ignore the force her father threatened. She twisted her arm free, squelching whatever fear her mind told her she should feel.

"Perhaps I am barren," she said, her own teeth as tightly clenched as her father's.

He sat back, and for a moment he seemed to consider her words. "It certainly isn't Selwyn's fault; he got that first wife pregnant five times. Lucky for you the old bitch couldn't carry the babes full term or you'd have to share that fortune with one of them." Then he scowled again and looked at Anne accusingly. "You'd better not be witholding favors from him. There's no reason for you to be barren; you're young and hearty. Get yourself a babe if you want us to hold on to his money, or the wretched Queen will take it all once the old man is gone. For your sake, you'd better not disappoint me in this—for your sake and your mother's."

Anne said nothing. Jarvis often threatened her and her mother. But Anne had no intention of telling her father she was a virgin still, even after more than a year of marriage. Although she had no doubt he'd blame Anne for "witholding favors," it was Selwyn himself who was incapable of performing nuptial rights. Selwyn had once wanted an heir more than anything else, but now he was plagued by fear and old age. He cared enough for Anne to be afraid she, too, would go the way of his beloved Celine, who'd suffered so many times and had at last died during the pain of childbirth.

Furthermore, Selwyn was sixty-two years old, certainly not the oldest person Anne knew, but his sickliness made him seem so. She doubted any woman could be tempting enough to one of such ill health; not that she had ever tried to tempt Sewlyn with her body. She cared for him, it was true, but their relationship was more like that of father and daughter—an affectionate father and daughter, nothing like the relationship she shared with her true father.

Whether it was his rare sobriety or eagerness for the coming night's business, Jarvis Melbourne was in a congenial mood. As he stood and headed toward the cushioned settee positioned in one corner of the room, he said amiably, "You shouldn't spend so much time out here by the coast, Anne. Go back to your husband. Go back to his bed, and stay there until you're with child."

Anne stepped toward the archway leading to the kitchen. "We'll be returning to Highcrest at week's end," she said. But to herself she noted it would do little good to return to her husband's bed. She'd been there only twice in the fifteen months of her marriage, both times within the first week of their private wedding ceremony. Both times Selwyn had done little more than touch her face with aged, trembling hands, and then he had sobbed. She'd sobbed with him the second time, not for her loss but for his. He'd given up on ever having children; he knew it was impossible now. Selwyn Thornton, one of the most powerful earls in England, had but one desire all through his life: to beget an heir. But all his wealth and power had done him no good.

Anne sighed deeply. She truly wished Selwyn could have the heir he longed for, and certainly not because of the inheritance that worried her father. But she knew as well as Selwyn himself just how impossible that was.

"The row of ash trees mark the boundary to Highcrest."

Christian Montaigne made no response to the stiff-backed, richly suited old lawyer across from him in the plushly upholstered coach. He looked out the glassed window, eyeing the trees ahead without a trace of outward emotion. Soon, he realized, he would meet the lord of this impressive estate. Not just any lord, this lord was his father.

Strange, this lack of emotion, he pondered to himself. He should at least hate the man, Christian supposed. But he didn't. His mother hadn't taught him to hate the wealthy Englishman who'd gotten her pregnant then abandoned her. And it was she more than anyone else who would have had that right. So he would meet this man with the same lack of real emotion he'd felt since first learning his father's identity.

Selwyn Thornton, third earl of Highcrest, one-time king's councillor and a former member of Parliament, a man of vast wealth, influence and power. It was hard to imagine that he, Christian Montaigne, one-time thief and sometimes scoundrel could be related to such a man. He supposed if he'd been born to Selwyn's proper wife that he would be the fourth earl of Highcrest. That made him smirk; he'd only just learned of the extent of his father's title and wealth. This might take time getting used to.

The older man beside him, Mortimer Melville, sat forward in his seat, leaning on an ornate, silver-handled cane. It was plain to see he was eager to reach their destination, no doubt because of Christian. Mortimer had been the one who found Christian back in France; since then the lawyer had fed him with information of Selwyn's wealth, as if sooner or later he was bound to strike some response. But Christian remained unimpressed, and more than a little wary of exactly why Selwyn Thornton was so eager to meet him.

"This house is his lordship's favorite," said Mortimer, "but he has another manor in the north, and, of course, a town home in London. He also has a coastal cottage, although he did give that to his wife."

Christian had spared barely a thought for Selwyn's wife until hearing of her just now. He wondered about his father's wife, the woman who had kept Selwyn from marrying Christian's mother so many years ago.

"You said my father is expecting me," Christian said slowly, "but what of his wife? You've said little of her. Perhaps because she is not looking forward to meeting her husband's bastard?"

Mortimer's face changed somewhat at the mention of Selwyn's wife; he smiled ever so slightly, and though he was quite an old man, he seemed to brighten just a bit. It made Christian wonder what sort of feelings the man had harbored through the decades for Selwyn's wife.

"Countess Anne is a grand lady," he said, "and greatly affectionate of her husband. She will welcome you just as your father will."

"I've yet to meet any woman who could welcome her husband's bastard," Christian commented, once again gazing out the coach window.

Moments later, Mortimer spoke again, although not of Selwyn's wife. Christian guessed old Mortimer did not easily tolerate idle chatter of Countess Thornton, and it made him curious about the woman. No doubt she was as old as Selwyn who, he'd been told by Mortimer, was past sixty. His wife must be someone special, indeed, to have instilled such loyalty and obvious admiration from someone as stodgy as Mortimer.

"If you look ahead," Mortimer was saying, "just through the trees, you'll see the high tower. Most likely we've been spotted already and the staff has informed his lordship of our arrival."

Mortimer was proven correct. By the time Christian's small party arrived at the tall stone gate surrounding the double-winged, multistory structure, there was a neat row of servants awaiting them. Some disappeared, leading the horses and carriage away, others offered cool cider or ale after Christian and the lawyer had barely stepped from the coach. One thing was certain, Christian thought as he glanced at the wealthy surroundings, Mortimer had not exaggerated about Selwyn's wealth, or about his father wanting to make him feel welcome. Such a warm reception renewed his cautious curiosity.

Christian tried to shake away the suspicions, yet it had seemed strange from the beginning that a man of Selwyn Thornton's wealth would want to meet one of his bastard sons. What could he possibly want from Christian that he didn't already have? He couldn't believe Selwyn needed another kinsman around; most wealthy people he knew had more than their share of poor relations feeding off their fortune. Mortimer had been open enough about the extent of the Thornton wealth, the history of the family line, and the power Selwyn possessed, but he'd said suspiciously little about the old man's immediate family. He'd acknowledged that Selwyn did, indeed, have a wife, but when asked about step-siblings, Mortimer had said nothing.

Christian emptied the cup of ale, then handed it back to the waiting maid, who smiled shyly up at him. He smiled in return, out of long habit treating servants the way he had liked to be treated in his youth when he'd spent some time serving others. "It was very good," he told her in impeccable English, rather than his native tongue of French. "Thank you for bringing it to me."

His courtesy only seemed to intensify the maid's shyness; she blushed and curtsied, and ran off to disappear behind the wide door of the manor house, almost losing the small mobcap atop her head.

The manor boasted formidable wealth, although it was built of stone rather than the more fashionable red brick. It seemed that each stone had been chosen not only for its size and strength, but also its hue, for there was a pinkish brown tint to the surface that suggested a hint of some mineral with which Christian was not familiar. It almost glistened in the daylight, like the sunstone he'd carried about as a child. Each window was filled with clear glass, except the one above the arch-shaped doorway. That one was splashed with color which, he noticed as he followed Mortimer inside the huge home, shed a rainbow of sunlit color upon the spacious inner hallway.

To one side of the hall was a high archway opened to a spacious parlor. With one glance, he sensed the opulence of this room, seeing the brocade settees, ebony chairs, lacquered tables and Venetian mirror overmantel.

On the opposite side of the parlor were three doors, arch-shaped like the door leading outside, but somewhat smaller in size. They seemed dwarfed by the height of the hallway, although even Christian, who was quite tall, would not have to stoop to pass through as he often did elsewhere.

Mortimer led Christian to the wide oak staircase at the back of the huge entrance hall. The fact that this all belonged to his father should have at least impressed Christian, as Mortimer had hoped; Christian had been in few French homes that could match this wealth. But he preferred to keep even that emotion in check; he was suspicious by nature and wanted to know exactly why his father had sought him out thirty-one years after he'd been born. Once he had answers to some questions like that, he would be free to react. For now, he was still curious over what sort of man his father was, and why he'd run out on Christian's mother if he knew she was to have his child. Thornton must have known, although his mother had sworn that his father had never acknowledged Christian as his. Until now—and again, he asked himself why.

At last Mortimer stopped; they stood before a closed door at the end of the open upper hall. Mortimer whispered when he spoke.

"His lordship resides here," Mortimer announced softly. "I am certain he's been told of your arrival, although he would no doubt wait patiently if you wish to freshen yourself before meeting him for the first time." For much of the journey from the coast, Christian had preferred riding his own horse rather than sitting within the confines of the coach and enduring its bumpy ride over rutted roads. Once on Highcrest ground, however, the condition of the roads had vastly improved and so when Mortimer had invited Christian to rejoin him in the coach, Christian had agreed, despite the fact Mortimer had used the opportunity to continue filling Christian's ear with further accomplishments and qualitites of Selwyn Thornton.

Christian grinned crookedly. "I may smell more like a horse than a man, but I'm sure he'll be able to tell the difference, unless his eyesight is gone. Lead on, Mortimer."

Mortimer had little opportunity to do as he was bid. Barely a moment later the polished wooden door opened noiselessly, and before them stood a tall man, gray-haired and a trifle pale, leaning on a silver and gold laden cane.

"My nose may not be as keen as it once was, but I still hear well enough through these thick walls. And I certainly see well enough to tell the difference between a horse and a man." He spoke somewhat roughly for one leaning so heavily on a cane, but in the next instant he smiled, staring straight at Christian. For a moment Christian would have sworn he saw a tear glisten in the old man's eye. "Most especially when that man is my son."

Selwyn Thornton held out a thick-veined whitish hand, and Christian accepted the clasp without hesitation. He'd expected his father to be weaker than this, from what Mortimer had said, although he did look every bit as ancient as Mortimer's description. But though his hand in Christian's was firm, he might have swayed just a bit as he leaned from his cane toward Christian. When he stood tall again, he placed both hands on the cane, then stepped aside to let Christian enter.

The sitting room was not what Christian would have expected for one so old. It looked as if the room had just been decorated, for the gold brocade cushions were still stiff, the green velvet draperies unfaded, the Italian carpet without wear. Perhaps the manor furnishings were periodically up-dated; certainly the Thornton wealth could afford such an indulgence.

Selwyn Thornton took a seat with obvious relief. Christian saw immediately that the man was weaker than he first thought, weaker perhaps than Selwyn wished to reveal. He breathed heavily, for just the simple exertion of moving from one end of the room to the other had sent what little color he'd possessed seeping from his face. Christian couldn't help but stare, searching for something familiar in him, some visible sign that he was bound by blood. And Selwyn, through his labored breathing, did the same. It seemed a long moment before anyone spoke.

"Mortimer," Selwyn said without taking his eyes from Christian, "you've done well. But for now, leave me with my son."

"Yes, my lord," Mortimer said, adding as he left, "I'm glad you're pleased."

"My son," Selwyn said, once they were alone. He seemed to savor the phrase. Never once had his gaze broken from Christian's. "You are my son, there is no doubt of that."

Christian took a seat opposite Selwyn. They sat before the huge fireplace, which spewed forth a great warmth despite the fact it was a comfortable May day. Christian fingered the amulet resting upon his chest.

"By this?" he asked, holding it up.

Selwyn's gaze left Christian's face for the first time. He laughed, though it sounded somewhat like a cough. "Hardly, although I do remember it. Your mother took it from me."

"She said you gave it to her. I guess you must have thought it fair payment for what you took from her."

"I hear scorn in your voice, my son, where there should be none. What your mother and I shared was a mutual pleasure—nothing more, nothing less."

Christian masked his emotions. Coolly, he said, "Perhaps, if we are to get on at all for my visit here, we should avoid talk of my mother for the present."

"As you wish," Selwyn said with a wave of one thin hand. "But please let me say one thing, that I am sorry she is gone."

"It was a long time ago."

"So I've been told. And you've been left to your own fortitude since you were ten—ten years old and without a sou to your name. Look at you now. You've captained one of the finest French ships—the only captain to outmaneuver England's navy. And you've been accepted by the finest families in your country."

"I've also been a thief," Christian added.

Selwyn only grinned. "I was told of that, too, and of your stay in prison when you were a boy. You can hardly be blamed for that. You did what you had to in order to survive."

"It seems you know all about me," Christian said. "But I know little about you—at least about why you've sought me out."

"I've been looking for you for nearly seven years."

Christian's brows rose. Mortimer hadn't told him that. It would have been difficult for Selwyn's men to find him in those seven years. With the war between their countries, he could imagine just how difficult it must have been for Selwyn's emissaries to continue their search. But that Selwyn would have been so persistent to find him under such circumstances was certainly unexpected news.

"Ah, so you do show emotion from time to time," Selwyn said, still watching Christian carefully. "You are surprised it's been so long?"

"I've said I do not wish to speak of my mother, yet I must after all. She told me long ago who my father was, but also that when she sent word to you of my existence, you scorned her by saying her child must be someone else's. If you would not acknowledge me then, why do you do so now?"

The many lines on Selwyn's face deepened into a frown. "I have lived to regret much in my life," he admitted, "and that is among my greatest regrets. The lawyers and my family convinced me all those years ago that should I recognize one bastard, every woman I'd ever . . . shall we say, enjoyed . . . would come to my doorstep with a child in tow and demand payment. I believed you were mine, even then, but they convinced me to have doubts. And then I met my wife, and marriage to her made me forget any love that went before.''

"That explains why you ignored me then; it does not explain why you've searched for me in these past years. Your lawyer answered none of my questions regarding this.''

Selwyn sighed deeply. "I wanted to meet you first, to know what sort of man you've grown to be. It is very important, considering what I intend to do. But I know already; I knew the moment I saw you. You've grown to be a fine honorable man.''

"Others I know might disagree with you," Christian said, barely loud enough for his father to hear.

A long moment went by as Selwyn gazed once again at Christian's face, as if fascinated by some vision of his past. Christian himself saw little resemblance, although he did admit Selwyn's pallor and age might have erased any likeness to himself. But he did not need physical proof that Selwyn was his father; his mother had told him long ago that this man was his sire.

He waited, and at last Selwyn spoke again.

"I have sought you out for many reasons, my son," Selwyn began. "It is my shame I did not recognize you when you were born, and ease your life as I should have. Yours and your mother's. I hope to make up for that now.''

Christian stiffened. "I have little need—or desire—to have you make up for past mistakes. My mother is gone, and it was she who deserved your help. I neither need it nor want it.''

Selwyn smiled, a sort of pleased, satisfied little smile. "Look around you, my son. See all that I have. Would you turn all of this away?''

"Is this a test of my nature, Lord Selwyn, even though you claimed to know me so well already? Perhaps to see if greed is one of my qualities?''

Selwyn gave another throaty laugh. "Not a test of your nature. Of that I think I know." A smile still lingered on his mouth, erasing some of the agedness from his face. "Can it be you haven't guessed why I've searched for you?" He held up a hand, referring to their surroundings. "This will all be yours one day—soon, I suspect. Every last shilling, every last piece of furniture. And that, my son, is a responsibility one does not pass on lightly.''

2

Anne pushed back the voluminous hood of her royal blue cloak. The day had turned out to be warm, after all, despite yesterday's cooling rain. She rode her favorite mare, a fine black filly who possessed more spirit than most female riders could handle, forced as women were by the confining skirts of traditional riding habits to sit sidesaddle. Nearby, Pel rode a mare Anne had given her soon after sending for her from the village to be her lady's maid. Between them rode Elsbeth. They often used one of Selwyn's carriages back and forth from the cottage, but with the spring weather so fine Anne had suggested they ride, sure as she was the fresh air and exercise would do her mother good. Elsbeth was silent as ever, but she rode the horse fairly well, and her cheeks were pink and her eyes sparkled blue. She looked rather pretty, Anne thought as she glanced her mother's way, and that made Anne smile. Her mother enjoyed little in life, and even though they had Selwyn to take care of them both, it sometimes seemed too late for her mother's good. But on days like today, Anne felt familiar gratitude swell in her heart for her generous husband.

"It'll be good to be back," Pel said, looking past the two grooms leading the way, seeing the high tower of Highcrest peeking through the trees upon the hill.

Anne laughed. "You didn't finish the statement, Penelope Escott," she teased. "You'll be glad to be back to see Gregory."

Pel's flushed cheeks and pleased smile admitted the

truth. Gregory Harlan, a Highcrest gatekeeper, would no doubt be just as happy to see Pel as she would be to see him, considering they were to be wed soon.

"I know I've said this so many times, Anne," Pel said, calling her by name rather than the "milady" and "madame" she used before others, "but I'm so grateful—"

Anne shook her head, cutting her off. "It's not my generosity, it's Selwyn's."

Pel shrugged, obviously unconvinced. "He's an upright gentleman, and kind, but he's no fit husband for you, that's for certain."

"Now, Pel—"

But Pel continued without pause. She still looked ahead rather than toward Anne, although a light of anger had settled in her eyes. "When I think of that father of yours, selling you into marriage to a man three times your age, it still sets my neck hairs on end."

"But look how nicely it worked out. I'm happy, Pel."

Pel snorted. "If you had any idea of what happiness really is, Countess Anne Thornton, you'd not be saying that now. Gregory might not be the richest man, nor the most handsome even, but he loves me the way I love him, the way you couldn't ever love that kindly old man up there." She pointed toward the stately manor house nestled on the hill ahead. "And, since you already know it, the way he loved his first wife—that's the way real love is. She may be dead these ten long years, but he loves her still."

Anne nodded, neither hurt nor angered by the truth. "I wouldn't want Selwyn to love me the way he loved Celine, Pel. You know that. I'm glad—relieved—he found he could only love me like a daughter."

"Lucky for you, or you'd have been in his bed every night this past year you've been wed to him, the way he's been praying for an heir."

"Hush, Pel!" Anne warned, glancing around. Only a few paces ahead were the pair of footmen who had acted as escorts from the seaside cottage. "Do you want that knowledge to get back to my father?"

"I doubt they'd betray you to *him*," Pel said, though

she lowered her voice to a whisper nonetheless. "Your father isn't very popular around here."

"Perhaps not personally," Anne agreed, "but with that allowance Selwyn gives him, he has money at his disposal, and that has often enough been reason for some people to go along with my father's wishes. Look how the village men sell those smuggled goods for him. He pays them to do it, so they hardly care what they're doing is illegal."

"I still don't understand why it's so important to your father that you share his lordship's bed," Pel complained. "He has enough money to keep him in his favorite wine the rest of his days, thanks to Selwyn. And I know he's not concerned over *your* welfare and future."

"Pel, why talk about this now? It hardly matters." She didn't want to admit the truth, that her father only wanted an heir out of Anne so he, through this heir, could be assured to control the entire Thornton fortune once Selwyn died. And considering how sick Selwyn had been, especially in the past year or so, his final rest was not too far in the future. Pel didn't realize that if there was no heir, no child for Selwyn to name as his benefactor, that the majority of the Thornton fortune would return to the Queen of England. And Jarvis Melbourne would once again be the improverished squire he'd been before that fateful day a year and a half ago when he'd first noticed the interest Selwyn had paid toward Anne.

Pel sighed. "You're right, of course. There's no sense talking about your father. It's just that ever since I found my Gregory, I ache for your loss."

"You needn't," Anne said, somewhat flippantly. She hated it when Pel talked this way. It was much easier to ignore the whole subject, even to herself. "I'll hardly miss what I've never had."

"But that's it, Anne! If only you knew—"

"Pel," Anne said her name with growing impatience, "do you really think that my father would have allowed me to wed whomever I pleased? Do you think it would have mattered if I'd been in love with someone, the way you love Gregory? Do you think that would have stopped him from selling me into marriage with Selwyn?"

Dejected, Pel shook her head, and there was a long moment of silence. Elsbeth Melbourne continued to stare ahead, as if the exchange between the two young women hadn't even taken place.

Anne, seeing her friend's unhappiness and knowing it was there only out of concern for her, spoke at last. "I know you want me to be happy, Pel. But some things are better not discussed."

Pel nodded, though the frown stayed with her, and Anne wished she could have said more. But she knew there was nothing else to say. There were times when she saw Pel with Gregory that she felt a stab of envy over the love they so obviously shared. Should she admit that to Pel? For what purpose? Anne knew Pel wanted her to have that sort of love in her life, but it was impossible. Anne had accepted that on the day her father coerced her into a loveless marriage; Pel should have accepted it long ago as well.

From his opened window, Christian Montaigne heard the clap of hooves on the brick pavement below and hurriedly slipped the white lawn shirt over his head. It was past midmorning, when normally half the day was gone for him, and he hadn't even had his morning ride. But he'd been up until near dawn with Mortimer, acquainting himself with the more intricate details of his father's businesses and estates. It was something Selwyn had wanted Christian to do from the first day more than a week ago when he'd arrived at Highcrest, but Christian had put it off, opting instead to get to know Selwyn himself first. And Selwyn had willingly obliged.

He went to the window, fastening the many buttons of his waistcoat. His father had told him that his wife would be returning today. The ladies had been expected yesterday, but the rain had obviously put them off. Christian was curious about meeting the woman Selwyn spoke of with such fondness. He'd learned his present wife was not the woman who had taken Selwyn's attentions from Christian's mother; Selwyn's first wife, Celine, had died several years ago. So the woman he would meet today was Selwyn's second wife, and everyone from Selwyn down to the lowest servant spoke of her with affection. Though Christian was eager to meet her, he doubted, no matter how kind-hearted the old woman was, that she would welcome her husband's bastard with open arms.

From his window he saw several riders passing through the courtyard gate. His gaze quickly scanned the footmen and a servant or two, and came to rest on the only woman who could possibly be Selwyn's wife.

Christian found her pretty, as he might have guessed from Mortimer's references to her. She sat astride a gentle chestnut horse, dressed in a light beige, linen cloak. Her hair was streaked with gray, her figure slight. It was hard to tell from the second floor distance, but something in her manner made Christian want to stare. The woman gazed ahead, almost as if her eyes were sightless. No one had mentioned any disability, so he quickly discounted such a notion. Perhaps someone had warned her of his coming, and her thoughts rested on something unpleasant. For that's what it appeared to him, as if she were troubled.

A younger woman helped her to alight, one Christian barely noticed at first, thinking her a lady's maid. But the cloak she wore was of indisputable quality, given the deep richness of its royal blue color. He could see her clearly, for her hood was pulled back and she wore no hat or powdered wig as many women did when wearing a riding habit. A light breeze blew her long, honey-blond hair from her face. She was truly a lovely creature, her skin smooth and fair, her cheeks rosened by the fresh air, and her lips smiling affectionately at the older woman, revealing even white teeth. Her eyes captivated him even from this distance. He could not tell the color, though he guessed they were light, but they were wide and honest—too large to hide the thoughts and feelings of her inner soul.

He scoffed at himself; what strange thoughts to have toward an unknown girl. Nonetheless, he finished dressing all the more quickly and headed below stairs, eagerly anticipating an introduction to the young woman.

Selwyn must have been forewarned of his wife's

approach, for he was dressed splendidly in a brocade coat, and waistcoat and breeches of matching damask. He looked far healthier than he had the entire week Christian had been with him, for although he still stood with the aid of a cane, his shoulders seemed straighter and his color a bit deeper, in contrast to the white cravat tied expertly at his throat. He stood just inside the open door of the large, marble-floored entranceway, and when he chanced to see Christian descending the stairs, he smiled broadly and waved his hand Christian to approach. Waites, Selwyn's personal servant, disappeared once Christian came to Selwyn's side.

"Come, my son, and meet my wife. Of her I'm sure you'll approve."

Three women soon passed through the doorway, one of which was the girl who had so intrigued Christian from upstairs. She was holding the arm of the older woman, and together they approached Selwyn. The eyes he'd guessed to be light were in fact a fair blue, the clearest blue Christian had ever seen, and just as large and guileless as he'd imagined even from a distance. Just now, as her gaze traveled from Selwyn to Christian himself, her eyes first held surprise then curiosity, and finally, he thought with some confidence, interest.

He smiled, for the briefest moment holding steady her gaze. Could she guess he thought her truly exquisite? It seemed in that moment he could hide nothing from her, he who was so good at hiding his thoughts.

It was she who broke the gaze, though not before smiling in return. A shy smile, he thought, or an uncertain one. An inexperienced demoiselle to be sure.

She kissed Selwyn's cheek affectionately, and Christian immediately guessed she must be a stepchild. Perhaps Countess Anne's child by a former marriage?

When she spoke, her voice sounded as sweet as Christian expected—smooth and confident, despite the demure smile of a moment ago. After the brief greeting to Selwyn, she spoke to the servant who lingered nearby.

"Pel, take Mother upstairs where she'll be more comfortable."

The servant immediately obeyed, and the older woman was led away, it appeared, never having noticed Christian's presence.

Selwyn spoke up. "There is someone very important whom I would like you to meet, and to know," Selwyn said to the young woman, lightly holding her arm.

Christian thought it a bit unusual that the older woman was being led away without a word, but since he was most eager to meet the young woman his father was about to introduce, he said nothing.

"This is Anne, my wife," was Selwyn's extraordinary announcement. "Anne, this is Christian Montaigne. Soon to be known by his rightful name, Christian Thornton. My son."

It appeared the introduction was as astonishing to the young woman as it was to Christian himself, for her wide, unfeigning eyes held the same amazement Christian was sure his own face revealed. He had no wits about him for the barest second; he wanted it all to be a mistake. But there was his father, with every right to place his arm about the young woman's shoulders as he was doing. His wife's shoulders. Good God, he'd been expecting to meet a stepmother, not some enchanting *jeune fille* who could easily haunt even his purest thought.

Ever polite, ever reserved, Christian recovered himself, he hoped, without too much embarrassment. He accepted Anne's outstretched hand and briefly kissed its top, unable to help welcoming the pleasant fragrance of lavender.

"You are shocked," Selwyn said to his wife, then frowned. "I should have sent word ahead to the cottage to warn you of Christian's arrival." Then he breathed deeply, obviously too pleased to dwell on his own lack of foresight. "But he is here, Anne! At last!"

Anne barely heard Selwyn's words, though she did sense his happiness. Her gaze, instead, continued to rest on the handsome young man before her. When she'd first passed through the doorway, she'd seen him immediately. Unwittingly, her pulse had raced before she'd even wondered who he was. He was tall, taller than Selwyn, and much

broader of shoulder. His waist was slim, his muscular legs
clearly outlined by the dark hose revealed beneath the close
fitting knee breeches. Strength exuded from him. But it was
his eyes which captured her attention, from the first moment
her gaze met his. Not so much their darkness but rather their
intensity, as if he was seeing her not for the first time. His
features were irrefutably handsome, his narrow nose, somewhat high cheekbones, wide, intelligent forehead, sensuous
mouth all surrounded those vivid eyes, eyes she could stare
into, mesmerized, as the rest of the world passed by unnoticed.

But the rest of the world demanded notice. Remembering Selwyn at her side, she rid her mind of the sudden and
almost overwhelming attraction this man brooked. Her
husband's son! She was silent after the introduction, for she
did not trust her voice. A moment ago the young man had
kissed her hand and she'd felt his lips, warm and smooth,
and was unable to stop herself from wondering what it would
be like to have those lips pressed to her mouth instead.
Belatedly, she chastised herself for such thoughts. She was,
after all, a married woman.

She turned a curious gaze to Selwyn, banishing the
memory of Christian's polite kiss from her mind.

"It's taken a moment to register, Selwyn." Then she
smiled. "It is extraordinary news."

Selwyn nodded his agreement. Anne knew that if it
wasn't for his ill health, her husband would be dancing like a
small boy who'd just discovered some treasure. When he
looked at his son, she could see strong emotion in his eyes.
"Mortimer is upstairs, still asleep," Selwyn said. "He and
Christian were up all night going through the books and so
forth. But come," he said, taking a step forward and heading
toward one of the arched doors to the right of the entryway.
"You must get acquainted with Christian before we talk of
all that. I am anxious for you to know him."

The room they entered was small, known as the
solicitor's salon, and normally used for business conducted
with Mortimer and other lawyers or Queen's officials. It was
not used often, as it had been years since Selwyn was an active

member of Parliament. Anne came there often because it was an intimate room lined with books, and she'd passed many hours sitting on one of the deeply cushioned settees, reading. The room was small only by comparison to the rest of the house, but necessarily so. Because of the business which had once been conducted there, there were no windows, no exit but for the single one off the hall, and a fireplace purposely made too small to hide anyone in its narrow chimney. The furniture was comfortable: plush, brocade-covered chairs, a long settee before the unlit fireplace, and a large, walnut writing cabinet against one wall, upon which sat several candles and a stack of books Anne had recently set aside to read. At the center of the outer wall was a huge desk, but it hadn't been used, she knew, since she'd come to live there. Lit by a crystal chandelier hanging above, the room was warm and inviting.

Selwyn was seated first. He leaned back, his breathing labored, and after a moment he rested his cane on the floor, obviously intent upon a lengthy visit between himself, his wife, and his son.

Anne was hesitant to sit, although she realized Christian must be waiting until she did so before taking a seat of his own. She took a chair near Selwyn, leaving the only vacancy farthest from her. Once he was seated, she took a moment to study him. She was struck again by his handsomeness. Was there a likeness between him and Selwyn? She thought not. But Selwyn obviously believed the lawyers had produced his heir. For Selwyn's sake, she hoped it was true. Yet something in her husband's words disturbed her. This long lost son had been going through Selwyn's books—perhaps anxious to learn about his inheritance?

Anne's gaze cooled as she submerged the wayward thoughts her silly mind had concocted. She wanted to be happy for Selwyn, for he'd found his heir, the heir that filled all his prayers. But she was cautious first.

"When did you arrive, *monsieur*?" she asked.

"Christian arrived last week," Selwyn announced. "Thanks be to God, Mortimer had more foresight than I've shown to you and sent word ahead. Otherwise, the shock of seeing Christian for the first time might well have been too much for me."

"You are French born then?" Anne asked Christian, hoping Selwyn would allow Christian to speak for himself. Obviously he understood English, but she wanted to hear his voice. A lot could be learned through a man's voice, she thought to herself. And it was for Selwyn's sake, of course, that she wished to know this man.

Christian nodded. "I was born in the county of Brittany." His answer was brief, but his voice was rich and unhesitating, his English without accent. His steady gaze lingered on Anne.

"Christian has done well for himself, despite having had precious few material advantages," Selwyn added. "Being a bastard could not have been easy, but now that I've found him, that has changed."

Anne tore her gaze from Christian's as her husband's words began to take meaning. "You will recognize him legally, then, to end his bastardship?"

"I've done so already," Selwyn said easily. He laughed. "There are many benefits of being a Thornton, one of them having my legal cases attended immediately. The papers have already been submitted to the House of Lords. So far as the law goes, Christian is a bastard no longer."

"I am happy for you then," she said quietly, letting her gaze return to Christian's. "For both of you."

Selwyn reached to pat her hand. "Now I know I've shocked you." He turned to Christian and said, "She is never so meek. Not that she wouldn't welcome you; Anne knows how long I've searched for you."

"It may not be the shock of my presence after all, Selwyn," Christian answered. His strong, deep voice matched the rest of him, and Anne found it exceedingly—annoyingly—pleasant. "Countess Anne has just returned from a journey. And though I don't know how far she's come, it may be fatigue, not shock, which makes her wish to put off cordial conversation with me."

"Of course," Selwyn said. "It seems I've been nothing but insensitive today regarding my wife. I'd hoped you could get to know each other, but I should have realized Anne would like time to rest.''

Selwyn was looking at Anne, who was having difficulty keeping her gaze from studying Christian. Was he truly sensitive to her—for she was indeed tired—or did he sense already that she was more cautious than her husband? Perhaps her suspicions made him uncomfortable? But even as she thought this, she discounted the notion. If anyone in this room was uncomfortable, it was herself. And for the silliest of reasons: she found Christian Montaigne over-whelmingly attractive. She must truly be fatigued, as normally she wasn't given to such infatuation. She'd thoroughly resigned herself to her marriage long ago.

She stood. ''I am, indeed, tired after the journey from the cottage,'' she said, smiling down at her husband. ''In fact, I shall retire for the evening and get to know your son better tomorrow, when I am refreshed. If,'' she added with the quickest glance toward Christian, ''that would be acceptable?''

Christian stood, although Selwyn remained seated, for it was too difficult for him to stand. Anne kissed Selwyn briefly upon his cheek, then bid good-eve to Christian.

He smiled disarmingly. ''I look forward to tomorrow, Countess,'' he said, and kissed her hand as politely as he had just minutes ago when first meeting her.

She withdrew her hand a bit more quickly than she had before. How ridiculously she was behaving! Why should a kiss, one so polite, send her nerves atwitter? Heavens, her mind must be weary, indeed. Tomorrow, she was sure, once she'd rested, she could put every emotion in its proper place and welcome Christian the way Selwyn had hoped she would.

She excused herself without another glance Christian's way.

Upstairs, Anne peeled off her riding habit. It was well past midafternoon, and it had long been Anne's habit to have the last meal of the day served to her alone in her room. She was sure Selwyn expected nothing different tonight, especially since she'd told him she was retiring for the night. So she slipped into a pale blue gown. It was loose and com-

fortable, and felt good after the heavy velvet suit she'd worn
all day. She sat before the warm fireplace, staring into the
orange flames. But instead of the dancing lights, she saw a
pair of dark eyes belonging to Christian Montaigne.
Christian Thornton.

She knew nothing about him, of course, except the
obvious. He was handsome and young, more than likely the
right age to be the missing bastard Selwyn had been searching
for so long. But something tugged at her mind, not so much a
warning as the same caution she'd felt when learning he'd
been studying Selwyn's books all night.

Selwyn was so eager to find an heir; it was his last
dream, his only dream. And since she trusted Mortimer
almost as much as Selwyn trusted him, there should be no
reason to doubt Christian Montaigne's identity.

Nonetheless, Anne couldn't help thinking that Selwyn
was too eager to accept him. It wasn't the Thornton wealth
or the title she felt so protective of. It was Selwyn himself.
What if he should find out Christian was some sort of
imposter, conveniently revealed after years of searching had
made Selwyn desperate—desperate enough to accept
someone with little evidence of kinship? She knew one thing:
if Christian was an imposter, and Selwyn found out, it would
surely kill him. He could not withstand such a loss.

The idea came suddenly, uninvited. But once it took
shape in her mind it became quite appealing. Perhaps it was
true that Anne didn't love Selwyn the way a woman should
love a husband, the way Pel loved her Gregory, but Anne did
honor Selwyn; she had much to be grateful to him for. And
she would not stand by and allow him a fatal disillusionment
if, indeed, he was headed that way.

How vulnerable he was, she thought. In Selwyn's
desperation to find an heir, he'd foregone investigation of
Christian's past. Mortimer's word was enough for Selwyn,
but the family solicitor was old and perhaps easily deceived in
this matter. He was almost as desperate to provide Selwyn
with an heir as Selwyn himself, simply out of pure love for
the man.

Besides, what harm could it do to have Christian's past

checked into by another lawyer? Someone who would not be so eager to believe Christian's story simply because of how deeply Selwyn wished to find his son. Selwyn need never know, not even, she conceded, if Christian did turn out to be an imposter. She truly did fear for her husband's health, should he learn Christian was not who he said he was. But if she were to discover a fraud, she could protect Selwyn—and his legacy.

She frowned. Mortimer would undoubtedly be quite rebuffed by the fact that she was double-checking his find. And he was a dear. But, blazes! He was too dear to this family, too dear to Selwyn. He knew how ill Selwyn had been, he had undoubtedly guessed Selwyn would not live much longer. Was he less scrutinizing in his search, purely out of the desire to see Selwyn's last wish fulfilled before it was too late?

The Thornton name and fortune was well-known, both in England and in France, Anne knew that. And the search for the lost heir was no secret. She herself had seen Mortimer escort a stranger out of his town offices—a man who claimed to be the bastard lost in France so many years ago. Couldn't Christian Montaigne be an imposter, as well?

But a persistent thought came to mind in between the dour cautions. Though she'd met Christian so briefly, Anne found it difficult to think of him as a fortune hunter. There was something about him that charmed her, something forthright and honest.

But how could she know any better than Selwyn, who was taking Mortimer's word for it?

Despite a certain amount of reluctance, her decision was made. Tomorrow, she decided, she and Pel would go into Wynchly. The lawyer she knew of was young and not as experienced as Mortimer, but he was free of the fierce loyalty that would mar his ability to see the truth.

Just then there was a tap at the door and, thinking it was her supper, Anne called for the servant to wait. Hurriedly she put on a heavy blue velvet wrapper, fastening it modestly to the throat. Then she opened the door.

Surprisingly, Selwyn stood there.

"May I speak with you?"

"Of course," she said, standing aside to let him enter. She closed the door behind him.

He eased himself into the seat she had just vacated, and she took the one opposite him. She noted his coloring, the best it had been for many months, and the renewed vigor, such as it was for someone so ill. And she once again had doubts about her plan for the morrow. Perhaps, even if it was a masquerade, it would be better for no one to know. Not even herself. She had never seen Selwyn happier.

"There are things I must tell you, Anne, so that as you get to know Christian, there will be no surprises."

"He seems . . . an upright gentleman."

"Oh, of that I'm certain," Selwyn said. "But do you realize that since I have made him my heir, he will be the next earl of Highcrest?"

Anne smiled, her eyes holding his and wanting desperately to banish whatever fears he might have had that this would upset her in any way. "Yes, Selwyn. And I am most happy for you, that your name and title will live on."

Still, Selwyn seemed unsure. "But do you see that the bulk of the Thornton inheritance—yea, this very house—will be his when I am gone?"

Anne did not lose her smile. "Do you remember when we were first married, you told me of the search Mortimer and your other lawyers were conducting? On our wedding day you said that you had ended their search, because of the hopes you had for me to produce an heir for you. No—" She held up a hand to still his protest. "I am not sorry, I hold no bitterness that we've had no chance for me to give you the heir you wanted. I told you that when Mortimer resumed the search a month after our wedding, and I mean it to this day. I want you to have your true son, your true heir. I have been no wife to you, Selwyn, but I have been your friend. I wouldn't be that if I harbored jealousy toward your true heir."

Selwyn stood, and so did Anne. Gently, he took her hand in his. "You have been a good wife, Anne. And a friend. I thank you for that."

He started to turn away, but halted. "You know that you will always be cared for, even after I am gone. Though Christian will hold the majority of my legacy, I have given you the seaside cottage, and no one can take it from you. And you will always be welcome in Highcrest, I will make assurances of that. As for your allowance, that will continue for the rest of your life. You need not fear for your future, my dear, yours or your mother's."

Soon after Selwyn left, Anne decided to visit her mother. The older woman's chambers were situated at the rear of the house, where the noises of the servants and household did not disturb her. There was an adjoining room in which her lady's maid always slept, but other than that this wing of the house was deserted. As Anne made her way past all the empty bedchambers, she imagined what Highcrest would have been like had Selwyn filled all the rooms with children, as she knew he'd hoped when he was a young man. During his years of marriage with Celine, Highcrest had been a happy place. Anne had visited once or twice when her father delivered his ill-gotten wine. But she'd been very young then, just a child of six or seven. Highcrest Manor had been new then, for Selwyn had built the estate for his Celine and their future. By the time Anne had returned, years after Celine's death, Highcrest had turned into the empty, lonely place it was today.

The servants had welcomed Anne as the new countess. They had brightened Highcrest with zealous cleaning and were eager to carry out her refurbishing ideas. Selwyn himself had insisted Anne redecorate the estate as she wished. But despite Anne's efforts to make the environment more cheerful, Highcrest remained the lonely home it had been on the day she moved in.

Her mother was eating supper when Anne entered. The older woman did not smile when her daughter approached, but she squeezed Anne's hand when she sat nearby.

And slowly, as if more for herself than for her mother, Anne told Elsbeth each and every thought she had. She started with the conflicting emotions regarding Christian Montaigne.

3

Anne stepped out of the carriage before either of the two footmen rushing toward her had the chance to help. She simply smiled at them and motioned behind her toward Pel, who welcomed their assistance.

"I won't need you till midday meal, Pel, if you'd like to see Gregory."

Pel's eyes sparkled at the idea. "If you're sure—"

"Of course I am," Anne insisted. "You could have spent the morning with him if Selwyn didn't object to my going to the village alone. This morning's visit to Wynchly took longer than I expected, and now you deserve some time to do as you please."

Pel was gone without further persuasion, so Anne headed toward the manor house. Her thoughts still raced, the visit to the lawyer's office fresh in her mind. She hoped she had made the right decision in hiring a solicitor to check Christian Montaigne's story, although in her heart she knew she acted only out of concern for Selwyn. But should he find out or, for that matter, if Christian himself should find out . . .

Just then, as if she had conjured him up merely by thinking of him, Anne saw him through the tall archway of the parlor. He stood before the unlit fireplace, as if deep in thought. One lean, long-fingered hand pressed the oak mantel, supporting much of his weight. Anne paused to look at him, not even unfastening the clasp of her cloak. He wore a green camlet coat over forest green cloth breeches and white hose, and high buckled shoes. The coat fit perfectly, smoothly following the wide line of his shoulders and tapering inward toward his slim waist. He wore no wig as Selwyn and most others did; he did not even powder his hair. But she found his natural hair appealing, thick and dark and long enough to be tied in a queue at the back of his neck by a black ribbon.

Just then he turned, perhaps sensing rather than hearing her presence. For the barest moment, still lost in admiring him, Anne said nothing, nor did she move. Strangely enough, when Christian saw her, he, too, was silent. Then, awkwardly, she stepped into the room and freed the clasp of her cloak.

"I was startled at seeing you here," she explained, adding, "that is, startled at seeing anyone in here. The parlor is little used these days."

He stepped forward and helped her from her cloak as if he'd spent some time as a valet—or even a lady's servant. His touch was so sure and gentle.

Christian spoke as he slipped the cloak off her shoulders. "I noticed Selwyn has yet to step foot within this room since I've come. Have I unwittingly treaded into a forbidden place?"

She shook her head, taking the outer garment and folding it over her arm. "No, Selwyn does not inhibit others from using this room, although he avoids it himself. There are many memories in this room, I fear, too painful for him to easily relive."

"I am surprised those memories haven't dulled through the years, most especially after having wed someone as lovely as you."

Anne glanced at him, wondering if he'd noticed—so soon—that the marriage she shared with Selwyn was not born of the same love other marriages were. "Selwyn and Celine enjoyed a long, loving marriage, although it was marred by unhappiness."

"Celine's inability to carry a healthy babe," Christian commented. "In that, she was much like your Queen."

Anne nodded. England's Queen Anne had carried and

lost no less than sixteen children, and the child who'd survived beyond birth did so most precariously, dying at the young age of eleven. Indeed, it seemed most difficult to carry a healthy babe.

"Do you enjoy living here?" he asked after a moment. They were sitting on the pair of chairs before the fireplace. "Sussex is isolated from the rest of England, so I've been told, by rough roads and uncomfortable travel."

"I've lived here all my life," she told him. "In Wynchly, that is."

"Wynchly is no London, that's true, yet it's a fair sized town with many people. But Highcrest is isolated even from that village, though not by poor roads. My father has made this manor a lonely place."

Part of her was tempted to agree with him, for she knew his words were true. But another part, more cautious, made her hesitate. Selwyn's marriage to her had not banished his loneliness or his desire to be alone. No doubt, Christian would think that odd.

"We live quietly," she said simply.

"My father told me you enjoy going to a seaside cottage about an hour's ride from here. Is that just as secluded?"

She nodded. "Very secluded." That was her refuge, the only place she knew her father would not threaten Elsbeth. He'd come to Highcrest on more than one occasion and happened to see his wife. The mere sight of him sent Elsbeth running to her apartment. Now, she feared, the cottage was no longer safe, as he'd recently encroached even on that.

"You have the graceful ways of a natural born countess, yet you don't seem to miss the social aspects nobility normally brings with it."

She felt her cheeks warm to a blush. "I am a squire's daughter by birth. And Sussex, as you say, is secluded. I have never had a busy social calendar."

"From a squire's daughter to an earl's wife."

Anne's gaze met his. He was looking at her closely with a scrutiny that seemed to read her every thought. It made the base of her neck tingle ever so slightly, and she shook the feeling away. Was his question more than a simple observation? If he had, indeed, surmised her marriage to Selwyn was not one of love, then what was he thinking about their marriage?

"Does rank impress you, then?" she asked, curiosity lending her boldness.

He eyed her closely again before answering, and for the barest moment she regretted her question. "Because you are a countess now, rather than merely a squire's daughter?"

"I ask in a more general term," she clarified. "Since, after all, you will be an earl yourself one day."

He smiled, and she thought he might have laughed, but something made him hold back. "A serious question deserves a serious answer, Countess. No, I am not impressed by rank; nor do I hold myself higher than I did a month ago, when I was still a poor French captain—made poorer still by the sad state of France's navy."

She was pleased by his answer, she couldn't help admitting to herself. But once again he studied her, and when he spoke, his voice was a harsh whisper.

"What about you, Countess? Do you hold yourself in higher esteem now that you are the wife of an earl rather than the daughter of a squire?"

She shouldn't have been surprised by the question; she had the feeling Christian would ask or say anything he pleased. And it was only fair to ask the same of her as she'd asked of him. Perhaps it was just that look which sent the twinge across her neck hairs again—that look that hinted he took further meaning from each and every word she spoke.

"I see myself no differently," she answered.

"Then it must have been a match for love," Christian said softly.

Anne's gaze met his. He *had* guessed her marriage to Selwyn was not a normal one.

Christian went on, "But what else could it have been? You are a very lovely woman, there is no trouble seeing why Selwyn came to love you. And he . . . is a kindhearted gentleman, one worthy of your admiration."

"And I do admire him," she said. She didn't look him in the eye when she spoke, and she chided herself silently.

This very morning she had enough caution of Christian to hire a lawyer to make sure he wasn't a fortune hunter; at the moment she felt he suspected *her* of that very malefaction. But if he had guessed already that she was not in love with her husband, what else could he think? Why else would a penniless squire's daughter marry a wealthy man she didn't love?

Anne heard the sound of shuffling footsteps and a thumping of cane in the hallway, and she knew Selwyn was looking for them. She couldn't help being relieved at having the conversation forced to an end. Though she had nothing to hide, she found the topic more than a little uncomfortable.

Christian, too, had heard Selwyn's approach, and both of them stood. As if in silent agreement, they walked toward the archway to exit the room Selwyn never used.

Selwyn hesitated at the archway, but when they stood before him he asked, "I hope you are not leaving because of me?"

"Wouldn't you care to go to the solicitor's chamber, Selwyn?" Then she added, to avoid even the slightest hint of embarrassment, "I'm sure it's warmer in there. I think there is a fire in the hearth."

Selwyn sent her an affectionate look, grateful for an offer kindly given. "You're very considerate of me," he told her, then looked again at Christian. "Has anyone told you why this room is seldom used?"

"Anne and I discussed it briefly," he said.

Selwyn gazed around the room, as if seeing more than the material things before them. Anne's memory of Highcrest Manor was limited from her infrequent childhood visits, but she did remember hearing of the parties Celine used to give, the evening receptions, the magnificent dinners for those few members of Parliament who ventured out as far as Sussex. She knew, however, it wasn't the socializing Selwyn missed; it was Celine's loss which still pained him. Anne could see it in his eyes.

Then Selwyn smiled, and the sadness in his eyes turned lighter. "It certainly looks like the parlor of a nobleman. But it's hardly been used as one." Then he nodded at Christian. "Perhaps that will change once you become earl of Highcrest."

Hesitant to respond, Christian remained silent. Anne wondered what he might be thinking. Wasn't he eager to take the place of a great lord, to be in deed as well as in name the true holder of one of the wealthiest estates in the county?

Just then angry shouts came from the entryway behind them.

"Get out of my way, lout! I'll find out the truth if you let me pass!"

To Anne's dismay, she recognized her father's angry tone immediately.

Selwyn turned toward the intrusion but remained silent. He waited for Jarvis Melbourne to notice them rather than calling out to the irate man. Anne was silent, watching as her father ducked into the solicitor's antechamber, ranged up the staircase, and finally spotted them in the parlor. She wished she could simply disappear, that she did not have to acknowledge the angry man headed their way as flesh and blood of her own. She felt Christian's eyes upon her, but dared not look to him.

Behind Jarvis was Mortimer, looking decidedly flustered.

Jarvis halted abruptly when he saw the trio. When he finally did approach, the look on his face was a mixture of anger, disbelief, and, Anne thought, fear. She knew why.

"So it's true," Jarvis said. His voice was unsteady, as if striving for control that was barely within reach. "You have taken a bastard in."

Selwyn leaned on his cane, a look of annoyance passing over his face before speaking. "I hope you have good reason to come barging into my home this way, Jarvis. If it's merely to meet my son, you should have sent word ahead of your arrival and I would have arranged a formal introduction."

Jarvis laughed. "Your son?" He eyed Christian. "I'd say he could be my bastard as easily as yours."

"Oh?" Selwyn said. "You were in France thirty-one years ago?"

"No, I wasn't. But how do you know *he* was?"

Selwyn opened his mouth to reply, but Christian spoke first. "He had my word," Christian told Jarvis calmly. "And if that isn't good enough for you, *monsieur,* I suggest you turn around and check with the solicitor behind you. *Monsieur* Mortimer has proof of my identity.

"I went to him as soon as I heard the rumors," Jarvis said, adding derisively, "he told me about the 'proof.' A few coincidences of your past whereabouts, a pendant you wear. Stories from people you could have paid to say anything. Do you think that's enough?"

Christian's face was emotionless. Anne saw his shoulders tense ever so slightly, and sensed he might be angry. But she would not have guessed it from his face, or his voice. When he spoke again, his tone was calm. "I haven't the faintest idea who you are, *monsieur,* nor do I especially wish to know. But if you are calling me a liar, a fortune hunter, then it is no less than my duty to call you out." Though he was without pistol or sword at the moment, to Anne he looked as dangerous as if he had a rapier poised for duel. And her father sensed that danger, too, Anne could tell. He was not so swift with a response.

At last Selwyn spoke up. "There will be no need for that, Christian, much as it might seem appropriate from Jarvis's behavior. Jarvis, you are a blunt and mannerless man, and I've tolerated you for many years because you've never given me reason to forbid you within my home. But listen to me well," he added, his voice growing stronger. "If you do not accept my son for who he is, and treat him with the respect which is due, then you will be forbidden from this domain, or any domain of mine. Daughter or not."

Anne felt Christian's eyes on her once again. "Daughter?" he said, his voice little more than a whisper.

Anne nodded, however reluctantly. But as unwilling as she felt within to admit the blood tie, she strove not to reveal her shame. "Yes, he is my father."

Gallantly, Christian stepped toward Jarvis with an outstretched hand. "Then I do heartfully apologize, for Countess Anne's sake, for almost calling you out, *Monsieur*

Melbourne. Let's put this unpleasantness behind us."

It was a long, awkward moment before Jarvis accepted Christian's hand. But although he acquiesced to the cordial gesture, the air did not seem any lighter.

"Actually, *Monsieur* Melbourne, you may not have to put up with my presence for much longer," Christian said, and all eyes went curiously to him.

"What do you mean?" Selwyn asked, alarmed.

"I wasn't going to tell you this way, Selwyn," Christian said. "Father," he added, and though it seemed awkward from his tongue, there was affection laced within the word. "But I haven't yet decided to stay in England."

Selwyn waved an unsteady hand. "Nonsense. This is your home now. You have duties here as the next earl of Highcrest."

"I had duties in France, too, Father," he said slowly. "I did have a life there, before you so generously offered me this one."

"What sort of life was that? How can it compare with this?"

"I had a partner, a man I was going into the shipping business with. And there were other . . . involvements."

"France has no navy to protect common vessels. That is, unless you intended privateering?"

"It has been done, for the good of France."

Selwyn scowled. He had paled the moment Christian had uttered his doubt about staying in England, and now he looked almost white. "If there's a woman you left behind, then send for her."

Anne could not help but look Christian's way. He must have seen her turn to him, for he glanced at her before answering, "No, there was no woman. None in particular." Then he spoke louder. "But I did have a life there, friends that are like family—and France itself. It's been my home, and has had my loyalty, even against England."

"Political loyalties? You would denounce me, and all of this, for politics?"

Christian frowned. "I have not denounced you. I would never do that. But men have been known to give up more for their country."

"Bah," Selwyn scoffed. "I'm too old and too sick to be hanged for treason, so I may say this, and listen well: family, not king or queen or country, should come first. God Himself would agree to that, my son."

"If the boy wishes to go home," Jarvis said with improper ease, "then let him. My daughter will give you an heir soon enough."

Jarvis, with his callousness, was the vent Selwyn used for his anger. Though his voice remained quiet, he was decidedly unsteady as he spoke. "I should have had you thrown out the moment you barged in here, Jarvis. So if you please, leave now, or I will see that one of my footmen shows you out."

"You're married to my daughter! Have you forgotten how you met her to begin with? That if it weren't for me—"

Anne stepped forward, wanting to avoid further argument. "Father, I think we should leave Selwyn and his son alone to discuss this in private." Because she doubted her father would follow orders from her, she took his arm. Callous he might be, but she doubted he would resort to physical resistance in front of Selwyn. Had they been alone and she tried such coercion, he would not hesitate to shove her away as harshly as his mood dictated; but he did have enough control, thank God, when in the presence of his powerful son-in-law.

"Mortimer," Selwyn called from behind as Anne led her father away. "See that Jarvis finds his way outside, will you? And that Anne, shall we say, remains unaffected by her father's mood?"

Anne glanced over her shoulder, wishing wholeheartedly that, for once, Selwyn wasn't quite so solicitous of her. How pitiable she must seem to Christian! But Selwyn's concern was not unfounded. He had noticed a bruise on her cheek several months ago, and though Anne remained silent about how it got there, Selwyn had guessed the truth for himself. Since then he'd made it common practice never to leave Anne alone with her father—a practice she had welcomed until this moment. What must Christian think of her and her family?

Anne let go of her father's arm once they neared the

door. She would have turned away without another word, but Jarvis grabbed her shoulders with unexpected swiftness.

"You get yourself with child, girl, before it's too late."

Mortimer stepped forward, and though he was hardly any match for Jarvis, he did represent a different sort of power. "Release her, Melbourne. And let's be on our way, shall we?"

With one last seething glance and a final, painful squeeze upon Anne's shoulders, Jarvis let her go. When the door closed behind him, Anne breathed a deep sigh of relief.

She was tempted to return to the parlor; she was sure she would not be turned away. But she did not want to intrude. And though she could not deny interest in Christian's decision to stay or leave, she had no real reason to rationalize that interest. For Selwyn's sake, she wished Christian would make England his home. But for her father—only because she feared for herself and her mother when her father didn't have his way—she hoped Christian would return to France.

There was, however, another reason she wanted to stay—a reason that came too easily to mind, a desire that had nothing to do with either Selwyn or her father. As she had made her way up to her bedroom, Anne tried to sort out the emotions she'd been denying since the first moment she saw Christian. She might have mistrusted him initially, she might still mistrust him, but she was also attracted to him. Though she had refused to reflect on such a notion until this moment, she knew it was true. If she'd let herself think about it yesterday, the first moment she'd seen him, she would have realized why she was so reluctant to doubt him.

Closing herself into the privacy of her room, Anne told herself she should feel shame. Christian was probably her husband's son. Her husband's! But hers was no normal marriage, no commitment of body or soul. And yet she couldn't deny her feelings regarding Christian. Her body played a part in these strange new emotions Christian stirred in her. Her heart fluttered at the merest thought of him; her palms sweated when she neared him; her limbs seemed to turn to the consistency of pudding at the slightest, most polite contact. And an overwhelming desire to explore these feelings, to discover where they might lead, was almost too tempting to ignore.

Anne laid aside her cloak at last, opting to change from her silken over-bodice to a plainer linen one worn over her petticoat skirt. She would retrieve her mother, she decided, and go outside to the garden. Perhaps the fresh air would do them both good.

She did just that, but to her own dismay she found her mother's silent company did not dispel thoughts of Christian Montaigne from her mind. As she walked with her mother's arm looped through hers, she forced deep, even breaths of the fresh air into her lungs, at the same time gazing at the lovely surroundings of Selwyn's private garden. The flowers were in early bloom, and occasionally she would stop and point out an especially beautiful sprig or blossom to her mother, who would smile her distant smile.

And once again, though she knew her mother would not respond, Anne began a conversation as if Elsbeth were the same person she'd been when Anne was a child. She confessed every thought, every feeling she could discern, speaking quietly and without pause.

"I should feel shame, of course," Anne concluded after a while. "Mother, I know what I'm feeling is nothing more than lust for a handsome man. I may never have felt it before, but it's surprisingly easy to identify. This feeling must be lust, the one that the church warns us of, and condemns." She smiled then, almost wickedly. "But I don't feel shame. In truth, Mama, I enjoy this feeling."

Anne glanced her mother's way. She sighed deeply, unable to prevent wishing one more time that Elsbeth could be the person Anne remembered from her childhood, the person Anne needed her to be. "Do you know who I'm talking about, Mother? It's Selwyn's son—his son, Mama. Legally, Christian is my stepson, unless the lawyer I've hired can prove him a liar. And I find that more difficult to believe every moment. Christian *must* be who he says he is. He must be Selwyn's son. Gad, but it's so ridiculous! If I don't learn to think of him in some sort of brotherly fashion, I'll be miserable the rest of my life, for he'll always be my husband's son.''

But it was useless, of course. She had to find a way to
squelch these dishonorable feelings, however impossible it
seemed. She'd never been acquainted with lust before, and to
discover the emotion about one's stepson—even if that
stepson was older than herself and a possible fraud—was
beyond tolerance! If he was indeed who he claimed, he would
always be part of her life through her marriage to Selwyn.
How could she allow thoughts like these when there was no
hope of fulfillment? When their relationship would be
confined to one of family bond only? She shook her head,
trying to expel the unpleasant thoughts. It did little good.

At last Anne returned her mother to her apartment, then
found her way back to her own room as well. The midafternoon meal would be served soon, and she would have to
change back into more formal attire. She took off the linen
bodice and stood for a moment dressed in nothing but her
thin lawn under-bodice and petticoat skirt.

Was it thoughts of Christian that made her more aware
of her own body, feelings he stirred within her that brought
new discovery? She found a brocade over-bodice to wear,
but hesitated before donning it. She looked down at herself,
seeing the curves clearly outlined by the fine lawn material.
Her mind wandered—sinfully, she knew—but she let her
thoughts sweep her away. Tentatively, she touched one
breast through the delicate fabric. She wondered what it
would be like to have Christian touch her there; she imagined
it so vividly the nipple immediately hardened to a tiny knot.
No one had ever touched her body, not even a lady's maid,
though she knew it was common practice of those born to
higher station to let others bathe them. But her body was a
virgin, indeed, every measure of it and in the purest sense.
For the first time in her life, she wished she was a virgin no
longer. And she knew to whom she'd like to surrender that
virginity.

Perhaps because her room seemed quieter and lonelier
than ever, when she heard her name, she first discounted it as
her imagination. Then it came again. ''Anne.''

Once again, it was as if thoughts of Christian could

conjure him. She waited silently for a moment, to assure herself she had indeed heard his voice, then opened the door of her bedchamber.

Christian was truly, miraculously, standing there before her. She was more than a little surprised to see him, most especially at her bedroom door! Hurriedly, belatedly, she slipped into the long-sleeved bodice and fastened it, for she saw his eyes fill with surprise as he gazed at her. But a moment later the look was replaced with one of such distress that any wayward thoughts were swiftly put aside.

"Come quickly," he said, his voice low. "It's Selwyn."

The words banished Anne's shameful thoughts, and her mind was plagued by worry and fear.

Christian led her in the direction of her husband's rooms, which were down the wide, carpeted hallway from her own room. "What is it?" she asked as they made their way hurriedly down the hall. "What happened?"

A pained expression covered Christian's face as he answered. "We were talking, and suddenly his breathing grew labored and he grasped his chest. I carried him to his room. He's had a seizure of some kind." They were outside Selwyn's door, and Christian hesitated before going inside. "Will you stay with him while I send for a physician?"

"Of course." She was frowning deeply, but his words penetrated her shock and reached her senses. "There is a physician here at Highcrest at all times. Perhaps I—"

"No," he said, gently restraining her. "You should stay with him. Tell me where to find the doctor."

"He uses the apartments at the opposite end of this hall," she said, pointing in the direction of the physician's suite of rooms. In an instant, Christian was gone.

Slowly, Anne entered Selwyn's chamber. It was dark, for Christian hadn't taken time to light candle or sconce. And it was quiet—deathly so.

She approached Selwyn's bedside, finding flint and candle on a nearby table. From this closer proximity she could hear his breathing, though the breaths were shallow and quick and obviously abnormal.

"Selwyn," she said his name softly, but did not touch

him. She was afraid even the slightest contact might pain him. Her heart ached for him, as he appeared so utterly weak.

His eyes opened and he tried to move, but Anne bid him lay back.

"I am all right," he said, though his unsteady voice belied his words.

"Christian went for the physician," she told him.

A moment passed, then he said quietly, "It will make no difference." His tone was one Anne had never heard him use before as he added, "Not this time." Only a moment ago, denying the pain, he'd told her he was all right. That was the Selwyn Anne knew. She eyed him closely at this latest statement, and eventually his gaze met hers.

"Anne . . ." he began, but just as he would have gone on, another pain struck him. He clutched at his chest, as if to tear out what caused the torment. Anne reached for him with a cry of compassion, wishing she could take the agony away. And just as she touched him, he fell deeply into the pillow, so still she thought him dead. But he continued breathing, however labored.

She barely heard the sudden noises behind her, barely registered someone gently leading her from Selwyn's bedside. There was a flurry of activity, servants scurrying all about, the physician and his assistant giving orders. And she was being taken away.

At first she didn't care that she was being led from Selwyn's side; she didn't want to see him suffer, she didn't want to see him die. And she was being held so firmly by such strong arms. It was a comforting feeling, warm and secure, as if protected from everything outside their embrace. She wished she could stay there, feeling this warmth, this strength.

But suddenly, without even seeing his face, she knew who was holding her. She withdrew from Christian's arms so quickly she would have thrown herself off-balance had he not reached out to steady her. But she shook off his concerned and gentle hands. She could not accept such comfort, most especially from him.

He looked surprised and even hurt by her obvious rejection of him, and she had to turn away from the sight.

"You're right to blame me, of course," he whispered to her back. "It was I who upset him, it was I who caused it."

Perplexed, she looked over her shoulder and saw such anguish upon Christian's face that she scoffed at herself for the fool she was. How could she explain to him the true reason she'd forced herself from his arms? That only minutes ago she'd dreamed of being held by him, and now, under the circumstances, it was her shame that sent her from him? And Christian thought only of Selwyn, as she should have.

She turned back to him immediately. "No," she said firmly. "That wasn't . . ." She halted abruptly. She could hardly tell him the truth. "It wasn't your fault," she amended. When he did not look at her, she added, "Christian, I certainly don't blame you. Nor would Selwyn, I'm sure. It wasn't your doing. You must believe that."

His face softened after that, she thought, with some amount of gratitude.

They were in the upper hall, just outside Selwyn's closed doors. There was little noise from inside.

"Has this ever happened before?" Christian asked at length.

Anne nodded. "About a year ago." She remembered the heart seizure well, although there was something different about this one. It was something in the way he'd spoken to her just before that second attack—a sort of hopelessness, or perhaps acceptance of what was to come. He'd fought it before, even when he'd thought his last dream of begetting an heir was over, when they'd been unable to consummate their marriage.

But then, she realized silently, he'd still had the hope of finding Christian. Was it possible, she thought with dread, now that he'd seen his last wish fulfilled, he no longer had any will to live?

She eyed Christian's handsome, worried face. It was a ludicrous thought. Certainly now that Selwyn had his son, whom he'd so obviously and quickly come to love, he had even more reason to live. He would want to share in

Christian's life, to see him take on the duties of an earl, to see him work and live . . . and love and marry, and father children of his own.

She spoke her thoughts as best she could. "Christian, he survived the seizure last year, and he will survive this one now because he has so much more reason to live. He has you, his son, whom he's awaited for so many years. He'll not die when he's just found you."

Christian slowly, almost shyly it seemed, took her hand in his, and Anne could not deny him. He needed the contact, she could see, and she wanted it as well. Although he was strong, at that moment he was drawing strength from her. Deep inside she felt a warmth from needing him and being needed by him, a mutual sorrow that provided a unique form of comfort.

Each passing moment weighed heavily upon Anne, as she was aware of the pain Selwyn must endure. But would he endure it? Could he?

Somehow the reality of Selwyn's illness seemed far harsher than Anne might have expected. He'd been sickly ever since she could recall. Yet she was not prepared to let him go.

Time seemed to escape meaning; it could have been hours or it could have been only minutes before Selwyn's door opened again. The physician's assistant came out, a grim frown on the young man's otherwise plain features.

He approached Anne and Christian, who had kept close but silent company. The assistant spoke to Christian.

"He wishes to speak to his son, my lord."

Anne touched Christian's forearm briefly, so gently the contact was barely made. But he turned to her expectantly, almost hopefully.

"Christian," she said slowly, knowing what she wanted to say and yet unable to express herself. "If he asks you to stay here in England . . ."

He nodded, covering her hand with his own. "I know."

Then he disappeared into the quiet room.

It seemed a very long time that Anne spent alone. A servant brought her a high-backed cane chair, another offered her a meal. She accepted only a cup of hot tea, barely tasting the fragrant drink. Her gaze stayed upon the closed door, wanting to go inside, yet reluctant to see Selwyn suffer so.

Part of her knew he was dying, had known for a long time. The last few days, in the presence of his newly found heir, he'd seemed healthier, stronger, but she knew that he was still as weak as ever. Perhaps he'd pushed himself too far in the last week, eager to get to know Christian in what time he had left.

Pel came, her eyes full of worry and sorrow. She said nothing, but merely squeezed Anne's hand, sat beside her, and waited.

At last the door opened, and the physician stepped out. He looked even more somber than his assistant had earlier, if that was possible. Anne approached him.

"He wants to see you now, Countess." As Anne stepped forward, he gave her pause by adding quietly, "I've given him something for his pain, but it's done little good."

She looked over her shoulder, feeling her eyes fill with tears. But then, facing the door, she breathed once deeply, fought back her desire to cry, and stepped inside.

She pushed the door closed silently behind her, shutting out the light from the wall sconce in the hall. The room was dim, vaguely lit by a single candle on the far side of the huge bed. She approached Selwyn slowly, her feet hesitant to bring her to his side where she would see him on his death-bed. For surely, she knew in her soul, Selwyn would not live much longer.

Then she noticed the silent figure in the chair, just outside the pool of light. She recognized Christian's broad shoulders, his large frame making the small bedside chair seem frail in comparison. For a brief moment, she'd forgotten he was still within the room, that it had been he Selwyn had wished to talk to most during this time. But she did not begrudge him. She was glad that Selwyn had found his son, glad they had found each other.

Selwyn lay still beneath the many blankets, almost as if Death had visited already. But in the opaque light she could see the slow, faint rise and fall of his chest, and she knew he still breathed.

"Selwyn," she whispered.

After a moment his eyes fluttered open. "Come closer," he said. As she could barely hear his voice, she knelt beside him. "You are kind," he whispered. His eyelids seemed too heavy to lift, and so he spoke with his eyes shuttered. "I see your unhappiness for me, but in truth, Anne, I am bound for a better place. Pray, do not mourn for me."

"Oh, Selwyn, do not talk this way," she said, though even to her the hope in her voice sounded false.

His hand, discolored and ever so frail, moved slightly closer to hers as if to take hold. But he could not muster the strength even for that, and his hand merely rested nearby. Anne gently took his hand in hers. "I will not last the night," he predicted.

Anne held back a sob. "Please, Selwyn, don't speak of such things."

"You have been a good wife, Anne, obedient and loyal. And when I am gone, you will marry again—"

"Selwyn—"

He went on as if she hadn't spoken. "I wish you to seek my son for advice in this matter." Anne's gaze went to Christian, but the dim light did not reach his face, and she could not see him clearly. He did not move; had Selwyn already warned him he would ask this of them? "He is like me in more ways than you know, Anne. Heed him as you have me, although no one, not even Christian himself, has any legal right to expect this of you once I am gone. But I ask you to go to him for counsel. He will prove wise, of that I'm certain."

He paused then and breathed once deeply then held it, a look of pain crossing his face. Then he continued.

"In the solicitor's chamber there is a volume I have written to you. Accept it as a gift of love, not as a command. And Anne," he added, his voice weaker still, "thank you. . . ."

With one last breath he lay still, utterly still, and Anne knew he was gone. She felt a single, hot tear run down her cheek, but she didn't brush it away.

Although she didn't hear Christian move, a moment later she felt his hands on her shoulders. She didn't resist him as he urged her to her feet to make room for the physician. This time, when he took her into his comforting embrace, she felt nothing but the welcome solace he offered.

4

Anne woke with a start. One glance toward the tall, mullioned window adorning almost the entire eastern wall of her bedroom told her it was well past sunrise, for the sky was already bright blue. She started to rise, but then remembering, she slowly leaned back into the pillow.

It was over. After a fortnight of visitors, lawyers, queen's representatives and other mourners, it was at last, finally, ended. Anne had no place to hurry to, no guest to see to. The last had left yesterday. Selwyn was reclusive to the end, but once he was gone it seemed he had many friends—perhaps now that he was no longer around to say otherwise.

Anne had barely had time to mourn Selwyn's loss; from the moment of his death she'd been accosted by servants, solicitors and the like, all having some questions as to Selwyn's final rest. There were funeral invitations to be printed, handbills to be sent, an elegy to be written and dispersed among the county. Besides that, it seemed a thousand other decisions had to be made, from the quality of funeral rings to be sent to various mourners to the choice of gloves and scarves and hatbands handed out at the funeral. Even before the last village official had visited Selwyn's body to assess cause of death and assure that he be buried only in woolen, according to the law, Anne had been approached by churchmen and merchants alike, wanting to know how the earl's wishes for his burial might best be carried out.

She knew Christian had averted many of those who requested her attention, but many of the lawyers and noblemen had questions of their own for him, and soon he was more in demand than Anne. Mortimer did what he could, but Anne knew from the start that the faithful old man was overwhelmed with grief at having lost Selwyn, his friend.

For two weeks, Selwyn's body had remained in the parlor he'd ignored since Celine's death. And for those two weeks, Highcrest had been the bustling manor Selwyn might have once imagined. People came from as far as London to see the great earl laid to rest. Many of the visitors were as curious about Christian as they were to see the body of the reclusive earl who hadn't been seen publicly for almost ten years.

At last, just two days ago, the mourning coach had carried Selwyn's ornate coffin along a slow journey to the chapel at Wynchly, with the coaches of all the mourners following behind. The bishop himself gave a Divine Service, and soon after that they had followed the pallbearers carrying the velvet-draped coffin to the wing of the chapel in which all Thorntons were entombed. Each of the guests and mourners were given a sprig of rosemary and, starting with Anne, each tossed the fragrant leaves at the foot of the burial vault. No one left until the grave was sealed. Then, since it was late evening, the guests returned to Highcrest for port or mulled wine, and then those who stayed were shown to their rooms. The last of the guests had left yesterday.

Anne rose slowly from bed. Today would begin her confinement: six weeks of mourning, during which time she would visit or receive no one. She sighed sadly. It would hardly differ from the secluded life she had lived before.

Nonetheless, Anne dressed without delay, thinking she would take her mother outside. It had been an especially lonely week for Elsbeth, who had kept to her room the entire time. She had been couped up in her small but comfortable quarters like a welcome prisoner. Anne had visited her daily, but she was eager to bring her mother's confinement to an end.

A servant was pinning back the side lappets of Elsbeth's mobcap when Anne entered her mother's room. Elsbeth had already been served a breakfast of hot chocolate, tea and toast, as evidenced by a tray near the fireplace. She had not eaten much of it, but Elsbeth had never been one to partake early in the morning. When the servant saw Anne, she smiled. Marta was a kindhearted soul who, unlike so many others, was not in the least bit afraid of Elsbeth or her mysterious silence.

"Your mother is happy today, Countess," Marta said, smoothing the fine linen fabric of the cap before stepping away to assess its position. "It's as if she knew you were coming to take her out today."

"Of course she knows, Marta," Anne said cheerfully, coming to hug her mother in greeting. "Don't you, darling? I told you yesterday that we would walk today."

Arm in arm, they left the servant behind and headed downstairs. The manor was already abustle with servants cleaning the parlor and adjoining dining room where so many large meals had been served. Even Celine's Chinese porcelain had been used, and a servant was carefully replacing the dishes in the sunlit alcove where they were usually displayed. Soon, Anne thought without a trace of a smile, the parlor would be empty again to collect dust, with nothing more than outside shadows occasionally crossing its walls and floor. Unless Christian wished otherwise.

The thought of Christian made her frown. He'd been kind, so kind, and mournful of Selwyn's passing, though he knew his father so briefly. But he was the earl now; it was official. The bastard son, Christian Montaigne, was now the fourth earl of Highcrest.

They left the manor house and headed toward the garden. Unwittingly, Anne squeezed the hand resting on her forearm. Her mother was dear to her—more dear than anyone else. Selwyn had told Anne only a day before his death that he would see to it that neither Anne nor Elsbeth would be in need once he was gone. Yet how could he have made such a promise? He was gone, truly gone, and she would miss the man who for the past year and a half was Anne's sole protection—protection from the villagers who feared Elsbeth, and more importantly, protection from her father.

She would miss Selwyn for the friend he was, but she would also miss the safety he'd offered. How could she depend on Christian Montaigne—Christian Thornton—for such a thing? A total stranger? True, he had been beseeched by Selwyn even upon his deathbed to give council to Anne in matters of importance. But she knew he had the power to deliver her back into the hands of her father. The earl of Highcrest could see many things done.

She sighed deeply. Though it may be in Christian's power to cast her from Highcrest, she doubted he would do such a thing. She knew little of him, yet she did not doubt he had a certain kindness to him. Glancing at the frail woman beside her, she frowned anew. As of yet, he knew nothing of her mother.

What if he were like the others, those who thought her mother possessed of evil demons who tied her tongue with their invisible rope of fire, making her speechless after so many years? Elsbeth had not been born with such an infirmity, many villagers were certain it was the power of evil which took her tongue from her.

Just then she felt her mother's hand tighten on her arm. Surprised, Anne looked up. But Elsbeth was smiling, watching a vee of geese fly across the sky. Anne patted her mother's hand, grateful for whatever enjoyment Elsbeth found. They flew so gracefully, from the direction of the coast.

Thoughts of the coast brought images of the cottage, and Anne took comfort in that. Perhaps she and her mother and Pel could move there. It was hers, after all, and with the monthly allotment Selwyn had provided for her, they could live comfortably. It was certainly a viable option, should Christian have any qualms about living under the same roof as Elsbeth once he knew of her illness. In that way, Selwyn could keep his promise. She and her mother would be taken care of, even if they chose not to stay at Highcrest. But, she realized with a sinking heart, that would by no means keep Jarvis Melbourne out of their lives.

The fresh air brought color to Elsbeth's otherwise pale features, and so Anne extended their walk. They did not go beyond the garden, but walking its entire length was more than enough for Elsbeth. At the far end of the flower and shrub garden was a grove of willows, where Anne and Elsbeth rested on the white wicker chairs. Elsbeth sat back in the tall, cushioned chair, and Anne thought she might have slept, her breathing became so easy. But as soon as Anne stood with the intention of moving her chair from the warm sun, Elsbeth's eyes darted. Hers was a volatile peace.

When at last they headed to the tall double doors of the manor, the morning was half over.

"Anne," called a familiar voice from behind, just as she was about to open the manor door.

Anne turned as Christian approached. He was finely but casually dressed in a white lawn shirt tucked into dark breeches and hose, without waistcoat or cravat and, as always, unwigged. He'd been riding, she guessed, for he came from the direction of the stables, and she'd seen him many mornings before, racing his powerful Arabian past the Highcrest hills.

He smiled broadly, but Anne gave only a meager nod in return. Elsbeth still held her arm, and she felt her mother's hand stiffen ever so slightly just as Christian drew near. Elsbeth did not like men; Anne guessed they all reminded her of Jarvis.

Christian bowed in Elsbeth's direction, which only caused her grip to tighten more.

"I have yet to be formally introduced to . . . your mother?" Christian said congenially. Then he spoke directly to Elsbeth. "I saw you the first day you returned with Countess Anne from the cottage, but you were obviously fatigued and whisked away by your servant."

Elsbeth never raised her eyes; she stared at the ground.

"Yes, this is my mother," Anne said. "We were just on our way to our rooms."

Her own gaze was as evasive as Elsbeth's. She was acting awkward—even foolish, she knew. But what else could she do? She was not prepared for this. She knew she had to tell Christian about her mother, but she wanted to think of a way to do it without making her mother's illness seem quite so mysterious. And she had yet to come up with such a way.

"Dinner will be served soon. I thought we might eat in the dining room—together. Will your mother join us?"

Anne forced a smile. "My mother takes a light breakfast in her room and rarely eats until evening."

Christian eyed Anne curiously, obviously sensing her unease. When he spoke, his voice was soft. "There are a few things I would like to discuss with you, Anne. You will come to the dining room, then? Alone, if your mother prefers?"

"Of course," she answered. Then, though she knew he would no doubt think it odd her mother was being "whisked away" once again, Anne did just that. She led her mother up the stairs and toward the back of the manor to her room.

Christian was already in the parlor when Anne passed through on her way to the dining room. He was seated in one of the high-winged chairs near the fireplace, a glass of Spanish madeira in his hands. He seemed to be studying the liquid or the fine crystal which held it, rather than drinking; but when he noticed Anne's approach he stood and set the glass on the oak mantelpiece.

"Would you care for a drink before we dine?" he asked pleasantly.

"Yes," she said, thinking the wine might help to calm her. She'd told herself as she dressed so carefully, adding the black widow's veil to the back of her head, that she would become accustomed to dining alone with Christian. It was only this first time which had set her nerves atwitter. Soon, she assured herself, she would not think twice about it.

She accepted the delicate crystal glass holding a moderate portion of the wine, wishing all the while she did not feel so tremulous inside. What was there to be nervous about, after all? She had better get used to being alone with Christian, and do it quickly. Her quivering insides would not tolerate such erratic behavior for very long.

They remained standing before the unlit fireplace, and for a moment Anne guessed they would have appeared a very odd sight to any newcomer, the way they both nervously stared at their wine rather than look at each other or begin a conversation. Christian, however, did not let the awkwardness last. He spoke as congenially, as if they'd known each other far longer than they had.

"I hope you don't mind my invitation to dine down here. Waites told me you normally eat in your room or in your mother's suite."

"Or with Selwyn," she added.

"Did you avoid the dining room because of Selwyn's reluctance to enter this parlor? Because it could only be reached by passing through here?"

Anne looked around the room. It was true, she rarely came to the parlor, but only because she had no business there, not because of any personal aversion to it. In fact, she always thought it a lovely room and had not touched it when Selwyn invited her to redecorate the entire manor. She had assumed the invitation included even this room, and for a while she thought a complete overhaul of the parlor might put him at ease if there were any occasion to enter it. But in the end, perhaps because she so quickly realized his marriage to Celine was not yet over just because Celine had died, Anne had left the room unchanged. Besides, the soft shades of green and dusty rose were too lovely to banish.

"Dining informally always seemed to fit the manner of life we've lived here."

"Then you would prefer to continue in that manner?"

The question, brief and to the point, seemed heavy with implication. Or was it merely that the question was accompanied by that stare, the dark hue seeming to deepen in that intense way?

She willed herself to be calm, letting her eyes meet his. "I think using the dining room is a fine idea."

"Good," he replied, his gaze still holding hers. Then he turned away from her and swirled the remaining liquid in his glass. "That brings us to one of the topics I wished to discuss."

"Oh?"

He glanced at her before continuing, and she wondered if she had imagined that he seemed a bit uncomfortable himself, almost nervous. But that, she thought, was ridiculous. Why on earth should he be nervous in front of her?

"Dining rooms are part of family life, are they not? And that's what we are—of sorts—you, your mother . . . me. A family."

Anne looked at him, unsure what to make of such a statement.

"You look surprised," he said.

"I suppose I am."

He laughed easily. "No more surprised than I should be. A few short months ago the closest I'd come to having a family was my business partner in Brittany. Now look at me—I'm a bloody earl!"

His astonishment at this twist of fate was obvious, but Christian had never revealed how he felt about that new title. And Anne's curiosity was irresistibly piqued.

"Now you're the one who sounds surprised. Yet you've had two weeks to get used to the title, and before that Selwyn made his wishes clear from the start."

"True enough," he agreed.

She smiled. "Yet it seems a short time ago for so much to have changed, doesn't it?"

He eyed her, then nodded. Clearing his throat, he said, "Tell me about your mother."

Anne was not prepared for the abrupt change in topic, even though she'd spent the better part of the morning trying to decide how best to describe her mother to Christian. The topic was inevitable, she knew.

"I do not mean to pry," he said gently, seeing her earlier unease return.

She shrugged, hoping she did not appear quite so rigid. "I just thought it a sudden change of topic."

"Not at all," he said. "We were discussing family, were we not?"

"Yes," she admitted, "we were."

"I could not help but notice she never joined any of the meals while we had guests during Selwyn's laying out, nor did she come to Selwyn's burial when he was laid to rest at the chapel. And since no one asked after her, I assumed

either Selwyn's former acquaintances know nothing of
her . . . or they know more than I do. Enough not to ask.''

"There is nothing to hide," she said, hoping she didn't
sound as defensive as she felt. Certainly that was stretching
the truth. She knew there was much to hide. "My mother
is . . ." Anne held back. Mad, would be the honest word to
use. But she couldn't say it—not aloud. And not to
Christian, not to the man who could, if he chose, hold their
future in his power. ". . . ill."

She looked up at him, wondering if he would press her
further. Would he want to know what kind of illness Elsbeth
suffered from? So many were wary of any illness, most
especially ones which were not easily recognized or
explained. And, upon learning the illness was not of the body
but of the mind—if he didn't guess as much already—would
he be like the villagers? They believed she was either
bewitched or a witch herself, and the punishment for witch-
craft was public hanging.

"I take it you have had the advice of the physicians?"
In truth, Anne had not. She said nothing.
A moment went by, during which Anne's already
faltering appetite dwindled away. She could not tell what
Christian was thinking.

"I've instructed Mortimer to send anyone who has
business dealings with the earl of Highcrest directly to me
rather than to him," Christian said at last, and Anne
suddenly let out the long breath she hadn't known she was
holding. He had, quite easily, changed the subject. "So
Highcrest may be a bit busier soon."

She gazed at Christian. He seemed to be entirely at ease,
and after a moment they found their way into the dining
room. Anne could not help but stare a moment longer as
they walked, amazement filling her. He respected her
privacy! He did not pry, he did not press her for information, he showed no sign of fear over her mother's
affliction. No one had ever shown such respect to her.
Certainly her father would never have accepted such vague
answers. Even Selwyn's protective influence required some
explanation. Not so with Christian. He saw she had little

desire to speak further of her mother, and respected that wish. It was a heady discovery.

He caught her gaze and for a moment it seemed to surprise him. He rubbed his chin with one long-fingered hand.

"Do I have wine on my chin?" he asked with a grin as he politely showed her to her seat.

She laughed. "No, of course not. I was just . . . surprised. It seems you will soon have Highcrest functioning the way it was years ago. And yet, a moment ago, you were uncertain of how well the earl's title fit you. But I am glad."

"I'm still not certain of such a fit, but it's mine." He gave a short laugh and sat down at the head of the table. Then he added, as if to explain the laugh, "When I was a youth, do you know what I wanted more than anything? To be part of the nobility I served—to have people serving me instead of the other way around."

"And now you have that."

He shrugged. "Through no power of my own, I'm sorry to say."

"It would be more enjoyable if you'd earned it?"

"Of course."

Anne was thoughtful for a moment. "I doubt those born to nobility, as you should have been, see it that way."

Sitting back in his chair, he studied her. "And how do you see it?"

She paused. "I . . . am not sure. I've known some who want wealth so much they would do anything to have it, no matter how foul a deed. And others I've met, like Mortimer, were born to wealth and work to keep it."

"You seem too young to have any knowledge of those who would do any foul deeds out of avarice."

Anne lowered her gaze. From a very young age, she'd known that her father would do almost anything for money. "Youth isn't always protected from the world around us." If only it were!

5

Jarvis Melbourne felt as if someone had struck his head with an axe. Each movement caused him agony. The pain behind his eyes darted with jolting speed to any part of his body he tried to exert, even with the utmost care. He was tempted to lie abed one more day, but knew he couldn't. The business ahead was far too important to put off, even another hour.

It had come to him last night. Amazing how even then, barely out of the throes of his longest drinking bout and still suffering from the horrible visions alcohol sometimes brought, he was able to concoct the greatest scheme of his life. And there was no time to lose.

He left his manor house and headed to the barn, commanding his sleepy stable boy to saddle his horse. He was tempted to shout at the slow moving youth, but knew the exertion would cause himself more discomfort than the lazy boy. Then, somewhat gingerly, he mounted the horse and headed toward Highcrest. Only thoughts of his scheme made the torturous journey bearable.

Anne watched in the mirror as Pel twined her hair up in an intricate knot, then affixed the widow's headpiece which came to a small V at the center of her forehead. It was not meant to enhance, yet Anne thought the headdress brought attention to her wide, soulful eyes—perhaps to see if she still mourned her husband.

It was early yet. She'd slept fitfully, her dreams

interrupted more than once by an array of unwelcome thoughts. Yesterday had been such an enjoyable day, due mainly to that long meal spent with Christian. Strange, she thought, it was as if neither one of them wanted the meal to end, and so the midday repast spilled well into the afternoon.

More than once she had let her gaze linger on him as he spoke. He was a handsome man, she could not deny it, and at times he would smile or tilt his mouth in such a way that she found endearing. His eyes haunted her. Sometimes he looked at her with a gaze she found intense, as intense as that first day they'd met. But almost as quickly as she recognized the look, it disappeared, and she would wonder if she'd imagined it.

But she did not let her mind dwell on his piercing stare, imagined or otherwise. She reminded herself she could be nothing more than friends with Christian. Any relationship besides familial would be extremely volatile, considering their relationship. Sharing the same roof, they must indeed preserve their family-by-marriage bond only.

By midafternoon yesterday Mortimer had arrived, and he and Christian had gone into the solicitor's chamber, leaving Anne to herself for the remainder of the day. But the afternoon's enjoyment replayed in her mind long into the night. She and Christian were swiftly becoming friends, she knew, but he also stirred such odd feelings inside her.

Those perplexing feelings had kept her awake most of last night. Surely it wasn't improper to enjoy Christian's company. After all, they would have to share the same roof for the rest of their lives, unless Anne remarried and moved elsewhere. She had told herself that remarriage was a possibility, although it seemed unlikely she would ever meet anyone to wed. Having once been a countess, she could hardly return to the village for courting, and Wynchly was the only place she knew besides Highcrest and her lonely coastal cottage. She could travel to London, she supposed, and thought that one day she might.

The idea of her own remarriage reminded her of Selwyn's last request, for Anne to seek Christian's council when selecting a new husband. She had remembered that

Selwyn had hoped for them to become friends. Friends, that was all.

During the night she had remembered the volume Selwyn had left for her to read. She'd decided to retrieve it first thing this morning.

As Anne made her way downstairs, a loud, disagreeably familiar knock sounded at the door. Jarvis Melbourne did not wait to have the door opened to him; he entered with a footman close at his heels.

"Tell your man to return to his stables where he belongs," Jarvis commanded his daughter as he caught sight of her coming down the stairs. "And then come in here where we can talk in private, uninterrupted."

As loath as she was to follow the orders, Anne recognized that her father's mood was one not to be reckoned with. She sent the concerned servant away and followed her father into the solicitor's chamber.

"Bolt the door," he commanded with a snarl, at the same time heading toward the wine Selwyn had always kept upon the mantel. Jarvis poured himself a glass of the reddish liquid, gulping it down far too swiftly to savor the superior flavor. He wiped at the beads of sweat on his forehead, and waited for the chamber door to be locked before he spoke in very hushed tones.

"Come closer, Annie, we've something to discuss."

The use of his pet name for her brought nothing short of mistrust to Anne. He wanted something from her, that was clear already. She frowned. Anne knew this was bound to happen sooner or later, and without Selwyn's protection, she was unsure how effectively she could put her father off. Certainly she'd been unsuccessful before having Selwyn's help. But that was long ago, she reminded herself. She'd been a child then. Surely she could handle her father now.

He poured himself another glass of wine and, surprisingly, poured one for Anne as well.

"You'd better have some," he said quietly.

Anne accepted the glass but did not drink from it. Her trepidation was growing by the moment. Unsmiling and rigid, she waited for her father to reveal what was on his mind.

"The bastard is still here, I take it?"

"Christian is a bastard no longer, Father. He is the true earl of Highcrest now."

"Bah," Jarvis scoffed. "What happened to his plan to return to France? To his beloved homeland he said would be so hard to give up?"

"He has responsibilities here."

Jarvis shot her a gaze as cold as ice. "Do you defend the bastard?"

She shrugged. "I am only telling you why he's decided to stay."

At that Jarvis laughed. "Because of responsibility? Are you really so foolish as to believe that? He's staying for the money, Anne, make no mistake about that."

Anne turned away, setting her untouched glass of wine on the marquetry design of a nearby table. She found a seat, and her father did likewise. They sat opposite each other before the fireplace, eyeing each other like adversaries. And, so often, that's exactly what they were.

"If you're worried that Christian will try to amend Selwyn's last wishes, you needn't, Father. He will honor our allowances, both yours and mine. He's told me as much."

Jarvis nearly exploded; his face grew oddly red, his bleary eyes widened to show more of the bloodshot white, his hands trembled noticeably. "Do you think I'll settle for that? When all of this—" he waved an unsteady hand while the other one threatened to spill the contents of the wineglass, "could have been mine?"

Anne stared at her father. Had he gone mad? The thought, even so brief, caused a cold shiver to pass through her from head to toe. She knew her father had always coveted all of Selwyn's riches, but they had never been within Jarvis's grasp. Highcrest Manor never would have been his. True, he might have tried controlling it through Anne, had she borne an heir, but that had not happened.

"Father," Anne said slowly, leaning forward. "You have always craved the Thornton wealth. I know that. But you must accept that it belongs to Christian now."

Suddenly, he laughed, a soft, cool little laugh that sounded far too self-assured for a man who believed he'd just lost a fortune.

"But not for long," he whispered. "That's why I've come. There is a way, Anne, for us to have it all still."

Anne frowned and shook her head. "No, Father. It is Christian's now. Why should this concern you so? Neither your life, nor mine, nor mother's, if you care, will change. We'll all be more than comfortable for the remainder of our days. We should be grateful to Selwyn's memory for that."

"You and your laziness! You would rather sit back and do nothing to regain what's been lost than do a bit of planning."

She sighed deeply. "Father, any sort of plan you've concocted to take the Thornton fortune cannot possibly be legal, therefore I do not even wish to hear of it. Just accept the way things are."

"Never! And you'll not only listen to what I've planned, girl, you'll participate to the fullest. For in truth, Anne, the entire plan rests on you."

She stood, turning her back on her father and heading toward the door. "Then I most definitely want no part of it."

She was halfway to the door when her father's painful grip upon her arm twisted her back to him. "Aren't you forgetting something, daughter?" he whispered, his foul wine-breath brushing her face. "Aren't you forgetting how you first came to this house, how you came to wed Selwyn to begin with?"

She remembered his threats all too well. She tried to force herself free, but he held fast, painfully so.

"You did what I told you then, and, by God, you'll do so again, if you want to see your mother kept out of the asylum. I'll put her there, Anne, have no doubt of that. And you can do nothing to stop me."

She took a deep, steadying breath. "I may not have the wealth of the Thornton name, but I have access to a portion of its power, Father. Mortimer Melville is dear to me, and I to him. He'll not let you—"

Jarvis scoffed. "Do you think I have only your mother's madness as evidence to put her away? If I reveal why it is she slid into madness, she will be locked away, perhaps even sentenced to die."

"What do you mean?" she demanded sharply. Did he know what caused her mother's madness?

Having her attention, knowing she would not flee without an answer, Jarvis let her go. He smiled triumphantly. "Your mother is a murderer, Anne. It's guilt—or God's punishment—which took her tongue from her."

"I don't believe you." She said it quietly, without hesitation and with utmost sincerity.

"Perhaps not, but the authorities will. I have only to show them the body of the man who disappeared three years ago—a smuggler, it's true, and a cheating one at that, but one of the queen's subjects nonetheless. His flesh will most certainly be deteriorated by now, but his bones are there, and so, I am sure, are the other items I buried with him—such as your mother's bloodied garments, and the cooking knife she killed him with."

Anne stared at her father with growing horror. She could barely speak. Her throat felt constricted with fear and revulsion. "You did this," she whispered. "You murdered the man and buried him."

He laughed easily. "What if I did? When your mother threatened to turn me in, it was the most effective way to shut her up. Quite successful, don't you agree?"

Something inside Anne threatened to burst. She wanted to scream, but the sound would not come. How she hated this man! Blood or no blood, he was wicked, and she would despise him till her dying breath. How could she have come from such a man's seed?

"You are a vile, hateful man. It would almost be worth an eternity in hell just to see you burn beside me."

Jarvis tried to touch her, to place a hand on her cheek or shoulder, but Anne pulled away.

"I learned long ago that those headed toward hell lead far more interesting lives, my dear," he said easily. "And since hell is something no one has guaranteed exists, I've decided to live for the present, not some ambiguous future. So spare me your judgment. There is no fear of hell in me.''

"I want you to leave, Father. Leave and never come back.''

He did not move.

"I will call Waites,'' she threatened. "And henceforth I'll leave orders you are not to step foot within these walls.''

Instead of moving toward the door, he returned to the wine decanter and poured himself another glass. "You are forgetting, Annie,'' he said as he settled comfortably into one of the high-backed chairs, "why I just told you that brutal little tale. It's fact, every word, and it'll do to keep you in line as well as your mother. So come sit with me and listen to my plan.''

Anne remained where she was.

Jarvis finished his wine and at last set the glass aside. Then he spoke, quietly, just loudly enough for Anne to hear from where she stood.

"You should have borne Selwyn's heir, Annie. Then we wouldn't have to go through with all of this. That's the key, you know, a child. And if that's what we need to keep this fortune, then that's what we'll have.''

Anne listened, but in the pit of her stomach, already burdened by what she'd just learned, grew a dread so real it threatened to make her ill. But she could not leave, and she could not call on the physical strength of Waites or one of the footmen to force her father away. For he would merely return again, perhaps accompanied by the authorities with charges against her mother.

"You shall announce that you are carrying Selwyn's child, Annie. The court will no doubt see that a legitimate heir should be recognized over an illegitimate one. Everyone will accept the fact that, should Selwyn have known you were carrying his child, he never would have chosen that bastard over your child.''

He spoke so calmly, so assuredly. He seemed to have it all worked out . . . except for one point.

Anne stepped forward and said quite flatly, "I am a

virgin, Father. And unless God sees fit to perform another miracle, I do not see—"

"Good God, Anne! A virgin!" He seemed momentarily surprised by her announcement. "You mean to say you never even tried—"

"Selwyn couldn't . . ."

Briefly, anger crossed her father's face. "Does anyone know? Other than you, about Selwyn's incapability?"

Although Pel knew, Anne shook her head. She would hardly endanger her friend by telling Jarvis of their shared confidences.

"Good," he said with relief. "Then we'll have no obstacles to clear away."

"There is one rather major obstacle, Father."

He understood immediately. "Something we shall take care of without delay. There are at least a half dozen men I can think of this moment who will be more than happy to perform the services, for the right price, of course."

Horrified once again, Anne gaped at her father. "Do you mean to say you would actually do such a thing? Pay a man to . . .to bed me?"

He looked at her as though totally unaware of the reason for her objection. "Why not? You're no child, Anne. You should've been bedded by Selwyn long ago. It's nothing to fear."

Anne shook her head. Indeed, her entire body trembled with shock at her father's plan. "I will not do it."

Jarvis glared at his daughter. In that gaze, Anne saw all the power of his treachery. He would not hesitate to have her mother put away, even sentenced to die. How could he be so cruel? But that was a question she'd asked herself a thousand times, and had never learned the answer.

"It may not work, you know," she said, clutching at one last strand of hope. "I've known married folk to go childless for years until their first babe is born. And if I do not beget within the next month or so, no one will believe it to be Selwyn's child."

"Then we have no time to lose, have we? I shall choose a

man by tomorrow night. You will have to go to that godforsaken cottage of yours and await him there. It'll do no good
to have the bastard seeing a man come to you."

"His name is Christian, Father," she said absently.
Why that seemed important, she had no idea. Certainly there
were far graver thoughts to fill her mind.

Jarvis didn't seem to hear her. He was smiling, so sure
of himself and his plan. "I'll return to see you tonight,
Annie, to let you know if I've chosen the man. Expect me
later this evening. I'm sure you'll be interested in my
choice!"

She glared at him. "I am not in the least bit
interested—in any part of this plot. I don't wish to know a
thing about whomever you think you might choose."

Jarvis suddenly held back whatever he'd been about to
say as an idea struck. He hesitated in silence, stroking his
chin and staring at Anne as though not seeing her. "You may
have an idea there, Annie girl. Perhaps it would be best for
neither of you to know the other." He was thoughtful a
moment further, then after eyeing Annie distrustfully, he
finally laughed. "Yes, that's it! I rather like the idea of being
the only one knowing the true parentage of the child. Far
safer that way, you know. Then neither one of you will go
ranting on with stories in the future—at least none you'll be
able to prove. Especially if the babe ends up looking like my
man instead of you or Selwyn." Jarvis looked so self-
satisfied, he was nearly beaming as he prepared to depart.
"You arrange for the darkest room in the cottage, Annie,
and I'll see he doesn't show up until well past sunset. That
way you won't be able to see his image no matter how close
he gets—and we know how close that'll be, don't we?"

After that he left, whistling a cheery tune.

When the door closed behind him, Anne felt as though
her bones suddenly turned to dust. She sank into the nearest
chair, exhausted. She didn't cry. She was burning with anger
and frustration at the power her father held over her. It was
different than the first time, when he'd forced her to marry a
man three times her age. She hadn't wanted to do that,
either, but at least it wasn't an illegal, ignoble thing to do.

This horrible plan of her father's filled her with despair and shame, for it was her very body she would have to use for such foul purposes.

She was unsure how long she sat there, alone, unmoving. She felt surprisingly calm, and guessed the true impact of her father's plot hadn't yet sunk in. She was to mate with a man, with a total stranger. The thought was so ludicrous she could not believe she would be forced to actually go through with it. Give her body to someone she didn't know? To someone she wouldn't even be able to see in the dark? It was preposterous. But a chill swept over her when she remembered the look in her father's eye. He was deadly earnest.

Deadly, too, was his threat against her mother. A sharp pain jabbed somewhere around her heart. She hadn't known there was an incident between her parents, one surpassing all others, which might have caused Elsbeth's flight into the silent world she now inhabited. Had she seen Jarvis murder the smuggler? Witnessed just how brutal the man could be? She probably did, and then threatened to have Jarvis put away—and out of her life. Anne's hands clenched into fists. Although she pitied the poor man he'd murdered, if there had ever been the possibility to see her father out of their lives, Anne wished she'd been aware of it. Perhaps she might have succeeded where her mother had failed.

But it was too late now. She believed her father had the evidence he claimed to have. There was no doubt he had covered his tracks well, and could indeed have Elsbeth take the blame. Too many people would be eager to believe such a thing of the strange woman who'd lost her tongue, the woman they believed possessed by evil demons.

When Anne stood, she found her legs wobbly. But, realizing that thoughts of her father would only increase her anger and frustration, she decided to make her way to her mother's room. She wanted to be with her, to take her in her arms the way Elsbeth used to console Anne years ago. Many a time Elsbeth had whisked her daughter out of reach of Jarvis's backhand, only to take the blow herself. Anne wished she could have protected her mother that way the night Jarvis had committed murder.

Anne shook away her unsteadiness. Certainly battling her nerves would not aid the situation. She had to protect her mother, that she knew, and if it meant dealing with her father, then she would do it. Anne would get through this . . . somehow.

She left the solicitor's chamber, her spirit still heavy, but determination slowly building. Just as she closed the door behind her, a movement in the parlor caught her eye. Mortimer was there, along with several of his assistants which Anne recognized. They were in deep conversation, with Christian in the center. The earl seemed entirely at ease and splendidly dressed in a blue silk waistcoat and coat, with a white cravat tied at his throat. How handsome he looked, even among so many other men, for there were a half dozen of Mortimer's young lawyers surrounding him. Christian, one could see after barely a glance, was not only the most handsome, but also the most appealing in an intangible way. It wasn't his fine cut of clothes or his height or his dark, natural hair which set him apart. He listened intently as one young lawyer reported on the estate. There was something in his presence that commanded notice, something quite compelling that wasn't easily ignored.

Yet there was also a new quality in his demeanor. Despite his air of calm, he stood a bit straighter than normal. Anne could tell that he was somewhat apprehensive, and the knowledge was not as surprising as it would have been before their long discussion of the previous day. He'd spoken yesterday of taking over the tasks Mortimer had handled, and though she knew he considered it his duty, she guessed he was unsure he could handle the tasks to his own satisfaction, since it was something he'd never done. There were many duties assigned to the active earl of this secluded section of England. Besides the possibility of entering Parliament, he had responsibilities right here at Highcrest and Wynchly, too. Solve the problems of an entire village? Judge them, help them, even punish them? God's blood, he'd said yesterday, it was like becoming a father to hundreds of offspring! It was a role in which he'd never imagined himself.

For the barest moment Anne forgot the deep morass of tribulation she had sunk into since her father's visit. She was tempted to step into the parlor and listen, for she was sure Christian would handle the new task of lordship far better than anyone might have expected, even Selwyn himself who'd been so positive of Christian's ability. But just as quickly as the temptation came, she banished it from her mind. Suddenly she realized that her father's scheme manipulated not only *her*. No, the whole crux of the plot was against Christian, to usurp the Thornton fortune which was rightfully his. How could she face him while trying to steal away his inheritance? True, he hadn't been an eager heir to the fortune, but it was his all the same.

He caught sight of her just as she was about to turn away. He smiled and waved, inviting her to join him, but all she could do was flee, tears of shame filling her eyes.

6

Anne stepped inside her mother's room, leaning heavily against the door behind her. It had been a long, troublesome day, and also a frustrating one. Anne had wasted hour after hour, trying without success to devise a way of escaping her father's ridiculous plot. Were there no solutions?

She knew her father well, and realized no mere argument would convince him to give up when he thought there was a chance of profit. The stakes were too high, the loss so great that he would try anything to win back the Thornton wealth. His avarice easily condoned the sacrifice of his daughter in order to keep his clutches on the Thornton fortune—a fortune that now belonged to Christian.

Anne's heart moved painfully within at the thought of Christian. An image of him had played in her mind throughout the day, mingling with the rest of her worries. How could she be so deceitful as to steal his fortune? How could she go through with something that would force an immovable wedge between them, whether or not the plan succeeded? She would always know that she'd acted against him. The agony of her guilt would not allow her to accept whatever sort of friendship he offered.

And now, standing before her mother, Anne's thoughts returned to Elsbeth. Now she knew the truth of why Elsbeth had finally broken under Jarvis's cruelty. Anne had been tempted to come to her mother earlier, to speak of what her father had told her, to whisper to Elsbeth that she knew of the anguish Jarvis had put her through. But Anne hesitated to bring up any reference of that horrible incident. She feared the memory would bring only pain to her beloved mother. She ached inside for Elsbeth. What torment Jarvis had put this woman through! Would it never end? Would they never be free of his wickedness?

Elsbeth sat with her maid beside her, both of them working diligently on the intricate embroidery designs in their laps. Only the maid looked up at Anne's approach.

"Your mother is working very well tonight," Marta said with a glance toward the embroidery needle practically flying through the air under Elsbeth's direction.

Anne said nothing. Instead, she continued to stare, her thoughts still wrestling with the burden her father had placed upon her. She knew there was but one thing for her to do; protect her mother, no matter what the cost. Even, she thought with the ache inside her sharpening, if that meant losing any kind of companionable relationship she might have had with Christian. Even if it meant stealing from him.

She moved closer to the pair seated before the fireplace, and that protective instinct made her want to hold her mother and make sure Elsbeth knew she was still loved, still cherished by her daughter. Theirs had always been a special relationship, much closer than many other mothers and daughters Anne knew of.

Elsbeth looked up just then, as if sensing the rush of loving protectiveness coursing through Anne. The older woman's needle paused in the air and Anne watched a slow smile spread across her mother's face.

"Mother," Anne greeted her, briefly touching Elsbeth's hand. But Elsbeth's smile faded gradually, and she returned her attention to her embroidery.

Anne frequently felt as if she were the mother looking in on her child's welfare. The thought struck her with new meaning.

Suddenly Anne realized that if her father's plan was to succeed, she herself would become a mother. Anne sank onto the chair behind her. In the future, she would have to protect not only Elsbeth, but also a tiny baby. Thoughts of a small, innocent child cast a new, even greater strain upon her. How could she be responsible for bringing some tiny person into this world—a child whose only purpose was to be used by Jarvis Melbourne? After that, what? How else would her father try to use the poor child, the false heir to the great Thornton dynasty?

Anne stiffened with anger against the whole situation. She cast aside her earlier frustration, summoning in its place firm determination. She'd wasted the day trying to think of a way to thwart her father's plan and still stay within the comfortable walls of Highcrest. But now she knew there was only one way to foil the wicked scheme. Suddenly resolute, Anne knew what she must do. It was an idea that had been on the edge of her mind throughout the day, one she had not allowed herself to entertain because it would be such a strain on her mother. But now, more desperate than ever, she gave in to it. Protect her mother she must, but surely there was another way besides going along with her father's wishes. She had to protect one other person as well—a child who must *not* be conceived. Now that she had faced the sole alternative, her mind worked quickly.

"Marta, I want you to fetch my mother's cloak, the beige one with the hood," she said as she stood.

Marta was slow to respond, obviously surprised such an order came so late in the evening. "Are you going out?"

Anne did not answer. Instead, she looked under the bed, the last place she had seen the travel bag Elsbeth used when going back and forth to the seaside house. Anne retrieved it, assessing its size with a frown. It was terribly small, but perhaps that was just as well. They couldn't be burdened by too much baggage. Yet, how much clothing would it hold? And how long would their toted possessions have to last them? The rest of their days?

Part of her wanted to hesitate, to reconsider their escape. There was such uncertainty ahead. She had a vague notion to find at least temporary refuge at a convent she'd heard of, a day's journey northeast. But would they find protection there? Would her father locate them and carry out his henious threats? Was this truly an escape?

A glance around her mother's suite reminded her how

content her mother had been here. It would be hard to take
Elsbeth away from the comforts of Highcrest. She'd heard of
the penurious life many convents provided for their flock. A
life of poverty brought one closer to God, so many were
known to say. Could her mother find any peace with such a
life? Or, if they went on to London, how could Anne make a
living for herself and her mother? Certainly they would know
no luxuries from now on, no matter where they ended up.

Anne shook away the doubts and uncertainty. Her
father had robbed them of the pleasant life they'd known for
so short a time under Selwyn's roof. They had no choice but
to leave.

When the thought of leaving Christian forever came to
mind, she cast it out without allowing herself even a moment
to dwell on it. She could not face that now; she needed all her
strength to do what she must to free them all from her
father.

Anne went to her mother's clothes chest and pulled out
several gowns. Out of the corner of her eye, she noticed
Marta leave the room, obviously in search of the cloak. Anne
began placing her mother's petticoats and bodices on the
bed, sorting through them and deciding which to take and
which to leave behind.

Before long Marta waited nearby, having returned with
the cloak slung over her arm. She stood ready to help, but
not interfering with Anne's efforts. At last Anne looked up
when she noticed that Elsbeth was also watching her.

Finally she stopped, laying aside the bodice she'd been
holding up for inspection. Anne approached her mother,
placing a hand on each shoulder. But just as she was about to
speak, a knock sounded at the door. All three looked to the
noise with surprise.

"It's probably Pel," Anne said, and Marta opened the
door.

But the shadow filling the door frame was far too large
to be Pel's. Unwittingly, Anne felt her heart move within her
breast. Christian entered.

Anne moved in front of the bed, ineffectively hiding the
evidence of their imminent departure. But even as she did so,

she realized the action was silly. She had to tell Christian they were leaving, and in such a way that he would not ask too many questions.

She saw her mother noticeably stiffen at sight of Christian. Elsbeth had never seen a man enter this chamber, and it obviously unsettled her.

"Christian," Anne greeted him, her unsteady voice belying her own unease at his presence. "Were you in need of something?"

He seemed momentarily uncomfortable, his gaze taking in the three women staring at him and the piles of clothing on the bed. "I was looking for you, Anne, and thought you might be here."

Anne had wondered if he would ask for some sort of explanation for her odd behavior of the day. After running from the parlor, she had continued to avoid him, going so far as to take both dinner and supper alone in her room, despite the agreement made the previous day about eating regularly in the dining room. But she knew she must face him. Cowardly behavior sat no better with her than dealing with the awful truth.

"I will come to the parlor with you," she said, then turned back to her mother. "I will return before you retire for the night, Mother. Wait for me."

Then she left with Christian at her side.

For one quick moment, seeing him walking beside her, so tall, so strong, she wondered if she could seek his help, his protection. She knew his nature well enough to believe he would want to help her; surely she hadn't imagined the true nobility in him. But almost immediately she shied from the thought of seeking his protection. Even if he did offer to help, she could not risk her father's evidence against Elsbeth becoming public knowledge. She doubted even all the wealth and power of the Thornton name would be enough to subdue a public outcry against her mother. If her father told his lies to the people of the village, Anne would never again be able to take Elsbeth outside, for fear some wild villager would act out his own judgment against her. And despite the fact she felt strangely attracted to Christian, it was also true that she barely knew him. How well she knew him in her mind! But in reality she'd known him for such a short time, too short a time to be confident of his reaction. Perhaps Christian himself might be one of those who would not know whom to believe, her strangely silent mother or all the evidences her father had against her. Anne wouldn't even blame him, not really. He didn't know any of them well enough to trust.

Christian spoke up, invading her thoughts. His voice sounded stiff, uncomfortable.

"In the future, I shall send your servant with my messages."

She said nothing, thinking it was an unnecessary consideration since she and her mother would soon be gone. She couldn't stop the spasm of pain that came with the realization. He wouldn't be sending any messages to her, nor would she be sending any to him.

They reached the parlor, where a servant appeared with a tray of tea and biscuits. The parlor was empty, without a trace of the business which had been conducted there earlier. Briefly, Anne wondered how the day with Mortimer and his staff of lawyers had gone. She was tempted to ask, but that might seem as odd as her earlier disappearance, considering she'd avoided the activity within the parlor all day.

"I thought you approved of having the parlor used as it should be," Christian began in a low voice. He did not take a seat, nor did he offer her one. "And for me to assume the responsibility of earl."

"I do." It was a simple statement, and a true one, no matter what her behavior seemed to indicate.

"That is difficult to believe, considering you fled from here with such distress upon your face this morning. It seemed as though seeing the parlor used again, in a way Selwyn never used it, upset you."

"That isn't what upset me."

Frowning, Christian let out a long breath. He was standing not far from Anne in the middle of the room and was eyeing her closely. "Anne," he began, "it is not my nature to press those who do not wish to speak. I consider myself a private person, therefore I am inclined to respect other's privacy as well. Including yours. But in this I am confused. If today's activities did not upset you, then why did you run off? Why have you avoided me all day? I've come to enjoy your company, and I had anticipated dining with you.''

Anne felt a sweep of bittersweet disappointment, swift and sure, fly to her heart and pull it downward. How she wished she could share more time with him! This day could have been as wonderful as yesterday.

She took a deep, steadying breath. ''I—I was not myself today. I cannot explain. Perhaps it is Selwyn's passing. I've been so busy up until now that I've barely had time to mourn him.'' Then she said quickly, seizing the opportunity to tell him, ''I've decided to return to the coastal cottage for an extended visit, at least for the accepted mourning seclusion.'' It was not the truth and she hated lying, but what else could she do? If he thought her safely within the cottage, he would not be concerned over her whereabouts. Eventually he would learn that she'd fled, but no doubt he would accept her decision. After all, even Selwyn himself said that Christian had no legal right to influence any of her decisions. ''I will take my mother, of course,'' she added.

She saw Christian stiffen, saw a stern disapproval seep over his face, felt an almost tangible wall rise between them. ''You plan to live there, instead of here, even after the seclusion period?''

''I—haven't decided.''

''Because of me?''

Her gaze flew to his. She wanted nothing more than to stay right here at his side—through the day, at every meal, always. It was so important to discover she was happiest when with him, but she could hardly tell him so. Her father had made it impossible for her to stay. Besides, even if she did not flee, even if she could have brought herself to go along with her father's awful plot, she could not have tolerated living beneath the same roof as Christain, could she? Didn't her father's plan make Christian an adversary of sorts? How could she nurture this friendship—if that was indeed all it was—when at the same time she was forced to act against him?

Lie, she told herself. Tell him you cannot live with him, that you do not care at all if you ever see him again. But she couldn't. His gaze still held hers, and she knew she could not lie. He would know.

"No," she answered, "it isn't because of you."

Her answer only seemed to confuse him further, and she wished she could explain. Instead, she rose to leave. Better to end this unsatisfying conversation than to add to it more questions, more confusion.

However, Christian detained her.

"There is someone waiting for you in the solictor's chamber," he told her. "He has not been there long. I wanted to speak to you first, I hope you do not mind."

Anne frowned. Her father, no doubt. He'd told her he would come tonight, most likely to make sure she was still willing to go along with his plan. Her gaze went reluctantly to the door opposite the tall parlor archway.

Christain spoke up. "It is a Mr. Bradley Gallen, Esquire."

Anne's heart sunk and leapt so quickly it caused physical discomfort. Gallen, here? The man she'd hired to check Christian's past? Did Christian know why the lawyer had come?

Christian moved nearer.

"The look on your face confirms my suspicion, Anne," he said softly. "You should learn to hide those eyes of yours if you ever want to succeed at deception."

"What do you mean?"

"Only that I assume you hired the man to check on me, since he's been in your employ since just one day after you learned of my arrival. Is this so?"

She lifted her chin ever so slightly. "I've done nothing wrong."

He tilted his head. "No, I suppose you haven't. Except mistrust my word, Selwyn's and Mortimer's."

"Any explanation I give you would sound hollow, I'm

sure. But when I hired Gallen, I did it with only the best of intentions.''

''Then shall we see what he has to report?''

''Both of us?''

''I've nothing to hide,'' he assured her. ''Let's see how thorough the man is. Perhaps he'll be good partner to recommend to old Mortimer.''

His cavalier attitude unsettled Anne. She'd been so concerned he would at the very least be angry, yet he sounded no different than usual. Perhaps, she thought with a trace of guilt, because he had the truth on his side? She knew that must be it; she didn't know exactly when she'd begun believing in Christian, perhaps she never really disbelieved him.

Just as they neared the solicitor's salon, however, the tall outer door to the manor's large hallway burst open. This time her father had not even bothered to knock. For Anne, he could not have arrived at a less opportune moment.

''Annie!'' He smiled a greeting, obviously in a merry mood. Anne frowned. He must have found a man for hire, the necessary stud for his plot. He stepped inside and slammed the door behind him. ''I came with fine news.''

His gaze swept to Christian's then, as if noticing him for the first time. He smiled smugly at the new heir, his eyes narrowing ever so slightly. Then he looked at his daughter again.

Just then Waites, obviously having heard the slamming door, appeared from the doorway beneath the winding staircase. He hurried forward to take the cloak Jarvis was hauling off his shoulders, but before accepting it he glanced Christian's way for approval. One nod was enough, though it sent a scowl to Jarvis's previously jovial face to see that Christian had been so thoroughly accepted as the new lord of the manor.

Jarvis turned his back rudely on Christian to face Anne. ''I would like a word with you, daughter. Perhaps in here?''

''Father—'' Anne began, hoping to hold her father back. But it was too late.

He stepped toward the solicitor's salon and opened the

door before any word could be spoken. Mr. Gallen stood in the center of the room, his head darting up from the documents he held in his hands.

"Oh? A visitor?" Jarvis said, eyeing Gallen. "But I know you," he said pleasantly. "You're one of the young barristers from Wynchly. Isn't your father Asa?"

Mr. Gallen nodded, but his gaze went to Anne as if confused. "Good evening, Countess. I've just returned from my journey. I hope the hour hasn't inconvenienced you."

"No," she answered, still wishing her father had not arrived precisely when he did.

"May I extend my deepest sympathy, Countess, over the loss of your husband."

"Thank you," Anne said.

"I may speak freely of our business, then?" the young barrister asked. He glanced toward Jarvis as he spoke, hesitant to speak before Anne's father. Obviously, the young man held the squire in low esteem. He did not, Anne noted, seem uncomfortable before Christian.

Anne hesitated, and Christian filled the void.

"Of course," he said. "Perhaps it would be just as well for your father to hear what your lawyer has to say, Anne. After all, didn't he hold as much doubt as yourself?"

"Doubt?" Jarvis repeated.

"Anne has hired the services of Mr. Gallen to find out if I am who I claim to be—the son of Selwyn Thornton."

Jarvis's brows lifted in interest, and his gaze fell once again to Anne. "You did that?" he asked proudly.

Anne did not answer, but her silence was enough. Something in Christian's voice told her he was not quite so comfortable with this as she first thought. Perhaps he did have truth on his side, but she guessed he did not like having to prove himself, after all. She heard it in his voice, in the animosity barely hidden when he spoke to her father, in the way he smiled but without a trace of warmth for either Jarvis or Mr. Gallen—or herself.

When they were all in the room, Gallen spoke up. He handed Anne a sheaf of papers. "I have recorded all that I found," he said.

Anne accepted the documents and scanned them briefly. They contained names and places and a complete chronology of Christian Montaigne Thornton's past. It was a document she would have liked to read immediately, had she been alone.

"If you will note the last page, Countess," Gallen invited, "you will see the conclusion I have come to. I am sure, once you've had a chance to read my report, you will come to the same decision yourself. Christian Montaigne is truly your husband's son."

From the corner of her eye, Anne saw her father move as if to grab the papers from her, but he held back. It seemed he was suddenly as adept at controlling himself when in Christian's presence as he had been in front of Selwyn.

Anne willed her hands not to tremble, although they threatened to. She wished she could tell what Christian was thinking. She wanted to speak to him alone, to have a chance to tell him why she'd chosen to hire the lawyer in the first place. But even if she had that opportunity, could she explain herself in a way that wouldn't sound distrustful of him? And, she thought with a heavy heart, what was the use? She was leaving. Christian Montaigne Thornton would not be a part of her life after tonight. She tried to ignore the cold feeling that thought left behind.

"Thank you, Mr. Gallen," she said briskly to the young lawyer. "I can see you've done a thorough job. Was the original fee satisfactory to cover expenses and your payment?"

"More than generous, Countess," he said, bowing formally. Then he said his farewells, paying Christian his due respect and barely saying a word to Jarvis. As Anne watched him go she remembered her plan to have Gallen locate her father's false evidence against Elsbeth. But she could hardly do that now, with her father there. Besides, she realized, she must reconsider that plan. Would she be able to afford his services now that she needed every resource for her surival?

An awkward silence filled the room once the lawyer was gone.

Jarvis broke that silence. "You can see now, Montaigne, I was not the only one to doubt your claims. Anne questioned your story and had you checked."

"And found out the truth," Christian answered, not taking his gaze from Anne. She knew he was staring at her, yet she was incapable of returning that gaze.

"You may as well know why she was desperate enough to hire a lawyer, Montaigne," Jarvis said. Anne barely listened. "Any woman would, in her condition. What else could she do, when she suspected herself with child? She thought you were a danger to her unborn heir, and as it turns out, her fears were right."

"Unborn child?" It was Christian's soft utterance which brought back Anne's senses. Her head shot up, and she looked at Christian, seeing his astonishment.

Christian's eyes stayed intently upon Anne, as if looking for the truth. But she could not utter a word.

"You are carrying a child?"

"I—I—" She could not speak coherently. How dare her father put his plan into motion! But how could she refute him, how could she speak the truth without endangering her mother, or making her father suspect she would not carry out the plan?

"Of course she is! She told me yesterday," Jarvis assured Christian, then admonished Anne somewhat firmly, "Tell him, Annie. You should have told him already."

She lowered her gaze, unable to confirm or deny her father's words.

For a long moment, Christian said nothing. At last Anne ventured a glance, and she was surprised by what she saw. Pain? But she could not be sure, either of the emotion or the reason it was there.

Then, softly, he asked, "Did Selwyn know?"

She knew some answer was expected of her, though she wished she could have avoided any participation in this ludicrous conversation. She shook her head, and thought she saw sadness in Christian's eyes. Of course! He was sorry that Selwyn had not known he was to have a legitimate heir. Had it

been true, it would have made Selwyn exceedingly happy,
Anne knew that. And Christian wished Sewlyn might have
known that happiness. He was not at all personally affected
by the thought of her carrying a child.

"Of course Selwyn didn't know," Jarvis said, a trifle
too loudly for the small confines of the room. "Do you think
he would have named you heir if he'd known a legitimate son
will be born to him?"

Another silence ensued.

"I trust you know what this means, Montaigne."
Jarvis's voice was low, but confident.

Christian did not answer, but Anne knew he was fully
aware of what it meant.

"You should have told him," Christian said hollowly.

Anne said nothing.

"She didn't want to get the old man's hopes up, in case
he lived," Jarvis said tactlessly. "What if she'd been
wrong?"

Anne lowered her head once again, shaking it once in a
weak denial. But she could say nothing.

"Did Annie tell you she would be going into confinement at the cottage?" Jarvis asked Christian. "A bit early, I
admit, but having a posthumous child isn't an easy thing, I
imagine. I'll be taking her there myself in the morning."

"No, Father," Anne said firmly. "I plan to leave very
early; Pel's Gregory will see us on our way."

"But—"

Anne shook her head, her gaze intent. She would win
this battle, as it was so vital to her escape. "You know
Mother will not accompany you."

Jarvis laughed, not quite embarrassed, Anne guessed,
yet sensible enough to see the awkwardness of how it must
sound to Christian. "My wife and I haven't gotten on for a
couple years now," he said to Christian. "Many more
husbands would live away from their wives, had they the
means to hire someone else to do their work, I tell you."

No one acknowledged the point.

Anne headed toward the door of the salon, anxious to
see her father out the door. "You may come to visit us at the

cottage, Father, but not until tomorrow afternoon at the earliest. We'll want a chance to settle in after our journey there.''

Jarvis followed her out. "All right, Annie," he said. "I will come to the cottage tomorrow afternoon." Then he glanced toward Christian who was watching them. Jarvis leaned down and as if well accustomed to affection, he kissed Anne's cheek. "Good night then, Annie."

Once Jarvis closed the outer door behind him, Anne turned back to Christian, who stood in the door frame of the solicitor's salon.

"It seems you are greatly affectionate of both your parents," he said, still watching her closely.

Anne did not reply.

"Although," Christian went on, "it seems a shame both your parents can find love only for you and no longer for each other."

"My father is a difficult person to love," she said in all honesty.

"Very noble of you to still love him, then."

She wanted to deny it; she wanted to tell Christian exactly how she felt about her detestable father, but she kept silent, seeing no purpose in such a revelation. She did not look at him.

Christian spoke softly. "No doubt you'll love your . . . your child."

At that statement, Anne did look up, hearing something strange in his voice. She kept her eyes on his, seeing once again just a hint of that former pain she'd noticed when her father first announced her pregnancy. She wanted to understand that look, to know exactly why it was there. But she dared not ask. In fact, she wanted no part of this entire conversation. It only made her more intrigued by him, only more enamored. And she must rid herself of this feeling, she must!

"I'm sure I will love any child I have."

"Of course."

She tried to skirt past him, but Christian spoke again, delaying her exit. "I will speak to Mortimer in the morning about the legalities of this.''

''Legalities?''

He sounded cold as he spoke, businesslike, as if discussing one of the village matters rather than something beneath his own roof. ''The inheritance,'' he said. ''What this will mean, should you have a son. A . . . half brother to me.''

Anne eyed him as closely as he had eyed her a moment ago. Despite everything, she had to ask, ''Does this upset you? Are you fearful of losing the title and fortune you so recently inherited?''

He laughed easily. ''A bold question, milady.''

''Too bold to be answered?''

He shrugged. ''What would be the point?'' he asked. ''Whatever happens will happen, no matter how I feel about it.''

Anne went to her own room rather than returning immediately to her mother's. She wanted to be alone, if only for a short time. It had been difficult to watch Christian being deceived, difficult to hold back the truth. But even worse than the deception was the pain her father's lies had caused Christian. Confusion rose within her. *Why* had he felt that pain? Was he only wishing his father could have known of the ''heir?'' Or was it something else, something more personal, a part of him wishing she wasn't carrying his father's child—because he was also attracted to her?

She forced the thought away; she simply could not spend her energy on this. It was all for naught. Even if, by some miracle, all the burdens her father had beset upon her were to disappear, she still could not indulge in such thoughts about Christian. He was her husband's son; they could be nothing more than relations-by-law. That had not changed just because she'd begun to want him as . . . as what? A friend? A lover? A husband?

Anne refused to answer her own questions. She had to act on the matter at hand; she had to begin her escape. Knowing her father, there was no time to lose.

Although there were many things she wished to take

along, she limited herself to three bodices, two petticoats and two under-petticoats. It was not the clothing that seemed so important, however, for the coming journey. She went to her jewel box and retrieved the items which would make her escape possible: a pair of sapphire earrings and an emerald brooch. She'd become accustomed to wearing many jewels while Selwyn's wife, but these costly items were the only ones Selwyn had bought especially for her. The others were kept in a separate box in Selwyn's suite. He'd given her free use of the Thornton jewels, even inviting her to keep them in her own room. But she'd resisted the idea, since so often when she wore them it was to dine in Selwyn's sitting room. She would simply don the jewel of her choice once she arrived.

And now, though she guessed even Selwyn himself would not condemn her for taking one or two of the Thornton gems for her escape, she knew she could not. The jewels she held in her hands were hers, bought especially for her use. The others were family jewels passed on from one generation to the next. They would be Christian's now, to give to his wife, and then to his daughter or son's wife. She swallowed hard at the thought. Then, summoning once again that former determination, she stuffed the jewels back into their soft velvet pouch and tucked it inside the satchel.

Briefly, Anne hoped for the day when she would have enough money to send someone back to Sussex to look for the evidence her father had against her mother. Only then would she be free.

Without even a last glance around the room she'd called her own for the past year and a half, she extinguished the candles and made her way toward her mother's room. There would be no farewells, no last good-bye to the person she would miss most. Tonight, past midnight but well before dawn, she would be gone.

7

Christian woke with a start, and looked quickly to the pillow beside him. Empty.

A dream, all a dream. He sat up and wiped his brow, unsurprised to find it somewhat damp. He rose from the bed and covered his nakedness, not caring what clothes he chose to wear. What he needed was a swim, a swim in icy water to drive this wretched heat from his body. Heat of passion, a passion he had no choice but to crush and dispel.

Had he said her name in his sleep? Had he called for her, laughed with her, this vision who was still so real it drove him from his lonely bed? He sat on a chair opposite the still warm mattress to put on his shoes, and he gazed at the furniture as if by being empty it had somehow offended him. The dream had been so real.

This was foolish! He'd never in his life had such trouble controlling his thoughts, even the thoughts he dreamt. And what agony that he could not control them now. Anne. Sweet, beautiful Anne, who haunted him to the point he wished he'd never come to know her.

He checked that thought. Would it be better never to have seen the sun, the stars, the highest mountain, if he could never see them again? More foolishness. He sounded like a bloody philosopher. No, Anne Thornton was more like an itch, and certainly it would be better not to have an itch at all if he could not scratch.

Christian made his way outside, intending to ride beyond the manicured grounds to a deep, tree-shaded pool he'd discovered soon after arriving at Highcrest. It was a peaceful place he'd sought many times since he'd met the lovely Anne Thornton, he realized with frustration. The cold, deep water provided meager relief, and as unsatisfying as it was, he took advantage of what it offered.

Not for the first time, he thought about going to Wynchly. It was not a small town, and he knew he would find every manner of woman there, from the coyest farm girl to the boldest barmaid. Perhaps one of them would welcome him and offer the kind of release he needed. But almost as quickly as the thought came, it disappeared. He would see Anne in the face of any woman now; she haunted him, even without knowing she was doing it. And he could not yet bring himself to use another human being in such a way—using one woman to be another.

But as he neared the stable, a despairing thought occurred to him. If he was unsuccessful at dispelling these thoughts about Anne, eventually he would have to find another woman to fill her place. He could not keep to himself forever.

He entered the stable, determined to think of Anne in a more familial way, like a sister, but his thoughts were interrupted when he noticed the two empty stalls. His pulse quickened before he was even certain of the reason. One of those stalls belonged to the horse Anne rode.

Christian called the stablemaster, and even to his own ears his voice sounded strained. When he even felt his hands trembling, he stilled them with pure fortitude. He would not give in to this feeling of panic, yet he knew the truth already. She was gone.

"Yes, milord?" the stablemaster said, out of breath. He might have come a fair distance, for Christian's call had echoed throughout the large, stone-walled stable.

"Where are the horses for those stalls?" he demanded, more sharply than intended.

The stablemaster looked quite anxious at Christian's concern. "Those are the horses the countess and her mother use, milord. They left during the night, well before dawn, I would guess."

Christian could hardly contain his feelings: desolation, emptiness, and an unutterable sadness. She was gone. Perhaps forever.

He turned to the stall belonging to his own horse, suddenly realizing he must have appeared foolish. He'd known she was leaving. Why did the reality of it come as a shock?

He handled the task of saddling his Arabian himself, rather than letting the stablemaster do it. Then he mounted the horse and rode from the stable, stirring up more dust than usual.

The quiet glen offered no peace that day. He stripped off his clothes and dove into the icy water, no longer to cool the passion but to drive away the sudden loneliness Anne's departure had created. He swam fast and hard, barely seeing where he was headed, then turned around and did it again. Instead of the water beneath him, he saw her face, haunting—always haunting. She was no guileful temptress, yet that was how she affected him. She was beautiful, indeed, and he wanted her, but she was sweet of nature and spirit and not a seductress. And pregnant with his father's child.

Reminding himself of that seemed to drain him of energy. He stopped his violent swim to tread water. The reality split into him, tearing into his heart. There could be no future for this feeling he seemed unable to control. She would always be the mother of his half-sibling. For him to harbor any feelings other than familial would be intolerable.

He made his way toward shore, still deep in thought. Is that why she left, why she could not share the same home as he? Last night she'd told him her departure was not because of him, and he'd believed her. When she said it, it was as if he could read her thoughts. And the thoughts he'd read had thrilled him; she wished she could stay with him, she wanted to be with him. But had he misinterpreted? If she had not left because she was hesitant about the feelings between them, then why had she left?

Part of him could understand why it might be easier to live apart; being close to Anne provided a bittersweet temptation. If they were never to openly acknowledge the feelings they shared, there would be no awkwardness, no pain.

But no pain? Hardly. There was pain in separation, deeper than he would have imagined. They'd never exchanged a word of love, not so much as a hint, caress or kiss. And yet her departure had hurt more than he cared to acknowledge.

Christian dressed, taking his time. It was early yet, there was no hurry in returning to the manor. Once dressed, he mounted his white horse and let the animal lead the way home at a leisurely pace.

But no matter how hard he tried to clear his mind, the realization that Anne carried Selwyn's child returned to him. A painful lump formed in his throat as an uninvited image of Anne coupled with Selwyn seared into his brain. But that thought he expelled, cursing his own imagination for providing the picture to begin with. Hadn't he told himself from that first moment, the moment he'd learned she was his father's wife, that any wayward thoughts of Anne were to be banished? Of course, he could be interested in her welfare, concerned over her future, for that was only fitting and Selwyn would have wanted it that way. But this jealousy . . . he must not merely hide it. He must be rid of it.

Perhaps, with a full day's work ahead, he could begin to think of things other than Anne. Briefly, he remembered what Jarvis Melbourne had seemed so eager for him to realize earlier. Anne's child would be the legitimate heir to Selwyn's estate. It was entirely possible that the tasks of earl he was so quickly learning would soon be usurped.

Mortimer was already waiting in the parlor when Christian returned.

"You are here early," Christian commented. It was just as well, he thought; he was anxious to start the day's work. Some distracting tasks were just what he needed to control his uncooperative thoughts.

"Perhaps, a bit," Mortimer said. "Swimming, my lord?"

Christian nodded, noticing a certain curiosity in Mortimer's tone.

"A fine way to start the day, I would imagine."

Christian returned Mortimer's interested stare. "Yes, it is."

A troubled frown tugged at Mortimer's wrinkled brow. "I have been told that the countess has left for the seaside cottage, perhaps indefinitely."

Christian felt suddenly rigid, not wanting to speak of Anne. But, unwittingly tormenting him, Mortimer went on.

"I was approached by a very agitated servant this morning. Pel is the girl's name. She came to me quite early and said her mistress had left for the cottage without taking her, which was unusual. She was quite concerned for the countess's well-being."

"I spoke to Anne last night," Christian said, at the same time wishing they were discussing business rather than the present topic. "She was bound for the cottage for several reasons. One, to properly mourn the loss of her husband."

At that, Mortimer frowned anew. "Yes, she has been too busy with the burial. But that unpleasant business is all over. Surely she could have stayed here, now that there are less demands upon her."

Christian shook his head. There was no denying it; Mortimer would have to know. Hadn't he told Anne last night that he would speak to the old lawyer about the legalities of her pregnancy? Nonetheless, it was more than difficult for him to speak of it. "She is in early confinement, Mortimer," he said stiffly. "Anne carries Selwyn's child."

At that announcement, Mortimer plainly gaped.

Christian added, "I was going to speak to you about it later, to have you inform the House of Lords so that Selwyn's last wishes may be adjusted accordingly by law as far as his estate goes."

"He made you his heir," Mortimer said, somewhat brokenly. "He loved you."

Christian nodded. "And he would have loved Anne's child, too."

"He didn't know, did he?"

"Anne wasn't sure until recently."

Mortimer laughed quietly, without humor. "Do you

know, Christian, I thought you and Anne . . . But, of course, that is impossible now, even with a special license to wed. It would be damnably uncomfortable, considering the blood tie of the child.''

Christian was momentarily surprised that Mortimer had linked Anne with him—even if he had done so himself more than once. But he said slowly, "It was impossible from the start, Mortimer."

"Was it?" he asked gently.

Christian nodded, then suggested they get on with their business.

Jarvis Melbourne was not quite as incautious as his daughter believed. She thought him too bold for attempting this plan, did she? He snarled, still watching the empty pathway at the base of the tall cliff leading to the cottage. He knew she thought his plan would fail, and now he knew why. She had no intention of arriving to fulfill her part.

He glanced at the bright morning sky. It was well past dawn, and if she'd left Highcrest as early as promised, she would have been this far already. He had no reason to trust her. He knew she would not go through with it. Perhaps he'd suspected it as early as last night, when she told him not to visit the cottage until well into the afternoon.

Jarvis spurred his horse to a trot, heading toward Highcrest. He would track her from where she'd started. And he would find her, he had no doubt of that.

Anne glanced at her mother anxiously, noting how tired the older woman appeared. Though Elsbeth had ridden a horse on various occasions, Elsbeth was not an expert horsewoman, and the effort exhausted her. Elsbeth had gotten little sleep last night. By the time Anne had returned to her mother's apartment suite the night before, it was almost midnight. Then, sending Marta away, Anne had explained her plan to her mother. They would leave three hours before dawn and head northeast, to a convent Anne had heard of. She clutched at her own bag, which held the jewels needed to buy asylum. It would cost both the earrings and the brooch,

no doubt, to buy secret protection. If her father did find
them, she would not depend solely upon the kindness of the
sisters. Expensive jewels would no doubt help to buy their
silence.

Anne did not tell her mother why they were forced to
leave; she could not bring herself to discuss it. Elsbeth
followed her daughter's instruction without question,
without hesitation, without remorse it seemed. She slept the
few hours they had before their departure, and when at last
they crept from her room and out to the stables, Elsbeth did
not spare a last glance behind.

Now, some four hours later and with several villages
between them and Highcrest, Anne began to breathe a bit
easier. There was no reason to fret, she'd kept telling herself
since leaving her room. No one in the manor would have
tried to stop their departure. Christian believed, along with
everyone else, that she was going to the cottage. The hour of
her departure was up to her. And so the stablemaster had
asked no questions as he sleepily saddled their horses, except
to inquire who would be escorting them. Anne had easily
replied she was to meet Pel and her husband Gregory just
outside the manor gates at Gregory's gatehouse. Once
beyond the sprawling lawn of Highcrest, they had seen no
one.

Yet Anne couldn't help constantly looking over her
shoulder for her father, wondering if he trusted her enough
to wait until the following afternoon to come to the cottage
as she'd told him. She doubted he would wait that long
before making sure they'd arrived at the seaside home, and
so for the first three hours she strove to put as much distance
between them and her father as possible, at the same time
taking care not to go too fast for Elsbeth's limited skill on a
horse. It was hardly a rugged pace, but it was steady, and the
journey combined with the limited sleep her mother had
gotten were taking their toll. For Anne herself, pure dread of
her father kept her going without thought to fatigue.

For her mother's sake, Anne pulled her horse to a slower
gait, and Elsbeth's mount did likewise. Anne leaned down to

retrieve a flask of water, and offered it to her mother. Elsbeth accepted it, her eyes never meeting Anne's.

They kept going, although not quite as unceasingly as before. Soon they would stop and Anne would give her mother some of the bread and cheese she'd taken for them. She was quite hungry already, but she knew the journey ahead was long, and hoped to spread out the rations accordingly. Anne was uncertain how far apart the inns were, and she wished to spare as many expenses as possible. Fortunately, the road was empty, although she guessed that would change as the day wore on. She had enough coinage to pay for a private room if one was available. Her only worry was for the obvious; two women traveling alone, without carriage or guardian, were easy prey for those without any scruples. She prayed they would be lucky enough to encounter no trouble on the way.

What was Christian thinking? she wondered, not for the first time. Throughout the hours as their journey continued, she could not keep him from her mind. He would assume she'd left for the cottage, of course, and more than likely would hardly miss her. He would be working with Mortimer again today. She liked to think of him doing that. She liked to think of Highcrest coming alive again under the capable instruction of an active earl, one who would not leave the business of village to others, one who would avail himself to other's needs and open his doors to anyone who came calling.

Soon after Anne and Elsbeth stopped to eat some of the food Anne had brought, they encountered their first fellow travelers. A small family, husband, wife, and one young child were on there way to Dover. They were traveling by foot and so before long as they talked with the family, Anne invited the child to ride with her, rather than having her mother carry the already weary child. The father needed both hands to pull a cart filled with their belongings. The young girl seemed quite excited to be riding a horse, her first such venture. She chatted happily, saying she'd ridden a cow once, but that didn't count. And never had she seen such a pretty horse, one so big. Usually the big horses carried men, not women, the girl had noticed. She felt very privileged indeed to have ridden on not just any horse, but such a large one at that.

Too late, it occurred to Anne that mingling with fellow travelers could well be her downfall. Suppose her father was to track her, as he no doubt would? Wouldn't it be wiser for her to keep to herself? How foolish she'd been! She should have kept up her pace and avoided all talk with anyone on the road who could give her father an identifying description and the direction they were headed. At least she had been wise enough to keep their destination to herself.

At last she let the girl down, for the family was stopping for a midday meal. They cordinally invited Anne and her mother to dine with them, but Anne declined, saying they preferred to keep going. Then, with a wave, they departed.

Just after sunset Anne and her mother came upon an inn called the Spotted Calf. Anne fairly ached all over from an entire day of horse travel, and she imagined her mother hurt even more. How wonderful it would be if she could order a bath at this inn! But, she noted after they'd left their horses to the attendant, the inn was small. She would be happy just to have a private room.

A slim, pinch faced woman greeted them just inside the public room. "What's your business, milady?" she said, respectfully enough but with unmistaken coolness. She eyed Anne and her mother warily, obviously assessing the worth of their cloaks, perhaps wondering where their escorts were. Women of nobility did not travel alone.

"We'd like a hot meal, a private room with a bed—and a bath, if available," Anne announced.

The sour-faced woman laughed, revealing an odd assortment of teeth. Those still intact were large, but there were several broken or missing, yellowed or black. "A meal, a bed, and a bath," she repeated. "Where do you think you are, milady? Windsor itself? We've got two rooms upstairs, one for the men and one for the women. You can fight for a place on the bed if you like. As for a bath, there's water out back for the horses. Soak yourself in that, though I do think it a might chilly and the water more than a bit dirty. You'd be cleaner not to bathe at all! The meal will be hot, of course, but that'll cost you extra."

Anne sucked back a sharp reply. She'd never in her life been spoken to in such a way, except by her father, and she expected it from him. She was tempted to issue a scathing retort, but thought the wiser of it. No use leaving a scene behind her to report back to her father.

"May we eat in the room upstairs, then?"

The large-toothed woman seemed to take offense at the very idea. "No, indeed; no food abovestairs! You'll eat in the public room, like everybody else."

Without a word, Anne turned to her mother and led her to a vacant table.

As promised, the meal was hot. That was, however, its only redeeming quality for the food was tasteless. She and her mother ate nonetheless, for the bread and cheese at noontime had been their only sustenance of the day.

Elsbeth ate slowly, and Anne was finished long before her mother. While she waited, Anne eyed the other occupants of the room. Most were commoners, as evidenced by their clothing. Some had come only to drink and pass the time. Others, she could tell, would stay the night. Briefly, she wondered if the family they'd traveled with during the day would come there to find shelter.

Her perusal of the room drew her attention to one man seated near the door. He'd been there since Anne and her mother had been served and, she now noticed, his gaze had met hers more than once. Did he look familiar? Perhaps, but she could not place him specifically. He was a small man, with a round face and dark, closely spaced, small eyes. Warily, she kept her gaze casually moving, not wanting to attract any attention.

She had already decided she would allow herself and her mother no more than three hours sleep. She would have preferred not to stop at all, but could not bring herself to press Elsbeth any further without resting on a real bed rather than out under the stars on the hard ground. Three hours would be enough time to rest themselves and their mounts, and still keep ahead of her father. Surely he was searching for her by now.

At last, her mother was finished.

"We'll go upstairs now, Mother," Anne said. "I'm sure we'll be able to sleep. At least it'll be safe and dry, and out of the spring wind."

She led Elsbeth toward the stairway, ignoring the man who had looked their way. But just as they reached the bottom stair, she noticed with growing dread the approaching shadow out of the corner of her eye. Still looking downward, she kept moving toward her destination, determined to let nothing stop them.

The man, however, had other ideas. With one quickened step he blocked their path, and though he was not tall for a man, he still stood as high as Anne, and was no doubt stronger. At last, Anne was forced to look up.

"Get out of our way," she demanded, deciding boldness was the best course of action.

He laughed, and she could smell wine on his breath. "What's your hurry . . . Countess?"

Anne's eyes momentarily widened at the recognition, but she strove to cover her surprise. "You are mistaken, milord. Now let us pass!"

She tried to skirt around him, but he held out his arm and Anne found to her dismay it was rock hard. She glared at him once again.

"What do you want?" she asked flatly.

His gaze skimmed her body boldly, completely oblivious to Elsbeth's presence. "Oh, milady, now that's a question with more 'n one answer. There are many things I could want from you."

"If you touch me, I shall scream until the sheriff of this glen comes and carries you away," she said, though it was a hollow threat since she had no idea if there was a sheriff within twenty leagues of here.

The threat had even less impact than Anne had feared. He hardly looked worried, his brows still smooth over his too-close eyes, the dirty teeth revealed by his lecherous smile only a shade lighter than his whiskery cheeks. He sighed.

"Well, since it's not my fancy to take a girl against her will, I'll let pass what's foremost on my mind. Instead, I'll just settle for the hefty reward your father's offered to bring you back." He laughed again. "You know, he didn't say what manner of health he wanted you in when you're brought back. My guess is he wouldn't care if I had my way with you."

Anne knew that he would not; in fact, a rape might very well suit his purposes. She swallowed down the fear threatening to erupt in her and spoke boldly. "If my father is offering a reward for my return, I shall pay you double if you keep our whereabouts secret—and forget you ever saw us."

He raised his brows, but said, "And where'll you get it, now that the bastard controls the Thornton gold?"

"I have money of my own," she assured him, hoping he would believe her.

He obviously did not. "I'll want payment right now; who knows when you'll be back in Wynchly to give me payment."

Anne thought of the jewels inside her pouch. She clutched at it, reluctant to give up any part of their meager holdings. She would have need of whatever offering she could give to the convent. The more she offered the better her mother's life would be there.

But the man standing before her was a more immediate threat. The earrings were of less value than the brooch. Would that be enough to satisfy him? She had no idea how much her father had promised him. If Jarvis still believed he would one day have control over the entire Thornton fortune, he could have promised this villainous wretch anything.

"Very well," she said stiffly. "I will pay for your silence." She fished inside her satchel, feeling blindly until her fingers closed over the small, velvet pouch. Then, without pulling the pouch out for the man to see, she found the earrings and withdrew them. One sapphire winked in the dim light, and it pained her to give the lovely jewelry to such a man. She would not miss wearing them, but they had been a gift from Selwyn, whom she admired, and she could not help wondering how their value would have made the sisters of the convent more willing to give her mother the protection and care she needed.

The man's eyes lit upon sight of the jewelry. He grabbed the gems immediately and stood closer to the light from a wall sconce to inspect them. "Ah, very nice, Countess. This will do, this will do." Then he looked her over once again, his gaze passing more slowly over the curve of her full breasts. "But you could have gotten rid of me much more cheaply, Countess. One roll would've done it, if you'd given in willingly."

Anne merely glared at him, then pulled her mother closer and led her up the stairs. She breathed easier once they were within the women's room, though it took awhile to still her trembling hands.

She frowned anew. The room was already crowded with travelers. Considering the discomfort of the quarters and the threat of the man she'd just paid off, Anne was tempted to turn on her heel and head out to the weary horses. But one look at her mother, who was visibly fatigued, made her change her mind. They would stay in the crowded room, most likely sleep on the floor, and she would just have to trust the lecherous man downstairs to keep his word and not turn them in to her father. Despite her gloomy thoughts, Anne nonetheless prepared to make her mother as comfortable as possible for the night.

The man belowstairs snickered once as he left the inn, patting the pocket holding the sapphires. Upon his face was a smile of satisfaction, happy the night had been so profitable. Soon, he thought to himself, just as soon as he informed Jarvis of where he could find his precious daughter, he would have the jewels and the reward to boot.

8

Anne woke reluctantly from a deep sleep, the squawling cries of an infant intruding on the wonderfully vivid dream she was having. Only a moment ago she'd been in Christian's arms, not quite kissing, but with the promise of one so real her lips still tingled from the memory. But now her eyes fluttered open, and instead of the rose-colored walls of her room at Highcrest, she saw the dingy, dark walls of the unadorned women's room at the Spotted Calf Inn.

She sat up suddenly, at once taking in not only the peacefully sleeping form of her mother still on the bed, but also the bright stream of sunlight pouring through the room's single window to the east. Not only had she slept past dawn, she had slept past the departure of several fellow travelers. The room was already less crowded, though the cries of the child being pressed against to his mother's breast made it seem as noisy as the night before.

Anne stood, taking no time to stretch her stiff limbs. She'd spent the night with one cloak beneath her and another folded under her head as a pillow, but still the uncarpeted floor was hard and unyielding against her already sore muscles. She was thankful she'd been able to find a place for Elsbeth in the large bed, thanks to the kindness of a younger woman who'd given up her place in deference to Elsbeth's age. And while Anne was fretful she'd let them oversleep, a small part of her was glad her mother had gotten more rest than Anne had expected to allow.

Elsbeth woke after a gentle shake to her shoulder. Anne

smiled, hoping to quickly reassure her mother in the unfamiliar surroundings.

"Good morning, Mother," Anne whispered. "We're a
bit late, I'm sorry to say. We won't have time for breakfast,
but I do have some bread and cheese left, so you can eat once
we're on our way. Come then, let's get your cloak. I'm afraid
it's wrinkled, but I think you should wear it nonetheless."

As she chatted, Anne had put on her own wrinkled
cloak, leaving it unfastened and the hood still draped across
her shoulders. Then she helped her mother with her cloak,
and they were on their way.

The public room belowstairs was loud with patrons
either just departing or still eating breakfast. Dishes clanked
and orders were shouted to the barmaid. The scents and
smells of coffee, tea, toast, beef steaks, and eggs wafted
through the air. It made Anne's mouth water, despite the
fact she remembered the poor quality of last night's dinner
only too well. Even with the tantilizing scent, she guessed
that breakfast would not taste as good as it smelled—certainly not as good as the food they were accustomed to back
at Highcrest.

She led her mother through the crowded room, keeping
a steady gait even when she felt her mother's step slacken.
Obviously Elsbeth was tempted by the aroma as well, but
there was no time. One look at the tiny watch in her bag had
told Anne it was well past seven of the clock already, and
they should have been back on the road hours ago.

Elsbeth must have seen him even before Anne, for she
pulled back first, more violently than any mere wish for
breakfast would indicate. Just short of the door, Anne felt
Elsbeth's sudden tug at the same time she saw the familiar
outline of her father's figure approaching from the side.

He stopped so close to her that his booted foot landed
on the edge of her floor-length cloak. "What's the matter,
daughter, did you lose your way to the Thornton cottage?"

Her father was quietly confident as he spoke to her, a
dark smile on his lips contrasting with the harsh glint of
anger sparkling in his watery blue eyes. Anne said nothing,
her heart in her throat, her mind reeling. Vaguely, she

realized she'd been betrayed and that her own mistake of oversleeping had only assured her father's success. But those thoughts she shoved to the back of her mind when she felt her mother's trembling hand in her own. When she turned to Elsbeth, she saw that not only her hands were quivering, her entire body was racked with shudders as she stared at the man who terrified her most. But she did not run or turn away; she simply stared, wide-eyed, and Anne was thankful that at least a small portion of her mother's strength remained in tact, enough strength not to run raving from the taproom—something Anne herself was tempted to do.

"We want no part of you or your plans, Father," Anne whispered, her voice soft but desperate. She had no wish to attract unnecessary attention. She'd learned long ago that public scenes added only shame to an already untenable situation. Once her father had hit her at the tavern in Wynchly when she'd come to fetch him. No one had raised a finger in her defense. The confrontation had merely begun a round of ugly gossip. Since then Anne sought to avoid any form of public outburst.

Jarvis laughed at Anne's words, taking her arm in a steely grip and propelling her outside. He spoke in her ear. "You have no choice, Annie my dear. I thought you understood that."

"Let us go," she cried, trying to wrench free now that they were outside the pub.

But Jarvis merely tightened his grip, and painfully so. He yanked her arm nearly out of its socket, so vicious was his force as he directed her toward the stables.

"You're a foolish bit of baggage, and it would be a great pleasure to never set eyes on you again—you or your mad mother." His tone was fierce, his eyes filled with anger. "But you're necessary for the time being, Annie, and I'll do what I must to make you carry out your part in my plans. If it includes beating you into agreement, then so be it. Just remember, girl, it'll be easier on you if you do this willingly."

They were at the stable where, perhaps not surprisingly, the horses belonging to Anne and Elsbeth were already saddled and waiting. A third and fourth horse were there as well, one belonging to Jarvis and the last to the small-eyed Judas of the night before.

Not a word was spoken as Jarvis threw Anne on the back of her horse then turned to Elsbeth. Anne nearly flew back to the ground to her mother's side, but Jarvis was too quick. Before anything could be done for her, Jarvis had grabbed Elsbeth and shoved her roughly into her saddle. Thankfully, Elsbeth gripped the sidesaddle hook and stayed aboard, showing more agility than Anne would have thought possible. But the fear on her mother's face was so real and so great, she guessed Elsbeth could have achieved almost anything at that moment, anything to escape the well-remembered wrath of Jarvis Melbourne.

Jarvis took up the rear, but one command to his beady eyed crony had them going at a much faster pace than Anne had set the day before. They never stopped or even slowed, not even when the horses began to sweat and their mouths drooled with foam. Anne kept a close eye on her mother, but Elsbeth had withdrawn so far into herself that she barely seemed to notice anything around them. She never looked away from the road ahead, not even toward Anne. She didn't seem to tire, though her stiff back was more likely from fear than tireless energy.

In considerably less time than it had taken Anne and Elsbeth the day before, they neared their destination just past noon. Jarvis led them toward the rocky, unkempt pathway to the seaside cottage, and Anne, despite her fatigue and her concern for her mother, did not enlighten Jarvis about the second pathway which would have offered a more comfortable ride.

However, before proceeding onward at this point, Jarvis halted the small party with a call from the rear.

"Baylor!" Jarvis hailed, and the man with the too-close eyes turned toward him. "Take the old one to my house, and give her over to the care of my housekeeper."

"No!" Anne shouted, leading her horse nearer to Elsbeth's. "Mother stays with me."

Jarvis leered at her. "You'll see her again, daughter,

provided you do as I say." Then he turned to Baylor again. "Go on, Baylor. Be gone with you."

Still Anne tried to prevent being separated from Elsbeth. With one gentle tap to her horse's flank, she had her horse between Elsbeth and Baylor. Out of the corner of her eye, she could see her mother holding tight to the reins, and for the first time since the beginning of this awful journey home, she saw the fear—sheer terror—upon Elsbeth's face. Anne could not, would not, let her go.

"You may as well start beating me here and now, Father, because I'll not let you take Mother away from me."

Jarvis took the invitation. He nudged his horse forward and the small, silver-handled horsewhip he held in his hand became a weapon instead of a tool. Anne barely felt the swift sting to her back, for the thick velvet of her cloak and the layers of clothing beneath prevented much contact. But she could not avoid the painful twist to her already sore arm as he grabbed her and pulled her from her saddle. Her sensitive mare reared, and she would have landed on the ground had not Jarvis already held her, forcing her to land in front of him, sprawled across his saddle like a sack of flour.

Anne continued to struggle, even when he used the whip ignobly upon her backside. Then she felt him kick his horse and they were off, up the bumpy pathway to the cottage with Anne's riderless horse led behind. She heard her father call to Baylor to continue on his way, and there was nothing more she could do but watch her mother being led away.

Just outside the cottage, Jarvis jumped to the ground and pulled Anne along with him. Then, with a rock-hard grip around her waist, he dragged her up the stairs to the door.

Mistress Markay, the elderly servant who watched over the cottage, opened the door moments after Jarvis's loud knock. She may have seen the appalling way Anne's father had delivered his daughter, yet she merely greeted them and offered tea. Anne barely knew Mistress Markay, despite frequent visits to the cottage. Oftentimes Anne invited the housekeeper to take a holiday to visit her daughter who lived in Wynchly, while Pel took over the domestic duties of the cottage. Mistress Markay kept the seaside home clean and well-provisioned and ready for Anne's visits on a moment's notice, so she had never had cause for complaint. Until now.

"Mistress Markay, I am here against my will," Anne began. "I wish for you to go to the bailiff—"

"Don't bother," Jarvis said. "The countess is merely distraught over the loss of her husband, what with the coming child and all. Don't pay her a bit of attention, Mistress Markay. Go about your duties and leave my daughter to me."

Mistress Markay left without delay, disappearing behind the kitchen doorway.

"That was foolish, Annie," Jarvis said, glowering at her. "Don't you know that even if she had gone for the bailiff, it would've done you no good? He works for me, have you forgotten?"

In fact, she had. Was there no escape?

"What are you going to do with Mother?"

He laughed, making his way toward the wine which sat in its usual place on a lacquered table before a gold brocade settee. "You're not to concern yourself with her, Annie. There's nothing for you to worry about, she's merely going home for a while—to visit her beloved husband."

Jarvis sat down, holding the crystal decanter in one hand and a full glass in the other, leaving the table free for one booted foot to invade. The delicate table creaked under the unaccustomed weight.

"What are you going to do with her?" Anne persisted.

Jarvis took a long swallow before eyeing his daughter. "Nothing," he said at last, then his gaze flickered with cruel warning before adding, "that is, if you perform what you're supposed to perform."

Anne glared at him. "You are a vile man, and I hate you."

He shrugged, taking another gulp. "I hardly care," he replied easily. "It isn't people I care about in this world."

Anne knew that only too well. She knew, too, that she had been beaten in this attempt to escape him, and there was no way out. Slowly, giving in to not only the physical exhaustion but also the desolation that came with submitting to her father, she plodded toward one of the chairs. She chose one far from Jarvis; she did not want to look at him. She sat on a high, narrow-backed, ebony chair near the window, seeing the bright sunshine beyond the delicate lace curtain.

"I will do as you say, Father," she said bereftly, "beginning tonight, if you wish. But you must promise me you will return Mother to me—in good health and untouched."

"Don't worry about Elsbeth," he scolded her. "She is too valuable to me to harm. After all, without her, how could I control you as easily as I do now?"

Anne felt her shoulders sag, and leaned forward to hold her forehead in her hands. There was nothing more she could do.

By midafternoon Mortimer's stomach was growling so fiercely even Christian heard it from across the desk. The noise seemed to resound in the small confines of the solicitor's salon.

A glance at the desk clock told Christian it was well past the regular dinner hour, and he smiled over at Mortimer who seemed to have ignored the rather demanding call of his stomach.

"Would you care to stop for dinner, Mortimer?" Christian asked.

Mortimer, too, eyed the clock, then turned his gaze to Christian. "You seem tireless today, my lord. If you'd rather work through the day—"

Christian shook his head. He'd spent the better part of the day working so diligently he hadn't had time to think. But now, even he was a bit hungry. After several hours of keeping himself as distant as possible from thoughts of Anne, he found the future did not seem quite as bleak as it had earlier. After all, she was not gone completely. He had resolved, somewhere between reviewing the accounts of the growing Thornton cloth industry and acquainting himself with a map of various sheep farms owned by him, that he would visit the seaside cottage before the week was out. Perhaps it was foolish not to try harder to resist this growing infatuation he had with Anne, but he felt himself giving in to it.

So many things were against them: their tie by marriage and, more importantly, the child Anne carried. But neither he, nor Anne could deny that there was something budding between them which was too precious to cast away. There were obstacles, to be sure, and if they were too great to surmount, then so be it. But he would not deny the attraction, and he did not believe Anne would, either, if confronted with the fact of his own feelings. They would face these feelings and decide from there what was to be done about them.

"I'll tell Waites to bring something in," he said, then stood. It felt good to have made a decision, and he was hungrier by the moment.

He stepped outside the small salon, summoning the footboy who was always somewhere nearby. Christian gave brief instructions, and the boy hurried off to do his bidding. Just as Christian was about to return to Mortimer, a knock sounded at the door. Christian hesitated as the butler's assistant went to answer it.

Curiosity brought Christian closer to the door, for obviously the visitor was somewhat suspect in the assistant's opinion, since he did not open the door very wide.

"What is it, Hadley?" Christian inquired.

Christian saw the visitor then, as Hadley opened the door wide enough for his master to see who was there. The man was quite likely of lower means, dressed in a working man's frock coat and with a jockey cap covering a somewhat worse for wear unpowdered wig. He was tall, but despite his poor clothing he had the air of nobility about him. Yet that was not his most noticeable quality. His face might have been handsome once, though age had not diminished his looks, for the man could not have been much past forty. Instead, it was a scar that marred his face, running deep and long from his left eye down the center of his cheek. The scar was disfiguring enough by itself, but coupled with the fact that the man's eyes held all the emotion of cold steel, his appearance could send even the boldest maiden into a dead faint.

Christian, however, was merely curious.

"He wishes to see you, my lord," Hadley said somewhat incredulously.

"I am Conn Guiscard," the man said in impeccable English, looking eye to eye with Christian. "And I have business with you, if you are the earl of Highcrest."

"That I am," Christian said.

"May we speak . . . privately, then?"

With a curt nod from Christian, Hadley let the mysterious stranger inside. Christian headed toward the parlor, but the man behind him gave him pause.

"We should go where we'll not be overheard, my lord. Is your house safe from ears in the walls?" He eyed Hadley, who lingered behind as he spoke.

With that Christian changed course. For some reason unknown even to himself, he gave great credence to this man, a perfect stranger. They went to the solicitor's salon, where Mortimer was still working.

"Whatever you have to say can be said before my barrister," Christian said.

"Who is this, my lord?" Mortimer asked curiously.

"Someone who says he has business with the earl of Highcrest."

The man's face did not alter from the unemotional facade he'd first presented as he spoke to Christian again. "You'd best hear what it is before you decide who should be privy to the knowledge."

"Very well," Christian said. Then to Mortimer he said, "Why don't you have Waites serve you lunch in the dining room? I'll join you shortly."

Mortimer left silently, although slowly, closing the door behind him.

Christian offered Guiscard, who stood barely an inch shorter than Christian himself, a glass of wine, which the stranger accepted. Neither man sat down. Christian sensed the man would not stay long—just long enough to deliver his message. Christian's curiosity was growing by the moment.

The man took an infuriatingly long sip of wine, compounding it with a leisurely swallow and a pause afterward as he eyed Christian with that calm, unemotional stare. The cold look in his eye never wavered.

Then he began, "You have in your acquaintance a man by the name of Jarvis Melbourne?"

Christian nodded once. His attention, already stirred, now sharpened.

"I, too, know the man. A greedy man, wouldn't you say?"

Christian spoke quietly. "I do not know him well."

The man smiled crookedly, and the scar down his cheek whitened. "You should know him better, earl of Highcrest, for he is your enemy."

"Did you come here to warn me against the man?"

"I am no angel of mercy, be assured of that," the man said. He took another sip of wine. "I'm here for myself alone. I've done business with Melbourne for several years now." He hesitated ever so briefly. "You are French, are you not?"

Christian nodded.

"As am I—or *was*. I'm not welcome in our homeland anymore."

"And why is that?"

"They do not welcome traitors."

Christian took the news without flinching. Though he could easily detest anyone who betrayed his country, curiosity kept such feelings in check. "Then why should I welcome you here?"

"I ask no welcome. I believe we can do business."

"What sort of business?" Christian asked skeptically. "Stolen wine? I'm aware that Melbourne smuggles French booty into this country. If you've come here hoping to deal directly with me rather than him, you've come to the wrong place. I want no part in it."

"A loyalist," he sneered. "But how loyal can you be, you who've given up your homeland in favor of an English title? Or perhaps it's the English money which keeps you here."

Christian was losing patience. He was not about to have his political loyalties judged by this villainous looking man. "It seems to me you have little right to cast a stone at me, since your own business shows loyalty to no one but yourself."

"Ah, so there you have it." Those dark, cold eyes glistened for the briefest moment. "Now you know all you need to know about me. We can speak about the business at hand then."

Christian was glad to hear it. "Get to it, man. You're wearing my patience."

"I was approached with a very interesting proposition late last night," the man began. "Melbourne knows exactly where my loyalty lies—in myself, as you just learned. He offered me a great deal of money if I were to perform one simple service for him."

"Which is?"

Guiscard took another long swallow of wine. Christian guessed that the man enjoyed keeping his listener waiting. Then he turned his soulless eyes on Christian again. "I am to come to a house by the coast, arriving well after dark. The door will be left open, and I will find a woman waiting for me. He told me nothing of her, except that I am to act as the stud to impregnate her." He looked at Christian as if searching for some reaction, obviously finding none, for he added clearly, "Melbourne promised a willing woman and an inordinate amount of money to bed her."

He continued on, still watching Christian closely. "Now why, I wondered, would Jarvis Melbourne pay a man to do such a thing? It couldn't be his wife he wants with child. They haven't lived together since that delectable young daughter of theirs wed into this rich Highcrest fortune." He waved a hand to include their luxurious surroundings, and his mouth turned upward at the corner once again. "Nor is Jarvis the family-type man, one who would want another baby to raise. Then I remembered hearing his daughter was widowed—and recently, too. I admit, I didn't learn about your involvement in all of this until this morning. I thought Melbourne's aim was to keep the queen from taking the

Thornton fortune into royal hands.''

Christian heard the words, but it took a moment for reality to sink in. Anne was not pregnant? For one, irrational moment, he felt relief. Anne was not pregnant! But as soon as that thought formed, along with it came the harsh realization that she was a fully willing partner in this scheme to *get* pregnant. Obviously the scheme depended more on her than Jarvis! Was it all her idea? To get herself pregnant and pass the bastard off as the Thornton heir?

Guiscard's voice was low as he added what Christian already knew. "It's you he wants to cheat out of a fortune; it's because of you he wants my bastard to take the place of the old earl's seed."

Anger churned inside him, yet he controlled it. Instead, he allowed a coldness to seep into him, permeating his entire being. His own eyes were no less steely than Guiscard's at that moment.

He turned from Guiscard, calmly walking round the desk and taking the seat he'd occupied the entire morning—the morning he'd spent trying to keep from thinking of Anne, beautiful, innocent Anne. Innocent!

A grain of doubt began to creep in. Was it true? *Could* she be part in such a plan? The Anne he'd become so infatuated with, the Anne with the guileless blue eyes that so fascinated him?

The stranger's voice summoned his attention. "You should have no doubt of the reality of this," he said, as if reading Christian's thoughts. "Where is the countess now, if not waiting at the cottage for me to show up this evening?"

There was sense in that, Christian had to admit. It gave credence to her seemingly sudden departure for the cottage.

"This information is worth your entire fortune," Guiscard said softly. "But I will settle for a mere portion of it. Say, ten thousand sterling?"

"I'll pay you," Christian said coldly. "But not until I am certain this is no fabrication."

"I may be a traitor," the man said steadily, "but I am no liar."

"Then there will be no trouble tonight, when I learn the truth for myself. You shall be paid tomorrow."

"You'd best not show up tonight, my lord," the man said warningly. "It may scuttle the whole plan."

"You've done that already by telling me."

"Oh, I'm still planning to go," he said with a new, lustful twist to his sneering smile. "I remember the daughter well. She'll be a fine one to bed, even if it will be in total darkness. I figure you can put an end to it all after they've already proven their intentions—through me bedding the wench, of course."

As Christian recognized the lust in Guiscard, his hands clenched into fists. But Guiscard's words took his full attention, for an idea was slowly forming.

"In total darkness?" Christian repeated slowly.

Guiscard smirked. "That slow-witted Melbourne actually thought I wouldn't figure out who I'm to bed—as if I wouldn't realize just how important it is for that daughter of his to produce an offspring, no matter where it comes from. Melbourne said I'm to know nothing about the woman, that I'm to perform the act in total darkness." A glint of lust ignited in his otherwise icy black eyes, and he added quietly. "But I remember her well enough. It'll be a pleasure indeed."

Christian's pulse quickened as he imagined this vile man with Anne. A surge of confused emotion rose, and a short-lived battle waged in his brain. He squelched any anger at the man's lust toward Anne; she'd earned any ignoble thoughts directed her way. She deserved to have this cur of a man bed her—deserved to be impregnated by him, and raise a son who would grow to be as much a blackguard as his father.

His mouth twisted to an ugly smile. Anne and her father had once made Christian feel as though he was the one not to be trusted, as though he was fully capable of pretending his way into being named Selwyn's heir. And all the time they—particulary Anne—was capable of something far worse than she and her father had even accused him of.

Christian spoke slowly, with a steady, unfaltering voice

and a tight rein on his emotions. "With the money I pay you, Guiscard, you will be able to buy any woman of your choosing." He sat forward, looking him straight in the eye. "I want to know the details, each and every one."

9

The sky was aflame with color, streamers of pink, purple, orange and fading blue. It would have been a lovely sunset to behold, on any evening except this one.

Anne turned from the window in her room with a scowl. Like a condemned prisoner. How much longer did she have? she asked herself for the thousandth time. It was past six already. Soon, she expected, her father's hired stud would arrive.

A light tap at the door called her attention.

"Your father awaits you downstairs, Countess," Mistress Markay announced through the closed oak-paneled wood.

Anne waited a full five seconds before answering. Then, calmly, despite her inner rage at her father, she told the servant she would be down shortly.

Anne was in no hurry to face her father again. He'd disappeared briefly late in the afternoon, and she'd hoped he would not return until morning. Sickly, she wondered if he trusted her enough to let his stud perform the task without looking over the man's shoulder.

Jarvis stood in the parlor, for once without a glass of wine gracing his hand. When she entered, Anne noticed the glimmer of anticipation in her father's eyes, and it galled her. *He's enjoying this,* she realized with vague surprise. It was like a game, and he hardly cared who he used and how.

"I've told Mistress Markay to keep to her own room

tonight," Jarvis said quietly once Anne approached. "Which room will you be using?"

Anne could not suppress a glare before answering, "My own."

"And which is that?" he asked impatiently.

"The first door on the right at the top of the stairs."

"Ah, that's good. He'll have no trouble finding that."

Anne shuddered, for even talking about what was to happen upstairs already brought a feeling of shame. Perhaps she'd been wrong to choose her own room; it might forever remind her of the horror that would take place there. But she had wanted at least the small comfort of familiarity, she reminded herself, and so she would not change her mind.

"You'll . . . spend the night as well?" Anne asked coldly. She hardly wanted him to, but she needed to know if he would be somewhere in the house.

Jarvis shook his head, at the same time leaving her side to go to the window and look at the ever darkening sky. "I'll be here long enough to greet the man, then I'll be on my way. I have other business besides this, you know."

She scowled; the business he conducted at night, if it was not smuggling, was drinking at the local pub. But she said nothing, for she was glad he would not be beneath the same roof when she submitted to his dreadful plan.

"It's dark," he announced, as if he were a child waiting for the Christmas Spirit to arrive at last. "My man will be here in an hour or so. You'd best have Mistress Markay attend to you now so she'll be confined to her room in time."

Anne hesitated before leaving, eyeing her father with nothing short of contempt. She wanted to say something, to tell him how she hated this plan, this deed, and him, most of all. But no words came, no words seemed strong enough. And, she realized with a heavy heart, what good would it do? She turned slowly away, in search of Mistress Markay.

Christian loosely held the reins of the dark horse he had behind him, gazing through the trees at the rocky pathway that Jarvis Melbourne was known to use from the Thornton seaside cottage. Guiscard had used that very pathway more than a quarter hour before, and soon, Christian suspected, Jarvis would be descending himself.

Inevitably, Christian's thoughts went to the cottage at the top of that cliff, more specifically to Anne. What was she feeling at this moment? he wondered. Did she feel anything at all, being so cold, so manipulative? How could he have been so wrong about her? God's breath, he'd had such dreams of her! How could he have thought those bright blue eyes so guileless, when in fact she was nothing more than an adept actress? A cold-blooded liar, even a thief? He'd been cautious of Jarvis Melbourne from the moment he'd met the man, but little had he suspected that his daughter was just like him.

Christian backed up a bit, enfolding himself and his horse further in the blackness of the forest as he saw the shadow of a rider coming down the hill. It was Melbourne all right, exactly on schedule. In a moment Guiscard should be arriving via the second pathway which led from the back of the cottage.

Christian spotted Guiscard before the other man saw him. Christian had taken a black filly from the Thornton stables rather than riding his snowy white and easily seen Arabian. That, combined with his black cloak made him almost invisible in the thick, shadowy forest.

"Guiscard," Christian called, using a low voice even though he was sure Melbourne was far out of range by then.

The Frenchman's head jerked around in Christian's direction, for he'd been about to pass by without having noticed him. He nudged his mount closer. Christian was already climbing on the back of his own horse.

"She is awaiting you, *monsieur*," Guiscard said with a crooked grin. "And I envy you, my lord, despite the gold you'll be paying me in the morning."

Christian ignored the comment. "Describe the house to me, and give me directions to the room."

Guiscard did so, succinctly and quietly. Then without a farewell, Christian tapped his horse's flank and was off.

The room was, indeed, in total darkness. Heavy velvet

drapes blocked any moonlight, and without so much as a hallway sconce to filter through the cracks of the door, Anne could not even see her own hand pass before her face.

Once Mistress Markay had been excused, leaving Anne in her high-necked lawn sleeping gown, Anne had waited a few minutes before going to the hallway to extinguish the sconces. Then she'd returned to her room, assured herself the windows were well covered, and snuffed out every candle in her room, save one. That she held in her hand and made her way to the bed, but with one vivid image of what was to take place there, she changed her mind and found a chair. Finally she had extinguished the last light and sat in total darkness for what she guessed must have been at least ten minutes.

She shivered, though she was not cold. After helping Anne into her nightdress, Mistress Markay had suggested a fire, but Anne had quickly rejected the idea. Anne could not tell if the room was cool; her nerves were so atwitter. Her hands and feet felt cold, but her palms sweated.

Just then she heard a creak. Was it only a normal sound in the night, or was that him, making his way up the stairs?

After another moment or two of silence, she decided the noise had been the wind on the roof, or perhaps a tree branch scraping the side of the house. He was not coming yet, she consoled herself.

But that consolation lasted less than a moment, as she heard a tap at the door. Her palms clenched into fists and, in a tiny voice, she called for the man to enter.

She heard rather than saw the door open. Although her eyes were well adjusted to the darkness, there was no light at all, and she could not even make out a shadow. She heard the door close firmly behind him.

He stayed near the entrance, she surmised, since she heard no footsteps draw closer. She was glad she'd decided to stay in her own room, as she would know exactly where he was, and how to make her own way around.

But those were foolish thoughts. They would have to come together, and she could not flee. Had she forgotten why they were there?

For a long moment Anne heard nothing save the violent pounding of her heart in her ears and her own uneven breathing. Part of her wanted to move, but she could not make herself stir. She felt powerless over her own body.

The silence stretched out until it became awkward. Anne could hardly make small talk, as even a prostitute might before such an event. At last, she shifted in her seat, inadvertently brushing an elbow against the candlestick she'd set beside her chair earlier. It fell to the floor in a clatter.

The man did not move as she bent and searched blindly for the fallen candle. But he did speak, and she stiffened at his voice.

"Are you hurt?" he whispered.

She could tell nothing from his low tone, though she told herself she didn't want to know even so much as the timbre of his voice. She had decided that if this awful plan succeeded and she did conceive a child, she wanted the baby to be hers and hers alone, without so much as a memory of the man whose seed had impregnated her. What value was there in knowing the identity of the man her father had hired? She could not reveal him later, as her father might fear, without putting herself in every bit as much jeopardy. After all, she was the one going through with the plot, no matter the reason.

"No, I am not hurt," she said, using a hushed voice as well. Then she sat straight, deciding to find the candlestick in the morning, saying, "You . . . you may sit. There is a chair two paces to the left of the door."

There was a low shuffle, then a squeak as the cane-backed chair accepted the stranger's weight.

The silence resumed, stretching out far longer than Anne expected, though, indeed, she had not known exactly what to anticipate. Certainly not this quiet stranger who seemed somewhat solicitious of her. Knowing some of her father's acquaintances, she had at the very least feared a hasty rape, with its only advantage being the swift delivery and a quick end. But this . . . it was as if the man expected *her* to . . . seduce him.

So she sat, and she waited. She'd be damned, to use one

of her father's epithets, if she was going to move first. Time seemed to stand still. The mantel clock ticked away the minutes, but it seemed an eternity between the quarterly chimes. What was the man waiting for? What was he thinking? Why didn't he get on with it?

Anne's chair, she knew, was considerably more comfortable than the cane and ebony chair in which the stranger sat. She considered inviting him to the settee opposite her chair, but quickly decided against it. This was, she admitted to herself, truly ludicrous. They were supposed to be . . . well, they should have at least been on the bed by now, but here they sat on opposite sides of the room like schoolchildren at their first party.

Was he playing some sort of game, she wondered? Her pulse, which had calmed in the last minutes of silent inactivity, now raced anew. Was this man purposely waiting, hoping to make her uncertain? Disorient her in some way? What sort of methods would he use to make her submit to him?

The chimes announced a quarter-hour had passed. Only fifteen minutes! Had the clocked stopped functioning properly? But time did pass, and Anne's nerves soon calmed once again. She might even have been close to dozing, though not for more than a minute or two. She grew more perplexed by the moment. What was wrong with the man? Hadn't her father explained in vivid enough detail what he was to do? No one, she decided, could be so dense not to have figured it out by now, even if her father had been uncharacteristically subtle about describing the task.

But she remained silent, inwardly triumphant her father had chosen a man so ill-suited to the job. It surprised her, considering how important this was to Jarvis, but she couldn't help being overjoyed at the unexpected turn of events.

At last, when the clock chimed eleven, Anne made the only move she could. If he was not initating his end of this, then certainly she wouldn't, either. For whatever reason, the man had obviously decided against bedding her, and that was just fine with her—more than fine, although for the barest moment she wondered if the stranger would betray her to her father. Was there something to be gained by that, for the stranger? She didn't think so.

Anne spoke. "You may leave now," she told the stranger. For a moment she heard nothing, and she wondered if he dozed despite the hard chair beneath him. But then he rose, and left silently. In a flash she went to the closed door behind him, listening to his retreating footfalls down the stairs and out the door.

She breathed a heavy sigh of relief and sagged against the door. This was far better than she'd dared imagine! Better than running away to escape her father! She could simply let the nights pass like this, and Jarvis would never be the wiser. He would simply think the stranger's seed never took root. And perhaps then her life could truly be her own, without her father manipulating her in any way.

Anne went to the untouched bed and sprawled across it. She could not help smiling at herself, having been afraid to come near this piece of furniture during the last hour. How lucky she felt! With this plan foiled, she was sure she could find a way to destroy her father's evidence against Elsbeth by the time Jarvis dreamed up any more schemes in which he needed her assistance. All Anne needed was time, and she had that now. Thanks to the intriguing stranger. As soon as posible, she would go to Gallen's office and hire him to locate the evidence Jarvis had against Elsbeth.

A frown tugged at her brows with thoughts of the stranger. What had been his motive? To double-cross her father? Likely enough. The type of men Jarvis knew were capable of almost anything, including taking payment and then holding out—just as the beady-eyed Baylor had done to her.

Soon after her head rested on the pillow, she fell asleep, the relief that filled her soul giving way to her exhaustion.

She wasn't sure what woke her, the rough jab in her shoulder or her father's sharp voice.

"Get up, girl!"

Groggily, Anne sat up and saw her father's snarling face. Then it all came back, and she feared the night's activity—or lack thereof—had been found out. Had the man her father hired double-crossed her, rather than Jarvis himself as she'd suspected earlier?

Anne slid from the bed when her father's bruising grip clamped around her wrist and pulled her up. He threw back the covers, shouting as he did so.

"This bed hasn't been slept in!"

She denied it immediately. "I . . . I set the covers back in place after he left," she lied, hoping her tone did not betray her.

"And did you change the linens, as well?" he asked, not looking at her but instead at the bed dressing. He seemed to be seeking something in particular, though what Anne could not guess.

"Why, no. . . ."

He eyed her with malice and suspicion. "I thought you said you were a virgin?"

Her heart jarred in her breast. "I—I am," she said, adding lamely, "I was, before last night."

He plainly did not believe her. "And you did not change the linens?"

She shook her head.

He eyed the bed once again, then said, "You're lying."

"No!" she denied. "He was here, you know he was."

Jarvis nodded, a cruel glint to his eye. "And holding back on me, no doubt for more money. But he'll not get away with this," he growled, aiming his cruel stare at Anne. "And neither will you."

He strode toward the door. "He'll be back tonight," Jarvis said, his hand on the gilt door handle. "And tomorrow, if there is no bloodstain upon that bed, I'll have a doctor in tow, to assure me that your maidenhead is, indeed, broken."

Then the truth sank in. Of course! She'd heard there was blood when a virgin was taken. Pel had told her of it when she and Gregory first came together. But she hadn't suspected her father would know of such a thing!

She sank down upon the bed as her father slammed the door behind him. All the joyous relief that had flooded her earlier disappeared before the sound of Jarvis's footsteps had even faded away.

10

Christian was perplexed. Last night, sitting in that detestably uncomfortable chair more than an hour, the anger—yes, even the repugnance—he'd felt for Anne had slowly changed to confusion. He'd waited for her to put her plan into action. Although he'd been uncertain whether or not he'd have gone through with it, he had waited for her to act.

And then, nothing. Minute after interminable minute, she did not move. Once he would have sworn she slept, as he heard her breathing become deep and regular. That's when the confusion was paramount.

He could not figure it out. If she was so anxious to keep the Thornton money through a false heir, then how could she have let the entire night pass without acting on her plot?

Christian sat in the solicitor's salon, a glass of brandy in his hand. He'd slept for an hour or two this morning after he'd gotten home, but the myriad of thoughts rambling through his brain woke him before he'd felt truly rested. At last, tired of tossing in his bed, he'd dressed and come downstairs, only to have his mind as cluttered as ever with the strange twist of the night before.

What would he have done, he asked himself yet again, had she tried to seduce him? Lit a candle, shown his face, accused her right then and there of the plot she'd concocted? That, indeed, was what he'd intended. But instead, the culpable little pretender had let the night pass without doing a single thing to proceed with her scheme.

Had Guiscard warned her? Christian doubted it. Guiscard knew he could get far more money from Christian, and guessed the avaricious Frenchman would rather be sided with the party having more wealth to dig into.

But what possible reason could she have had to let the night pass without going through with what she'd already paid a man to do? It rankled him.

Perhaps she was having second thoughts, doubts about the morality of what she intended. How could she be so devious as to use her body in such a way? To use motherhood in such a way? He had no unnatural esteem for motherhood but, perhaps because he'd lost his mother so young and she had been all he had, he did have a view of it that brooked a certain amount of respect. And Anne, the Anne he thought he'd been coming to know, would not create a human life simply to be used. Once again, unbidden, the image of Anne's bright blue eyes came to him. From that first moment he'd spotted her, he'd thought her eyes were a clear passage to her soul, a soul which was pure and uncorrupt.

But he shook off those thoughts. He'd learned, hadn't he, that she was none of those things? That she was, if nothing else, as avaricious as someone like Guiscard, perhaps more so? Not for the first time, his heart hardened against her. There was no room for doubt, despite last night's surprising twist. She might have had qualms about the actual act of coming together with a total, unseen stranger. But he would not forget that she'd concocted this scheme herself. He guessed, if she could get over any squeamishness about being bedded, she would still go through with the strategy to gain control of the Thornton dynasty.

Waites called from outside the door, saying he had a message in hand.

"Bring it in," Christian called. A moment later the tall servant entered, a sealed envelope in his hand.

Christian tore it open. The note was from Guiscard.

Monsieur, I could not risk being seen with you. What's wrong, did you turn shy? You'd best

take her tonight if you plan to go through with
this, or my neck will be endangered. And I
assure you, if my neck is—so is yours.

G.

Christian crumpled the note, frowning. Vaguely, he was
surprised Guiscard would be bold—or foolish—enough to
threaten him, but that was not what intrigued him most
about the note. Obviously Anne had told Jarvis of the lack of
success of the night before, and they were displeased. What
had she expected? Was a rape more to her taste than having
to seduce the man she'd paid to bed her?

His jaw clenched. What a confused little liar she was, on
the one hand having full participation in a plot to steal his
fortune, and on the other having some sort of specific
expectation about the actual act. It hardly made sense! Well,
if it's a rape she wants, then a rape she'll get.

Anne spent the day in her room. She tried not to be
more disheartened than she had been yesterday at this time,
for she was only right back where she was twenty-four hours
before. But that brief calm she'd experienced in the early
hours of the morning, that vision of hope she'd endured her
father's plan without actually going through with it, made
the reality of it now seem even worse than the day before.

How she wished she could escape! But she was trapped,
she knew it. Her father had not assigned her a guard. She had
a horse and food and clothes, even the remaining costly
brooch, all at her disposal. But she couldn't leave, and her
father was fully secure and disgustingly happy in that
knowledge. He had her mother.

Anne stood at her window, looking out at the western
sky much as she had done the day before at roughly the same
time. There was no lovely sunset to view this time, for the sky
was laden with clouds, thick and gray and gloomy. At last
she turned away, pulling the heavy, emerald green velvet
draperies snugly into place. By the time Mistress Markay

came to unfasten the back laces of Anne's bodice, the room was already cast deep in shadows.

Mistress Markay was a taciturn older woman. Missing the company of a friend, Anne was tempted to speak to her, but held back. Anne's mood was too low to carry on any sort of conversation. She made but one statement, and that was to remind Mistress Markay to stay within her room throughout the night. Briefly, Anne imagined the servant must wonder why she was being confined to her room, but it was not Mistress Markay's place to question, and Anne was hardly willing to give any explanation.

Soon after Mistress Markay departed, the room was in total darkness but for the single candle Anne once again kept lit. Tonight, knowing her certain fate, she went to her dressing table and pulled from a drawer a tiny vial Sewlyn had given her the first night they were to have been together. He'd told her, gently and as subtly as possible to spare her further embarrassment, that she should rub some of the sweet-smelling oil between her legs, and it would ease the passage when they came together. She had done so that first and second night of their marriage, but Selwyn had never been able to teach her if it would, indeed, do as he promised. Tonight, she thought as she swallowed a painful lump, she would find out.

Her hands trembled as she applied the cold, thickened oil. Despite its age of more than a year, it still smelled of lavender, and Anne was reminded of that night with Selwyn. She'd been afraid then, too, but in a different way. She'd barely known Selwyn, but surprisingly enough guessed he would not have hurt her. But he had done little more than stroke her face with trembling hands, and in the end he'd sobbed for what could not be. He had cried for the children he would never have.

That thought brought Christian to mind, and inexplicably she pulled her hand away from her most intimate part, as if embarrassed to be thinking of him while doing such a thing. But his image came to mind before she could prevent it. She wondered what it would feel like to have him stroke her there. She was far too nervous to feel or even imagine any pleasure, but Selwyn had told her that the act of lovemaking could be one of the greatest joys a husband and wife could have together. And she knew she would have liked to discover if that were true . . . with Christian.

But she banished him from her thoughts. She could not allow any image of him, most especially tonight. Not when she must do what she must do.

She wiped her hand on the small towel resting on her dressing table, then carried the candle with her as she made her way to the bed. Exiling all thought from her mind, she threw back the covers to the very edge of the bed, then lay down. Finally, she leaned over to the table beside her and blew out the candle. The room was in total darkness, and she waited.

The noise, when it came, was slight, but enough to send a rush of nerves sliding down Anne's spine. She heard the door handle move and she trembled, clutching her hands upon her chest, only to feel the erratic pounding of her heart. She moved her hands away from the reminder of just how uneasy she was.

This time the man didn't knock, but merely slipped noiselessly into the room. For a moment there was silence, then in a deep, low voice he spoke.

"Direct me to you," he commanded, and there was such quiet force in his voice that Anne was hesitant to answer. But she knew she must.

"I am here, on the bed. It is directly in front of you—perhaps four paces if you do not take long strides."

She heard him step, surprisingly sure-footed for someone in an unfamiliar room in total darkness. Then she heard him draw near. She could vaguely smell the not pleasant aroma of saddle leather and perhaps soap, a musky scent that she thought for a moment was familiar.

But then all thought scattered as she felt the bed sag beside her. Part of her wanted to bolt, but she willed herself to stay, knowing the consequences if she disappointed her father yet again.

"I can only guess you want this quickly and without

care," the man said, his tone still low but harsher than
before. "You should have told me last night, milady, that
this was how you wanted it."

Suddenly she felt a firm grip on her wrist, and from
there he seemed to know immediately where the rest of her
body was. His mouth came down on hers with such pressure
that she was driven deeply back into her pillow. His lips were
hard and dry, and the force behind them bruised her. He still
held one of her wrists, but her other hand was free and, after
the initial shock of his brutal kiss, she tried pushing him
away. He seemed not even to feel her resistance.

With his mouth so tight against her own, she could not
speak, but she did moan—a pathetic, wimpering little sound
that sounded foreign to her own ears. She had never felt so
totally overpowered—not even by her father, who had
threatened to beat her numerous times.

Her sound of protest seemed to reach him. He lifted his
mouth only a breath away, but far enough to allow Anne to
speak.

"No! I—do not want it like this," she said, hating
herself for begging but desperate to forestall him. She was
breathless from his assault, and gasped for air. Her breasts
rose and fell with each deep breath, beneath the stranger's
chest, rock-hard with muscle. This man, surely, could kill her
if he so chose.

"Then how is it you would like it, milady?" he asked
hoarsely. Though she could not even imagine what he looked
like, she knew the words had been accompanied by a sneer.
"You chose not to seduce me. Shall I seduce you?"

"No . . . I just . . ." She wanted to scream the truth, to
shout that she wanted no part of this at all, that she was here
against her will and no matter how much he was being paid it
was still a rape. But she knew she could not. Her mother's
life was at stake. She took a deep breath to steady herself. "I
want this to be over as quickly as possible. I . . . I will lie
back and you . . . you may do it when you are ready."

Then she shut her eyes tightly, despite the fact she could
not see, anyway.

There was an agonizingly long span of time in which

nothing happened. The stranger did not move, nor did he speak. Anne wondered if he would leave, he sat so long, seemingly contemplating.

He had mentioned seduction. Was that the only other way, other than rape, that this man knew? She knew nothing of how a man became excited and ready to bed a woman. Did they need violence or passion along with it? Couldn't they just do it?

Obviously not, he was taking so long. It was up to her, truly up to her. And since violence was out of the question . . . She took a second deep breath, hating each moment which passed. She could easily grow to hate all men, she thought. She hadn't expected her father's plot would take so much more effort than she'd originally feared.

Slowly, she reached out to touch him. She had no idea how to seduce a man, but she assumed some contact was in order. Her hand brushed his chest, and she felt the smooth fabric, perhaps camlet, of his coat. Then she touched his face, ever so gently, and found he had a lean, strong jaw, and smooth skin with just a hint of roughness to it. So, he had not shaved for the occasion, and for some reason she found that funny. But she did not laugh.

She had touched little more than his chin before she felt his hand on hers, drawing her away. When he let her go and did not touch her in return, she moved closer to him and touched him again, this time letting her fingertips trace the smooth skin of his lips. She brought her other hand upward, too, and let her palms rest on his cheeks before sliding back into his hair. She found it tied in a queue and, more deftly than she would have guessed possible from her own nervousness, she released it from the ribbon.

She had not bargained for this, had not expected that she must play such an active role in this most detestable part of her father's plot. But what amazed her even more was that it was not at all so abhorrent as she would have guessed. Though she could not see so much as a shadow of the man, from the limited contact they had, she knew much about him already. She knew he was strong and lean and clean-smelling;

his hair was clean as well, and though she guessed his coat was of fair quality, she assumed he could afford no wig, since those of her father's acquaintances rarely had much money. She found she was glad he wore his own hair, for she knew it was the custom of men who wore wigs regularly to shave their head. And a shaven head could not possibly be as pleasant to touch as his thick, sweet-smelling hair.

But this was ridiculous! she silently scolded herself, appalled at her own thoughts. Was she some kind of whore, enjoying this as she was? She started to pull away, ashamed at herself. Perhaps she should let him rape her, she thought desolately. At least then no part of the shame could be hers.

But he resisted when she withdrew. He caught her hands gently this time and replaced them around his neck. Then, softly, his mouth came down on hers.

If she had not expected any of this, neither had she expected a kiss to make her tingle. His lips were warm, more tender than she would have believed possible only a minute ago when he'd kissed her so fiercely. At first he hardly touched her, letting his mouth barely caress hers with tiny, brief grazes that left her wanting more. Then he closed in on her lips, still gentle, but more lingering. A moment later she was startled, feeling something smooth and wet—his tongue! It brushed her lips, and she was astounded by the intimacy.

"Open your mouth to me," he whispered, and she did so without thought, forgetting the dismay of moments ago, the admonitions against taking pleasure in something she should not be enjoying.

His tongue against hers felt wonderfully enticing, as it explored the inside of her mouth slowly and at perfect ease. She allowed her own tongue to slide around his and once, quickly, to venture past his inviting lips and into his mouth. But she felt too unsure, too shy, to linger.

Reluctantly, she did not protest when his mouth left hers. His kiss found its way over her cheek, slightly down her neck and back up again, to her ear, which he kissed as intimately as he'd kissed her mouth only a moment ago. She felt herself leaning toward him, almost pressing herself to him, she wanted to be so close. She could not seem to stop herself from melting against him, her entire body growing pliant at his touch.

They were still sitting, and now he took her fully into his arms and shifted their weight to lay back. He held her close as he kissed her, one arm around her and one hand stroking her hair, which she'd left loose for the night. How she wished this could go on! Forget the reasons, forget why they were here, she only wanted this pleasure to last and let the rest of the world be damned.

Gradually, his free hand left her hair and caressed her face, stroking one cheek gently and then touching her neck. His fingertips brushed the top of her gown, fastened with the tiny buttons at the throat. Deftly, he loosened her gown, freeing each button one by one. She barely noticed, until he reached the last button which was just below her navel and she realized so much of her body would easily be exposed to him. She felt suddenly shy, having thought this deed would not be quite as thorough as it was turning out to be. She tugged her mouth from his, with one hand pulling the gown closed again.

He was gently persistent, taking that hand in his and kissing her fingertips. Then, still holding her hand, he kissed her mouth again and, little by little, she relaxed once more. His kiss moved on, traveling lower, reaching her neck and nuzzling beneath the open collar. His hand never left hers, even as his kiss went ever lower, until reaching her breast. She sucked in her breath at such contact, feeling his lips upon one taut peak. Her breathing resumed slowly, irregularly at first. She never would have dreamed she would be allowing —aye, enjoying—so many intimacies. She had thought to be over with it as quickly as possible . . . but now, she wouldn't have minded if it would go on throughout the night. Something had grown inside of her, perhaps from the very first gentle touch, that was now fully identifiable. She desired this, her body wanted what this man was doing, she wanted to go on with it, to carry it through to the end. Perhaps Selwyn had been only partially right—joy could be found between man and woman, not only man and wife.

The stranger loosened her hand only long enough to free himself of his coat and waistcoat. A moment later he slipped away, and she heard the soft whisper of more clothing as it sank to the floor. Then he laid beside her again, and her hands brushed against naked flesh.

She should have been shy, but she was curious. The darkness gave her fingers boldness, and she touched his chest, finding it hair-roughened and as rock-hard as she'd suspected through his clothing. Her hand skimmed his shoulders and crossed something not so smooth as the rest of him. A scar, crescent-shaped, she discovered in her sightless exploration, along the back of one shoulder. Then, when he pulled at her gown, she squelched the last of her admonitions and aided him in discarding the last garment between them.

She relished the feel of his body against hers. His arms were as hard as his chest, his legs long and firm, with hair that tickled against her own, softer limbs. Briefly, she wondered if his hair was dark or light, but then he was kissing her again and it blocked out all thought.

One hand gently caressed her breast, and she swelled at the touch, her breathing once again becoming ragged. She wanted this, oh, how she wanted this! She didn't let herself think, she only felt, and she could only marvel at the magic he created in her.

Her entire body seemed as if under a spell, enchanted by this man's touch. Wherever his fingers grazed or lingered, the spot seemed aflame, and she fell deeper into the spell his lovemaking wove. He kissed her breasts again, nibbling tenderly and sending wave upon wave of delight through her body.

Then, while still kissing her, his hand skimmed further downward, stroking her hip, her belly, her thigh, until she thought she would burst if he did not find the center of her desire. When he did, she shivered at her own response, so thoroughly did it penetrate. She had spread oil between her thighs, but she felt tenfold wetter, and could only guess nature had supplanted the aid she'd used. When his fingers lightly explored her, she held back her breath altogether, letting it out slowly in one low-pitched sigh.

Anne thought she would simply melt in a pool of her own desire, so pliant to him did she feel. Her body felt hot where it met his, along the entire length, but in a moment when he shifted, separating them for a moment, she felt cold where he no longer held her.

Tenderly, he spread her legs, and she felt him kneel between them. Then, with one hand beneath each buttock, he pulled her slightly upward against him and she felt his manhood, hard and as hot as she, at the feminine entrance. He pressed against her, but after a moment withdrew, and Anne might have squirmed, for she felt herself slide back fully upon the bed.

"You're a virgin," he whispered, and though she did not know his hushed voice well, she heard the astonishment.

"Yes . . . I am," she admitted. "But . . . I mustn't be, not after tonight."

His touch seemed to change then, at first almost imperceptibly, but she did not imagine it when he pulled her back against him, this time a bit rougher.

In a flash he was inside, with one quick stroke. She had told herself earlier it would hurt, for where there was blood there was pain, but she'd forgotten and, she thought somewhat begrudgingly, she might not have felt it at all had he just continued and not paused to announce what she already knew.

But after a moment she forgot the pain. He eased her back and held her close, but she barely felt his weight upon her. His hair-covered chest caressed hers, and his mouth came down on her own. Even if it was a bit rougher than before, she didn't mind. Her fingers brushed again that crescent-shaped scar, and she welcomed the shape of it—for it was uniquely his. A fire was building in her loins, stoked by this man, whose every movement gave her pure pleasure. He plunged deep inside her, and she felt more of his weight when his arms came around to hold her beneath her hips, teaching her to meet each of his thrusts. She did so with a willing heart, for each drive added to the fire already burning out of control deep within her. It grew and grew, seeming to cast her entire being into flames. The pace quickened, and before long she did not need his assistance to meet his thrusts, though she enjoyed the feel of his fingers on her backside and she did not want him to remove them. All of it together, his fingers, his hard chest, his deep kiss, his manhood buried deep within her, combined to take her outside herself, carried away in pleasure that seemed almost too great to bear until it exploded from her middle, permeating outward and upward to reach her stomach, her chest, her arms and legs and toes. Her entire body a mass of such exquisite pleasure, she fell back deeper into the pillow, not even aware that both his thrusts and her own, meeting his, had stopped.

Neither moved for a moment. Anne felt his weight and she still took pleasure from it, though she knew if she allowed herself to think about each of her reactions to him, she would be appalled at her behavior. She was damp with sweat, both his and her own, seemingly from head to foot. Her hair clung to her forehead, and when she lifted one hand to wipe it away, the man shifted off her.

The air felt cool where he'd left her body exposed but, still covered by the total darkness, she did not hurry to find a blanket or wrapper. Instead, she merely lay back, luxuriating in the astonishing feelings she'd just discovered—through him.

Perhaps that was why she was surprised to hear him dressing already. She sat up, wanting to say something but unable to choose any words that conveyed her feelings. For, in truth, she did not know what she felt. She didn't want any part of this, she loathed and detested all the reasons this man had come to her. But she could not deny the awful truth: not only did she want this man to stay, she wanted him to hold her again, to restoke that incredible fire he'd ignited in her only moments ago.

What could she say to a man who'd given her so much, although she did not know him, could not see him, would never see him? Tentatively, she reached out, but he had already stood, and her touch could not reach him.

"For a virgin," he said coldly, "you seem to have a natural knack for this sport, my lady. You were born a whore."

A moment later she heard his retreating footsteps, but she could not move, could not speak. She was frozen in place, her hand still outstretched.

The word seemed to echo in her head. Whore. He'd called her a whore . . . but what else must she be, to the man who'd been paid to bed her? What else, indeed, even to herself?

At last she fell back, limp, and still unclothed. Tears sprang to her eyes, and she had no strength to hold them back. His words rang in her ears as if he were still there, labeling her over and again. Whore . . . whore . . . words that, despite her pain, she could not deny.

11

Anne barely tasted the chocolate she sipped. She wasn't at all hungry, but had accepted the cup of steaming chocolate to stop Mistress Markay from offering yet again something for Anne to eat. "A body needs sustenance," she'd said, "especially one as thin as yours." Coming from Mistress Markay's plump form, it was obvious she firmly believed in plentiful sustenance. So at last, more than an hour past noon, Anne had agreed to chocolate and toast, hardly a hearty meal, but enough to satisfy Mistress Markay for the time being. She was like a mother, wanting her child to eat. That thought made her heart twist, so worried was Anne over the treatment and well-being of her own mother.

Anne sat in the parlor, trying without success to banish last night from her mind. But it all came back, over and over, with disturbing clarity. Each renewed memory of it brought a hot flush to her face, and her insides twisted with nausea. She could not help but be appalled at what she had done. She'd actually enjoyed it! Enjoyed bedding with a perfect stranger, enjoyed having her body joined with a man she did not even know.

The stranger's words still haunted her. He'd called her a whore, and she knew it was true. Last night after he'd left, she'd crawled from the bed, which was still warm from their passion. Welcoming the darkness, she did not light a candle. She had found her discarded nightgown and slipped back into it, then made her way to one of the chairs. She would not return to sleep in that bed.

This morning her father's pounding at the door had awakened her. The room was still dim, with only a few narrow shafts of sunlight sifting through the gap in the draperies. He had not bothered to wait for her call to enter; in a moment he stood before her, towering over her bed. Then he'd looked at her, huddled in the chair with her arms hugging her knees. He'd smiled a triumphant smile. She'd never hated him more than at that moment.

And what of tonight? she wondered now. Her mouth compressed into a harsh frown. Tonight, she resolved with a will of iron, nothing will happen. Tonight and all the nights to come, until her next monthly flux and she convinced her father it was too late to conceive and have anyone believe it was Selwyn's child. If the stranger expected to be seduced—or even find her willing—he was in for a surprise. Instead, he would see himself back on that hard ebony chair for the night.

The thought put a cynical smile on her face. She hated herself for how she had reacted to him, but wasn't he just as much to blame? After all, he'd called her a whore when it was his caress that had set her aflame with desire. And though she didn't know the way of men, she thought he'd enjoyed their coupling, too. Did that make him some kind of lecher?

She hadn't heard the summons at the door until seeing Mistress Markay hurrying to greet a caller. Anne's heart skipped a beat, fearful for a moment that it would be her father, back to torment her with another of his knowing smiles.

But it was not Jarvis. Instead, she heard the polite voice of a manservant, and a moment later Mistress Markay entered the parlor with a folded note in her hand.

"A message for you, my lady," Mistress Markay announced. "From the earl."

Anne set aside her chocolate, appalled that her hands shook so fiercely that the delicate china clattered in her ears. Mistress Markay seemed not to notice, however, that Anne's hands still trembled ever so slightly as she accepted the proferred message. The servant merely handed her the note, then added, "He did not wait for an answer, Countess."

Anne nodded, her attention already focusing on the note. "Very well, Mistress Markay. You may return to your duties."

Anne unfolded the note.

> I plan to ride to the coast today. I hope you will not mind if I visit you at the cottage. Expect me around two.
>
> Respectfully,
> Christian Thornton

Anne read the note with a mixture of dread and anticipation, then, with a glance to the clock sitting on the parlor mantel, the dread increased tenfold as she realized it was near two already. She grimaced, thinking that while the note was cordial enough, it was still somewhat overbearing. He had not given her the slightest chance to refuse his visit.

She did not want to see Christian, and she knew it was because she felt so overwhelming impure, so guilty over what she had done the night before. This whole plot was against him, and what had she done? Fallen into the stranger's arms and delighted in his every caress.

But even while these misgivings surfaced, she couldn't help wondering why he was coming. Was he making the trip out to the coast especially to see her? She hadn't even said good-bye, not properly, anyway. Had that bothered him in some way, so that he wanted to see her now? Perhaps to ask if she'd made her decision about how long she would be staying at the cottage?

It was ludicrous to think he might miss her, but could it be possible?

She had little time to dwell on such questions, however. There was barley enough time to return to her room, change into a gown and over-bodice of somber black mourning damask more suitable for visitors than the linen clothes she usually wore at the cottage. Then she added the faintest touch of powder to her already smooth, white skin and tied up her golden hair in a neat chignon. Just as she was inserting the last pin in her hair, she heard the summons at the door belowstairs and knowing Christian had arrived, she nearly dropped the pin from her suddenly trembling hands.

Anne entered the parlor a few minutes later, hoping she did not look quite as flustered as she felt. Christian stood by a window, sunlight setting dark bronzed highlights aflame in his queued hair. He wore a blue coat made of frieze, dark breeches, and contrasting white hose. And never, Anne decided as she saw him step through the entryway to greet her, had he looked more handsome.

"Good afternoon," he said, turning from the window to face her fully. As he watched her approach, his intense gaze was more noticeable than ever. For a moment it made her want to shiver.

"Have you dined?" she asked politely, quelling the nervousness his visit—and his stare—caused her.

"No, I haven't," he said. "But do not trouble yourself."

"Oh, it will be no trouble at all. Mistress Markay loves to feed people," she told him, smiling.

Anne headed for the kitchen, but Mistress Markay had anticipated such an order and was already bringing out flatware and dishes to the small alcove off the parlor which served as a dining room. The competent servant left Anne nothing to do but entertain her guest.

She took a seat before the windows, welcoming the warmth of the sun. Christian took the brocade chair opposite her, and she could not shake the feeling that he was eyeing her a bit more closely than usual.

"Did you enjoy your ride to the coast?" she asked conversationally.

"Actually, I haven't been all the way to the coast yet. I came here first." His dark eyes bore into her.

"Did you . . . wish to speak to me about something?"

"You left so suddenly the other day, and at a rather unusual hour."

"I prefer to travel when the roads are quiet." Never

mind that the road between here and Highcrest was little used, except by the few servants living at the manor.

"And you didn't allow any footmen to accompany you."

Anne managed a smile. "Have you come here to berate me, my lord?"

Surprisingly, he stood and looked out the window once again, presenting her with his stiff back. "No," he said over his shoulder. "I just wanted . . . to see you."

She noted the brief hesitation in his voice and wondered at it; he sounded almost unsure of himself. But, of course, there was no reason for that, and she convinced herself she was mistaken. There was, however, one advantage to having him stand with his back to her. His piercing gaze was directed elsewhere, and it made Anne feel immensely relieved. She relaxed just a bit. Perhaps if she did not think of all the problems her father had foisted upon her, she could enjoy Christian's visit.

"Are you settling into the duties of earl?" she asked pleasantly.

"Well enough," he said, still not looking at her.

"I think Mortimer will one day work himself to heaven. He'll do it to you, too, if you let him."

He glanced at her over his shoulder and said with one skeptically raised brow, "Concerned?"

Confused over the cool tone of his voice, she hesitated before answering, "Of course . . . that is, I do not wish anyone to work themselves into an early grave."

"How kind of you," he said in a low, unfriendly way.

Anne stood, puzzled by his behavior. He was acting as if he had come unwillingly, as if he didn't want to be there visiting her. She hadn't asked him to come!

Deciding it was better to confront rather than avoid what seemed obvious, she asked, "Christian, something is troubling you—and it seems to have something to do with me. What is it?"

He faced her, his countenance once again void of all emotion. She hated it when he wore that mask; she could read nothing of his inner thoughts.

"Nonsense," he told her, looking her straight in the eye. "I came here to see that you are well and ask if there is anything you would like from the manor. One of your servants seemed quite upset over your quick departure. Pel is her name, I believe. Would you like me to have her sent here when I return?"

Indeed, Anne would have liked that very much. But under the circumstances that was out of the question. Pel would never be as meek and unquestioning as Mistress Markay, remaining in her room if she heard any noises from upstairs during the night. And for Pel's own sake, Anne could not risk having her concerned friend here.

"No. Pel is to marry soon," Anne explained. "I did not wish for her to leave the side of the man she is to wed."

"You will be staying here indefinitely, then?"

A moment ago she would have said no, only for the six-week mourning period she had originally told him of. By then her monthly flux will have long been returned—for it was due by the next full moon and already the sphere was growing more round during the night. Once her father's plot against Christian failed, she could return to Highcrest. But now, seeing Christian in such a strangely antagonistic mood, she hesitated.

"I still haven't made up my mind."

He shrugged as if it hardly mattered. He had started to turn away again when Mistress Markay called their attention.

"I have a bit of dinner here, if you'd care to partake, my lord, Countess."

The two went to the dining alcove. Had her mood been lighter, Anne would have laughed at what Mistress Markay called "a bit of dinner:" steaming baked shrimp, duck with onion sauce, potatoes in cream, hot bread, a variety of vegetables swimming in cheese or butter, along with tea and coffee and more chocolate for dessert.

"Will your mother join us?" Christian asked before nearing his chair.

The question, innocent enough, sent a wave of worry rushing through Anne. She did not want Christian to know

Elsbeth was at her father's. He might require an explanation, considering he was aware how Anne's parents felt about each other.

"This is my mother's nap time," Anne said, truthfully enough. Did he have to know she was not taking her nap upstairs? God, she prayed, please let her mother be napping peacefully at her father's!

Christian accepted Anne's words, and they began their dinner in silence.

At last Anne spoke. She wanted to chat with him, to enjoy the same easy conversations she'd had with him back at Highcrest. She wanted to banish this coolness in him, even though she was uncertain why it was there. And his silence only seemed to intensify his black mood.

"What was your mother like?" she asked curiously.

He seemed surprised by her question. "She died a very long time ago," he said softly.

"But surely you remember her well; she was your mother."

"Yes, I remember her."

"Then tell me of her. That is," she added, "if you wouldn't mind."

He eyed her. "Why do you wish to hear of a woman who was in your husband's past?"

Anne had not considered that connection. She'd thought only that the woman was Christian's mother, forgetting entirely that the woman was also a former paramour of Selwyn's.

But she was undaunted, saying, "I am not troubled by those whom Selwyn loved. He loved Celine throughout his marriage to me."

She said the words honestly, without pain.

"And you never begrudged him this?" Christian asked.

"One cannot be forced to stop loving, even if that person is dead."

"You speak wisely for one so young."

She lifted her chin slightly. "I shall be eighteen soon." Then she realized he had successfully diverted her from asking any more about his mother. She did not press the issue, however, knowing she would not have liked to be pressed about her own mother.

"Tell me how you learned to speak English so fluently," she said after a moment, still hoping they could enjoy a cordial conversation. "If you were poor most of your life, how did such a penniless Frenchman come to know a foreign language?"

"From my mother," he said. Then he asked, "Do you really wish to hear of this? Of her?"

Anne nodded without hesitation.

Christian seemed to relax then, speaking freely. "She was orphaned herself at a very young age, but she'd been a pretty, affectionate, child, and an old gentleman from her village had always been fond of her. When her father died, he took her in. He'd been a university scholar for many years, and was educated in languages and sciences. He taught my mother to speak four languages, how to read and write, how to speak to any nobleman from England, Russia, Italy or Holland. I think that was one of the things which drew Selwyn to her. She was a French peasant who spoke to him like an English noblewoman."

Anne smiled. Christian had loved his mother, she could tell. Soon their conversation became easier. Anne asked more questions, and Christian did not seem at all loathe to answer her. Dinner stretched out, and Anne, despite the fact she had not been at all hungry, found she'd eaten a hearty portion of every single dish offered.

Finally Mistress Markay brought out a tray of sweet-meats and small sugar cakes. Christian helped himself to one of each variety, and Anne surprised herself by enjoying one sugar cake and a cup of chocolate.

Anne laughed after one of Christian's amusing stories, then said impulsively, still smiling, "I think I will return to Highcrest in less than six weeks, my lord. I miss sharing my meals with you."

Instead of the expected pleasant reply, Christian stiffened at her words, as if suddenly reminded of something that troubled him.

"Whatever you wish, Countess," he said coolly, his

tone harsh and indifferent. "Selwyn made sure in his last wishes that you are always to be welcomed at Highcrest."

"And you would welcome me for that reason only?" She couldn't hold back the question.

An impersonal shrug was his only answer. Suddenly, the atmosphere between them turned awkward again.

Anne glanced at the tiny locket watch she wore around her neck. Past five already! It would grow dark in a few hours. Her father may stop by again before nightfall, and she did not want him to see Christian there. The afternoon had been so wonderful . . . until this moment.

"Perhaps you should be going, my lord," she said without looking at him. "It is a fair ride back to the manor, and if you leave now you will arrive before nightfall."

She spoke with as cool a tone as he himself had used earlier. Given his last reply, she doubted that he wished to linger in her company, anyway.

"Yes, I wouldn't want to be caught here after nightfall." His stiffly issued statement confirmed the fact that his mood had, indeed, gone chilly again.

He stood, and Anne felt both relief and regret as Christian took his leave. What a confounding man he was! He'd been so cool when first seeing her, then he'd proceeded to cordially enjoy a meal with her. Then he'd turned cold again. How did the man think?

He took his leave with the briefest of farewells. Anne watched him from the cottage door as he mounted his horse, a different one from his Arabian, she absently noted. She did not return to the cottage until he was well down the hill and out of sight.

12

Once Christian was at the base of the pathway leading down the hill, he directed his horse toward the coast rather than to the road leading back to Highcrest.

It was a scant five minutes before the grassy earth turned rocky, and he was within sight of the channel. He let his horse walk slowly as he made his way to an old cabin he'd spotted yesterday while awaiting darkness. It must have once belonged to a fisherman or perhaps a smuggler, for it was near the water, yet set far enough back to be hidden by the trees. Though it appeared abandoned, it must had been used relatively recently, for there was only a slight buildup of dust over the bare wooden floor.

Christian saw to his horse, leaving him saddled, but giving him fresh water from a pouch he'd tied over the animal's backside. Then he took cover inside the deserted house.

He sat on the floor, leaning back against one of the walls. Then, with his head resting against the wall, he closed his eyes and let the afternoon replay in agonizing detail.

He would've liked to curse at her, or shake her, or demand she tell him the truth. How could she look so innocently beautiful when inside she was as deceitful as a snake? She had held one friendly conversation after another, breaking bread with him as if there were nothing more between them than a family friendship.

He cursed aloud, standing and pacing as a vision of her face, smiling and lovely, came to him so vividly it made him ache inside. Blast, but he had wanted to tell her! He wanted to tell her it was he who came to her the night before, he who had taken her virginity. God! She didn't even know. She didn't know who she had given herself to for the very first time.

It had sickened him all night and all morning, until he'd given in to his frustration and scrawled off a note to her, saying he would visit. He'd had to see her, had to see if she would be any different after what she'd done. After all, she may not know it was he who'd taken her virginity, but she knew who this plot of hers was pitted against.

And there had been no change in her. Her eyes, those tempting, innocent blue eyes held no more malice or intrigue than a tiny babe's. Her smile was as fresh, her manner as congenial. Damn! He'd been a fool today. He hadn't meant to stay longer than a few moments, to see her and connect in his mind the angelic face he remembered too well to the deceitful wench he'd bedded the night before. He had even been prepared to tell her everything, to expose her plan. Wasn't that what he'd intended to do last night?

He'd been weak then—more than weak, he'd been a fool. Last night, when he neared her on the bed, his full intention was to play it only so far, long enough to know for certain she would actually go through with it. Then he was to have lit a candle, and oh, how he would have enjoyed seeing that cherubic face then, when she discovered him instead of some stranger! He had tried to resist, although he admitted not very hard, when sensing how willing she was. But she'd touched him, and that had been his undoing. Once her fingers had brushed his mouth, once she pressed herself close, he was doomed.

And she'd been a virgin! That was the most astonishing thing in all of this. He might have pulled back, halted what had at the moment seemed inevitable, but when she'd told him she must be a virgin no longer, any semblance of reason had snapped inside him. He'd almost hated her for what she was doing. And, hating himself as well, he'd succumbed to the pure lust of it and gone ahead, rather than pulling back and revealing to her that he knew exactly what she was about.

Yet along with even the most uncharitable thoughts of her, he could not deny that part of him was relieved she'd been a virgin. He hated to admit it, but it was true. He was glad she'd never bedded with his father, glad she didn't carry any other man's child. More foolishness, he chided himself. Was he still feeling that useless infatuation for her, even after what he knew of her now? That she was a deceitful, conniving fortune hunter?

Then a vision of the night before came to him, of the desire she'd stirred in him and the passion he'd sensed in her. He should hate her, he knew, but he didn't. Even now, thinking of what they'd shared, he wanted nothing more than to go to her immediately and find the same passion he'd found the night before. It wasn't just the pleasure of it, he realized. It was her, the passion in her, the ardorous way in which she welcomed each of his caresses. Was she so adept at lovemaking, even though she'd held on to her maidenhead, or was he right in thinking she had discovered passion last night for the first time? He shook his head, not knowing what to believe. He wanted to think she'd never been so much as touched by another man, that the first stirrings deep inside her had been created by him. But, he realized with a sinking heart, she could have deceived him in that, too.

He shook off any traces of dust from sitting so briefly on the floor and banished as well any more thoughts. Dwelling on Anne Thornton would lead only to pain, if he could not rid himself of this foolish confusion. Indeed, there should be no question at all; she was a liar and a fortune hunter. That should end any confusion, for he could never come to love someone such as that.

He sneered at himself when the word love came to mind. Surely he'd never entertained thoughts about the innessential emotion. It was lust he felt for her, nothing more. And lust was all he needed. After all, if she wanted a man to bed her, he could satisfy his lust and foil her plans all at the same time.

It was growing dark. Despise her he might, but he wanted her. And soon, once again, he would have her.

* * *

Christian made his way noiselessly to the room. He was sure of the way by now, his third time. Last night he'd barely knocked, but tonight he was more solicitous. He wondered what kind of greeting she would give this night.

He tapped on the door, and a moment later she called to him. He entered, but even in the total darkness he sensed she was in the chair and not on the bed. Her voice had come from the corner of the room.

He stood in silence. He did not like to speak, afraid she might come to recognize his voice. But, he consoled himself, he was the last person she would expect in this room; he had little fear she would suspect him.

"You may sit on the chair," she told him after a moment.

He did not obey. Part of him rebelled at the idea. Was he to spend the night on that hard chair again? He had to admit he was fully expecting a repeat of the night before, and the idea that it was not to be brought more disappointment than he cared to realize. Besides, what sort of game was this? He had hoped, on that first night, that she'd changed her mind and would not go through with her plans. But last night had shown him she had few qualms about her scheme. She'd enjoyed it, he knew she had.

"I was not paid to sit on a chair through the night, my lady," he whispered, somewhat firmly. Then he took two steps closer. Her voice made him halt.

"Stop," she said, and it almost sounded like a plea. He could imagine her holding up one delicate hand, as if that would have been enough to stave off a man who wanted her, the type of man without a scruple whom she'd had her father hire for the job. But Christian stopped.

"I—I am not ready for you tonight."

Christian smiled. "Do you mean that lavender oil you used last night, my lady? You hardly needed it."

"No! No . . . I do not want this tonight."

Christian paused, uncertain. Was her plan dictated by her passion? Was she only going through with it when her body wanted a man? It was hardly as cold-blooded as he'd expected, but it was no less dispicable. "Should I leave, then?''

"No," she said. "Please . . . just sit and do not come nearer.''

He was confused, but he did as she asked and returned to the annoyingly unwelcoming chair.

This night was even longer than the first. Christian shifted position often, trying to find a comfortable spot on the unyielding chair but to no avail. Minutes passed and neither spoke, the only sound being his own restlessness. He couldn't be sure, but he thought she started each time he moved, and after a while he tried to remain still. It was as if she was frightened of him, frightened he would force her to the bed as someone like Guiscard no doubt would have done. And though he might despise her, he had no wish to terrify her, so he tried not to move. There was no comfortable position to be found, anyway.

He wasn't sure what he expected on this night—well, he had expected to be bedding her again, but he had wondered if she would be as amorous as she had been the night before. Certainly he had not expected this meek, shy person she presented tonight. She seemed more frightened tonight than she had been on that very first night—at least then she had trusted him enough to actually sleep. Tonight she seemed more like a frightened rabbit, and her extreme mood swing confused him.

A morbid and disheartening thought came to him. He knew little enough of her family; her father was an avaricious squire, and her mother suffered an illness of the mind. Could it be possible, he wondered with dread, that Anne truly was a product of her parents, avaricious like her father, and unbalanced as well? Why else would she present such opposite traits? During the day she was as innocent as an angel; that was the Anne he could love. But this whole plan suggested she was as avaricious as her father. And now this odd behavior . . . one night hot and passionate, the next frightened of an act she had enjoyed the night before. The facts did not fit into place, not in a logical sense. And one explanation could be that she was as mad as her mother.

But he rebelled at the very idea. It simply could not be;

the Anne he knew at Highcrest, the Anne he'd spent that very afternoon with, was not unbalanced. She was spirited and bright, often witty. Deceitful or not, she did possess many admirable traits, as well. The Anne he knew simply could not be mad. Surely he would have seen some sign of it before now.

He cast the idea away, refusing to even entertain such a ridiculous thought. And so the confusion returned. None of this, he thought, made any sense. But with resolve he told himself it was not necessary to understand the peculiar workings of Anne's mind. Enough of the facts were clear: she was planning to usurp the Thornton fortune. Hell, he thought to himself, he wasn't sure he wanted it—but he'd be damned before he'd let someone steal it. Even someone as beguiling as Anne.

A while later, sometime after midnight he knew from the chimes of the clock, Anne spoke again.

"You may leave," she told him in a low voice.

Once again he hesitated to obey. "Perhaps I should not bother to return tomorrow, my lady." He sounded snide, even to himself. "I would get a better night's sleep in my own bed."

"You must come," she said, and he wondered at the sharpness in her voice. She sounded almost desperate. "And you must say nothing of what goes on here to my father, or he'll have you imprisoned for not living up to your part of the bargain."

"I'm only too willing to perform what I've been hired for," he whispered smoothly. "Only say the word."

"Please . . . just go."

He shook his head, too confused to make sense of it. Then, silently, he slipped from the room.

13

Seated at the table across from Jarvis, Anne eyed him over her cup of tea, feeling nothing but venomous hatred. And yet she remained calm to the core. She didn't mind hating her father. It hardly mattered that she hated him even more now that he was manipulating her so thoroughly—but, she thought with a tight little smile, not entirely successfully. She hid well the single grain of satisfaction this knowledge made her feel. She'd given up her virginity, but that was all. She would not allow the man he'd hired another chance to impregnate her. Her father had succeeded, but only so far.

Jarvis had just finished a sumptuous supper of five courses, of which Anne ate relatively nothing. He took note of her meager appetite, not out of concern, she knew, but only because bringing it to her attention was another way to taunt her. He'd said she may be eating for a babe now, and should nourish it well. She'd cringed, and subsequently had not let another bite pass through her lips.

While she sipped her tea, Jarvis drank a third glass of port. Mistress Markay had left the bottle behind at Jarvis's request, and so Anne knew they would not be disturbed for the time being. Now was the time to speak her mind.

"I will be returning to Highcrest in two weeks' time, Father."

He looked at her suspiciously. "How do you know you'll be finished with business here by then?"

She didn't want to blush, but nonetheless felt her cheeks warm when answering. It was a far too personal topic to discuss very easily with one such as Jarvis. "I will know by then if this has been successful or not." Then she added, eyeing him icily, "You'll agree, I know, that to extend this another month would be foolhardy. Selwyn has been dead for more than three weeks already."

He shrugged, obviously unconcerned.

Anne, however, continued. "I will return to Highcrest, and I expect to have Mother at my side."

"Don't worry about her," he snarled.

Anne leaned forward, her iron-willed control of her hatred almost snapping. "Why shouldn't I? You haven't answered one of my questions regarding her, you won't let her come here, you won't even let me see her. After all you've done to her—to us—tell me, why shouldn't I worry?"

He waved a hand at her as if to dismiss her melodramatics. "She's back in her home, a familiar place." Then he glared at her. "She's happier there, I'd wager, than in the godforsaken rathole you would've ended up in if you'd succeeded in running away. So don't talk to me about how worried you are, you weren't worried when you dragged her along with you."

Anne said nothing, though she felt not one smidgen of regret over her actions. Her father could never make her feel guilty about stealing away with her mother in tow; she knew Elsbeth would be far better off with her, even in some rathole, than back with Jarvis himself. It was love she needed most of all, not familiar surroundings—especially the surroundings of a home in which she'd known only suffering.

Jarvis stood, a contented look replacing the scowl he'd aimed at her a moment ago. He rubbed his stomach as he stretched, saying, "I shall have to compliment Mistress Markay on the fine dinner, Annie. A wonderful cook, that one. Perhaps I shall persuade her to come work for me."

Then he found his cloak and headed for the door, for the sun was just about to set. Before leaving, he glanced back at Anne who had followed him to the door.

"Have a pleasant evening, daughter," he said with a twisted smile. "And let's hope it's a successful one."

Once the door closed behind him Anne turned away in

disgust. Then, hearing Mistress Markay clearing away the supper dishes, she joined the older woman. For a moment she was tempted to help the servant with the dishes, as she would have done had Pel been there. But she could guess Mistress Markay's reaction to a countess clearing away dirty dishes, and decided not to risk the woman's apoplexy.

Instead, she said, "Why don't you clean up in the morning, Mistress Markay? It grows late already, and I'm sure you've spent the entire day in the kitchen creating that wonderful meal. Wouldn't you just like to retire for the night?"

The plump woman merely smiled, and her gray eyes never left the task at hand. "I don't mind, Countess. I was glad to have someone to enjoy my cooking for a change." Then, as if startled by her own words, she added, "Not that I've any complaint of serving you here, my lady."

"No offense taken, Mistress. But please, I would prefer if you'd go directly to your room rather than linger to put things in order tonight." One glance at the darkened window told Anne it would be far too risky to let the woman remain up and about for too much longer.

"Very well, milady. I wouldn't want to be making any noises to disturb you, if you've a mind to go to sleep early tonight."

"Thank you, Mistress Markay. And good night."

With that, Anne watched the woman head to the back of the first floor, where her room was located.

Anne went upstairs, feeling little else but fatigue. It would have been splendid, she thought, to be able to go to her room and do nothing but sleep the night away. But nighttime was when her nerves began their frenzied vigil; the darkened hours were hell to her these days.

Still, she was too tired to muster the anxieties of previous nights. If only she could be sure her father wasn't having the cottage watched, then she could simply send the hired stud on his way before even offering him a chair.

It was entirely possible, though, that Jarvis had hired someone to make sure his stud arrived and stayed long enough to perform what he'd been paid to do. For that reason alone, Anne knew she must allow the man to stay, even if it did send her into a fit of nervous energy.

She closed herself into her room, beginning the nightly chore of setting the heavy drapes in place, changing into her nightgown, and extinguishing all but one candle for the time being as she waited. She had to admit she'd been more nervous last night than that first night. On the first night she'd been sick with worry, afraid the stranger would be forceful. But despite her fear, she'd been worried on only one level—afraid of his intentions. But last night was different. It wasn't only the stranger's intentions she'd battled—she'd fought her own desire, as well.

She sat down on the bed, smoothing the cotton quilt with one hand. How well she remembered what had happened two nights ago! Too well! But last night, knowing she had only to give the slightest signal and he would again show her that wondrous world of passion she'd only just discovered, she'd been just as afraid of herself as she'd been of him.

She'd told herself it was possible he would force her, even though so far he'd shown no sign of wanting her unless she was willing. But somehow, after what they'd shared on that second night, she wondered if he thought he had some right to her—especially since he was being paid to repeat such an action in the first place.

But the worst of it was that if he'd been more forceful, she could not say with any certainty that she would have fought him. That was her shame. She wanted no part of this; she wanted no further chance given to her father's devious scheme. But somehow, late at night, knowing the stranger was there, not seeing him but hearing his voice, smelling that vaguely familiar scent of horse and leather and soap about him, she remembered too well the feelings he'd stirred in her. It was almost enough to banish all the moral and inherent objections she had to this whole plot.

But then she would remember Christian, and it was somehow easier to resist the stranger. Last night, when once she had closed her eyes and imagined herself allowing the stranger to do what he'd come here to do, she had in the next instant remembered Christian. And that had cooled her shameful instincts. This whole plot was, after all, aimed against Christian.

Since yesterday she'd also battled with one question niggling at the back of her mind. When Christian had visited her, she had enjoyed his company every bit as much as she had at Highcrest. What was it about the man, she wondered, that could make her feel as though everything she said was interesting, every laugh somehow special, every smile some sort of a prize to behold? It was so easy to be with him, to savor every moment in his presence. How could she forget what she'd felt for him? How could she let herself be carried away by pure lust, pure carnal and selfish longings, when she was at the same time unwillingly nurturing a deep affection for Christian?

It was such a quandary! She knew she had no future with Christian, knew that any infatuation with him should be quickly stifled. But she could not stifle it with the stranger! That was an even more hopeless quandary! She knew nothing of the man except that he had a family. Jarvis had wanted to make sure the man he hired for the job was capable of producing an heir, and so he'd chosen a man who had sired three sons and two daughters. He was a family man! She squirmed in her chair. There was little trouble guessing why he'd been so successful in producing so many children; if he was even half as solicitous of his wife, surely she would welcome him to her bed each and every night of their wedded life!

Determinedly, she told herself she needed only to get through this awful plot of her father's. She truly doubted just one mating with a man, no matter how virile, would cause her to be with child. And once this was over, once she'd found the evidence her father had hidden and she was at last free of him, she would go to London. It would be an exciting adventure, she told herself. She'd never been there before, but Selwyn had told her it was a busy, bustling city that never rested. He'd never liked it, preferring instead the quiet Sussex life. But she was sure that amid the lively city of London, she would manage to forget both of the men who threatened to turn her inside-out. Being a widow in an exciting city would certainly keep her too occupied to pine over any man.

While Anne daydreamed of various escapades in London—parties with other nobles, even an audience with the queen—time escaped. But when she heard the light tap at the door, she hurriedly extinguished the last candle and called for the man to enter.

Tonight the man took a seat on the hard ebony chair without even waiting for directions from Anne. That made her relax, for she was quite flustered that he'd come so close to opening the door when she still had a candle lit. Thankfully, she hadn't been able to see the man, and she was relieved. Even though she would not be bearing his child as her father wished, she still did not want to know a thing about him. He might have in reality taken her virginity, but Anne, who had wanted to give herself to the man she loved, repeatedly told herself that she was still pure. In her heart, she convinced herself, she was a virgin still. As she had given herself to him only upon her father's coercion, she did not want to see the man's face.

It would remain like some bad dream—even though, she had to admit, the nightmare did contain more than a few moments of glory. But those she steadfastly refused to remember. And she had to maintain a rigid control if she was ever to allow herself to love anyone in the future.

Anne was not nearly as jumpy as she had been the night before. The man was quiet tonight, not like last night when she'd heard a hint of force in his voice. Tonight he seemed almost docile, sitting silently in the chair without even shifting. And soon, quite without realizing it, Anne was comfortable enough with his presence to give in to her fatigue. She leaned her head back on the soft cushion of her winged chair, feeling her own breathing becoming more and more steady.

Her mind filled with images. Christian was there, smiling and laughing. He looked at her with that ever intense gaze of his, his eyes golden like a cat's, and full of what she could only describe as love. It shone from him, in his smile, in his touch, in his words. And she reveled in it.

Then, suddenly, he was replaced by a faceless man. She had wanted Christian, but this man's presence was welcomed as well. He, too, was strong, and though she could not see his face, she knew he was handsome. He was ever so gentle with her, and though he spoke not at all, she trusted him and wanted him to hold her. They did nothing in her dream but hold each other, yet it was sensual. The desire was there, she could tell; her body yearned for his just as his did for her. Then he touched her breast with his mouth and the passion was unleashed. How odd it was, this dream filling her body and mind. First the stranger kissed her with his unseen but sensuous mouth, then Christian was there, first with a smile, then with a kiss. He, too, touched her breast with his mouth, and the Anne in her dream moaned with ecstasy.

Her arms twined around his neck, letting her fingers curl into his hair, one hand freeing the thick queue at the back, while the other caressed the strong corded muscles of his neck. How real it seemed, this dream that made the hard sinew of his shoulders come alive beneath her touch. One hand slid downward, and she even imagined the smooth linen of his shirt straining against his chest, and the quickening beat of his heart against her palm. The Anne in her dreams was bold, and she unbuttoned his shirt so she might feel his skin. His body was hard, even to his flat stomach, but the hair covering most of his chest felt pleasantly soft to the touch.

She wanted to kiss him—needed to kiss him. Her lips fairly ached for the feel of him, and she lifted her mouth to his. Surprisingly, he drew back ever so slightly but then, knowing her need, he fulfilled it. His lips were gentle against hers, too gentle, and she wanted more. She pressed herself closer, letting her own lips crush against his, relenting only enough to explore him with her tongue. Anne knew she was behaving shamelessly, wanting him with such carnal fierceness. But it was only a dream, after all, and she had no power to hold herself back. Nor did she wish to.

This time it was Anne's kiss which roamed and explored, Anne who seduced him with her touch. Her lips left his mouth, trailing downward as she opened his shirt wider. She kissed the strong column of his neck, the hard muscles of his chest, and the pulsebeat of his heart, reveling in the knowledge that it pounded far more erratically than normal.

She pulled the linen shirt from his breeches, letting her hands linger over the smooth skin of his stomach. Then, slowly, one fingertip slid along the edge of his breeches. She wanted to be inside, to touch even that most intimate part of him. The top buttons of his breeches opened easily then. Hesitating only a moment, she let her fingers find the buttons which would open him to her. Tentatively, she stroked him, and heard a deep intake of breath. It was not pain but pleasure which made him sigh, and that was enough to add to her boldness. She wanted to free him of his breeches.

The remaining buttons came away as easily as the first two. He helped her then, and his breeches and underclothing were pushed away. He was hot and smooth, hard to the touch. She had the wildest urge to kiss him there, but held back thinking that, even for a dream, that was too far to go.

But with that thought, something tugged at her consciousness. How could she be dreaming, she wondered, with such vivid detail of something about which she knew so little? She had never touched the stranger the night they came together, not like this, and yet her fingers now explored him and knew him in intimate detail. How could she imagine something so thoroughly having had such limited experience?

Her mind was hazy with desire, and she didn't care to know the answer. Somewhere deep inside she was aware this could be no dream, had perhaps been aware from the very first touch, but it was too late to care. There was no room for reason when her entire being was filled with longing.

The stranger tugged at her nightgown, which was twisted around her hips. Together, they lifted the gown over her head and it went the way of the breeches on the floor. His shirt, too, was discarded, and then they were in each other's arms. Anne reveled in the feel of his body next to hers.

His kiss was harder this time, but wondrously so. He kissed her mouth, nibbled her lip, let his tongue tease hers. Then he moved on, just as she had done before. But his kiss lingered on her breasts, taking first one nipple and then the other, sending tremors of pleasure along her veins as he suckled so gently and expertly. This, surely, was no dream.

His caress moved from the breast he weighed in his hand to press gently against her flat stomach, then to slide along the smooth skin stretching over her ribcage and down the curve of her hip. Then, at last, he found that core from which burned the fires he ignited within her. She writhed at his touch, pressing herself against him. She reached down to touch him again, and while he sent shivers of exquisite delight from the workings of his fingers, she sought to do the same with her own caress. And clearly, by his ragged breaths which matched her own, she was equally successful.

She seemed to anticipate his movement, and when he shifted ever so slightly she was already opening her legs to him. He knelt between her thighs, spreading her wide, and a moment later they were joined. He leaned forward, and her legs slid around his, entwining him just as her arms went about his shoulders. Their mouths met as if reading the next move of the other, and slowly at first, then more steadily, the rhythm between them built.

Nothing Anne knew was like this discovery. This time there was no pain as they became one; there was only an intense need, a longing inside to have him right where he was, deep within as if filling a part of her made only for him. That intensity only built and built long before it would diminish, as his thrusts carried her upwards, sending tingles from head to foot, growing so acute she thought she could bear it no longer. Then at last it peaked, and the gradual descent was almost as exquisite as the glorious ascent had been.

For a long while neither moved. He might have attempted to remove his weight from her, but Anne prevented it by tightening her hold on him. She didn't want it to be over; she didn't want it to end. She knew already that the end would be too hard to bear.

And so he stayed atop her, and she shifted a pillow beside them so he might relax and lean some of his weight to the side. But they remained joined as one, and they slept.

Anne wasn't sure what woke her. Surely it wasn't the chime of the clock which struck three. She'd slept so often in this room that the chimes had long since ceased to disturb her. Then she knew; it wasn't the stranger's weight upon her, for it was a comfort to her. He felt warm, and she welcomed his closeness. And she barely felt constricted by him, for she knew without doubt that he had awakened already and was holding yet more of his weight from her.

No, his weight had not disturbed her. She'd been awakened from within, from deep below where something inside her had grown hard once again. And her body, even lost in sleep, had already responded to him. She was moist and ready, and before she even knew what she was doing, she squirmed beneath him as if to demand deeper entry.

The stranger needed no further invitation. Almost instantly, both were hot with passion. Thrust for thrust, they met each other as they climbed back up that plateau of pleasure. It stretched out, until both bodies were damp with sweat and the scent of their lovemaking permeated the room.

At last, emerging from the ocean of mindless passion, Anne let the stranger shift away. Her breathing sounded as labored as the stranger's, and she felt the cool rush of air when they parted. Then the middle of the bed sagged somewhat, and she knew he was sitting up. She knew, too, that he would leave.

She would let him go this time; she had no choice. Nor did she have a choice in the shame she would no doubt feel once he was gone. But she pushed that premonition away and reached for him. Her fingers brushed his shoulder, and she felt the scar she'd noticed on that first night. He did not move as she caressed the crescent-shaped brand, and she closed her eyes as she touched him. She could not and would not see his face, but this part of him she knew. It would have to be enough.

14

Anne folded the quilt neatly on the foot of the bed. The room looked as it had when she'd first come to the cottage over two weeks ago. Strange, how it could look the same after having been the very place in which so much had happened to her.

She tied back the heavy drapes at the window, but little light trickled in. It was a dark, dreary day, and the sky looked like a dirty gray blanket. But she told herself the sun would shine soon, just as, she prayed, she would have nothing at all to fret over.

She'd been looking forward to this day since arriving at the cottage days ago—so many days ago! And, she told herself steadfastly, it would be her day of triumph. Today she expected her monthly flow.

How pleased she would be to announce that her father's plan had failed. And there was nothing, she assured herself, he could do to manipulate her further. His final attempt to control the Thornton fortune was over, and that meant she could at last have a life of her own. Soon, she consoled herself, she would have her mother back, and together they would return to Highcrest, where Elsbeth would be most comfortable and Jarvis would have the least amount of access to her.

She'd refused to let herself think about Christian, but along with thoughts of Highcrest he came inevitably to mind. She did not, however, let herself worry; she hadn't forgotten her plan to go to London. She was sure she could arrange to

use Selwyn's town house if Christian himself had no
immediate plans for the place. She and her mother would be
happy living there, she thought. Perhaps, if Elsbeth never
again saw Jarvis, she might even one day recover from the
horrible memories that seemed to imprison her now.

Thus Anne started the day in higher spirits than she had
enjoyed for quite some time. She'd slept no later than she
had the previous days, but she no longer felt the fatigue she
had that first week.

She squelched unbidden thoughts of the stranger. He
had continued to come nightly, but Anne allowed him to stay
only one hour—more than enough time for any possible spies
to be satisfied. Since that night two weeks ago when her
dream had led her into seducing the man, she had kept a
strict rein on her senses. Nothing, she thought to herself,
was worth the shame she'd suffered upon realizing what
she'd done. She'd actually seduced him! All but verbally
demanded he bed her! And when it would suit only the vilest
of purposes—not just to satisfy her own lust, but to satisfy
her father's plot! She must have been mad to let another
night of passion erupt between herself and the stranger.

And so the rest of the nights had all passed in silence.
Now they would come to an end—but not too soon for
Anne. Today she would tell her father that his plan had
failed, and he would tell the stranger never to come to the
cottage again.

She refused to dwell on the fact that she would never
again be with the stranger, never have the chance to see his
face, hear his voice, know who he was. She had only to
remind herself yet again that he already had a family of his
own. She'd been nothing more than a temporary mistress to
him, albeit an unidentified one.

Nor did she let herself think too much about Christian.
He had not visited her again, although in a bittersweet way
she wished he would have. Perhaps he hadn't missed her at
all. Nonetheless, she planned to send him a message that she
would be returning to Highcrest before the week was out.

Anne ate a full breakfast that day, finding herself
famished now that she was so sure the end of her father's

plan was in sight. The stranger need not even arrive this night; she was sure she would be able to tell her father by this afternoon that she had not conceived a child.

However, as the day wore on, Anne became more and more concerned. There was no sign of the change in her body. She told herself worrying would do no good; Pel had once told her that she'd missed her monthly flow due to grief when she'd lost her father. Perhaps Anne's regularity was interrupted by the upheaval her father had put her through.

Matters only worsened when her father came for supper that night. He wasn't in the room two minutes before he stared at her hopefully.

"Today was the day, was it not?" he asked, his eyes gleaming avariciously. "You said you would know today."

Anne blanched, so reluctant was she to give in to any possible suspicion. Her monthly flux was late—only late! It would be here before morning. "I—do not know for certain one way or the other."

He raised a brow, interested but still cautious. "I'm no doctor, Anne, but it seems to me if you aren't bleeding, then the babe has taken seed."

"It's too early to tell," she told him, trying to sound sure of herself. But in all honesty, she'd become as frightened as a sinner at the last judgment. She had never been late. She was as regular as the sunrise, no matter what crises her father had put her through.

Suddenly Jarvis brightened, obviously deciding to be hopeful instead of angry. "By God, girl, if you've no sign by tomorrow, that must certainly mean we're in luck! Ha!" He clapped his hands together once and rubbed his palms together. "This was far easier than I imagined! And to think I've been losing sleep to come up with a way to extend this out one more month." He laughed again, clearly convinced Anne was with child.

But Anne cooled his ebullience. "You're getting carried away with your hopes, Father. I assure you, by tonight I'll be flowing like the river Thames itself."

He glared at her. "Watch the way you speak, young lady. Those words are hardly befitting a countess—the mother of the next earl of Highcrest.''

But Anne doubted the improperness of her words was what had bothered him. Jarvis was hopeful to believe the plan had already worked—if only he knew just how remote the possibility of conception chance was!

"Just tell your man not to come tonight, Father," she told him. "One more night won't make any difference, anyway."

"Tired so soon of the pleasures of the flesh?" he taunted. "And here I thought I'd done you a favor, getting you a Frenchman and all."

"A Frenchman?" she echoed, snatching with more eagerness than she should have allowed at the hint of the stranger's identity. Questions gnawed inside her, she wanted so badly to know more about him. But she held back, and the curiosity on her father's face made it easier to say nothing.

"So, perhaps he was not so inept, after all. Enjoyed it, did you Mistress Virgin-Widow? Maybe you'll thank me for this one day."

"Never," she hissed, glaring at him with all the hatred she felt inside.

Jarvis laughed but then, taking up his cloak after only having discarded it a moment ago, he spoke. "I think you've done well enough, Annie. The fear on your face tells me that even you think our plan has succeeded. So I'll forgo one of Mistress Markay's excellent suppers and find the man I've hired. I'll tell him he's done his duty and need not come to you tonight."

He headed toward the door, but with his hand on the door handle he added, "But I tell you, Annie, if you have not conceived after all, the man will be coming hereafter for the next month. Be assured of that."

Anne locked the door behind him, wishing she could lock it against him for the remainder of her life. She knew such thoughts were foolish; a simple locked door would never be enough to keep her father out of her life. She sank against the cool wood, her forehead pressing into one varnished panel.

Nonetheless, she was glad he was gone for the time being. Gladder still to have the rest of the night to herself. It was relaxing to linger in the parlor as the sun was setting. She had no need to rush Mistress Markay to her room, to assure herself the door had been left unlatched, then hurry up to prepare herself. She let Mistress Markay serve her supper in the parlor, and the servant fairly beamed over how much Anne ate. It was good to see her appetite so improved!

Anne tarried long over her meal before she realized she was actually loath to return to her room. But why should she be, tonight of all nights? She could spend the entire night blessedly alone!

She carried her supper dishes to the kitchen, and Mistress Markay clucked over the fact that she was doing a job fit only for servants like herself. Anne brushed away the scolding, but did not stay to help clean up, knowing the older woman would sooner resign her post than allow such a thing.

Anne returned to the parlor, lighting a lamp and choosing a book from the tall, wooden cabinet. She sat down to read, but soon tired of the tale for it was one she'd read many times and knew it almost by heart. At last she extinguished the light. The cottage was quiet; Mistress Markay must have finished cleaning the kitchen and gone to bed. No doubt she would stay there no matter what, still following the strict orders Jarvis had issued when Anne first arrived.

Anne had no idea what time it was when she headed toward the stairs. She was not tired, but thought she might sleep anyway if she went right to bed. She should welcome a complete night of slumber.

Just then she heard a small click at the door. It was dark, but the sky outside had cleared during the evening and now the moon cast a silvery light which filtered through the unshaded window from the parlor. She froze, one foot on the step in front of her. Someone was trying to get in!

She'd never worried over any type of intrusion at the cottage. Although it was a remote place, everyone in the county knew it belonged to Selwyn. No one would dare risk a crime against his property, at least no one had ever risked such a thing before.

But she quickly pushed that thought from her mind. She doubted an intruder would come so early in the night, before the inhabitants had had much chance to go to sleep. Surely it was far safer to come in the small hours of the morning, when detection would have been far less likely.

There was, however, another possibility. Only one person would come to this door after nightfall and expect to find it open. Had her father been unable to contact the stranger, to tell him not to come tonight?

Anne swallowed hard. She had only to open the door and stand face to face with the man whose touch had the power to cast all reason from her brain, who ignited such passion in her that she could forget every moral fiber in her being and even betray another man for whom she had come to care so quickly.

She stepped toward the door, even as she did so telling herself she should not give in to the temptation. Hadn't she held herself back each and every night so far? Not only from repeating the passion she knew he could give, but also from lighting a candle and looking upon his face? Why was it so much harder to resist now?

She did not know—perhaps because she might never see him again, or because even if her father's plan had succeeded and she did carry his child, Jarvis would see fit that he never set foot in England again. He would return to France, and be forever out of her life. The man to whom she'd given her virginity with wild abandon, without having even seen his face. Suddenly she could not bear it. She must see him.

With one quick flip of the lock, she opened the door. But the man was already turning away, obviously deciding his services were no longer needed. He was more than an arm's length from her, with his back to her. Anne's eyes took in this first glimpse of him as eagerly as any lover would toward the object of their passion. He was tall and broad of shoulder, his dark hair tied back in the familiar queue. A long cloak hid the rest of him, but she knew his body well enough. It was his face she longed to see.

"Wait!" she called, breathless with anticipation.

At last he turned to her, and her eyes widened in astonishment.

"Christian! What are you doing here?"

He stood and stared at her, as if totally at a loss for words. Then, stepping closer, he almost filled the doorway.

"I was riding," he said slowly, eyeing her. "And my horse had an accident."

"Oh! Are you hurt?" She looked at him, her pulse quickening with concern.

"Perfectly all right," he assured her. "My horse threw me . . . and then he ran off. He's probably back at the High-crest stable by now, comfortable in his stall."

She gazed at him, worry still coursing through her. "No doubt the entire staff is up in arms over your riderless horse returning. They'll be out searching for you."

"No doubt," he quietly agreed.

An awkward moment passed as Anne recognized that intense gaze of his. Would it never cease to fascinate her, to raise her curiosity? Then she remembered her manners.

"Come in, my lord," she invited, stepping aside to let him pass. As she went for a candle she explained, "I did not hear you knock; you quite frightened me. I thought you were an intruder!"

She saw his frown just as the candle ignited. "Then why ever did you open the door?"

"I—I suppose it *was* a foolish thing to do," she said lamely, then led him into the parlor and lit several lamps. Surely Mistress Markay was following her father's directions to the letter, for even with the obvious noises of a visitor she had not roused herself from her room.

Anne faced Christian once the room was ablaze with light. "You're sure you're not hurt?"

"Quite," he said tersely. "And I should clarify, so that you don't think yourself going deaf, that I did not knock just now. I saw that the house was dark and hoped the door would be left unlocked so that I could come in without disturbing anyone. I was about to go around to the kitchen entrance when you opened the door. It's too late for me to set out for Highcrest tonight, so I will borrow your horse tomorrow, if I may, and return to the manor then. If that is all right with you?''

"Of course," she said. "Is there anything I can get for you for now? Are you hungry?"

"No. I supped early and took an evening ride—a foolish thing to do, as it turns out. Once it grew dark, the horse I chose to ride was more anxious to return home than I was, and it decided to go back with or without me.''

"How long have you been on foot?"

He hesitated before answering, as if calculating. "An hour or so, I'm not sure."

"Well, you'll be comfortable here for the night. It's a good thing you found your way here, or it would have been a long night in the forest."

He nodded.

"Are you sure I can't get you anything?" she asked again. She was so happy to see him, having forgotten completely about the stranger and her hope of learning his identity. It was far better not to know, she hastily assured herself. And to have Christian's company instead was more than enough consolation. "A cup of ale, mulled wine? Some brandy?"

He contemplated a moment. "How about mulled brandy? If you'll join me?"

She hesitated for a moment, then smiled. "I would like that, but we'll have to prepare it ourselves. Mistress Markay has gone to bed and I assure you, nothing disturbs her until morning."

"Lead to the kitchen then, Countess. I haven't been an earl long enough to have forgotten how to fend for myself."

Before long they found two glasses, a pan for warming the liquid over the glowing embers of the dying kitchen fire, and all the necessary spices, Christian assured her, to concoct the finest mulled brandy in all England.

"It has to be just the right temperature," he told her as he swished the brew in the pan over the cookfire.

"I think it needs more cinnamon," Anne said, standing over Christian's shoulder.

He frowned at her. "A critic already and you haven't even tasted it."

A moment later he declared it finished. They had, however, made far too much for only two glasses, and Anne searched hastily about for something else to put it in, coming up with a very proper looking teapot.

Christian did not hesitate to pour the brandy in the unconventional server. "It's a good thing your Mistress Markay is a sound sleeper. Any dedicated housekeeper would have our necks for abusing the china this way."

She laughed and scooped up the two empty glasses before leading the way back to the parlor. Once there, Christian poured them each a steaming, healthy portion, and cautioned Anne to wait a moment before tasting.

"Well?" he asked after she'd sampled the drink.

"Well?" she repeated, smiling mischievously at him. She knew he wanted her opinion, but she delayed long enough to irritate him.

"More cinnamon?"

She shook her head. "It's perfect the way it is. Why would you want to spoil it with more cinnamon?"

He grinned at her, falling in with her playful mood, then took a sip himself and, without a trace of humility, pronounced it superb.

"Having you come here tonight will save me the trouble of sending you a messenger in the morning," Anne said. "I've decided to return to Highcrest for the last weeks of isolation, if that is agreeable to you."

"Perfectly," he said over his glass. "It's been every bit as quiet at Highcrest as this place must be."

"Do you have plans to change that in the future?" she asked curiously. "I mean . . . to have parties and the like?"

He shrugged. "Not for a while; it isn't customary too soon after a death, of course. But eventually, perhaps. Would that bother you in any way?"

"No, of course not," she said. "You are the earl now. It is certainly your decision to make. Selwyn and Celine used to have some very fine parties, although few people made the long trip from London. But there are enough gentry around

Highcrest to make an interesting evening, I'm sure."

"You must help me, then," he suggested. "Since you've lived here all your life, you would know best whom to invite."

She laughed lightly. "Hardly. I would know all the villagers who are most fun, of course. But I don't know any gentry. I may be a countess—dowager countess," she clarified. "But I've lived as a squire's daughter—one who never had the money, or the acquaintance of other gentry in the county."

He still seemed interested. "Then tell me, if you were to invite the villagers who would be fun, as you say, who would they be?"

She contemplated. "Well, Pel, of course, and her Gregory," she began, then named a few more, ending with Mortimer. "He's gentry through and through," she said of Mortimer, "but he's as much fun as any villager I've ever known."

"He's fond of you, too," Christian observed.

"He wasn't always," Anne said. "He was very much against my wedding Selwyn, although he never raised an objection to Selwyn himself. He knew how Selwyn wanted me."

She glanced quickly toward Christian when she realized what she'd said. How strange it was to discuss Selwyn to Christian, his son! And how loose her tongue felt. She must not allow Christian to refill her brandy again. The first glass had already gone to her head.

"Why did Mortimer doubt you?"

Anne shrugged, too late realizing the movement was one she'd picked up from Christian. Did he know, she wondered, that he'd affected her, even down to unconsciously mimicking him? "He didn't like my father. He still doesn't."

"He held you in suspicion because of your father?"

She nodded, then added with a smile, "But then he got to know me, and we've been friends ever since. It's really very simple. No great scandal there."

Anne noticed Christian's face change ever so slightly. He seemed to be scowling, though it was such a minute change she could not be sure. But when he spoke, she was certain. His tone had lost its warmth.

"What is it Mortimer holds against your father?"

Anne bit back an endless list of grievances one could hold against Jarvis Melbourne. "It's a personal thing, I suppose," she said evasively. "Mortimer just doesn't like him."

"It hasn't anything to do with the money, then? The Thornton money?"

Anne eyed him quickly, nervously. "What do you mean?"

Christian took a long sip of brandy, draining his glass. "Only that Mortimer might have been wary of a fortune hunter. He does seem protective of the Thornton interests."

Anne stiffened in her chair. The fact that he'd hit exactly on the truth made her far too uncomfortable to tolerate. "Of course Mortimer is protective of the Thornton wealth; he has been overseeing it for many years!"

Christian's gaze held hers steadily. "Then it seems logical he would want to see it protected."

Anne gripped her glass, looking at it rather than Christian as she said quietly, "Are you accusing me of being a fortune hunter?"

Christian's voice was just as low. "I thought we were discussing your father?"

She stood, placing her glass with a thud on the table before them. "It isn't my father who wed Selwyn! How can you accuse my father of fortune hunting without accusing me as well, since it's I who wed into the family?"

Christian remained seated, although it was considered highly improper for a gentleman to do so once a lady had risen. "You seem quite defensive, my lady. Why don't we change the subject?" He sighed aloud. "Let's see . . . the weather is always a safe topic, although it's been so rainy lately that could hardly warrant anything interesting. Ah, I have it," he said in a cold, tormenting voice. "How about if we discuss your baby? Have you chosen any names for this step-sibling of mine?"

Anne spun around to him, her hands clenched in fists at

her sides. He was blatantly disrespectful, not only in the way he remained seated, but also in choosing such an improper topic! Men simply did not discuss a woman's pregnancy! But it was hardly the insulting social ramifications which affected Anne. It was as if he suspected the whole awful plot!

"I—I think I shall retire for the evening, my lord," she said tightly. "I am suddenly quite fatigued." Her fury was blatantly obvious.

She turned away, and suddenly, before she'd even heard him move, Christian was standing in front of her and blocking passage from the room. He'd discarded his brandy and, miraculously, all traces of coldness from his face as well.

"I'm sorry," he said, and he was so close she could smell the spiced liquor on his breath. It was surprisingly sweet, reminding her of the brandy's pleasant taste.

But Anne did not look at him; she could not. After all, his suspicions would not have bothered her had she been innocent.

"I—I really am quite tired, my lord," she whispered.

Still, he did not move. "You really should learn to call me Christian," he said softly. "Considering we're family."

Anne did not reply. Their former conversation still stung. She knew she must leave the room, as her knees felt as though they might give out any moment.

"Just one thing," he said as he stood aside. "I want you to know I'm glad we're a family, Anne."

She could not resist looking at him then. His eyes were clear blue, so devastatingly handsome she felt she could stare into them for an eternity. But best of all, he seemed sincere. Reluctantly, she tore her gaze from his.

"Good night, Christian," she said over her shoulder.

"Good night, Anne."

15

Christian nudged his horse's flanks and both his own horse and the one he led behind increased pace. This journey back to Highcrest would have been laughable, he thought, if it wasn't so damned deceitful. Here he was, unnecessarily borrowing Anne's horse just to cover his lies of last night. Obviously something had gone awry, as she hadn't been expecting her late-night caller. Not that it would've mattered to him. The last week or more of visits had been downright boring. He shook his head. This was the most vexatious situation to figure! The woman was an absolute enigma!

Nothing made sense. She'd given her virginity to a perfect stranger in hopes of becoming impregnated by him. If she was willing to go that far to enact this plot of hers, why hadn't she used his "services" every night thereafter? He could understand that first night's hesitation. Perhaps even someone as deceitful as Anne had had qualms about giving away her virginity. But once that was done, why hadn't she continued with it? Tried every night for the success of her plan? His mouth tightened and he sneered—mostly at himself because he knew he would have enjoyed the task far more than he cared to admit. More than she? He doubted it. Her passion had been every bit as real as his own on the three occasions they'd come together.

That was what vexed him so. If it had been enjoyable, and if he'd been willing to perform the service she and her father had been paying for, then why had she allowed only three tries at this plan's success? Did she know her own body so well that she could guess when she was ripe for a man's seed?

He told himself yet again that he should despise her. But last night, when he'd looked into her guileless eyes, laughed with her, and welcomed her company, had he hated her then? Hardly. Last night he realized how easy it would be to care for her, how perfectly right it felt to be with her late at night, all alone, raiding the kitchen to share a glass of brandy. For a few brief moments it had been as if they'd known each other forever; being together had felt so perfect.

Then he'd remembered. How could he have forgotten, even for a moment? The memory of it made him cold, the way he'd caught back his eager enjoyment last night. And so he'd taunted her. Even now, his heart twisted inside when he remembered the look in her eyes, the hurt he'd created intentionally. He'd felt like a cad when he'd seen that pain, no matter what the facts were, no matter how justified the attack.

But justified he was. He had every right to hurt her, and it shouldn't matter to him one bit if her blue eyes looked like two huge, melancholy puddles.

Yet as he came within sight of Highcrest, his thoughts were strangely mixed. He should hate her, but he couldn't. Certainly he shouldn't tolerate this weakness he had for her—the very weakness which made it so difficult for him to hate her the way he should. He cursed himself. He should forget the passion she'd stirred in him. He had to remind himself of the reason he'd bedded her to begin with. But instead, all that came to mind was kissing her, holding her body against his, and joining with her, discovering a fulfillment he'd never felt before. That combined with the blind infatuation he felt for her made it impossible to control his wayward emotions. He couldn't forget he was besotted with her like the most callow youth, and most especially he could not forget the passion he'd felt in her arms.

He'd wanted many women in his life, and had had most of them, but none had ever felt quite the same as this. Christian was sure it was only because of the intrigue, the fact that she hadn't the faintest idea it was really Christian himself who would have the last laugh in this.

But, in truth, he'd wanted her the moment he'd first laid eyes on her, long before he'd known what kind of person she was. That was the worst of it: he wanted her every bit as much, despite the knowledge that she was a lying, deceitful fortune hunter.

There was but one solution to the whole dilemma, he thought. If he could not eliminate—indeed, could not even control—the ever growing fascination he had for the woman, he had no choice but to penetrate her deceitful exterior. He wanted two things from her, and one—the one which even now made him sit upon his horse more stiffly than usual—was to bed her again. But he wanted it to be in broad daylight, when she knew exactly who was stirring her deepest passions and desires.

With a stubborn set to his jaw he realized that wasn't all he wanted. He wanted the truth from her. He wanted to hear from that sweet, delectable mouth of hers the whole dastardly plot to pass off her bastard as Selwyn's heir. He wanted her to come to him with it—to trust him, to beg his forgiveness and cleanse herself with a confession.

And then what? If she somehow came to care enough for him that she felt guilty over what she'd done, guilty enough to reveal it all and ask his forgiveness, would he give it? Perhaps. But perhaps not. It would be good to have that power over her, to have something—other than his money—that she would want.

And what of a child, the bastard she hoped she carried? His child, if indeed his seed had taken? His jaw clenched again. That would be the key to all of this. If she did confess all, if she did show some sign of purity, some small glimpse of conscience, then he would reveal whose child she carried, and they could both raise the child together as the next heir of Highcrest.

If, on the other hand, she did not come to him, did not show him some sign of goodness in her soul, the child—their child, if there was one—would still be legitimized. That was one way to repay her for her sins against him. He would simply take the child and raise it as his own. While she, the deceitful mother, could very well rot at her seaside cottage, observing her child from afar.

But even as he made such coldhearted plans, part of him rebelled at the very idea. Part of him—that weak, silly, infatuated part—already believed there was goodness in her. Perhaps, if he could get her to admit it all, to come to him with her plot rather than continue trying to fleece him, they could find some semblance of honesty between them and start from there. He had little doubt she had some feeling for him. He hadn't imagined the glow in her eyes last night while they shared their brandy. Nor had he imagined the passion she'd felt when in his arms.

But he scoffed at himself. He wanted no part of such lily-livered thoughts. Was he too cowardly to enact the plans he knew she deserved? If she was cold enough to bring a child into the world only to gain control of the Thornton fortune, wasn't it in that child's best interest to take it away from her? To raise it without the avarice she'd obviously been nurtured on?

No, his mind was made up, and the future was clear. He was, after all, giving her a fair chance. If she proved herself fit to raise a child, he would be happy to allow that, even help her and be the child's father.

If, on the other hand, there was no child and she invented some sort of fabrication of miscarriage rather than confessing the truth, he would tell her he'd known all along exactly what she'd done. And then he would banish her from Highcrest, regardless of Selwyn's last wishes. Christian was earl of Highcrest now, he could bloody well decide who lived there and who did not.

So there it was. He would woo her, charm her, inveigle his way into her heart so that she confessed all to him. And if she did not, she would be banished from all Highcrest holdings—except the cottage, which was hers.

He had reached Highcrest. At least he'd made a decision about what he was to do next. He would give this task his best effort, and that part of him so childishly enamored of her would make it an easy and delightful task. Besides, wooing her would accomplish not only a confession; it would get her into his bed, which was, he admitted, exactly where he wanted her.

Anne, dressed in a black riding suit and a three-cornered hat, headed from the cottage to the stables. A groom had returned the filly which Christian had borrowed that morning, and she couldn't resist the urge for a short ride. She was badly in need of escape from the cottage and all the memories it now held.

A young stableboy had been sent from Highcrest to assist Anne on her journey back to Highcrest. Obviously Christian had not approved of her unconventional journey to the cottage a couple weeks ago and was making every effort to allow her the opportunity of a fully chaperoned return. But she was glad of the boy's presence now, for her horse stood ready and waiting for Anne's ride.

The weather was changing, judging from the partially blue sky and dramatic mixture of puffy white and dark gray clouds billowing up above. Nonetheless, Anne could not tolerate another long afternoon in the cottage. Besides, she had business to attend to. Now that her father had loosened his rein upon her somewhat, she could venture alone into Wynchly. There she would find the Barrister Gallen once again. She nudged the filly to a quick sprint away from the cottage grounds, and Anne decided even if it poured on her she wouldn't care. This was better than being couped up inside, and far too important to postpone.

The rain held off all the way to Wynchly. Anne found Gallen's office without delay, however, since she did not wish any of her father's cohorts to see her in the village.

Anne was thankful to discover that Barrister Gallen was in his office. Both happy and flustered to see her, he fussed over which seat she should take and offered her tea, which had long since gone cold. Upon realizing his mistake, he apologized profusely, but Anne assured him she'd rather go without than have him trouble himself over brewing a new pot.

Anne did not stay in his office long, still afraid of her father's wrath. Briefly, with a carefully worded prelude swearing him to secrecy, Anne told Gallen the whole sordid story of the murder her father had committed. She asked Gallen to find the false evidence Jarvis had buried and bring it to her, so that she could destroy it herself. Nothing short of that would calm her worry over her mother's welfare.

Gallen was as solicitous as ever, not even raising a judgmental brow when Anne divulged every last detail. Perhaps Gallen knew her father well enough not to be surprised over the tale she brought. Whatever the case, he was sympathetic to the end, and promised he would find the evidence and also a way in which to place the blame where it rightfully belonged, upon Jarvis. But Anne was not quite ready to wage a war against her father. She was so used to defending herself from him that she was not yet prepared to attack. Nonetheless, she told Gallen to do all he could.

She left his office feeling considerably better than she had in days.

But true tranquility eluded her. Two men dominated her thoughts on the way back to the cottage, both of whom created no less than havoc within her heart. The stranger was gone from her life. She had only to tell her father she had conceived, and the man would never again have need to sneak into her bedroom.

She hadn't conceived, she told herself stubbornly. It was true that her monthly flux was late, but she didn't *feel* pregnant, therefore she told herself she wasn't. Her breasts felt tender, but that was because her time of the month was on its way.

She would lie convincingly to her father, however. Anne would tell him she was with child in no uncertain terms, and he would tell the stranger to be on his way and never set foot in this county again. And Anne would never see him again. Not that she had seen him at all—not really.

He was such an intriguing man. He'd been well paid to take her, yet he'd done so only on three occasions, and only when Anne herself had made it clear she was perfectly willing. She felt her cheeks warm even now when she remembered the passion that had erupted between them. One hand left the reins of her horse, and she put her palm to one shame-warmed cheek. The memory still tore at her. Part of her was appalled that she had behaved so disgracefully, and another part of her—stronger at times than any shame—wanted only to repeat that very behavior . . . to know again the stranger's heated embrace, to feel his lips on her breast, his caress over every measure of her body, his body joined deeply with hers.

It was exactly that, she told herself as she gently urged her horse to a faster pace, which she must forget. The stranger was gone. She must not let his memory touch her in any way. If she did not expel him from her mind, she would never be free to truly love anyone else. And in spite of her father, she hoped one day to do that very thing.

The hope of love brought Christian to mind. Last night had been both wonderful and horrible, all in the space of a meager hour of his company. She'd been so happy to see him, and during the first minutes they'd been together she'd wanted nothing more than to be with him forever, to be his friend, his late-night companion, even his wife. For a very short time it had felt as though they were the only two people on earth. But then he'd changed; he'd grown cold before her very eyes. Or had it been her imagination? Had her own guilty conscience made his words seem like insults, his smile like a sneer? Hadn't his last words to her been that he was glad they were a family now? Would he have said such a thing if he despised her?

By the time she reached the cottage it was drizzling again, and she felt a bit chilled. But that chill penetrated her to the core when she saw her father's horse at the trough just outside the stable of the seaside cottage.

Reluctantly, Anne let the groom take care of her mare and made her way to the cottage. But there was no use avoiding the inevitable, she thought. Just before entering, she squared her shoulders and took a deep breath. She needed to be confident in her lies. Her father knew her well.

He was at the table eating when Anne found him. But when he saw her approach, he immediately stood, a look of such profound anxiety on his face that Anne wished she had the nerve to let him sweat just a little bit longer.

She eyed him viciously. She would put his mind to rest, all right. With lies. How welcome would be the day—in a safe month from now—when she would tell him the truth, that in fact she was not with child after all and must simply have miscalculated. The thought of it made her tingle with anticipation.

"Well?" He stood, holding his napkin and oblivious to the fact that his chin was covered with grease from the roast duckling he'd been eating.

"Where is Mistress Markay?" Anne asked, her tone idle.

"In the kitchen, where she belongs," he snapped at her. "Get to it, girl. Have you conceived, or not?"

She looked him squarely in the eye, feeling nothing but vengeful hatred. "I have."

"Ha!" He dropped the napkin and clapped his hands together with pure glee. Then, his hands shiny with grease, he clasped her shoulders and shook her happily. "Good girl, Annie! I'm proud of you!"

After that he turned back to the table for one last swallow of wine, then headed toward the door. He called to her over his shoulder.

"Take care of yourself, now Annie. Go ahead and finish that meal. We can't risk your health now."

She halted him with a scathing reply. "The best way to insure my health is for you to stay away from me," she said, adding with as much conviction, "and for you to bring Mother back to me."

He was plainly too overjoyed to take her wrath to heart. "Oh, I'll have her brought to you right away, daughter dear. And as for my company, I know we haven't always been like father and daughter, but you'll not be hearing a complaint from me. No, indeed. You've done me a great favor, Annie. One I won't soon forget. So if you'd rather I didn't visit so often, I'll just come round now and then, to make sure you and the babe are doing well. What kind of father would I be otherwise, Annie?''

He had neared the door. Before leaving, he added one last comment. "Eat well, daughter. I'll visit you at Highcrest before too much time has passed.''

"I want Mother here right away!'' she called after him, but she spoke to the closed door.

16

"Mother!"

Anne rushed out to the carriage just as one of Jarvis's footmen helped Elsbeth to the ground. Anne swept her mother into a hearty embrace, so overjoyed to see her safe that she held her close for a long, happy moment. Then she held her back at arms' length to look at her.

"How are you, Mother?" she asked worriedly. "Are you well?"

Anne's heart twisted inside. Her mother did not even look at her or spare her one of the smiles she'd used while living at Highcrest. She had been away little more than two weeks, yet she seemed to have lost weight and, if possible, added a dozen new wrinkles to her aging face. Her mouth was drawn, her cheeks pale, and the look in her eyes woefully distant. Silently, Anne cursed her father. Elsbeth hadn't looked so out of sorts since leaving his wretched home more than a year ago. Two short weeks back there had sent Elsbeth once again deep into a distant world no one but Elsbeth could occupy.

"Come inside," Anne whispered, still holding her mother close. "Mistress Markay has a fine supper waiting for you. You'll eat for me, won't you, Mother?"

Silent as always, Elsbeth did not answer. Anne led her inside the cottage to the table where Mistress Markay had already placed a steaming bowl of chowder, warm, buttered bread, and a cup of tea. But to Anne's dismay, Elsbeth showed no interest in the pleasantly fragrant meal.

Seated close by, Anne took a spoon in hand and raised a portion of the chowder to her mother's lips. But Elsbeth's mouth remained closed.

Anne resisted the urge to succumb to her raging emotions: renewed hatred of her father, frustration over her mother's illness, panic that Elsbeth may never eat again. Instead, she placed the spoon back in the bowl and gently took her mother's hand. She stroked the age-spotted skin and spoke softly in her mother's ear.

"You're back with me to stay now, Mother. He won't ever take you from me again. I won't let him." Then she added, in as light a tone as she could muster, "Now, if you'd rather take a nap than eat, that's all right for now. But I want you to promise me you'll eat before you retire for the night."

Elsbeth made no indication that she was even listening.

Anne helped her mother upstairs to the room she always occupied, helping her out of the stiff bodice and full skirt and into a soft linen gown and wrapper. Then she bid her mother to lie down, and stayed with her until certain she was asleep.

As Anne returned to her own room, her concern for her mother overshadowed the myriad other worries which had burdened her recently. She hoped life at Highcrest would help her mother. Anne knew Elsbeth was comfortable in her apartments there, with Marta to attend her. She took some solace in such hope. Tomorrow they would return to Highcrest. It could be exactly what Elsbeth needed.

By midmorning the following day, Anne and her mother were cozily esconced within the luxurious confines of one of the Thornton carriages. Anne had succeeded in getting her mother to eat a meager breakfast of toast and chocolate. Anne herself had skipped the meal entirely, so overcome with worry for Elsbeth that she felt quite nauseous.

Despite her own lack of cheer, Anne chatted amiably on the journey to the manor. She was desperate to present a calm facade to her mother, and each word that came from her mouth extolled the happy times they would have back at Highcrest. The weather was warm enough for frequent outings if Elsbeth so chose, and soon Pel would be marrying Gregory, and Anne wanted Elsbeth to help stitch her a set of bed linens, quilts and pillow shams and the like. Anne decided what her mother needed now was to be busy with pleasant tasks; that was the only way to forget her brief sojourn back into the hellish past of living at Jarvis's home.

The carriage slowed and Anne peered out the window, knowing it was too soon to have reached Highcrest already. Then she heard a footman from the rear stoop of the carriage call the explanation.

"A rider ahead, Countess," he announced. A moment later he identified the approaching horseman. "It is the earl."

Anne's pulse raced at the news. She willed herself to be calm, but her stubborn heart still raced. Her traitorous stomach seemed to flip immediately, and her ungovernable hands shook until she balled them into tight little fists.

The carriage halted, and a moment later she heard the hoofbeats of a horse alongside the carriage window.

"Good day, Countess," Christian greeted, politely saluting her first and then her mother with one sun-bronzed hand to the tip of his three-cornered hat. "I saw your approach and decided to greet you early."

With a quick glance to make sure her mother was not upset by the man, Anne smiled somewhat tremulously and leaned toward the window. "Don't stay out too long, my lord," she chided him gently, and found to her own relief that her voice didn't sound nearly as unsettled as her stomach felt. "Or is this mount not afraid of the dark?"

For a moment he didn't catch on, then he laughed and patted his Arabian's powerful neck. "This one has yet to show fear of anything."

"Like his master," Anne said, before she'd even realized the words were too personal to politely emit. But Christian seemed pleased by them, and she did not regret the comment.

"Will you sup with me this evening?" he asked.

Anne nodded without hesitation, forgetting entirely that only last night she had resolved the best thing to do where

Christian Thornton was concerned was ignore him entirely.

"Then I will see you back at the manor house shortly." Once again he tipped his hat at her, then with a quiet command the huge horse beneath him cantered away, taking Christian off the road but back in the general direction of Highcrest.

The carriage reached Highcrest soon after, but Christian was nowhere to be seen upon their final approach. Anne stayed with Elsbeth that afternoon, hoping her presence would help her mother feel more settled. Although Elsbeth ate lightly, any sustenance she accepted gave Anne hope. For herself, Anne was ravenous by midafternoon, and although she knew she would be eating supper with Christian, she had a hearty snack of sweetbread with oysters, tea and almond cake.

An hour before supper, Anne left her mother for her own room, having ordered a bath for herself. She'd remained in her travel clothes through the afternoon, not wanting to leave her mother even long enough to change her attire. Now within the privacy of her own quiet room, she welcomed the perfumed heat of the bathwater, and let her servant scrub her hair until it, too, smelled of lavender.

Pel came to help her dress and style her hair. Upon their reunion Pel had drawn her into a sisterly embrace, and Anne had been tempted to spill out each and every problem tugging at her very soul. But she'd kept silent.

"Something's troubling you, Anne," Pel said as she eyed Anne's reflection in the mirror. She was in the process of pinning up Anne's hair into an intricate style of curls and ribbons, and though the task demanded attention, her sharp eyes seemed to miss nothing in Anne's behavior.

Anne tried to smile but failed. "Why do you say that?"

"Because since I walked through the door you've said less than ten words. And because your eyes are drooping, and not due to sleepiness. You're trying to hide the fact that something's wrong."

"I suppose I shouldn't try to keep things from you, Pel," Anne admitted.

"Then there is a problem."

Anne merely shrugged. She wanted to say there were several, not just one. But she wasn't quite ready to reveal all. Anne still felt ashamed at what she'd done.

"I'm worried about my mother," Anne said. "Have you seen her since we returned?"

"No, I haven't." Then she smiled, obviously in an attempt to brighten the conversation. "She probably missed having me and Marta taking care of her."

"Oh, I'm sure of that," Anne said in a harsher voice than she intended.

Pel put the last pin in Anne's hair and then came around to face Anne directly. "Why did you leave without telling me?"

Anne looked at Pel, who always said what was on her mind. This was the first time Anne had ever kept anything from her friend, and it didn't sit well. But she couldn't talk about it. Not yet.

"I knew you would want to come along—well, perhaps not want really, but feel it was your duty."

"Of course I would've come along!" Pel said. "And wanted to, not because of duty. I've always accompanied you to the cottage."

"But you're to be married in less than a month. I thought you should stay here with Gregory."

Pel laughed. "Is that the reason?" Then she smiled with a loving glint to her eyes. "To be honest, Anne, we did spend a lot of time together. It was . . . well, wonderful."

Anne reached out and squeezed Pel's hand. "I'm glad." And in truth, she was. At least someone she knew and loved was happy.

With her hair done, all that was left of her toilette was to step into her petticoat skirt and fasten a chintz stomacher to the gap of her black satin bodice, lacing it to fit snugly to her waist. The style pushed up her generous breasts, to which she added a lace modesty piece. Though the current rage was to do without a modesty piece, it seemed out of sorts with the mourning attire she wore.

"You're the picture of loveliness, even in black," Pel

said admiringly as they studied Anne's reflection in the mirror. Anne's tiny waist looked even smaller with the layers of underpetticoats filling out her skirt. She was dressed entirely in black, from the modesty piece at her bosom to the laces in her hair and down to the black kidskin slippers adorning her feet. She'd never worn much black in the past, and even now after wearing it every day for over a month, she was startled by the contrast of her milky white skin. Her hair also added to the contrast, the flaxen gold shimmering with soft highlights. The only spots of color on her entire being were her blue eyes, and perhaps because of the lack of color elsewhere they looked much brighter, much bluer.

"It's time for supper," Pel said.

Anne's stomach danced at the announcement. She suddenly felt quite shy, without really knowing why. Then she knew. The memory of what she'd done came rushing back to her. She'd participated in a plot against Christian. What was she doing, having supper with him? Was she mad to spend time with him? She should avoid him at every cost, stay far away from him and his penetrating gaze.

But at the very same time, she had to dine with Christian. She wanted to spend time with him, share conversation and laughter and thoughts. That was the shame of it; she shouldn't spend even so much as a minute with him, but she couldn't seem to help herself.

"I'll wait up for you," Pel said as Anne made her way to the bedroom door.

Anne spoke over her shoulder, as much to herself as to Pel. "I won't be long."

Christian was waiting in the parlor. As always, he looked devastatingly handsome. He was dressed in a gray demask coat and breeches with a black waistcoat; his hose and cravat were white, his buckled shoes black leather. He looked wonderfully masculine, his dark hair neatly tied back in a queue. When he saw her he stepped away from the mantelpiece and approached her with that ever intense gaze in his eyes.

"Good evening. May I greet you properly?" He stood quite close, so close she could smell soap and just a hint of cologne. Her heart fluttered when he placed his hands on her shoulders, half on the material of her gown and half on her exposed skin . . . skin seared by his touch. "With a kiss?"

Anne could not respond. She felt as though she were glued to the floor, and only by force of will did she remain standing. She wanted nothing more than to lean in to him, let him embrace her fully and kiss her in any fashion he wished. But she controlled her unruly thoughts. He meant only to welcome her as a member of the family.

What should have been a chaste kiss became a provocative encounter for Anne. He brushed his lips against hers, barely touching her. With his long fingers resting ever so gently upon her shoulders, he let his thumbs move in a deliberately enticing circle. He had only to widen that circle to touch the tip of her breasts just beneath the top of her bodice. Even through the modesty piece, his touch felt sensuous. And Anne wanted more.

She cursed herself silently. What had she become? She pulled away, stiffly. She didn't let herself speak, not trusting her voice. But inside she condemned herself—and the stranger—for awakening something within her that she would never, ever be able to ignore from now on.

"Would you care for some wine?"

Anne's glance shot to Christian. He was already turning away, heading for the table which held the delicate decanter of crimson wine. She eyed him with nothing less than envy. That kiss had done nothing to him, left no effect whatsoever. His voice was as calm as ever, his gait as smooth, his hands as they poured the wine just as steady as if he'd kissed his sister instead of . . . instead of what? She hardly knew how to think of herself when it came to Christian.

"Yes," she managed to say, and her voice was low so she could hide any unease.

He handed her a generous glass and then sipped from his own.

"It's claret," he said as if in apology. "I hope you don't mind. I know French wines are considered unpatriotic these days."

Anne hardly paid attention. She took a sip, and it

warmed her to the core. She welcomed the feeling, and resolutely pushed away her nervousness.

"I shouldn't think that would bother you at all," Anne said. "You are French."

"Half-French," he corrected. "And no, it does not bother me at all. I was thinking of you."

"I am patriotic, my lord, be assured of that. But this war . . . I am not so sure we should have entered into it at all. It doesn't seem to be our business."

"Then you wouldn't mind if the king of France succeeds in setting a Frenchman upon the Spanish throne? Austria cares very much."

"And well they should, being so close. But we are English; we live on an isle. We are our own empire."

"You sound like solitude is what you want for your country."

She shrugged. "Perhaps I do."

Christian paused, eyeing her. Anne felt the uneasiness creep up once again under that stare, but she squashed it with heroic determination.

"I haven't known many women with whom I could discuss politics," he said.

Deciding it would be far preferable to talk about him than herself, Anne asked, "I suppose you've known a great deal of women?"

"My share." Then he added with a grin, "Well, perhaps more than my share. But only because I like women. Many men I know don't like women—oh, I don't mean they prefer men's company in every aspect, but they use women for whatever suits them and they go on with other pursuits. Money, hobbies, politics, whatever. Have you known any men like that?"

Anne nodded. Her father fit that bill to perfection.

She was truly curious now. "If you like women, why haven't you ever married?"

"Now that, my lady, is a question I've devoted some thought to. Why, indeed? It deserves a serious answer."

"And do you have one?"

"Of course. I have great respect for the holy sacrament

of marriage," he explained. "The vows taken are not to be scoffed at, and should be respected to one's dying day. It's because of my respect of that vow I have never taken it. Knowing myself, I do not believe I could fulfill such a vow."

Her mouth turned up at the corner, but not exactly from pleasure at having learned something of him. "Because you like women too much?"

He nodded.

Anne did not allow her gaze to stay on him. Those eyes, so like gold, were too captivating. She raised one hand to refer to their surroundings as she spoke. "Surely now that you've all this, you'll be wanting an heir."

It was the wrong thing to say, but she realized it too late. She knew it the moment his gaze intensified upon her own.

"You are the one with the heir, Countess," he said softly, and for a moment she thought she saw a hint of anger in his compelling eyes. But whatever the emotion was, it disappeared before she could name it with any certainty.

"Perhaps we should have our supper," Christian said after a moment of awkward silence.

Anne was only too glad to end the current conversation and have the meal to divert their attention for the time being. When Christian spoke again, it was as congenial as ever.

"Waites told me there will be a wedding among the servants soon."

Anne relished the new topic. "Yes, between Pel, my maidservant and Gregory Harlan, one of the gatekeepers, the one who lodges at the gate house. He has served Highcrest Manor for years now."

"This Pel—" Christian said.

"Penelope Escott," she said.

"She seems to be more than a servant to you. She is the one who came to Mortimer on the day you left for the cottage. She was quite concerned over your welfare. It seems you never go there without her."

It seemed odd indeed to be discussing such matters at the supper table; surely no earl and dowager countess had ever made a habit of such a thing! But to Anne, who felt she was discussing friends and not servants, the conversation flowed easily.

"I thought she might like time with Gregory instead. With me off to the cottage, it gave her more free time to spend with him."

"Very kind of you," Christian remarked.

Anne felt herself shrink inside; kindness had actually nothing to do with it. She knew Pel would've fought her father's plot fervently—more fervently than Anne could have risked, for her mother's sake.

"Pel and I grew up together. Her family lived near my father's house."

"I see," he said. "Perhaps, in that case, you would like to invite them to have their wedding party here."

She gaped at him. "Here?"

"Why not?" Then, seemingly as an afterthought, he said, "Oh, because of the mourning period? If the wedding is to take place after the sixth week of isolation, I see no reason why we could not have a small gathering here. In a modest way, of course."

"But . . . but a servant's wedding at Highcrest? It—it's simply not done."

"Why not?" he asked again. "Didn't you once tell me you paid no attention to rank?"

"I don't," she insisted.

"Then why the fuss over this?"

"I was thinking of you," she said. "If you are to be accepted at all by other nobility, you certainly couldn't—"

"They would frown on this sort of thing?"

"Undoubtedly."

"Hmm," he said, but it seemed as if the decision had already been made and he was merely humoring her by considering the dire consequences of her warning. "There's but one thing to do," he said easily.

"And that is?"

"Not invite them."

At her shocked expression, he laughed. As if anyone would have considered inviting them to begin with!

He placed one of his warm hands over hers, and spoke softly. Every other thought seemed to disperse, and for a moment she knew nothing but the fact that he was holding her hand. She stared at the sun-golden tone of his skin, the soft curling hair that vaguely shadowed his wrist and back of his hand. She found herself wanting to place her other hand on top of his, to stroke him and let her fingers entwine with his. But she did not move.

"Have you learned nothing about me, Anne?" he whispered. "I could hardly care what others think of me. I may be an earl now—for the time being anyway—" they both ignored the reference to the child she was supposedly carrying, "but I used to be just a plain old working man. My title may have changed, but I'm still just me. Christian Montaigne or Christian Thornton. Same person."

His gaze held hers so steadily, she felt as though she could sit there forever and simply stare into those eyes. His hand tightened ever so slightly upon hers, and she felt an intimacy rise up, engulfing them in a tiny world that no one outside the dining room could ever enter.

"And now . . ." he said softly.

"Yes?" She couldn't help feeling expectant.

"We should have dessert."

17

As Pel's wedding day drew near, Anne's mourning isolation came to an end. Anne might have welcomed Pel's wedding—certainly the end of isolation would brook no great change in the quiet life Anne lived at Highcrest—but each day that passed brought one more grain of worry that Anne's monthly course was simply not late. It was not coming, at least for the month of April.

It had been over four weeks since she'd surrendered her virginity, and her monthly flux was more than a week overdue. Still, she clung to the fact that she didn't feel any different. She'd had an upset stomach or two, but she convinced herself it was simply due to worry over her mother's welfare. And since returning to Highcrest, Elsbeth had settled somewhat, eating a bit more, which made Anne relax. She'd felt robust herself, eating with a healthy appetite. There simply was no sign, except for her lack of bleeding, that she had conceived. And she prayed she had not. In fact, she continued to assure herself that she had not. Surely she would feel different if she were carrying a child, even after only a few weeks.

And so she went about the days without too much concern. It was easy to find other things to occupy her thoughts. Christian had been so wonderful since Anne's return that he filled her mind instead of memories of the stranger and any possible outcome from their mating. She had once told herself to steer clear of Christian, and with a halfhearted effort she had tried. But he seemed always to

anticipate her activities and be there to meet her, riding his
Arabian when she went for a jaunt on her mare, or waiting
for her in the garden when she walked, or in the solicitor's
salon when she stole there to read a book. She had thought,
at first, that the meetings were by chance, but after the third
day of riding together Christian told her he had purposely
waited for her so they might share their daily rides together.

And the time they shared was precious to Anne. He
could make her laugh with the greatest ease; he listened to
her when she wanted to speak; he made her feel as though
whatever she said, no matter how trivial, was of great
interest. And even when they didn't speak at all, the silences
were far from awkward. There had grown between them a
feeling of companionship, one which Anne knew she would
be miserable without.

She no longer tried to keep herself from seeing
Christian. While it was true that she'd had more than one
dream of his kiss, it was also true that he'd been the perfect
gentleman. A brotherly sort, to be sure. Other than that first
day when he'd welcomed her with a kiss, he hadn't so much
as touched her to dismount from her filly. He always allowed
the grooms to do that. Oh, there were times when that
intense gaze of his could have seen into her very soul, but it
was obviously her imagination if she thought it to be sexual.
Simply wanting Christian to be interested in her as a woman
didn't make him so. He was friendly, warm, even
affectionate, but always a gentleman. And she told herself
that was as it should be. They were, after all, related by
marriage even if her husband was deceased. For propriety's
sake, she mustn't allow herself so much as the briefest
thought which was anything besides brotherly.

It was midmorning and Anne was dressed in her riding
suit, the only piece of clothing not black being the white
steinkirk knotted at her throat. She passed the parlor on her
way toward the door, but paused when she spotted Christian
talking to Waites. Christian, too, was dressed in a riding suit,
and so she decided to wait for him since it was obvious he
once again intended riding with her.

'It mustn't be too fancy or she'll think we're violating

the mourning period," Christian was saying. "Why don't you see the servant girl? Pel is her name. She'll have a list."

"Sounds like you're planning a party," Anne said as she stepped into the parlor.

Both Waites and Christian looked as though they'd been caught stealing sweets before dinner when they saw Anne approaching them.

"And so we are," Christian said after the briefest pause. "Don't you remember? We decided to celebrate your servant's wedding here at Highcrest."

Anne was perplexed. "And the two of you are planning it?"

Christian laughed. "You make it sound as though we're two priests planning a Jewish wedding."

"Which is about as likely as an earl and his valet planning a servant's wedding," she said. "Why don't you leave the wedding to Pel and her family?"

Christian raised his hands in supplication. "I was just trying to be helpful." Then he turned to Waites. "Perhaps it would be enough to simply let Mistress Escott and her family know our doors are open to her." He turned to Anne for approval. "Enough?"

"More than enough," she said.

They made their way out to the stables. "Don't tell me you still think it's improper for Pel to celebrate her wedding in the Highcrest parlor," he said as they walked out into the bright sunshine.

"Not improper," Anne said. "Just . . . unusual."

"And what's wrong with being unusual?"

"Nothing," she said, somewhat defensively.

"Now don't get argumentative," he chided her gently.

"I'm not argumentative!"

"Good," he said, taking a light hold on her elbow. She glanced down at the contact, for it was the first time he'd touched her in days. "I don't want anything to mar this day."

"Why today?" she asked, somewhat breathlessly. "In particular, that is?"

He shrugged easily. He was very close and she could feel

the pull of her skirt as it swished against his leg closest to her.
"Because today is the last day of isolation. We shall all
continue to miss Selwyn, of course, but I know as well as you
what he said on the day he died."

"Which was?"

"Not to mourn him; he goes to a better place. Have you
forgotten?"

"No, of course not," she replied. "But I didn't think
you'd heard him."

"I did, and I intend to follow his instruction. Do you?"

She was always somewhat taken aback by his abrupt
questions. "I won't do anything to disgrace the Thornton
name," she said.

He stopped abruptly, and she nearly bumped into him.
"Won't you?"

She wanted to shrink from his suddenly black
expression; his golden eyes looked fierce, his brows drew to a
deep frown. Wind whipped at his tied hair and a few strands
came loose, and for a moment he looked almost wild.

"What . . . what do you mean?" she asked.

Just as suddenly as the look appeared, it vanished. He
smiled, loosening the hold on her elbow which had tightened
almost painfully.

He smiled mischievously. "You mean you won't wear
red to Pel's wedding?"

"Is that what you'd like for me to do? Wear red instead
of black?"

"The color would suit you," he commented as they
continued walking. "But no, that isn't what I had in mind."

"What did you have in mind?"

His shrug was familiarly noncommittal. "Let's ride to
the pond today," he suggested as a groom greeted them with
their saddled mounts.

Anne willingly agreed. The pond was a favorite spot of
hers.

The water was placid but for a few peaceful ripples
marring the smooth surface. It was a warm day, and before
long both Anne and Christian had discarded their coats.

"I'll tell you one thing you might do," Christian said after a moment, watching the water rather than Anne. "Against tradition, that is."

"What?"

"Take off your shoes and your . . . your hose, and dip your feet in the water. I'd bet it would feel cool and welcome on a day like today."

In fact, Anne had done so on more than one occasion last summer. But she could hardly admit it, and never, ever would she have considered doing such a thing with anyone present—least of all a man such as Christian!

At her hesitation, he said daringly, "Are you afraid?"

"Of what?" she asked quickly, proudly.

"My question exactly, of what?"

That was enough. Anne sat on the grassy bank and slipped off her shoes. She reached under her skirts for her garters and, still keeping herself modestly covered, she removed her white hose and tucked them into her discarded shoes. Then, barefoot, she remained seated and looked at Christian boldly.

"And what of you, my lord?"

That was all the invitation he needed.

It was almost sinful, Anne thought, to enjoy something so much. The water felt marvelously cool and refreshing. She held her skirts high, but retained propriety by allowing the water to cover whatever her hiked up skirt would have revealed. Perhaps it was the very unseemliness of it, the fact that no earl should have ever asked a lady to do such a thing, and certainly no lady should have ever agreed. But as they waded in the shallow water, all Anne could think was that she'd never delighted herself more.

"Have you ever been swimming?" Christian asked.

"Oh, no, you don't," she said teasingly. "I'll wade up to my knees, but you're not getting me in any deeper than this."

He laughed at her conclusion. "Did I ask?"

"No, I've never been swimming. I think I would probably drown—or get eaten by fish."

He laughed. "Fish wouldn't have you. They prefer bait that's smaller than they are."

She looked toward the deeper section of the lake, a frown forming. "Still, they might bite."

Christian laughed again. "You really would be afraid, wouldn't you?"

She stiffened at his humor. "I prefer to have the water I bathe in scented like lavender, not fish."

"Hmm," he considered the statement. "I must admit, if I were to take you in my arms, I would prefer the scent of lavender, too."

Anne did not look at him even though she felt his gaze on her. She knew, if she looked at him, he would see that his words had affected her, and she didn't want him to know.

"Anne," he whispered her name and she had to force herself not to turn to him. She didn't want to look into his eyes; she didn't want to see his face, didn't want to feel her very insides melt in utter and indefensible admiration of him.

"Yes?"

"Don't be alarmed," he said gently, almost erotically, "but there is a shadow behind you. I think it's a fish."

It took a moment for the meaning of the words to sink in, so hypnotic was his tone. But once it was clear that there was a fish nearby, she lost all control. She screamed, dropped her skirts into the clear blue water and raced to shore, nearly tripping as her heavy, water-logged skirt hampered her footing back on land.

Christian's laughter was the first thing she heard once she dropped to the ground, ending her frantic run. And as he approached, she glared at him accusingly.

"Did you do that on purpose?" she asked mistrustfully. "There wasn't really a fish at all, was there? You just thought it would be amusing to see me in terror."

He dropped to the bank beside her, the entire length of his hard body shaking with mirth. "It was a fine sight, to be sure," he said, then held up his hand in defense. "But there really was a fish. Honestly."

She continued to eye him warily.

"You're a mess," he said, and once again his voice sounded too sensual to be ignored.

Self-consciously, she glanced down at herself. He was right. Her skirt was soaked more than halfway up, and now had little pieces of grass clinging here and there.

"Maybe you should take it off," he suggested. "Until it dries."

She swallowed hard. "I—don't think that's necessary."

He shrugged as if it hardly mattered, and that was what bothered her so.

"I suppose we should wait here until it dries then," he said after a moment. "Otherwise we may raise a few eyebrows back at the manor, and even the most loyal servant can have a loose tongue."

"I—I can wait alone, if you've business to attend to and cannot spare the time."

"Don't be silly," he said. "I'm not leaving you here alone."

"Why not? I've ridden out here by myself many times before. There's no harm in it."

"Suppose a giant fish jumps out of the water and eats you?"

She laughed and shook her head at him.

"I'll stay," he said. "I want to."

"Good," she replied, her eyes riveted to his. "I'm glad."

It was past noon by the time they returned to Highcrest. Soon after, Christian disappeared into the solicitor's salon and Anne went to dine with her mother. But Anne knew they would see each other again at supper, for it had become the custom for them to take the last meal of the day together. It was a custom she knew she was becoming far too fond of.

One thing was odd, though. Today Christian had seemed different somehow, not quite so brotherly. And, Anne realized, she had liked that very much—far, far too much, in fact. But was it because of her imagination, or simply his admitted affection for women in general that his voice sounded so sensual? Perhaps it was not personally

aimed her way at all. She really must make a greater effort to
spend less time with Christian. Regardless of the fact she
often felt pangs of guilt over what her father had made her
attempt against Christian, he was after all still her deceased
husband's son. Therefore, he was unavailable to her—not
that it appeared he had considered such a thing. Anne knew
she was alone in whatever infatuation she felt for him,
certainly the feeling wasn't returned. It seemed obvious to
her he wanted to build a relationship, one of trust and
affection, a friendship, she assured herself, and nothing
more. It was all they were entitled to, being of the same
Thornton name already.

Still, she couldn't help remembering the sound of his
voice when he'd suggested discarding her soiled skirt until it
dried. But she reminded herself that a mere moment later,
after her denial, he'd shrugged as if it were of no difference
to him at all. That's what she must remember, she told herself, that she could have been of no more sexual interest than
a sister when faced with the prospect of partially disrobing
with him nearby.

Throughout that night as she tossed in her bed, Anne
forced herself to think only of the proper aspects regarding
Christian. It was a battle fought without success, however,
for the moment she fell asleep her traitorous mind created
images she blushed to recall in the morning.

Pel came early to help Anne dress and to style her hair.
Anne welcomed the company, for it took her mind off the
struggle she'd waged through the night.

"It's a lovely day," Pel greeted her as she drew back the
draperies at the window. "You're lucky."

"Why is that?"

Pel shook her finger at Anne. "Have you forgotten?"

Anne was immediately stricken. "Today isn't your
wedding, is it? Oh, Pel, what are you doing here serving
me—"

"No, no, it's not my wedding, silly! That isn't for two
days yet. Today is your birthday!"

Anne sank back to the edge of her bed in relief. "Oh, is
that all?"

"Is that all!" Pel remonstrated. "You're eighteen today. Aren't you happy?"

Anne shrugged. It hardly made any difference to her; she'd never in her life celebrated a birthday. Her mother used to give her a special sweet after dinner, but because her father never had the money for a party, her birthdays had always gone by unnoticed for the most part. Not that he would have spent money on a party for her, anyway.

"Will you wear color today, Anne?" Pel asked as she opened the tall doors of Anne's wardrobe.

Anne sighed, catching sight of the lovely gowns hanging from pegs in the wardrobe. "Isolation may be over, but it's still customary to wear black for a year, you know."

Pel looked as disappointed as Anne felt. "Not even for your birthday? I'm sure Selwyn wouldn't have minded."

But Anne shook her head. "Maybe for your wedding I'll wear a ribbon . . . a red ribbon," she added, smiling to herself. "That's as far as I'll go to break tradition."

Anne's former resolve to avoid Christian was surprisingly successful that day—due in no part to herself. Christian simply was not to be found, even though to her own shame she looked for him more than once. She dared not ask Waites; that she would not allow herself.

But by supper she could not contain her curiosity. The entire manor's staff seemed to be acting more than a little strange. Waites and the others were exceptionally quiet, and Anne thought she saw more than one upstairs maid steal a quick little smile her way. Only Pel, as talkative as ever, remained the same.

"Maybe I'll take my supper up here in my room," Anne said when Pel came to help her change for dinner. "I don't really feel like changing my clothes. It's been such a quiet day."

Pel looked oddly upset by Anne's suggestion. "Then the very thing you need is to get yourself dressed in the finest gown you have—the finest black one, if you must. Mustn't get lazy, you know."

Anne looked at Pel with her head cocked to one side. "Lazy? Aren't you the one who tells me I interfere with the servants too much as it is? Just ask Mistress Markay—"

"All right," Pel capitulated. "Perhaps lazy wasn't the right word. But you really should take supper downstairs; I think I saw the earl heading for his room awhile ago. Most likely he'll be changed and waiting for you in no time. You wouldn't want him to be eating by himself, now would you?"

"I went riding by myself today," Anne said, and even to her own ears she sounded like a little girl who was sulking over the lack of attention she'd been getting.

"Sounds to me like you could use some company then."

Anne brightened. "That's a fine idea," she said. Then, despite the fact that inside she knew whose company she desired most, she asked, "Why don't you take your supper up here with me, Pel?"

But Pel shook her head. "I'm promised to Gregory for the evening."

Anne sighed. "Very well. If you're sure you saw Christian—I mean the earl—back within the manor?"

"I did, indeed. I'm sure he'll be waiting for you for supper."

Anne let herself be changed and freshened, her hair twisted once again into an intricate coil of heavy blond curls. She wore an open gown of black satin with a matching black petticoat; it was often hard to tell that she'd changed at all since all her clothes these days remained black. This gown, however, was slightly different in style from the more demure gowns she'd been wearing. The sleeves reached only to her elbow, and were trimmed in a delicate ruffle of black lace. The bodice, too, was edged in lace, eliminating the use of a modesty piece despite its rather daring plunge which revealed a generous portion of her breasts. She wore no jewelry, not feeling bold enough to use the Thornton jewels which now belonged to Christian. It was a pity, however, because the low cut of the gown begged for something sparkling at her throat.

Ready at last, nearly fifteen minutes past the usual supper hour, Anne made her way downstairs. Odd how quiet the house seemed; there were no sounds of cooking from the kitchen, no servants passing her in the hall. It had been a strange day from the start.

Just as she reached the bottom of the stairs, however, she heard the hushed voices of more than a few people. The sound came from the parlor and, curiously, she headed that way.

"She's here!"

The voice came from the familiar housekeeper Mistress Lindall, and she sounded quite agitated. The parlor was filled with people, servants, villagers, even Mortimer and his assistants. And in the center, towering above most others, stood Christian. When he caught sight of her he laughed and headed her way.

"You spoiled the surprise," he reprimanded her affectionately. "You were due fifteen minutes ago."

"Surprise?"

Now it was Christian who seemed surprised. "For your birthday, little goose!"

Anne's eyes widened as she surveyed the room. Everyone was looking at her, smiling or sending some sort of well wishes.

"This is for me?"

Christian laughed and gave her a brief hug. "The surprise worked, after all."

Then Mortimer stepped forward as did many others, with a kiss on her cheek or a squeeze of her hand. When each and every one of them had expressed their kind thoughts, Christian raised his glass and made a toast, wishing Anne the happiest of birthdays.

Christian led Anne aside, taking her elbow. He whispered in her ear. "Before you scold me about the improprieties of having a celebration so soon after isolation, let me remind you it is *after*."

Anne stared up at him, too overcome to even think of scolding him. He caught her glance and held it, and Anne knew she would never be content unless he was always part of her life and she could look into that gaze.

"Happy Birthday, Countess," he whispered. Then, quite unexpectedly, he pressed a small, flat box into her hand.

"What is this?"

"A present, of course. What would a birthday be without presents?"

Anne could have told him, for that was exactly the kind of birthday she'd had thus far. She stared at the box, covered in red cloth and surprisingly heavy for its size. To her dismay, she felt tears moisten her eyes.

"Well?" Christian asked when the moment stretched out. "Aren't you going to open it?"

Wordlessly, she nodded. She lifted the top of the box and nestled inside on a black cushion sparkled a large blue sapphire imbedded in the center of a silver rope necklace.

"Christian," she whispered with awe. Never had she expected such a thing—not the celebration and certainly not a gift as exquisite as this. "It's lovely, truly lovely."

His face was very close to Anne's. "Not as lovely as your eyes. That's why I chose the blue sapphire, you know. Because it reminded me of your eyes."

Anne gazed at him, feeling so aflutter she nearly swayed toward him and into his arms. But she held herself erect, grateful they were surrounded by a roomful of people. It gave her the strength she needed to behave the way she should.

Pel had followed her downstairs and was now approaching her with her own happy wishes. When she saw the sapphire, she immediately volunteered to clasp it around Anne's neck—a task Anne might have preferred Christian himself perform, but considering the battle she already fought to keep herself out of his arms, she was glad Pel was there to do it.

Not much later, Christian led Anne to her chair at the long table in the dining room while the rest of the guests followed suit. The sidetable was laden with food, which several servants immediately offered.

Since Christian sat at one end and Anne at the other, conversation between the two was impossible with twenty people seated in between them. She was relieved, however, in a vague way, since having his presence so near was wreaking havoc inside her. She would at least be able to carry on an easy conversation with those seated around her. Mortimer was at Anne's right, and she patted his hand affectionately.

"Was this your idea, Mortimer?"

He smiled, the wrinkles around his mouth deepening into ready laugh lines. "I wish I could take the credit, my lady. But the truth is, it was all his lordship's idea."

Anne's incredulous gaze flew to Christian, who was just taking his seat. "Christian's?"

Mortimer nodded. "He's become quite happy living here, my lady. The entire village has quickly grown fond of him. A fine heir to Selwyn's . . . er, I beg pardon, my lady." His ancient face looked immediately distressed. "I've forgotten, for the moment, that you carry the heir."

"Selwyn," Anne said slowly. "I should like to speak to you about that matter."

She wasn't sure how far she would go, certainly she had no intention of revealing the truth, but she did wish for more information. Information she prayed to God she would have no need of.

"Yes, my lady?"

They spoke quietly, and the rest of the table chatted on in pleasant company, oblivious to their conversation.

"If my child is a girl, will Christian retain the title?"

Mortimer frowned. "I cannot say for certain, this is of course up to the courts and how they decide to divide Selwyn's estate. There is a chance Christian will be allowed to keep the title, yes. The inheritance may be divided equally, or perhaps the bulk of it granted to your daughter if the courts deem it is fitting, considering your child is the legitimate one."

"And if the child is a boy?"

Mortimer smiled and raised one hand as he spoke. "Then it will all go to your son—with perhaps a reasonable allowance set aside for Christian. I myself can see to that, if you would not mind."

Anne swallowed hard, even though the news came as no

surprise. That was exactly what her father hoped for, wasn't it? She looked at Christian, who at that very moment was smiling her way. Anne hurriedly averted her gaze, despite the awkwardness of it. Her fingers rose to touch the sapphire fastened to her throat. It was too much to bear, she thought. He was, without doubt, the kindest, most wonderful man. Not to mention the most handsome. He haunted her dreams almost nightly. How could she live with herself, knowing she was the integral part of a scheme to rob him blind?

18

Pel's wedding day arrived and, much to Pel's own consternation, Anne acted as lady's maid to the happy bride. They were in Anne's room, and Anne was unsuccessfully trying to style Pel's hair. She sighed with annoyance when a stubborn curl refused to obey her fingers.

Pel laughed. "I've made a much better lady's maid than you ever would," she teased. "Why don't you let me do it myself?"

Anne gave in, realizing it would be in Pel's own best interest to let her do just that. A few minutes later, Pel's hair was artfully arranged by her own nimble fingers.

"Well, at least I'll be able to lace your chemise," Anne said when Pel stood. Then, once Pel's undergarments were in place, Anne went to retrieve the gown Pel would be married in. It was a gift from Anne, a lovely creation of silver and white lace. But just as Anne turned back to Pel, the garment in hand, she swayed dangerously as everything went momentarily black.

"Whoa!" Pel said, grabbing Anne's arm. "Sit down for a minute," she commanded.

Anne did so, only because the dizziness had been unexpectedly overwhelming.

Pel tried to make light of it. "Overworked already," she said with a grin. Then she frowned. "Don't you think this is taking your father's act of a false pregnancy just a little too far? That is," she added, "if it is false?"

Anne raised tormented eyes to Pel's. "If?"

"Well," she began slowly, "I've never been pregnant, but my little brother is eight years younger than I am. I remember my mother swooning more than once from carrying him."

Anne moaned, and sagged forward, holding her forehead in her hands. "It's true," she said in a muffled, fear-filled voice. "I can't deny it any longer, not even to myself. I truly do carry a child."

"But how?" Pel's question was obviously shocked. "I thought it was all a delay tactic, until your father concocted some insane way of declaring Christian Thornton a fraud?"

Anne shook her head miserably. "The plan was for me to leave a true heir—to have a baby."

"But *whose*? Certainly not Selwyn's!"

Anne stood, the dizziness gone. She spoke with her back to Pel, unable to face her with the truth. "My father hired a man. . . . He came to me at the cottage and . . . and . . ."

Pel came up behind Anne and put an arm around her shoulders. "You don't have to tell me any more," she said shortly. Then she hugged her close. "You poor thing."

Anne resisted the sympathy. "Poor thing! I did it! I went through with it."

"For a good reason, no doubt. Did it have something to do with your mother?"

Anne nodded.

"Reason enough."

Finally Anne turned to Pel, relief, affection, gratitude all swelling in her heart and pushing tears to her eyes. How wonderful was Pel's friendship. Conquering her tears, she said, "This is unfair of me, to burden you with all of this on your wedding day."

Pel gave her another quick hug. "I'm just sorry you've had to go through all of this."

"I don't want to think about it," she said brusquely, once again retrieving Pel's dress. "That's how I've gotten through every day since the beginning of this: by thinking about something else. Sometimes . . ." she said with a trembling voice, "sometimes it even works."

* * *

Pel's wedding ceremony was held in the Highcrest chapel, a small stone structure a short distance away. The sky threatened rain, and so a Thornton carriage took the bride, Anne, and Pel's mother, who had come to be with her daughter to the chapel. Christian was already at the church, along with the groom and several guests.

Anne couldn't help but shed a tear or two as she watched Pel take her vows. Pel's love for Gregory, standing tall and handsome beside her, was so obvious it reminded Anne of the void she'd felt in that part of her life. Unwittingly, her gaze went to Christian, who was seated beside her. Strangely enough, that void didn't feel quite so deep anymore.

Afterward the entire company returned to Highcrest Manor. An assortment of delicacies had been set out for the guests but, according to Pel's wishes, the celebration would be brief and quiet. While she was grateful to the lord of the manor for his generosity, she nonetheless did not feel entirely comfortable and planned to leave somewhat early with her groom. She'd told Anne it would be just as well with Gregory. He was every bit as anxious as Pel herself to begin their marriage.

Many of the guests had departed before four o'clock. Pel and Gregory were gone as well, but Mortimer and a few of the villagers were still lingering over a glass of sherry. Anne had just said farewell to a woman she'd known since childhood when she saw an impressively rigged carriage pull up before the manor. The door of the house was ajar in anticipation of guests' departures, and so Anne had no trouble seeing the caller alight from his carriage.

Anne did not recognize him. He was tall and thin, dressed handsomely in fawn-colored breeches and a somewhat darker coat and waistcoat. As he approached she noticed his features: not plain, exactly, but not really remarkable. His eyes were the exact color of the hair that rather carelessly peeked out from the sides of his wig, a washed out brown instead of the gold she'd come to admire

so much in Christian's eyes. He was not broad of shoulder
like Christian, and she guessed he might be a just bit shorter,
as well. Then she caught herself. What was she doing,
comparing this man to Christian? Had she completely lost
control of her senses?

The man bowed formally before her, and smiled a rather
pleasant smile. His teeth were not white—not as white
as . . . she stopped her thoughts. "May I help you, sir?" she
asked.

"I am looking for Countess Anne Thornton."

"I am she."

His smile broadened. "I hoped that the moment I saw
you. I am Newell. Newell Franklin."

Anne continued to gaze at him, but it was obvious the
name was supposed to mean something.

"Lord Newell Franklin?" he supplied hopefully.

Anne shook her head apologetically. "I'm very sorry,
Lord Newell . . . er, Lord Franklin, but I am at the dis-
advantage here."

"Selwyn sent for me."

Her face showed enlightenment, and she chose her next
words carefully. "I'm so terribly sorry to have to inform
you, Lord Franklin, but my husband has passed away."

"Oh, but I know that, Countess. That is precisely why
I'm here. I did think, though, that you would be expecting
me." He looked around the entrance foyer. "Is there some-
place we could talk? Privately, that is?"

Curious, but also aware of propriety, Anne thought of
the solicitor's salon. She also remembered that Mortimer was
still in the parlor and thought of asking him to join them.

Her plan was unnecessary, however, for just as she
turned toward the parlor, Christian emerged. He eyed the
newcomer with interest, glancing back to Anne for an
explanation.

"This is Newell Franklin," she said. "Lord Franklin,
actually. He has asked to speak to me."

"Oh? What about?" Christian eyed the stranger with
what Anne could only describe as an intimidating stare.

Franklin seemed to stiffen at Christian's presence. "It's a private matter."

"Nothing so private that you'll keep it from family, I'm sure?" He directed the question to Anne.

"Of course not. In truth, Christian, I don't know what this is about."

"Family?" Newell repeated.

Anne made the necessary introductions. "This is Selwyn's son, Lord Christian Thornton."

Newell gave a bow of his head respectfully, seeming somehow relieved that the connection to Anne was so proper.

"I should like to speak to the countess in private, my lord. If that is permissable?"

"It most certainly is not," Christian said firmly. "We shall all go into the salon and learn what this is about."

"I only wish to spare my lady's embarrassment," Newell explained. "Since it's obvious Selwyn did not inform her of what he was about before he died."

But Christian was already at the salon door. Newell and Anne had no choice but to follow him in.

"Well?" Christian asked briefly once the door was closed behind him.

Newell shifted his weight from one foot to the other and gripped his three-cornered hat rather firmly.

"This really is quite embarrassing," Newell began.

"Then perhaps it would be best if you got it over with as quickly as possible," Christian suggested. His tone, however, was hardly sympathetic.

Newell bristled, and when he spoke it was in a somewhat more steady voice. "I received a letter some time ago from Selwyn, who was a close associate of my father's at one time when they both served Parliament. The letter implored me to arrive here at Highcrest after the six week mourning of his death, to meet his widow."

"To meet me?" Anne asked with surprise. "But why?"

"He was most concerned over your welfare, my lady. He said in the letter that you would be in need of a husband.

When he first contacted me he was unaware of his son."
Newell glanced briefly to Christian. "I believe his initial
intentions were to see you remarried quickly, so as to assure
the smooth running of his estates. But a more recent letter,
written not long before he died, told me of his son and that I
needn't concern myself with the burden of worrying over the
entire Thornton fortune. But that I should still consider
myself one of the suitors for your future."

"*One* of the suitors?" Christian asked. His face, for the
moment, was full of surprise.

"I was under the impression that Selwyn chose three
men in all, men he knew were of impeccable character and
may prove of interest to the countess."

Anne took a seat in a rather unladylike fashion by very
nearly falling into it. "Do you mean to say that Selwyn chose
men to be my husband?"

"It sounds bizarre, I admit," Newell said. "But Selwyn
explained it rather neatly. Sussex being so secluded and all,
he thought it wise to provide you with what he believed the
best London has to offer. I am proud to say I am one of
them."

Anne was speechless, so great was her surprise.
Christian, too, was silent, though he had managed to wipe
clean any emotion from his face. He was leaning against the
closed door, arms crossed in front of him, and he looked
totally at ease.

Newell spoke up again. "He was really very fond of
you, my lady. He extolled your beauty, and I must say he did
not exaggerate in the least."

Christian ignored Newell's gushing compliments and
spoke. "What exactly convinced you to take part in such a
scheme, Franklin? Aren't there enough *femme fatales* in
London these days?"

Newell stiffened. "Respect for the friendship between
my father and Lord Selwyn was the reason."

Christian sneered. "And nothing at all to do with the
fact that—initially at least—Anne was the only heir to one of
the greatest fortunes in England?"

"Positively not!" Newell exclaimed, clearly affronted by the notion.

Christian stroked his chin, as if in thought. He glanced from Newell to Anne and back to Newell again. "And there are two more just like you on their way from London as well?"

"I cannot say, my lord," Newell said curtly. "I don't know if the others agreed to come."

Anne stood, knowing but one thing. She hardly wanted a husband chosen for her. Her father had done that for her once; she would not allow anyone to do it again! Not even if Selwyn had done so out of kindness.

"You are not aware, then, that I carry Selwyn's child?" she said.

Obviously he was not. He blanched.

"There may come a time, Lord Newell," Anne said, "that I will be interested in remarrying. But certainly not while I carry Selwyn's posthumous child. I am terribly sorry you've made the long trip from London, but under the circumstances I would say it was useless. Thank you for the respect you've shown to Selwyn's memory by fulfilling his wishes, but I think it would be best for all of us if you would return to London."

"I—I—"

"Let me show you to the door, Newell," Christian volunteered after a wink in Anne's direction.

Newell was out of the salon, indeed, out of the house, within moments.

Christian returned to the solicitor's salon and closed the door, coming to Anne who had not moved a muscle.

"He thought I was expecting him," Anne said slowly, confusion making her frown. It was so unlike Selwyn not to have told her what he'd been about.

"I'm sure Selwyn acted only out of fondness for you. Newell was right about that."

"Oh! The journal!" Anne popped from her chair, looking around the room with sudden intent. "He told me to read his journal, and follow what it says. Do you remember?''

Christian shook his head. "I couldn't hear everything he said that day. Where was he to have left it?"

"In here! Somewhere."

After a thorough search, Anne found it in the bottom drawer of the huge maghogany desk. She opened it eagerly, and read the words of the final entry aloud.

> Three men of my choosing will call on you, my dear. I know it is most unseemly for a man to choose his wife's next husband, but ours has been a warm and caring friendship and I am too well aware there are few local prospects for a countess in Wynchly. You mustn't take this as coercion, my dear. I know how you would resist that. That is why I've selected three men for you to choose from, more choice than you were given the first time. Please know that I do this in love.

That was all it said; hardly enough explanation, but sufficient warning to be sure. Anne caught Christian's interested gaze.

"The first time?" he repeated curiously. "Didn't you choose to marry Selwyn?"

Anne hedged, closing the journal and returning it to its place in the desk. "I—don't know what he was referring to."

She stood, intent now on leaving the room. She was tired after the long day, and definitely did not want a confrontation with Christian.

But he stopped her with one statement. "I thought we've built a friendship between us, Anne."

She faced him. He was too important for her to ignore. "We have."

"One built on trust?"

She nodded.

"Then why don't you tell me the truth?"

"About what?"

"Everything." He said it so clearly, so firmly, that she

wondered if he could only be referring to what was in the journal.

"There is nothing to tell." She said it in a low, almost sad voice. Certainly she had no choice but to evade his question. She would not have him know she'd married Selwyn only because her father had manipulated her into it. It might lead him to suspect other things, as well—and she couldn't risk that.

"I see," Christian said. He did not look at her.

"I'll be retiring for the evening now, if you don't mind."

She opened the door, but Christian spoke once more. "No doubt your pregnancy is fatiguing."

She glanced over her shoulder. He sounded somewhat angry, but she could tell nothing from the cold expression on his face. "Yes," she agreed, then left the room.

19

"Selwyn was right about one thing," Mortimer said to Christian, who stood at the parlor window watching the retreating carriage. "The men he chose were beyond reproach."

Christian turned to Mortimer, unsmiling. They had just sent the last of the three men whom Selwyn had chosen as possible suitors for Anne on his way. This last fellow they had not even bothered introducing to Anne, who was upstairs napping. "Why are they beyond reproach?" Christian asked, unconvinced. He hadn't liked this business from the start. There was something decidedly suspect in titled noblemen coming all the way out to Sussex to be considered as husbands by a woman they'd never met. "Because they still offered themselves despite the fact Anne is no longer sole heir?"

Mortimer nodded. "That is, you'll agree, a fine test to have put them to."

"So what are you saying?" Christian asked through clenched teeth. He felt himself stiffen from head to foot, though for the life of him he couldn't explain why the topic was so unpleasant. "That the men are fitting prospects for Anne, and that she should consider them?"

"Well," Mortimer began slowly, "of course, I agree with her ladyship that she must wait until after the birth of her child. But yes, I do think any one of the three men Selwyn chose would be fitting."

Christian managed an indifferent shrug. "It hardly

matters now, does it? That was the last of them. I doubt they'll grace Sussex with their presence again, no matter how loyal they feel to Selwyn's memory.''

Mortimer poured himself a glass of wine, silently offering one to Christian, who refused. "It may be the last of two of them, anyway.''

"What do you mean?"

After a long sip, Mortimer explained. "Only that the first one who came—the one I have yet to meet, a Lord Newell something-or-other—''

"Franklin," Christian supplied.

"Yes, that's it. Lord Franklin. He's staying in Wynchly.''

Christian's brows rose in surprise. "Is he, indeed? It's been three weeks since he first arrived to announce this preposterous plan of Selwyn's. He hasn't shown himself since.''

"I sent one of my men to inquire after his intentions when I first learned he'd stayed behind," Mortimer said. "It seems the young man in quite interested in Countess Anne after all, despite the fact she carries another man's child at this very moment. His intentions were to wait until the other two gentlemen had come and—he hoped—gone as well. Now that they've retreated, he'll probably return to reissue his interest.''

"That's ridiculous!"

Mortimer watched Christian closely, his glance moving from Christian's irate face to his clenched fists. "Are you sure you won't have some wine?"

Christian immediately noted the older man's scrutiny and obvious conclusion that he needed a drink to bolster him. "No," he said firmly, then took a seat before the unlit fireplace.

Mortimer sat across from him. "You've been nearly as prickly as Countess Anne herself these past few weeks, my lord," he said. "It seems to me you've taken great care to avoid her, since her birthday, and it's making both of you most unhappy.''

Christian's gaze held Mortimer's. "You're very

observant," he said without emotion.

Mortimer looked pleased that Christian didn't deny the truth. "Then you admit you are avoiding her?"

He shrugged, noncommittal.

Mortimer went on. "I don't pretend to know all that goes on in this house, or what words have passed between you. But," he added, and his tone seemed to take on a warning edge, "I hold Anne in high esteem, and she deserves only the best and kindest treatment. God knows she hasn't had that before."

"Are you inferring that I haven't treated her well?"

Mortimer waved a hand. "I only know that if you've given her a friendship and then withdrawn it without reason, it's hardly fair."

"Just where are you getting your information, Mortimer? Do you have spies even within this house?"

He shook his head, amused that such a suspicion was even mentioned. "I am merely an observant man—one of the reasons Selwyn trusted me with his entire fortune while he was alive. I saw the friendship which was growing when Anne first returned from the cottage. And I saw it disappear for no apparent reason. You've known from the beginning that Anne carries your father's child, therefore it cannot be awkwardness over that. I confess, as observant as I am, I've been unable to decipher the reasons for this distance between you." He paused long enough to eye Christian closely once again. "The strangest part of it is that it's not what either of you seem to want. Countess Anne mopes about, watching out for you. And when she does catch sight of you, she's happy one minute then withdrawn the next. She's getting as adept at avoiding you as you are of her." He took another sip of wine, adding, "It makes no sense. Especially since your eyes are every bit as much slaves to her presence as hers are to yours."

Christian scoffed, although inside he was cringing at the truth behind Mortimer's words. "You take your powers of observation too far, Mortimer. I think half of it is your imagination."

Mortimer only smiled, obviously confident he knew

what he'd been talking of. He took another sip of wine, finishing the last of it, then stood. When he spoke again his voice was serious.

"I have been a loyal servant of the Thornton family for most of my life. Your father was my friend, more than just my employer. I will, no doubt, serve the Thornton family until my dying day. But hear this, my lord: Countess Anne is a worthy woman and deserves the kindest treatment. Do not trifle with her affections if you have no intentions of carrying through to a respectable end."

With that he left, and Christian watched his departure disturbed by what had obviously been a warning. But Christian had no intention of following the lawyer's concerned advice; in fact, he greatly doubted the perception of Mortimer's observations. Mortimer, it was clear, was entirely fooled by Anne's supposedly guileless nature. But Christian knew better.

Mortimer, however, hadn't been entirely deceived. It galled Christian that he who had once bluffed his way through more than one game of chance could be so transparent about a woman—a woman he kept telling himself he should despise.

It was true, however, that he'd spent the better part of the last three weeks carefully avoiding her. And his own irritable temper proved he hadn't enjoyed it in the least. What he *had* enjoyed was riding with her, sharing supper with her, having tea in the afternoon with her. But that had stopped when he came to the conclusion that the trust he thought they'd built did not in any way penetrate that lying facade of hers. He asked her outright that day to spill it all, to confess to him anything which he might be interested in knowing about her. And she'd refused. She'd explained nothing. How carefully she guarded her secrets! And with good reason, he supposed, considering the size of the Thornton fortune. Obviously it meant more to her than any trust they had been in the process of building.

Even while he avoided her, on those few occasions he'd chanced to spot her, he'd eyed her closely. Was she indeed pregnant? She hardly looked any different, though it was barely two months. She did take frequent naps, he noticed, and she ate well, which would seem to indicate she was taking special care of herself.

Christian had a whole host of mixed emotions regarding that subject. If, indeed, she had conceived, he was still fully resolved that unless she showed some sign of worthiness, he would take his child, whether a boy or girl, and raise it on his own. Anne herself would be banished from Highcrest. As the days wore on and she still showed no sign of conscience, his resolve grew more and more firm.

There was only one regret in his withdrawal from her company. He had been so respectful of her while trying to build trust between them that he'd been foolish enough to have missed out on every chance of bedding her. And that he regretted with an overwhelmingly physical ache. He still wanted her, and wanted her badly, even if he did despise her. He had half a mind to do exactly as he wished, devil take any qualms about it.

Christian left the parlor for his own rooms, intending to change his clothes and go for a ride. One thing niggled at the back of his mind, the knowledge that Newell Franklin had elected to stay in Sussex rather than returning to London. Why should it bother him so? Christian hardly cared if, sometime in the future, Anne sunk her clutches into some unfortunate lad.

Anne rode carefully along the rutted field. When she'd first realized she was carrying the stranger's child, she had ridden every day like a madwoman. If she lost the baby, it would be too late for her father to force her into another try at conception. But even a harmless fall from the back of her horse hadn't threatened this child nestled so snugly in her womb. All she'd succeeded in doing was bruising her wrist, though when she'd climbed back on her horse she was surprisingly shaken. As much as she hated every aspect of her father's scheme, she discovered during that fall that she would not have been happy to lose the life she carried. Already, though she showed no outward signs, she thought of the baby inside her as a tiny little person, one who needed to be nurtured and protected, someone who would be hers and hers alone to love.

Inevitably, the stranger came to mind often. More than once she was tempted to seek out her father and ask for the man's identity now that she was sure she carried his child. But two things held her back, one being the assurance that it was better to know nothing more than she did, and the other that her father had left her blissfully alone since the success of his plan, and she did not want to do anything to change that.

Sadly, she knew why the stranger came to mind so frequently. It wasn't only the reality of carrying his child. The truth was the stranger's memory was no longer blotted out by Christian. In the last three weeks, Christian had been nothing but cool to her, and she couldn't help feeling the loss. She missed the Christian who could make her laugh, the Christian who made her feel so wonderfully special. The Christian she had dreamed of and dreamed of still, who would take her in his arms and love her the way the stranger had.

She missed the time they'd spent together. She continued to ride on a daily basis, although more gently now that she realized she wanted her child, despite her father's plans for it. She missed Christian's company on these rides, for her visits with him had quickly become her favorite time of day.

She'd cut her rides short since riding alone, but today she was not quite so eager to return to the manor. She'd gotten into the habit of napping, feeling so fatigued lately, but she'd napped earlier and wasn't at all tired now. So instead of heading back to the stables, she went to the pond. It was a warm day, and she fondly remembered the morning she'd waded in the water with Christian.

Today was even warmer than that day had been. She glanced around, tempted to take off her shoes and do it again. But then she remembered the fish, and wondered if she could set aside her misgivings long enough to enjoy the cool water.

"Contemplating swimming?"

Anne spun around in the saddle, surprised to hear Christian's voice. He nudged his horse from the cover of the trees.

She was unashamedly glad to see him. "No, but I was thinking of testing the water to my knees again."

He smiled, and she welcomed the difference from the past days of chilly receptions. His smile was like sunshine after a winter of cloudy days. "Don't let me stop you. I'll watch for fish."

"Will you join me?" she asked, his cheerful mood making her bold.

Much to her delight, he dismounted and headed her way. When he stood beside her, holding out his arms to help her alight, she slid into his embrace as if it were the natural thing to do. But the rush of blood through her veins was anything but natural.

He held her close an instant longer than necessary. Then, taking her hand, he led her to the grassy bank.

"You've been avoiding me," she said to him. She'd been troubled during the last few weeks, even while telling herself it was best not to see him. But she couldn't help thinking there had been a reason he'd stayed away, one she couldn't figure out.

"So have you," he said, giving absolutely no sign of enlightenment for which Anne had hoped. He knelt before her once she was seated. "Can I help you?"

Before Anne had a chance to answer, Christian's hands were on her soft kidskin shoes, unlacing the ties. It seemed to take an inordinate amount of time, and his gaze met hers often. It was, she could not deny, an almost sensual experience, despite the fact his fingers never touched her skin. And, a moment later when he held her ankle and slipped the shoe from her, it felt as though all the blood in her body surged to the spot where he held her ankle.

Then he did the same with the other shoe, and Anne merely sat, as if mesmerized, watching him. Perhaps that was why when his fingers slipped up under her skirt, she did nothing about it. But then, realizing he sought her garter, she drew back, shocked.

"I—I will do it," she said breathlessly.

But Christian did not listen. He smiled, shaking his head very slowly. His eyes held hers so steadily, she felt as if she were in a trance. She could barely believe this was happening, that his hands were on her so intimately, and yet she was powerless to stop him. He pulled away one garter from just above her knee, then the other, and a moment later was unraveling her stockings in agonizingly minute sections. He brushed her skin often, and his fingers felt cool against her suddenly heated flesh.

When he was finished, instead of inviting her to the water or turning to rid himself of his own hose and shoes. he helped her only halfway up, so they were both kneeling and facing each other. They were very close, so close Anne knew if she were to take a deep breath her breasts would brush against his chest. But the very act of breathing seemed too complicated for her to conquer at the moment. She gazed into his eyes, the golden flecks hypnotically intense.

"Why . . . are you doing this?" she asked after a moment. Her voice was barely a whisper.

"Doing what?" he asked, in a low but innocent tone.

But Anne did not doubt what was happening; surely this was not her imagination, the sensual way in which he'd helped her out of her stockings, his intentionally close proximity at this very moment, the blatant fire in his eyes. She could not be imagining everything, as wild as it all seemed.

Then he belied his innocence and kissed her. At first only his lips touched her. But, when she didn't resist, his arms encircled her and he pulled her nearer, closing the tiny gap between them. His arms were strong, holding her, but his hands did not remain idle. He pulled her arms up around his neck and then, ever so slowly, let his hands slide down the sides of her body. His hands rested at her waist, but it wasn't long before his touch slid back up along the swell of her breasts.

His mouth played havoc with her senses. His tongue teased hers, and it felt smooth and warm inside her mouth. He withdrew only a bit, as if inviting her into his mouth. And

Anne wanted desperately to do so . . . but she held back.

"Wait," she said, leaning back. Her arms withdrew from around her neck and, halfheartedly, she pressed her palms against his chest, holding him away. But he still remained far too close for her to think clearly.

"Why?" he asked, his gaze as intense as ever. His mouth—the very mouth which only a moment ago felt so wonderful upon her own—was smiling appealingly.

Then, even as she was trying to form the next words, a protest to be sure, his hands were at the laces of her bodice. He did not work quickly, but instead each movement was deliberate, confident of her acquiescence.

"I—I don't understand."

"No?" He grinned at her as though his intentions should be obvious. And, indeed, they were.

"But why? We—we've never—"

"Haven't we? It seems to me this is what we've wanted for a very long time now. Both of us."

"No. . . . No . . . I can't."

But her protests were weak, and a moment later her breasts were free as he pushed away the unfastened material of her bodice. His heated gaze left her face then, to openly admire what he'd just revealed. Then, with a gentle touch, he took her breasts in his palms and let his thumbs tease the already taut peaks.

"You've very lovely," he told her, looking straight into her eyes. Then he pressed her into his arms again, and her breasts rubbed against the slightly rough material of his silky camlet coat. She wished, insanely, she could feel the touch of his chest against her instead.

Holding her close, kissing her into submission, he lowered her to the ground and laid beside her. With his lips still on hers, one arm remained about her as his other hand explored first one breast, then the other. Unwittingly, she arched under his touch, pressing herself closer to his hard length. She wanted this, she couldn't deny it. Every sane and sensible thought was banished from her mind as desire engulfed her.

The tie at the back of her skirt came free as easily as her

bodice had. The garment was loose about her, and his hand caressed her stomach, still flat as ever. His touch was dizzingly effective in destroying any thought of withdrawal. And yet, stubbornly refusing to be conquered, a small tremor of uncertainty trickled into her senses. Yes, she wanted this, reveled in his merest touch. But not forgotten were the long days he'd avoided her, and without even the vaguest explanation. Why was he here now, seducing her—even if she was enjoying it every bit as much as he? The doubts and questions would not be ignored.

That alone might not have been enough to lend power to her protest. Somehow, amidst the haze of longing, she remembered she carried another man's child. She was not well versed in the state of pregnancy; her mother had never spoken of the care that a woman should take to protect her unborn child. Might the culmination of passion—the very act which made her loins ache overwhelmingly—be dangerous for the tiny child in her belly? Mere weeks ago she wouldn't have cared. She would have welcomed any act which might free her of her father's plot. But now, loving her child as all her own, she could do nothing which might jeopardize its welfare. Fear for her unborn child was enough to dampen her growing desire, and it spread like a cooling rain throughout her heated veins.

"I—can't," she said, more firmly than before. Then she said softly, "The baby. I don't want to hurt the baby."

Christian's kiss, nestling along the curve of her breast, froze. She felt him stiffen within her arms, felt him withdraw in spirit before withdrawing physically. She was, therefore, unsurprised, when he faced her with a mask of cold indifference.

"Ah, yes, the little heir to the Thornton fortune," he said with a blatant sneer.

Anne sat up just as he did. She didn't bother to refasten her clothing. She pulled it closed but kept her gaze on him.

"It's the baby, isn't it?" she asked. "That's why you've been avoiding me?"

He stood, retrieving her discarded shoes and stockings and tossed them in her lap.

"Fix your clothes," he commanded, ignoring her questions.

She moved to lace the back of her skirt first, knowing she couldn't properly fasten her stomacher with it open. But when she removed her hands from her bodice, it gaped open once again and her breasts spilled forward. Christian's eyes went automatically to them, but a moment later he turned his back on her, whether to give her privacy or because he couldn't stand the sight of her she could not tell.

With her skirt inexpertly but adequately tied, she stood and refastened her bodice with the same imperfection which came of speed. Then, fully covered, she walked around Christian to face him. She would have this out, whether he wanted to or not.

"I don't understand you," she said, her voice barely steady. "I told you long ago that I carried a child—"

"Selwyn's child," he corrected.

"Yes," she repeated firmly, because she knew she must. "The heir."

He said nothing.

Anne continued. "What I don't understand is why you've been so kind to me, so friendly, as if you truly wanted us to be a family, of sorts. And then you withdrew without a reason. And today you act as if—as if—"

"I wanted to be your lover? Well, surprise, surprise, my lady. I do," he said with an unholy glint to his eyes. Then he added, glaring straight into her eyes, "And you want it, too."

Her hands clenched each other in a firm grip, squirming under his words because they were so true. She averted her gaze from his as she spoke. "I can't deny that, after what's taken place just now." Then she looked at him. "But it's wrong, don't you see? If we want each other so much, we should—we should be married first."

That statement penetrated his artful mask. "Married?" he repeated, aghast.

She let her hands fall to her sides, and stood tall against his surprise which was so obviously insulting. Her words came through stiff jaws. "Is that so outrageous?"

He sneered at her. "Your husband is dead less than three months, and you're already proposing marriage to another man."

"I didn't propose!" she insisted. "I merely stated that if we want to bed each other so badly, we should be married. That is, after all, what's known as the act of marriage."

"My, my," he said. "I didn't know you were such a prude."

"That's not prudish! It's proper."

"Proper! For a man to marry his stepmother?"

She glared at him for that. "I would hardly call myself your stepmother."

"By law that's what you are," he reminded her.

She turned away from him and headed for her horse. "This is a ridiculous conversation. You know as well as I do that if we truly wished to wed, we could procure a special license because we are not bound by blood. But do not," she stated firmly, eyeing him once she'd neared her horse, "confuse this for a proposal on my part. I may want you in the most carnal way, I admit, but the only way you'll get me is to wed me."

She placed one small foot into the stirrup and swung herself up into the sidesaddle with so much grace she was proud of herself. Then she glared down at him.

"I believe you were right to avoid me if you knew something like this would happen between us, my lord. From now on I think it wise if we both avoid each other."

Then she kicked her horse's flanks and was off at a greater speed than she'd allowed herself in quite a few days.

20

Christian brushed the dust and grass off his breeches, dust kicked up from her hurried departure and grass from the frustrated interlude of moments before. Devil take her, he thought savagely as he grabbed the reins of his horse and swung upon its back. Then, heading in the opposite direction, he too kicked his horse's flanks.

She guarded her body like the purest virgin! He, who had taken that virginity and tasted her passion, knew better than to believe the act she'd just played. And yet, damn, but she was good at playing the innocent!

He rode hard across the hills, going no place in particular. When at last he slowed his mount to a trot, Christian was in as black a mood as ever, and fortunately for Anne he had no idea where she was or he would have gladly sought her out and wrung her neck. First he would've taken her, and then he would've wrung her neck.

He'd known the moment he'd seen her near the water's edge that he was going to approach her. He'd wasted far too much time trying to build a trusting relationship. It had gotten him nowhere; he had no reason to believe she was any closer to telling him the truth. So when he'd seen her today, he'd had but one thing on his mind: to build the kind of relationship he'd wanted since first setting eyes on her.

And it had worked, for a time, anyway. Taking her today certainly wouldn't have been rape. If mention of the baby—his baby!—hadn't made him so irate, he would have hushed her naive protest and made love to her in the most gentle manner to assure that no harm would come to their child.

Of all the impudence to mention marriage! She who'd been married and never known the marriage bed. She who had paid a man to take her virginity! She'd sounded like the most proper little maiden, protecting her virtue as if it were her last possession. And he knew better than anyone else exactly why she'd surrendered her virginity. She'd given it up to him for the vilest of reasons; to steal an inheritance—his inheritance.

He glanced at his surroundings, realizing he was on the north end of Highcrest. Pulling his horse around, he headed back toward the manor house. No, he would not wring her neck, much as he would've liked to a moment ago. And he wouldn't rape her, either, despite the ache that still permeated his body at not having her. She wanted him to avoid her. Well, that would be easy. It was exactly what he intended doing. Otherwise, he might very well carry through on at least one of the vile acts which tempted him just now.

As days passed and Anne saw less and less of Christian, she grew more and more morose. The afternoon by the pond lived in her memory, haunting her daily and nightly. Why had the mention of marriage been so ludicrous to him? It was obvious he wanted her. Could he never learn to love her? Was that why he'd almost laughed at the prospect of marrying her?

It cut her, the knowledge that he'd never even considered marriage to her and obviously never would. She had thought, during those initial days they'd spent together—and because of her birthday celebration—that he at least liked her. The excuse of their relation by marriage was certainly no reason for him to entirely discard the notion of marrying her. He obviously found her attractive. Why did he only want to be her lover, and nothing more?

Such questions did little for her self-esteem. Even while she missed him, she was glad she didn't have to see him, to see his eyes and remember that he thought her good only as a mistress but never as a wife. She was like every other woman

of his past, those he'd referred to once before. He liked
women, he might even like her, but he knew marriage was
not for him simply because he liked women as much as he
did. It was a hard kick to her pride to realize she meant
nothing more to him than any paramour from his past.

And yet, something about the fact that he liked women
so much did not make sense to her. Since he'd arrived in
England, he'd been the perfect gentleman, with her—until
the episode at the pond—and with every other woman as far
as Anne knew. Unless he and his partners were amazingly
discreet, Christian had been celibate since becoming the earl
of Highcrest.

Perhaps that was it, she pondered. Perhaps, since
becoming entitled, he had decided to act more gallantly
toward women. But that only increased her unhappiness.
Certainly he *should* be thinking of marriage—but marriage
to her was the last thing in the world he wanted.

It was for that reason she was so glad she'd resisted
giving in to him. She didn't want to be just another lover.
But that wasn't the only reason she was glad they hadn't
made love that day. As the days passed and she became more
aware of the child growing inside her, she knew she would
never do anything to jeopardize its safe haven within her
body. She remembered too well how fervid passion could
get. Surely it wasn't safe to allow her body to be joined with
another while she carried life inside her. And so, as her
breasts began to swell and her belly gradually lost its flatness,
she told herself the passion she so desired with Christian
would have led only to regret.

She still wore her mourning clothes, although soon Pel
would be tying the waistlines a bit higher to accommodate
the slight thickening of Anne's stomach. Knowing Anne
already loved her coming child despite the circumstances of
its conception, Pel did all she could to make sure no doubts
or uncertainties of the future marred that maternal feeling.
She herself was hoping to bear a child soon, and so it was
easy for her to be excited over Anne's baby.

Nearly a month went by, a month of trying unsuccessfully to forget the waterside interlude with Christian. A

month in which Anne had seen almost nothing of Christian that, sadly enough, did little to expel him from her mind. He was not with her physically, his presence was strong in her mind.

Anne was in the parlor with Pel, busy working on clothes for the baby, when Waites brought a message. Anne set aside her needlework to accept the folded note, but before she'd even opened it she knew who had sent it. It was not the first such message.

"Lord Franklin is persistent if anything," Anne said as she refolded the note which asked, once more, for her to see him at teatime.

"I thought he would've given up long before this," Pel said.

Anne frowned. "So did I. Obviously, refusing to see him hasn't been enough to get my message across. Maybe I should talk to him, and tell him outright there is little reason for him to remain in Sussex."

"He should have gathered that for himself by now," Pel said.

"I hate to think of him staying in Wynchly all this time," Anne said with a sympathetic frown. "He's an earl, you know."

Pel laughed. "Are you feeling sorry for a member of nobility?"

She shrugged. "I suppose I shouldn't. It's entirely up to him where he sleeps at night." She paused, looking toward the window. She knew the inn at Wynchly was hardly fit for a man of Lord Franklin's rank. "And yet . . ."

Pel's attention returned to her needlework as she spoke. "See him if you like, then. If it'll ease your conscience. I see no harm in it."

That seemed to settle Anne's mind. She called Waites back and told him to accept Lord Franklin's wish to arrive at teatime that afternoon. Since it was nearly that time already, Anne went upstairs to freshen herself, leaving instructions for Mistress Lindall to prepare tea for two.

Newell Franklin arrived nearly fifteen minutes late. Anne sat in the parlor waiting for him, unable to stop wondering if some harm had befallen him. He'd been so persistent, she could scarcely believe he would be late except for some sort of mishap.

When he arrived he looked decidedly flustered. His cravat was askew, having been improperly tied. And the wig he wore once again showed signs of his natural hair peeking out at the temples. He had under his arm a flat package wrapped in soft cloth, and in his free hand he held a three-cornered hat, which Waites did not bother to take from him upon Newell's entry. He looked, Anne admitted, quite handsome, even if it did appear as though he'd dressed himself after a lifetime of being dressed by servants. Waites had brought Newell to the parlor, then discreetly disappeared.

"Forgive me for being late," Newell said almost breathlessly. Then he grinned, and Anne could only call his expression boyishly sheepish. "The truth is I was not expecting you to let me come. I've grown accustomed to your refusals, polite though they are."

"That's something I wanted to discuss with you, Lord Franklin," she said. She gave him an apologetic smile she hoped portrayed both kindness and a warning that he would not like what she had to say. "But first, let's have tea."

They sat opposite each other, Anne on the settee and Lord Franklin on a winged chair. He placed the package beside him and his hat on the floor.

"You must excuse my servants if they are unaccustomed to receiving visitors," Anne said, seeing Lord Franklin place his hat at his feet. "They are adept at their jobs, though it is so rare we receive people here that they often forget what is expected of them with certain duties."

"Quite all right," Newell said, at the same time accepting the steaming cup of tea Anne offered.

"I agreed to see you, Lord Franklin—"

"I would be happy if you would call me Newell, my lady," he said eagerly.

Her smile grew somewhat smaller. "I think it better if we keep to formalities, considering what I wanted to tell you."

He replaced his tea on the table between them and held

up a protesting hand. "I know what you are going to say, my lady. You think it best for me to return to London, do you not?"

Anne looked at him, surprised not that he'd guessed, but that he admitted such a perception. "That is exactly what I wanted to say."

But Newell shook his head. "I cannot."

"Cannot?"

"I think my father was relieved more than anything else when the letter from Selwyn arrived. Sussex! Far enough away, considering the conditions of the roads between here and London, to have me well outside society's scrutiny."

Anne grinned, for Lord Franklin was so obviously at ease. He spoke as if they'd been friends for years, in spite of the fact his confession was something she should, as a lady, disdain. "You speak as though your father has reason to be all well rid of you. I thought Selwyn chose only men above reproach for me to consider?"

"Oh, that I am—or was, when Selwyn wrote. But just before I left . . . well, there was a slight problem with a wager I made. A ridiculous affair actually, and totally unfair to me. My father thought it best for me to keep to myself for a while. Where better than Sussex?"

"Where, indeed?"

"I hope you don't mind my candor?" he asked.

"Of course not; I welcome any honesty."

"I'm glad. Then you won't mind if I say, in all honesty, that you are the loveliest woman I have ever seen? The loveliest woman I have ever painted?"

She felt uncomfortable under his praise, but curious nonetheless. "Painted?"

Immediately he leaned aside to retrieve the cloth-wrapped package and handed it to Anne.

"I brought this for you, my lady. It's one of the ways I spend my days, waiting for you to accept my company for tea."

Anne untied the loose knot and slipped the cloth from a lap size canvas. Anne turned it over to see the surface, and gasped at what she saw.

It was the likeness of herself—only far more beautiful, she thought. Her hair was free of any chignon, and flowing as if a slight breeze was in the air. She was smiling contentedly, with a look in her eyes Anne could not quite describe—more peaceful than happy, almost serene, she would say. An emotion she hadn't felt since . . . she couldn't remember ever feeling serene—not the way this portrait depicted it. It was very appealing, and for a moment she wished she truly was the woman of the portrait. But she knew she was not, even if Newell Franklin thought so. She looked at Newell, curious as to why—and how—he had captured such an emotion upon her face.

He seemed suddenly shy of his work. "I painted it from memory, my lady, and you must admit I didn't have a great deal of time with you in which to make that memory."

Anne nodded. "It's lovely, Lord Newell. Lovelier than life."

"Oh, no!" He stood to emphasize his protest. "I was just thinking how pale the portrait looks in comparison to the reality of your beauty."

Anne gazed at the painting, flattered but frankly doubtful that she resembled the exquisite portrait.

"You are very talented," she said. Then when Newell took his seat once again she added, "Perhaps one day you will be famous for your paintings."

He smiled humbly beneath her praise.

Just then the door of the manor house slammed shut and a moment later a dark shadow whisked by only to stop short and end up at the parlor entrance. Christian stood there in riding clothes which were sullied by an afternoon's worth of dirt. He still held his silver-handled riding crop, and as he crossed his arms in front of him, he let it dangle along one hip.

"How very quaint and cozy," he observed, watching the two sharing tea.

Anne swallowed hard. She hadn't seen Christian in days and wished she didn't have to see him now. The merest glance he sent her way made her extremely uncomfortable.

There was but one thing to do; she had to avoid a scene.

"If you would like to have tea, my lord," she said, "we will still be here after you change your attire."

"Oh, will you, indeed?" he said, stepping inside the room. He laid his crop on a sidetable and then neared them, choosing to take a seat next to Anne on the small settee. Then he looked at the silver tray holding the china service and said with perhaps a bit too much disappointment, "There're only two cups. Obviously one of us wasn't expected," he said while looking at Newell.

Newell seemed to blanche before Christian's stare, and Anne couldn't help feeling sorry for him. "I sent word to Lord Newell that his company would be welcome this afternoon."

Christian raised one brow and eventually his gaze turned to Anne. "Then I take it I am the uninvited one? Hmm," he said, looking between the two of them before settling his gaze once again upon Anne. "This should be embarrassing, I suppose, although I have become quite accustomed to having tea with you, my dear."

Anne's eyes widened ever so slightly, but she bit back the surprise caused by his words. He was acting so strangely! They hadn't shared tea since . . . since those days so long ago when he'd acted friendly toward her. "As I said, my lord, should you wish to change your attire—"

Christian glanced down at himself unself-consciously. "I'm quite comfortable, thank you. Will you ring for Mistress Lindall? I'm sure she'll be happy to bring another cup."

Anne did so with reluctance, using the small silver bell which sat on the edge of the table. The bell was easily heard. Anne did not look at the servant or, indeed, anyone else as she gave the order for another cup. She didn't want Christian to stay. He was acting decidedly odd.

"And would you bring some of those devilishly enticing cucumber rounds of yours?" Christian asked, his tone so merry Anne was tempted to look at him. He was enjoying himself so much. "Perhaps Franklin would like to try one, as well."

"Yes, my lord," Mistress Lindall said. "I shall bring a tray."

The servant left, and Anne felt Christian's gaze on her. When she looked at him at last, however, she saw that he was staring not at her but rather at the portrait she held against her chest.

"May I see what you have there?" he asked. Then, without waiting for approval, he gently pried the canvas away from her. The touch of his fingers against her breasts where she'd held the portrait was as shocking as a sudden fire on the dry brush. She was grateful she was already sitting, for surely her limbs would not have supported her at the moment.

Anne could not resist the temptation to look at him as he had his first sight of the portrait. But she remained unsatisfied. His expression told her nothing, although he did gaze at the canvas for several long moments.

"This is quite good," he said, and Anne didn't doubt his sincerity. For Newell's sake, she was relieved.

"Thank you," Newell said. He sounded stiff; it was obvious he was no longer enjoying the tea party. "It is a gift for her ladyship."

"Kind of you, Franklin," Christian said. "Highcrest will be all the lovelier for it, for when the countess is out, we will still have her portrait to behold."

"It is up to Countess Anne where she chooses to display it, of course," Newell said. "She may want to keep it some-place more private than a hall in the manor."

"Oh, but this should be displayed somewhere for all to see and admire," Christian countered. Then he stood and placed it on the mantelpiece. "Perhaps here for the time being, until we find a permanent place for it."

"I think Countess Anne should really decide—"

But Christian ignored him entirely. "Have you any others, Franklin?" Christian asked with interest. "Not of Anne, I wouldn't expect, but anything else which might be interesting? You're good enough to be commissioned, do you know?"

Anne spoke up. "I really don't think someone in Lord Newell's position would consider painting for money, my lord."

Christian frowned, nodding. "I suppose you're right. You do remember the rules of society better than I do, my dear. But tell me, Franklin, do you have any other paintings?"

"A few," he said coolly. "I've been enjoying the Sussex countryside while I've been here."

Christian sat beside Anne once again, this time so close his thigh pressed upon her skirt. She was tempted to move away, but knew she would only call attention to his close proximity. His nearness, however, shattered her concentration.

"Is that why you've decided to stay so long in Sussex?" Christian asked. "To paint the countryside?"

Newell did not reply. He looked from Christian to Anne, somewhat at a loss for words.

Mistress Lindall entered, carrying a tray laden with several small cucumber slices topped with herbs and cheese. There was also a china cup and saucer for Christian. Anne poured, conscious all the while that Christian's thigh was nearly touching hers. But she did not spill a drop, and was quite proud of herself for the accomplishment, considering her hands trembled and her insides felt afire.

Christian took a napkin and a cucumber, but instead of tasting the snack for himself, he offered it to Anne. He was smiling in the most ridiculously friendly fashion and, Anne decided, she did not like it at all.

"She likes these almost as much as I do," Christian explained to Newell. "Take it," he said gently. "You know you must think of the baby and eat enough for both of you."

She took it, not because she wanted it, but because she wanted to stop him from leaning so close as he offered it to her. This was some sort of jest, she decided. He was acting most outrageously—and she didn't like it one bit!

Then he took a cucumber round of his own and devoured it in one bite, afterward washing it down with a long sip of tea. He had a fob chain hanging from his waistcoat, from which he took out his pocket watch. Noting the time, he gazed up at Anne.

"Shouldn't you be upstairs?" he asked. Then he looked at Newell. "She usually naps just after tea, and it's getting late. I'm sure you understand, considering her condition."

"Of course," Newell said, though his face was slow to show enlightenment. He was eyeing Christian most suspiciously. At last, he stood. "I should be on my way, then."

"Let me walk outside with you," Anne volunteered.

"I would welcome your company," Newell said happily, the first sign of a smile on his face since Christian had entered the room.

Christian did not bother to stand as they made their exit, but he did call after Anne in an affectionate voice, "Don't be long, my dear."

Anne glared at him over her shoulder and left with Lord Newell at her side. She escorted Newell outside and waited while a footman fetched his carriage, which had been brought around the side of the house.

"He acts very . . . friendly toward you," Newell said with a brief nod back toward the manor house.

"Selwyn's last words to him were to see to my welfare," Anne said. She hoped the explanation was satisfactory to abate whatever conclusions Newell had drawn from Christian's far too familiar treatment of her. "I'm afraid Lord Christian takes those last wishes a bit too far at times."

"Be careful of him, Countess," Newell whispered.

Anne's gaze shot to his. "Why do you say such a thing? You sound as if you're worried over my welfare."

Newell hesitated, eyeing the door of the manor as if he expected Christian to emerge at any moment. "There's no danger, I'm sure." His tone was hardly convincing. "It's just that he seems overly possessive of you. And the look in his eyes when his gaze is on you . . . I didn't like it."

"Why?"

"I've seen it before," he said, "but mainly in men whose vice greatly outweighs their virtue."

"He's always been a gentleman," she said, though she

didn't look at Newell as she spoke. It was true, for the most part.

Newell was bold enough to take Anne's hand in his. "Just beware of him, my lady." Then his carriage pulled up before them. As the door was opened by a footman, Newell spoke again, this time with a lighter tone and a smile. "I hope you don't let him bully you into hanging the portrait where *he* wants it. It belongs to you, after all. You should say where it will hang."

She nodded, smiling at him. "Thank you for the portrait, Lord Franklin."

"Newell," he corrected, then stepped into the carriage. He waved at her as the horses pulled the rig into motion.

Anne returned to the manor house, but the smile she'd aimed at Newell disappeared when she headed back to the parlor. Christian was still there, just finishing another cucumber round.

"Was there a reason for that display?" she asked through clenched jaws.

He looked up at her innocently. "What display?" he asked, finishing his tea and briefly wiping his napkin over his mouth.

"The display that implied we're practically lovers?"

He grinned. "Haven't we already declared that's exactly what we'd like to be? Lovers?"

"Positively not!"

Christian shrugged. "You're a bit sensitive, I think. I acted only in congenial friendship. I'm sure his lordship doesn't think anything odd."

"He does, indeed. He just now warned me to beware of you."

Christian rose and he took steady steps toward her. "I've underestimated the milksop. At least he's observant."

"You have no reason to dislike him," Anne said, though control of her thoughts threatened to disappear as she watched him coming near—too near. "Lord Newell is a kind gentleman. You could learn from him."

"Could I, indeed?" He stood very close to her, so close she was tempted to take a step backward. But she stood firm. "Actually," Christian said softly, "I don't dislike him. He's a talented artist."

"Then you shouldn't have sent him on his way."

"I merely pointed out that you usually nap at this time of the day. And that's true."

"I think you should leave it up to me whether or not I will take a nap. And where I shall be hanging my portrait."

He glanced back at the portrait sitting on the mantel-piece. "I was merely praising him for his talent, saying that it should be displayed where others can admire it. Where's the harm in that?"

Then his gaze returned to her, looking at her in that intense way she found so disconcerting.

She looked away from him. "It was the way you said it, the way you acted toward me."

"How was that?" He was still far too close for Anne to think clearly.

"Possessively. You acted possessively." She wished she didn't feel so quivery inside. "Lord Newell noticed. He—he didn't like it."

Christian raised one brow. "Oh? What if I said I didn't like him visiting here?"

"Why should that bother you?"

"Selwyn did ask me to give you counsel," he said. "And you are an expectant mother."

Anne squared her shoulders. "Lord Newell is well aware that I carry a child and that there could be no possibility of forming any sort of relationship until well after the child's birth."

"You do remember, don't you, that Selwyn bade you to come to me when choosing a husband?"

"I doubt he meant to have a man of his own choice double-checked by you."

"Perhaps I am to be the insurance that his choices are all that he hoped. Perhaps that is exactly what he wished—to have the men he chose double-checked. If he was fully certain about them, why would he have asked you to come to me at all?''

"When the time comes for me to choose a husband—*if* that time comes," she clarified, "I will do so on my own, without any counsel from you. No matter what Selwyn said.''

He shook his head in reproach, but he was smiling. "You've lost respect for his memory very quickly, my lady. Even while you carry his child."

Why did every reference to her child make her wince? Was it only a guilty conscience that made her want to squirm under his perusal?

"I have a great deal of respect for Selwyn's memory," she told Christian. "However, I don't think it's necessary for me to have your approval of whomever I choose to marry. Even Selwyn himself knew that, and said as much on his deathbed."

"So he did," Christian admitted. Then he grinned. "But in spite of your objections, I intend to watch over you as Selwyn asked."

She scowled at him. "Just as you did that day at the pond?"

Christian's smile faded. For a moment she thought he would issue an angry retort, but instead, very slowly, he raised a fingertip to her chin. "I only wanted to please you."

Then he kissed her, and at the first moment contact was made, Anne had to steel against pressing herself into his arms. Instead she stood, rigidly erect, willing herself to resist the wondrous magic of his lips on hers.

He made it nearly impossible, for his mouth was gently insistent. A moment later, he let his tongue slide along her lower lip before seeking entrance into her mouth. Her teeth were clamped tight, and so he nibbled at her lip and teased her with his persistent tongue. His hands rested on her shoulders, but he did not pull her toward him; it was as if he expected her to capitulate any moment, as if certain she would fall prey to his kiss and let herself fall deeply into his arms.

And how she wanted to! But with more strength than she thought she possessed, she remained standing, stiff. Perhaps because she knew she couldn't go through with it, for the sake of the baby growing within. It lent her a surprising amount of willpower, just enough to be the victor in this battle of her senses which Christian had set off.

At last, when Christian realized she would not surrender as easily as she had before, he lifted his mouth from hers. But he hardly looked defeated.

"You protect that little heir of yours quite fiercely, Anne," he whispered. "I know as well as you, though, if you realized our lovemaking would bring it no harm, we would be upstairs in no time at all."

"No," she said, holding her chin high. But she was quaking inside.

Christian's gaze held hers, and she knew he could see through her meager guard. He was right and knew it just as surely as she did.

21

Anne didn't bother to see her father out. Today's visit had been the second since the beginning of her pregnancy and, thankful though she was that his visits were infrequent, she nonetheless hated each and every one of them. His questions of her welfare and the child she carried only angered her. She knew only too well that he cared only because of what she and her child would bring him. And so when her father left her in the parlor, she did not bother to follow him from the room.

Once she heard the front door close behind him, however, Anne stood from the seat she had so stiffly occupied while Jarvis had been there. She would visit her mother's room. Seeing her father always left her with the desire to comfort Elsbeth.

Elsbeth had just awakened from a nap when Anne entered the room. Anne smiled at her mother, and Elsbeth offered a subdued grin in return. Since returning from her brief visit to Jarvis's house, Elsbeth had slowly settled back into the more comfortable life at Highcrest. She was eating more, and occasionally she even smiled, as she did now. But much to Anne's sorrow, she still was not quite the same as before going back, even though it had been nearly four months.

"We're going for a walk, Mother," Anne said. "Out to the garden. Would you like that?"

As always, she received no response, but Elsbeth did not protest when Anne placed a shawl around her mother's

253

shoulders. It had taken Anne nearly two weeks to get her
mother out of her Highcrest apartments; Anne knew Elsbeth
feared she would be returned to Jarvis if she left her comfortable rooms. But through patience and perserverence,
Anne had gotten her mother to enjoy walks in the garden
once again.

Anne chatted when they reached the garden. She spoke
of Pel and other villagers Elsbeth would know, carefully
avoiding any mention of Jarvis or even Christian—although
she skirted the latter subject for her own protection rather
than her mother's. It was an especially lovely day, and Anne
thought her mother was truly thankful for being outdoors.

By the time they came inside, it was near teatime. As
they stepped inside the large hallway, Mistress Lindall was
waiting near the parlor archway with a steaming pot and
several of Anne's favorite scones.

"I thought you would be back by now," Mistress
Lindall said, taking the tray into the parlor.

"Mistress Lindall," Anne called after the servant, "I
think we should have the tea in my mother's—" But she
stopped short when she saw Elsbeth looking very intently at
something in the parlor. Before giving further instructions to
the servant, Anne's eyes followed Elsbeth's gaze.

She stared at the small portrait of Anne, which was still
on the mantelpiece where Christian had left it so many days
ago. Anne watched, barely breathing, as Elsbeth took her
hand from Anne's arm and walked toward the fireplace.
When Mistress Lindall noticed, she, too, watched the woman
who never did anything of her own initiative.

Elsbeth was short, far shorter than the tall mantelpiece.
She did not touch it, but merely gazed up at it with just a hint
of a smile on her face. Anne stepped beside her mother and
reached the small painting.

"Would you like to have this, Mother?"

Elsbeth accepted it, and with one free hand she stroked
her daughter's cheek. Though she remained silent, the slight
contact was enough to send quick tears to Anne's eyes. She
hugged Elsbeth to her, as close as she could, as Elsbeth held
the portrait in between them.

"We'll have tea right here, after all, Mistress Lindall," Anne announced, feeling so buoyant over her mother's behavior that she thought it would be all right.

Mistress Lindall nodded approvingly and then left the two alone.

Anne led her mother to the settee, taking the portrait and leaning it against one of the chairs nearest Elsbeth. Then Anne took a seat across from Elsbeth and poured the hot tea, all the while telling her mother where the portrait had come from.

She was tempted to tell her mother that she may one day meet the artist if she wished, but she knew how uncomfortable men made Elsbeth, and so she held back such an invitation. Besides, she hardly knew Lord Newell. She would have to know him far better before she decided to allow him knowledge of her mother. She didn't want him returning to London with stories of Anne's mad mother. Anne still clung to the hope of making the city a home for herself and Elsbeth one day, and she hardly wanted any stories to precede them.

Just then Mistress Lindall returned to the parlor and approached Anne.

"Waites would've come to announce a visitor, my lady," she said with a glance to Elsbeth, "but he knows his presence makes the madam ill at ease. Barrister Mortimer is looking for his lordship, but wondered if he might have a word with you first."

Anne's brows drew together in a frown. She didn't want to leave her mother alone, but certainly she couldn't have Mortimer join them. Her mother would hardly welcome his presence. "Tell him to wait in the solicitor's salon." Then, as Mistress Lindall was about to leave, Anne called after her, "Where is his lordship?"

"I do not know, my lady. Barrister Mortimer was not expected, therefore he is prepared to wait."

"Tell him I shall be there directly."

Anne eyed her mother; she was content, sipping her tea and occasionally glancing at the portrait beside her. Anne didn't like to leave her mother unattended. Yet she knew she would be right across the hall, and for only a moment or two, as long as the business with Mortimer would take.

Anne stood. "Mother, I will be across the hall for a few minutes, and then I'll come right back. Will you wait here for me, and finish your tea?"

There was no response, of course, and with one long look to make sure Elsbeth did not seem in any way adversely affected by the announcement, Anne left the room.

Mortimer stood when Anne entered the solicitor's salon, having made himself at home in a large winged chair before the desk.

"How nice to see you, my dear," he greeted her as she took the seat opposite the one he'd just vacated.

"You, too, Mortimer," Anne said with a smile. "I'm surprised you have any business with me, however. Usually you come only to see Christian—his lordship."

Mortimer noted her familarity with Christian's given name, but he said nothing. He took his seat once again.

"I would much rather come to see you, my lady," he teased. "His lordship may send the female population of Wynchly atwitter, but personally he does nothing for my heartbeat."

Anne's smile wavered, somewhat in spite of herself. The knowledge that perhaps the entire female population of Wynchly was interested in Christian made her undeniably uncomfortable.

"What can I do for you, Mortimer?" she said, hardly wanting to discuss Christian.

"I've a bit of news—rather unpleasant news, actually. A warning, of sorts, or perhaps a caution."

"Against whom?"

"Newell Franklin."

Anne's brows raised in surprise. "What has he done?"

"Well, nothing a sentence in debtor's prison might not cure."

"Debtor's prison!"

"It seems the untarnished Franklin name has come across its first smudge. Newell is here escaping the consequences of being unable to pay a wager he made to one of his cronies. That is my caution to you, my dear. Beware of him; he may have set his sights upon the Thornton wealth.''

Anne did not speak immediately, weighing Mortimer's news. She liked Newell, despite the warning. Besides, hadn't Newell himself referred to some sort of bad wager as being another reason to stay in Wynchly?

"He mentioned some sort of trouble when he came to tea the other day,'' Anne said.

"Yes, I was told he'd come to visit you. That's why I thought to tell you about the financial aspect. The Franklin wealth has been dwindling through the years; bad investments, extravagance, and unwise spending have all contributed to it. It seems Newell hasn't quite realized his family will be nearly impoverished if he continues to make outrageous bets.'' Mortimer sighed. "The sad part of it is that my sources tell me their estate could be saved with a bit of planning, if they had the sense to hire someone to manage their money for them. But the Franklins have never been ones to go on a budget.''

"Newell told me he thought it best he stay away from London for the time being. He was really quite honest about it.''

Mortimer leaned forward in his chair. "I'm glad to hear it, my lady. But there are many other places he could go besides Wynchly.''

Anne's gaze met his. "Do you think he intends following up on Selwyn's wishes for the sake of the Thornton money?''

Mortimer nodded, but added, "Of course, you are a lovely young woman, and he has been known for his flirtations with various women in London. It's entirely possible he is smitten with you, especially considering he now knows of the child and is still here hoping to court you.''

"Even though the child will be the heir,'' Anne said slowly.

Mortimer's face grew more serious. "But it's true that if the courts decide in favor of your legal heir, as we expect, the legal guardian of this child will have control over the vast Thornton money until the child is of age to control it himself.''

Anne knew that only too well! Was Newell, too, after the Thornton money?

She stood. ''Thank you for the warning, Mortimer,'' she said, ''but I really don't think it was necessary, after all. I like Newell, it's true. But for now only my baby is important to me. I certainly have no desire to consider marriage—to anyone.''

Mortimer stood as well, and took her hand in his. ''Of course, my dear. I understand completely. You could hardly muster thoughts for one man while carrying another man's child.''

Anne lowered her eyelids, feeling immediately ashamed since she had done exactly that every single day. Damn Christian Thornton! And the stranger! And especially, most especially, her father for this whole situation.

''I must rejoin my mother for now, Mortimer. I hope you won't mind waiting here for his lordship?''

''Of course not,'' Mortimer said. ''My main reason was to see you, though, so if he doesn't return soon I will go back to my offices.''

Anne left the solicitor's salon and headed back to the parlor. She wasn't troubled by the news Mortimer had brought—not exactly, since she didn't really care if Newell Franklin was a fortune hunter or not. She liked him, but could hardly even imagine entertaining romantic notions of him.

No, what bothered her most about Mortimer's news was that it simply added Newell to the list of those she knew who wanted money above all else. A list on which Christian Thornton did not appear. Her father and all his cronies wanted nothing more than wealth; they thrived on greed. She herself cared nothing for money but she was being manipulated because of it. Even Mortimer, the old dear, lived his life taking care of money, guarding it so carefully. But Christian was different. When Selwyn had named him heir Christian had even considered returning to France and not collecting the huge Thornton holdings. Imagine being able to turn one's back on that! He hadn't done it, that was true, but Anne thoroughly believed he would have, had Selwyn not been so devastated over that very possibility. And more recently, when learning about Anne's child and the fact that he would be losing the Thornton money after all, he'd made no fuss, no plans for counter suits to have the courts uphold Selwyn's last will naming Christian himself heir. He just accepted the loss of a considerable fortune as if it hardly mattered. She couldn't help admiring him for that, considering everyone else became so greedy over the slightest possibility of possessing the Thornton inheritance.

Anne's thoughts were cut short as she stepped closer to the parlor archway. She stood gaping at what she saw.

Her mother, teacup still in hand and looking quite at ease, sat opposite the very subject of her thoughts. Christian drank from his own cup and was speaking in a very low voice. She stepped into the room, unable to wipe the surprise from her face.

When Christian caught sight of her he stood, although his movement was slow as if not to startle Elsbeth who was watching him rather than Anne.

"Good afternoon, Anne," Christian said. His voice was calm, and he was smiling. "Your mother and I were just having tea."

"So I see," she said, staring at her mother. Elsbeth did not look at either of them. Instead, she glanced from her teacup to the portrait resting at her side. When Anne came closer and took a seat on the settee beside her mother, Elsbeth glanced once at Anne, then at Christian, then, still calmly, back at the portrait. Christian's presence did not bother her in the least!

"I saw your mother in here alone and came to join her," Christian said as he took his seat once again. They both watched Elsbeth.

"And she . . . welcomed your company?" Anne asked somewhat incredulously.

"Well, I wouldn't say welcomed," Christian said. "She wouldn't look at me at first." Then he directed his words to Elsbeth. "Would you, my lady? But then when I complimented the portrait you're admiring, you almost smiled.

That," he added now looking at Anne, "is when I took it upon myself to join your mother for tea. She hasn't seemed to mind."

"No, I would say she hasn't. I'm amazed."

Christian grinned. "Not everyone is adverse to my company, Countess."

Anne glared at him. She wanted no part of his humorous charm. He who wanted to bed her, then discard her! "Mortimer is awaiting your presence in the solicitor's salon," she said coldly. "I believe you've kept him waiting long enough."

Christian's grin turned to a full smile at her obvious coolness. "Perhaps you and your mother would care to have supper in the dining room?"

"No," she said firmly.

He stood then bowed. "Very well, Countess. Good afternoon, my lady," he said to Elsbeth. Then he left, the refusal for supper obviously not bothering him in the least.

22

It was still dark, though the eastern horizon held an ever widening pale glow promising sunrise. Anne could just barely see it from her window.

This was the third morning in a row she'd awakened before dawn; not that she was particularly fond of sunrises, she just didn't seem capable of sleeping past five in the morning these days! Her hand stroked her tummy tenderly, as if the tiny baby inside could feel the caress. The early morning wakefulness didn't bother her, however. She thought she might sleep through the night if she could resist her afternoon naps, but those naps served more than one purpose.

She sighed deeply. The naps in the afternoon at least gave her someplace to go in which he would not be able to follow. Not that he ever followed her, but he did seem to appear wherever she went.

She'd lit several candles upon waking just a short while before. In the last three mornings she'd amused herself with reading or sewing. But today she found herself inexorably thirsty. She knew the entire household would still be asleep and so, not wanting to disturb anyone, she slid her feet into soft slippers and threw a shawl over her loose lawn gown, then made her way downstairs.

She wasn't sure what alerted her to someone else's presence once she'd reached the bottom of the stairs. Perhaps she'd heard a noise or some other sense had warned her. Knowing her way to the kitchen, she had not bothered to take a candle and so the area was dark. She could make out certain shadows from the single wall sconce at the top of the stairs, but for the most part the downstairs hallway was black.

Then a noise came from the solicitor's salon. She wasn't afraid, only curious as to who might be up and about at such an early hour. She approached the salon and pushed at the door; it swung open easily on the oiled hinges.

There was a fire in the small fireplace, or the remnants of one. One thoroughly blackened log remained intact, still burning amidst a bed of glowing embers. It shed enough light upon the small room to give her a clear view inside.

Then she saw him. Christian was sound asleep in one of the large winged chairs before the desk. His head rested comfortably to one side, slightly tilted. There was an open bottle of wine on the floor beside him and a glass overturned at his feet. When she neared him, she stepped on the wet stain the wine had left, and it seeped through the thin kidskin of her slipper. Perhaps that had been the noise she'd heard, the glass of wine being tipped over by his foot.

"Christian," she said gently, but he did not stir.

Almost timidly, she touched his shoulder but still he remained deep in sleep. She hesitated to touch him again, not sure she wanted to wake him. She remembered waking her father once from a drunken sleep, and he'd thrashed out before he knew who she was, hitting her savagely across the face. Of course, she wasn't sure that this was a drunken slumber, but the evidence did seemed to indicate as much.

Besides, she told herself, what was the harm in leaving him there? He didn't look uncomfortable, even though he would be better off in his own bed. Slowly, she retreated, unable to shake the disappointment. But even as she defined the feeling, she scolded herself for it. Why should she allow his company now, in the early dawn, when she could not allow it during the day's more respectable hours? Why was the loss even greater now?

She had gotten no further than a few steps away, toward the door with the light of the fireplace behind her, when she heard his voice.

"Wait," he said quietly. "Don't go."

She stood still, facing him. In the dim light she could not see his face clearly; she saw that his eyes were open, and he gazed directly at her in that intent way of his.

Suddenly self-conscious, she stepped in front of the empty chair opposite him, knowing the firelight behind her would have illuminated her shape beneath her gown. And with her ever growing tummy, swelling breasts, and thickening hips, she didn't want him to see her.

He stood when she moved, approaching her. He didn't pause until standing directly before her, close enough to make her pulse speed and her breathing become erratic. She wondered if the nearness affected him at all, as he still hid his emotions behind that intense mask.

"Why did you move from the firelight?"

She lowered her head, but he put a finger to her chin and she had no choice but to look at him. She did not answer, though.

"Your body is lovely," he whispered. "Still lovely. I think," he added, bringing his face even closer, "that it will always be lovely, even the day before you deliver."

Then, gently at first, he kissed her. She didn't struggle. She couldn't; her body wouldn't let her. She wanted him to hold her, to press against her, to envelope her in his arms. And when his kiss deepened, she opened her mouth to him, wanting to taste him.

But, too soon, contact was broken. He pulled his mouth from hers and with a frustrated little laugh he still held her against him.

"I want you," he said, almost angrily. She didn't understand his fury. "I want you too much."

Then she felt only coldness as he took his warm body away from hers and left her standing all alone in the dim light of the salon.

Shaken as much by the abrupt departure as the desire which had ended so quickly, Anne waited a moment before returning to her room. She waited until she was sure he had time to reach his own room before venturing near the same stairway he would have used. She shook her head in confusion. What had stopped him? Surely nothing would have come of it, she assured herself. Nothing more than a kiss. But why had he stopped himself?

She would have to increase her resolve to avoid him. He wanted her, and the reminder of that only made staying away from him even more difficult. But resist him she must, since the way in which he wanted her had no future, and certainly no honor. He wanted to use her body for a few fleeting moments of passion. And that she would fight with her every breath.

Well after the sun had risen, Anne once again left her room, this time fully dressed. She would not ride that day, she decided. Instead, she would take her mother for a walk and exercise them both. Since that encounter by the riverside, she knew there was the possibility she might run into Christian on her morning jaunts. And she didn't think she could bear that today.

Anne went into the dining room and rang for Waites. She would have a full breakfast before her walk. As always, it seemed she was famished.

Mistress Lindall answered the call.

"I would be happy to bring your breakfast, my lady," Mistress Lindall greeted her cheerfully.

"That would be fine," Anne said, but added, "I'm just used to Waites greeting me first thing. He's well this morning, I hope?"

"Oh, he's just fine I would imagine, going off to France for the first time. Of course, what with the ill feelings between our country and that one, he could've had a better time to visit, but Waites promised nonetheless to bring back the latest news and fashions—"

"Waites is going to France?"

"Left already, Countess!" she said excitedly. "With his lordship, early this morning. Just after dawn, I would say. The earl woke some of us and asked for a few preparations, then invited Waites to accompany him. And off they went."

"To France?" She couldn't seem to grasp the reality of it. Christian had left? He was gone, without even a good-bye?

"That's right, my lady. Quite a surprise to us all."

"Did he say . . . is he coming back?"

Mistress Lindall laughed. "Of course. He's the earl!"

Anne shifted uncomfortably. "I mean, did he say when?"

"No, my lady. But I shouldn't think he'll be gone for too long."

"Why is that?"

"Oh, Waites didn't pack many of his lordship's belongings. That would suggest a short trip, wouldn't you say? And what with the two countries being at odds over Spain . . ."

Anne nodded, though she stopped listening soon after that as Mistress Lindall served breakfast in a most chatty manner. He was gone. She kept saying it over and over, as if to make herself believe it. The fact that he'd taken few possessions meant nothing; he could easily buy whatever he needed once he reached France and stay there indefinitely. Indefinitely! Suddenly her healthy appetite had abandoned her.

The huge pink sun balanced upon the tip of the highest hill on the receding landscape; it resembled a colorful ball, precariously resting on the nose of some odd-shaped circus seal. In between the land and the boat were the deep black waters of the channel, taking him home.

Home? Was France home anymore? The question surprised him, so much that he looked over at Waites as if afraid the vulnerability that question brooked somehow showed on his face. But Waites looked like an overgrown child embarking on his first adventure; he sported a youthful grin and the merry eyes of someone who'd finally received the present they'd always longed for. He obviously had no inclination to read Christian's mind.

Christian himself had little enthusiasm over the thoughts crowding out any eagerness he might have had to be returning to the land of his birth. It had been a sudden decision, and the moment the boat pulled out of the dock, he'd wondered if the decision had been *too* sudden.

But he knew he couldn't stay at Highcrest. He needed time away, time to gain control over his increasingly ungovernable feelings regarding Anne. He'd made a vow to stay clear of her, only to break that very resolution. He couldn't seem to help himself. This morning, however, it had all come to a boiling point in his head. He'd seen her standing there, his child growing in her belly, and he'd felt something so intense it had frightened him. Whatever the feelings were, whether hate or possessiveness or even love, guilt was the feeling that had won out in the end. He'd been part of a plot that had resulted in a child. He'd seen the reality of her pregnancy for the very first time, and it had almost overwhelmed him. For the first time since learning of this twisted plot, he realized an actual human being—his child—would be the result. He hadn't meant to let it get that far! He hadn't even meant to bed her, not at first. He'd intended to expose the plan, expose her for the deceitful witch she was, renounce any possible bastard she might conceive, and that would've been the end of it.

But no. He'd had to bed her, had to fall prey to his own weakness for her and actually ended up aiding her in this plot! He wanted to defend himself, asking himself who would have thought their coming together only a few times would result so conveniently in a child? But it did no good.

All along he'd doubted that she had conceived his child. But it was true, he'd seen that for himself this morning. And all the thoughts and plans he himself had made, those of taking the child and raising it himself, seemed so cold when faced with the reality of it. What kind of parents did this child have, one who could conceive solely for money, another who could cold-bloodedly take that child from its mother? Even if that mother was totally unsuitable?

And yet, even with all that going through his mind, he had looked upon her this morning and wanted her. This very morning, he had wanted her more than he'd ever wanted any woman. He'd seen evidence of their child, proof of her treachery, and still, he had wanted her. He would have taken her right then and there, right on the floor of that small salon, if he'd let himself have his way. He wasn't sure, even now, of what stopped him. Maybe he really did despise her as he told himself he did; or maybe the guilt he felt at his own part in the success of her plan made him hold back, so disgusted was he at himself.

That was why he'd left; he'd had no choice. Sooner or later, he thought, he would have ignored the guilt, penetrated her defenses, and bedded her. It was inevitable. But that was precisely what he could not do. He still planned to take the child as his own, despite the cold-bloodedness of his scheme. But it would be far worse, he thought to himself, to let someone so avaricious raise his child. Besides, Anne wanted the child for one purpose: to steal Christian's inheritance. With that plan failed, she would have no use for the baby. He realized she may very well hand over the infant of her own free will—or else, he decided, she could be her father's cellmate at Newgate.

The thoughts were all so bleak. But they shouldn't be, he told himself. Hadn't he realized long ago that marriage wasn't for him? Now, thanks to Anne's treachery, he would never have to marry to provide an heir. She had done so for him already, without the restrictions marriage implied. He smiled crookedly. He should be glad. Glad . . .

"I'm glad you could come to tea today, Lord Franklin," Anne said politely. She wished she could mean it, but after Christian's abrupt departure yesterday, she was still somewhat in shock. She hardly felt anything. Except perhaps loneliness.

Newell grinned. "To be honest, I was fearful my requests would be denied again. I'm afraid I was bold with some of my advice the last time I came to tea."

"Not at all," she assured him, pouring him a full cup of tea and handing it to him.

She noticed he'd been looking around somewhat anxiously since first entering the room. She couldn't help feeling amused, but didn't allow herself to reveal it. After all, it was hardly flattering to Newell that his dread of seeing Christian was a source of entertainment.

"Lord Christian has gone to France," she said conversationally, sparing Newell's pride. "He left yesterday morning—quite unexpectedly, in fact."

"Oh?" Newell's brows rose with interest, but at the same time he looked undeniably relieved. "Rather a strange time for a visit back home, I should think. What with the strain between our countries at the moment."

"Yes," she agreed. "But I don't think this visit had anything to do with political loyalties." She felt her heart move slightly in her breast. If her guess was correct, the only reason he'd left had been because of her. And the fact that he could no longer stand to share the same roof with her.

"Just homesick, then?" Newell asked.

She nodded, even though she could hardly imagine self-reliant Christian feeling such an emotion. No, it was far more likely he was having trouble accepting the fact that she would not become his mistress. And his repulsion of marriage was too great, therefore he removed himself from the temptation. No doubt he would be back once the temptation to bed her was no longer there. But she could hardly explain all this to Newell.

"I wanted to thank you again for the portrait," Anne said, eager to be on to another topic.

Newell glanced quickly up to the mantelpiece, as though having forgotten the portrait's existence. When he found it gone from where Christian had placed it, he looked pleased.

"Have you decided where you will hang it, my lady?"

"My mother showed such interest in it, I made the portrait a special gift to her. I wanted to thank you personally because the painting has been a source of joy for her, and for that I am grateful."

"I would be happy to do another. One of her, if you like."

Anne shook her head. "No, I think one is enough. And mother has never been one to be the subject of anything, even a portrait. But thank you."

There was a long pause, and Anne stirred her tea. Perhaps it had been a mistake to accept Newell's request for tea. She felt strained at having to carry on a conversation she had no real interest in. She could have simply sent him a note of thanks for the portrait instead of inviting him to the manor. But she had hoped his visit would help banish the loneliness she felt from Christian's departure. So far, the visit had utterly failed in tht regard. Right now she wished only to be alone.

Then Newell cleared his throat, shifted in his chair to sit more erect, and sat his tea back on the table between them. "I hope you will allow me to visit on a regular basis, Countess Anne. Anne? May I call you Anne?"

She nodded, though something told her she should have refused.

"I know we've met only on a few occasions, Anne," he said, "but I must tell you, I find myself extraordinarily happy when in your company."

Anne smiled. "Perhaps you're just bored with Sussex, my lord. I am merely a source of entertainment—entertainment you must miss after living in London so long."

He shook his head vigorously. "Oh, I'm sure it's not that—although I must confess there are certain aspects of London I miss. But I haven't been bored here. My painting keeps me busy and I must say I'm pleased with some of the work I've done. Your portrait, to name one. I'd like to do another, with your permission."

"I would think doing the same subject twice might prove tiresome."

"Oh, no! Not when you're the subject," he assured her. "But I would like you to sit for me. I'd like to see if I could better capture your beauty this time."

Anne laughed a little self-consciously. "I'm sure I'll prefer your imagination, Lord Newell. The portrait you've given me already is lovely—far lovelier, as I told you, than reality."

"And again, I disagree." He grew more serious. "Let me do this, Anne. Please."

Anne considered it a moment. Perhaps it would give her something else to think about, something to take her mind off . . . well, things she should not be thinking of. And Newell was a pleasant person, one she liked, despite Mortimer's warning. Besides, he'd never once given any indication he wanted more from her than she was willing to give. What was the harm in it, after all?

"Are you sure you'd like to paint someone in my condition?" she asked at last.

His eyes swept her, and for the barest moment she thought she imagined something sexual in the look. But when his eyes met hers, they held only admiration.

"You are a beautiful subject, my lady. And if I may say something delicate, your condition hardly shows. Your face will dominate the painting—although I would like to do a full portrait."

Anne frowned. "That would take time, wouldn't it?"

His glance fell to the floor and he looked unsure of himself for a moment. "I must admit, I'm a slow painter. The small one I did of you took two weeks, and I worked on it every day."

"I'm afraid I couldn't come for sittings. I'm not riding much these days and the roads are so bumpy I would fear for my child if I traveled too often back and forth to Wynchly."

"Oh, I would be more than happy to come here—to paint here. It's what I'd hoped for, in fact. My room in the inn at Wynchly would not accommodate a large portrait." As if sensing her next question, he added, "I would simply have the necessary articles delivered here, and I'd come for a sitting whenever you'll have me. Once a week, twice a week . . . every day if you like."

She paused, considering.

"It would give me great pleasure to do this, Anne," he said. "And I think you'll like the results."

"Very well," she said suddenly. She smiled. "I think this will work out very nicely."

"Wonderful!" He stood, so happy with the news. "I'll have everything brought over tomorrow, and we can begin when you like."

Anne saw him to the door, and once there he took her hand in his and pressed it to his lips.

"I will see you tomorrow," he said. Then he was gone.

23

Summer ended and autumn passed in a blaze of color. Anne had always preferred spring to autumn, spring with its new life and bright skies. But this year fall was different for her. She felt a sort of kinship with all the trees and plants that were dying in such a grand way. If it were spring, perhaps she would have felt a kinship with that, too, because of the baby growing inside her. But with fall she felt a part of herself passing; she was changed now, soon to be a mother, no longer a child herself. And part of her would die just like the trees outside her window.

As week after week passed and her body grew and grew, her emotions seemed to magnify as well. When she passed a mirror or glass and caught her own reflection, she didn't recognize herself. Her belly was so large she often wished her pride would allow someone to help her when she stood from a chair, or rose from her bed in the morning. Her face was somewhat swollen, as well as her hands and feet. She felt ugly and ungainly, and had not allowed Newell to finish his portrait. He'd begun with her full approval, and as the early days went by she was glad for his company, happy to have him there to divert her attention from all that bothered her. But as her belly grew, she knew the last thing she wanted was someone staring at her to record her image. And so she'd told Newell she couldn't allow him to visit until after the child's birth.

It wasn't only feeling alien to her own body which bothered her; what troubled her every bit as much was

Christian's long absence. He never wrote, never contacted her or anyone else in the household. He did correspond with Mortimer, she learned, but that only increased her despondency regarding him.

But, she realized, now that her body had lost whatever grace it may have possessed, she should be glad he was gone. Certainly she didn't want Christian to see her this way. She knew he had wanted her in the same carnal way she wanted him. If he was trying to escape that desire, he should see her now. Surely that would have killed whatever desire he'd had.

Occasionally her thoughts would return to the stranger, to the father of the child she carried. He'd been a gentle lover, and she was glad for that. Sometimes she still was tempted to ask his identity, but she dared not. This child was hers and hers alone, and in spite of the ugliness she felt while carrying it, she loved the child all the more because of the tender way in which it had been given to her.

How she wanted this child! She longed to hold it in her arms, to feel its smooth skin, to hear it breathe, to nurture it at her breast. However, Anne did not allow herself thoughts of the actual birthing. The nearer the time came, the more her thoughts went to Celine. Celine, who had lost so many babies; Celine who had suffered through every pregnancy; Celine who had died during the throes of labor. Anne had known some pain in her life—her father had hit her often enough to conjure pain—but even his most brutal blows had resulted in nothing more than a minor bruise. Anne had no idea what real, prolonged, pain was like, or how she would react to it. And that frightened her.

As the weeks passed she tried to keep so many things from her mind: the stranger, the birthing, and Christian.

Anne was in the parlor when Christian returned. It was cold, autumn having given way to an early winter, and she sat before the fireplace with a shawl around her shoulders. She felt very old as she sat there, her feet near the hearth and her hands folded in her lap. She felt old because she was so tired, and here it was only eight o'clock. She'd had dinner already and would go to bed shortly.

When the door opened she heard Waites's voice first.

He was saying something about drawing a nice hot bath for his lordship. For a moment, Anne wondered if she'd dozed and had imagined Waites's voice, as it had been so long since she'd heard it. But when she heard Christian's voice, she knew he'd come back at last. At once she sat up straighter, pulling the shawl tight at her swollen bosom.

"A bath would be nice," she heard Christian say. He sounded almost as tired as Anne felt. Her heart twisted. Wasn't he well?

"And a late supper?" Waites inquired.

"No—yes, bring a bottle of port. All that time in France and not one glass of English wine. I find I've missed it, after all."

Anne heard Waites laugh, then she saw his shadow pass the parlor archway, totally oblivious to her quiet presence.

Christian, however, did not pass the archway. Her heart pounded within. He may have been drawn to the fire crackling in the parlor's hearth, as he headed straight to the parlor rather than up the stairs to his own room.

Christian stepped into the room and almost immediately his gaze caught hers. He stopped. He did, indeed, look tired, and thinner, too. He needed to shave; there was a dark shadow on the lower half of his face. He still wore his coat, which he'd been unbuttoning as he stepped inside the parlor. But when he caught sight of her he just stood, his fingers still on the middle, cloth-covered button.

Anne wanted to rise, to move closer to him, to greet him with some sort of contact. But she remained seated. The one thing she did not want him to see was the ignoble way in which she rose from a chair.

"Hello," she said softly. She wished she could say more, but even that single word was an effort to her constricted throat.

"Good evening," he said. Then he resumed unbuttoning his coat and pulled it off his broad shoulders. He draped it on the back of a nearby chair. But he did not approach her. She wondered if he would just leave, go to his room as he'd told Waites he would do. A moment passed, and he showed no sign of retreat. Then he spoke, and in the silent room even the quiet tone of his voice sounded loud.

"Are you well?" he asked.

She could not speak. She nodded, still staring at him, happy and frustrated at the same time. How wonderful it was to look upon him again! How much more wonderful it would be to touch him, to put her arms around him, have him put his arms around her. But she couldn't move, wouldn't let him have a better view of how she looked.

"And the baby?"

"Fine," she said, her voice barely a whisper.

Just then Waites appeared behind Christian, a bottle and glass balancing on the tray he held in his open palm.

"Should I take this upstairs—?" He stopped abruptly, seeing Anne for the first time. "Oh, my lady! How good to see you again, Countess."

Anne wanted to smile, but her lips seemed to be made of cold clay which would not conform to her wishes. And her eyes could not leave Christian's.

"Welcome home, Waites," she said.

"I'll take the wine, Waites," Christian said. He was having no trouble speaking or smiling or moving, Anne noticed with envy. He slid the tray smoothly onto his palm and gave further instructions to Waites over his shoulder. "Bring another glass."

But Anne found her voice. "No," she said. Christian's smile diminished somewhat, and she felt glad he valued her company. "I have tea here, Waites. I don't like to take spirits anymore while carrying the baby . . . it puts me to sleep."

"Very well, then, Waites. You can settle yourself from the journey. I won't need you again tonight."

He bowed slightly toward Anne. "Good night, then, my lady. It is very good to be home again."

He was gone then, and Anne wished he wouldn't have left quite so soon. She hadn't expected Christian to return—oh, she knew he would someday, and had lamented each day of his absence. But he'd been gone so long she'd given up hope he would return any time soon. And now here he was, looking dishevelled and devilishly handsome. And she still wanted him; despite her protruding belly, despite her disatisfaction with her body, she wanted him.

Christian settled the tray on the table before Anne, then he went to the fireplace and added another log, waiting a moment for it to blaze cheerily. He poured himself a glass of wine and sat on the chair opposite her.

He looked so content, Anne felt a twist at her heart. Was this what it would be like, she wondered, to have a husband come home to her? One she couldn't get enough of? One her eyes wanted to devour?

"How was France, my lord?" she said, tearing her gaze from him and staring instead at her teacup.

He leaned his head against the back of his chair, and she thought again how tired he looked. There were shadows under his eyes, and his movements seemed slow. But he'd never been more handsome and she'd been starving for the sight of him.

"France was . . . busy," he said. "I had loose ends to tie up."

"Then you are finished with your business there?"

"Not finished, exactly," he said, looking at her. "But it is taken care of."

"And Highcrest is your home now?"

He paused, still gazing at her. "I thought that was clear when I told Selwyn I would stay."

Anne's lids fluttered downward. She'd been afraid his return to France would become permanent, as Selwyn was no longer at Highcrest to make Christian stay.

"Did you think I would leave Highcrest because of the baby?" Christian asked quietly. "Because it will be the heir upon its birth?"

Her gaze flew to his. "I did not know why you left England, my lord. But I did not think worry over losing the Thornton money had anything to do with it."

"No?"

"Did it?"

He shrugged, staring at the fire. Then he said, "No."

"You left very suddenly," she said.

"And now you know it had nothing to do with coveting your baby's inheritance."

"Then why did you leave?"

He didn't answer right away, as if wondering if he should tell her. "I think we both know why I left."

Now it was Anne's turn to stare at the fire rather than Christian. "You needn't have gone all the way to France, my lord, to escape any carnal feelings for me. My pregnant state would have solved the problem, if only you'd waited a few more weeks for it to become more obvious to you."

Suddenly he laughed, not loud, but it was so unexpected she started. "Do you think being pregnant makes you less desirable?"

She didn't answer; the truth seemed obvious.

Christian rose from his chair to come to her side. He sat next to her on the settee, even closer than he had that day Newell had come for tea so long ago. Once again his leg pressed against her thigh. Then, slowly, he moved even closer. He let his lips brush hers briefly, and for Anne the sensation was both alluring and unseemly. She wanted to succumb and to resist, part of her wanting him so badly she ached, the other part too caught up in her own insecurity with her body to even think of being a passionate woman.

But Christian did not demand she choose which emotion to follow. He lifted his mouth from hers, then stood.

"Nothing has changed," he said, and it seemed as though it was as much a revelation to himself as it was to her.

Then, without a word, he left the room.

Anne sat stiffly in the chair, her lips tingling, her heart racing, her thoughts jumbled. She knew one thing only: for the past month or more, she'd felt utterly ugly. Christian had been home barely ten minutes, and part of her already felt like a desirable woman.

She was relieved, however, that he'd left the room first. After a while, once her heartbeat had slowed and her breathing had calmed, she struggled to her feet and made her way to her room.

Anne woke early the next morning. She'd slept only fitfully, as was normal for her lately. But there was one slight difference: the baby was somehow heavier, pressing lower than before. It made finding a comfortable position entirely impossible.

When she finally arose from her bed, she wanted to dress and hurry downstairs, but purposely controlled those feelings. She forced herself to stare at her reflection in the mirror, reminding herself how unattractive she'd become. She should not want Christian to see her at all. But last night's kiss had left more impact on her than she'd guessed. She no longer felt so ugly; her thoughts were undeniably happy, her mood light. He'd seen her at her worst, and still wanted her.

Pel helped her dress. Anne continued wearing mourning clothes, although the gowns she wore these last days of her pregnancy were more like loose-fitting shifts. She thought it odd indeed to be wearing black while carrying life, but she knew she must conform to custom. Because of her father she felt she'd gone against enough rules of society already. Pel tied Anne's hair back in a braid, then wound it into a coil. Adding a shawl to her shoulders, Anne made her way downstairs.

Christian was in the dining room when Anne entered. An array of food was already spread out before him, eggs and fruit, bread and hot coffee. But he had not as yet served himself and he stood, smiling, when Anne approached.

"Welcome home, my lord," she said with downcast eyes as she took her seat.

When they were both seated, they spoke. "I thought we said our greetings last night," he whispered.

She looked at him. "Yes, I suppose we did."

He offered her the platter of eggs, then spoke casually. "Did you miss me, my lady?"

Once again, her gaze met his. He didn't look so tired this morning. He actually looked cheerful and boyish and achingly attractive. And his flirtatious attitude was wonderfully familiar.

She stared at him and said, "No, my lord, I did not miss you. Should I have?"

He shrugged as if her denial didn't really matter. "I will

be more honest than you, Countess, and tell you that I did in fact miss you while I was gone. In fact, I'd intended to stay through the end of the year, but returned early."

"Because you missed me?" she said in complete skepticism.

"Yes." His answer was firm, and for a moment she almost believed him. But she quickly reproached herself. He wanted her in one way only, in a way he could not possibly have her, most especially now.

Anne's plate was nearly full, she realized she had no appetite. She didn't think it odd, considering Christian's return had sent her emotions atwitter. But how was she to get through the meal? She suddenly wished she'd possessed the willpower to remain upstairs in her own room until sure she would not have to share any time with Christian. How silly she was; she wanted him home, but didn't seem capable of bearing his company.

"I imagine you will be seeing Mortimer today," Anne said, taking a sip of her coffee.

"I sent word to him of my return. I think it's a safe guess that he'll be arriving here sometime this morning." Then he added, "I may have gone for a couple months, Countess, but I didn't shirk my duties here."

"I know that," she said. "Mortimer mentioned to me once that you'd been in contact with him."

"Regularly," he replied.

"So you didn't abandon Highcrest altogether."

"Not at all."

Just then Anne felt something strange in her middle. It wasn't pain, actually, just a tightening sensation which made her hand go reflexively to her stomach. Oddly enough, her protruding tummy felt hard, rather than pliant to the touch, certainly more firm than it had before.

"What is it?" Christian asked, immediately attentive and concerned.

"Nothing," she replied. "A hunger pang, perhaps."

"You haven't eaten a bite since sitting down," he chided her. "Would you rather have Mistress Lindall prepare something else?"

Suddenly the thought of more food, or, indeed, any food, made her feel nauseous. This is ridiculous, she told herself. Why was she forcing herself to sit at the breakfast table when she certainly had no intention of eating? Just so she could share Christian's company—when it was obviously his very presence which stole her appetite?

"I think I will have breakfast later," she said, standing. She knew Christian was concerned, but she didn't want to stay another moment. She wished it were summer; she would like to take a walk, do something. She suddenly felt very restless.

Christian stood as well, and followed her when she headed toward the parlor and the outer hall.

"Anne." His voice was full of worry. "Is something wrong? I mean, is it time for the baby, do you think?"

She was startled at his observation, but she kept walking. If she could not walk outside, she would walk upstairs, as she'd done before on days of inclement weather.

Anne gave a brief laugh at Christian's distressed countenance as she headed toward the stairs.

"It is not time for the baby, my lord," she told him, though after a moment she wondered if she should have lied. Selwyn had died precisely nine months ago. She had planned to convince those around her that the baby's arrival was already late. "Can't you just believe that I found your company insufferable and I wish to get a bit of exercise?"

"Anne."

It was clear he didn't believe her insult; he was truly anxious over her welfare and that touched her heart.

"I'm fine," she assured him. Then, standing at the base of the stairs she glanced upward. "This may sound silly, my lord, but in the past few weeks when it's been so cold, I've walked the length of the upper corridor rather than going out to the garden for a walk. That's exactly what I intend to do now. It makes my back feel better."

"Your back does hurt, then?" he asked, still solicitous.

She smiled. "Not so much. I just feel like walking."

He took her hand and started up the stairs. "Then I'll accompany you."

Anne permitted him to walk beside her up the stairs, but at the top she stopped. "Your breakfast is getting cold, my lord. Why don't you go back to the dining room?"

He faced her. "I'm not hungry."

"Now you're acting quite foolishly." She started to walk, but turned back to add somewhat harshly, "You know, Christian, if anything goes wrong—you'll remain the sole heir."

"Don't say it!" he chided her, and his golden eyes darkened ominously.

Even as she spoke, Anne felt a deep sense of regret at her words. A jest like that at such a time was entirely without humor.

She did, however, wonder at Christian's behavior. He did, indeed, seem concerned, not only of her welfare but also of the child's. And that seeded a deep sense of guilt in her, knowing this child's existence was to do nothing more than steal Christian's rightful inheritance. At least that was how it had begun, in her father's mind.

"Please," she said, earnest now because self-reproach was welling in her. She didn't want to see Christian; she couldn't bear to be the benefactor of his kindness and concern. "Go back downstairs. I'm sure Mortimer will be here soon."

"Mortimer can wait," Christian said. Then he placed her hand on his arm and directed her ahead. "Now, which way would you care to go, madam? To the right toward the window, or to the left to the portraits?"

She sighed, knowing she would give in. She was as helpless at resisting his kindness as she'd been at resisting his kiss. "To the portraits."

They walked slowly, and all the while Anne was conscious of the compatible silence, her arm securely entwined with his. But when they came to the long section of hallway wall which held the portraits of various Thornton ancestors, Anne regretted having chosen this direction. The portrait of Celine, one of the more recent additions when compared to those which had been in the Thornton family for the last one hundred years, was a portrait which never failed to ignite all

Anne's fears about childbirth.

When they came to the portrait she couldn't help but stare, transfixed by it. She didn't want to stop and look at it, didn't want to talk about what she felt, but something inside made her do just that.

Christian saw where her gaze was directed.

"That is Celine, isn't it?" he asked.

Anne nodded. "Do you know how she died?" Anne asked Christian, unable to stop herself.

"Yes," he said slowly, watching her stare at the painting, "I do."

"Do you know how many babies she lost? Step-siblings, to you?"

"Not exactly," he said, his voice becoming terse. The topic made him uncomfortable, Anne could tell. He tried to start walking again, to urge her along, but she remained frozen in place, still staring at the portrait. It had been painted years ago, when Celine was young, perhaps Anne's age. She was lovely, with chestnut eyes and hair, a sweet smile, and ivory skin. She would have made a loving mother, Anne could tell just by the expression the artist had caught in her eyes.

"Five," Anne answered. "She lost five babies, and with the last she died, too. There were plenty of doctors around, but they couldn't do anything. Selwyn told me she suffered for two days . . . two whole days. She bled to death, and the baby suffocated. They tried to take it when it was obvious Celine wouldn't make it, but it was already too late. The baby was dead already—"

"Stop it," Christian said quietly, his tone more firm than ever. Then, without allowing her resistence, he turned her around and headed in the opposite direction, toward the windows.

There was a moment of tense silence until Christian spoke again. When he did, his voice was steady and calming. "Anne, it's true I don't know much about the birth of babies, but it does stand to reason that if you were going to have some problem, there would have been some indication of it. But you've been healthy through these months, haven't you?''

She nodded.

"And the baby, he moves around and you can feel his life?''

She nodded again, then said with a slight smile, "Or *her* life.''

He grinned, glad her recent moments of morose thinking had ended. They stopped walking, and Christian placed his hands on her shoulders. "If it means anything, Anne, I'm glad I came back in time to be here for you—if you're afraid. I don't know if I'll be any help. A moment ago you had to calm *me* down, but maybe we'll find we work well together. We can take turns soothing each other. All right?''

She laughed, for the idea of calming Christian down, even though it was true she'd done so a moment ago, seemed so ridiculous. It was true, he did act as if he cared about this baby. And that made her feel warm from head to toe. There could be only one reason for that, and that was because he really did care for her.

But before Anne could reply, another strange tightening gripped her stomach, this time a bit stronger. Her hands went automatically to her middle once again.

Christian watched, and immediately he paled somewhat. "I'm taking you to your room," he announced. "Then I'm sending someone for the doctor." He hardly looked at her as they made their way to her room. He seemed intent on figuring out the best course of action, as if there were some strategic way in which to birth a baby. When they reached her room, he led her to the bed and headed back to the door.

"I'll get Pel," he said, "and your mother, too, if you like. Do you want your mother?''

"Yes," she replied immediately, without thinking, but as soon as he'd turned his back to carry out her wishes, she called him back. "No, not Mother. I don't want her to see . . . it may be too much for her.''

He nodded in silent agreement, then was gone.

Barely a few minutes later, Pel came, wide-eyed and

concerned.

"His lordship said it's time!" she said, looking every bit as worried as Christian had. Obviously, Christian was not as adept at calming others as he had been calming Anne herself. "He sent Gregory for the doctor. Why did we ever let that doctor move from Highcrest? We should have kept him here, just like we did when Selwyn was sick. Then we wouldn't have to wait for him now."

"Pel," Anne said in a level voice, knowing her friend's concern caused her prattle. "I'll just need help getting undressed. I'll wear a lawn gown—and then, I'd like you to put a few layers of sheets on the bed so I won't soil the mattress."

Pel let out an exasperated breath. "Imagine worrying about a mattress at a time like this! Especially when that little heir who'll supposedly soil that mattress can bloody well buy a thousand new mattresses!"

"Pel, just do as I say," she said, already reaching to the back of her neck to unfasten some buttons.

A few moments later, when she was just sliding the mourning gown from her shoulders, the door burst open and Christian stood there. When he saw her undressing he gaped a moment, then started to retreat. But even as he showed the good sense to remove himself, he looked somewhat dumb-founded.

"I'll wait outside for a moment," he mumbled.

"Yes," Anne said, feeling considerably calmer than he looked. "Perhaps you should."

Once the door was closed, Pel whispered, "Do you mean he's going to be here during this?"

Anne smiled, amused at Pel's reaction. "For a little while."

But in the end, Christian did not leave, after all. He pulled up a chair at her bedside and held her hand, smoothed her sweaty hair from her face, and spoke to her in a sur-prisingly calm voice, considering how distressed he'd been earlier. The physician told him to leave once, but Christian ignored him and, whether because Christian was an earl or because he looked terribly stubborn, the doctor didn't persist.

And Anne was more than grateful for his presence. He talked to her through every painful contraction, and urged her on when she began to push. He sometimes looked as if the pain touched him as well, but when Anne had the time to look up into his eyes, he would banish whatever worry or fatigue he felt and smile assuredly. She was glad for that.

Later, what might have seemed like an eternity turned out to be only a few hours, and when Anne heard the healthy squall of her son, she forgot the pain, forgot the relief that it was over, forgot everything but the joy at finally holding her baby in her arms.

Christian looked every bit as relieved as Anne. He smiled with surprising tenderness at the child Anne held in her arms, and one final time he smoothed Anne's hair from her face.

"He's a handsome, healthy boy, Anne," he said. "And you're a beautiful, healthy mother."

She gave him a weak smile. "A tired one, anyway." She glanced toward the window. When had the sun set? It was dark already. When she looked back at Christian, he was staring at the child, almost in awe. Even in her weariness, she was amazed at the expression in his eyes; he looked at the child almost lovingly!

"You had better get some rest yourself, Christian," she whispered after a moment of studying him. "Or you'll be the doctor's next patient."

Christian left when Pel came to take the baby, to wash it and dress it and bundle it in soft, warm blankets while Anne slept. As Anne watched Christian leave a feeling of such love swelled in her heart. At that moment, she could not have loved him more had he even been the child's father.

24

Jarvis Melbourne slid unsteadily to the ground from the back of his horse and tottered toward the steps of his modest manor home. His wig was off-center, the white, once-immaculate curls were frayed and loose. He'd left his overcoat at the inn, but the cold did not penetrate the coat and waistcoat to touch Jarvis's liquor-heated veins.

His first visit that day had been to Highcrest. The minute he'd heard the doctor had spent the previous day attending the countess, Jarvis had rushed to see about Anne's welfare. The ride to Highcrest had been an anxious one, he was so eager to know if his plan had succeeded. And how it had! In such a grand way! Even now, hours later and a bottle later, he could still feel triumph swell in his heart. Not only had the child been born early—not late, as Jarvis had feared could happen—but it had been a boy! A strong, healthy boy who was so obliging of his grandfather to arrive early, lending a bit more credence to this whole magnificent plan.

Jarvis laughed as he stumbled inside his home, leaning against the door behind him. A boy! A boy to inherit it all, the money, the title, the power. Thanks be! Jarvis would not have to deal with the women of his family much longer! At last he would have a man to guide, to shape, to steer toward taking the helm of power under Jarvis's expert tutelage.

He lurched toward the stairway, but any control of movement seemed to have deserted him once inside the safe confines of his own home. Too much wine again, he thought. That certainly must change, now that he had the great burden of seeing after his grandson's interests.

But for now, unable to move himself upstairs, he collapsed against the bottom stairs, a hard bed to be sure, but Jarvis didn't care; he couldn't feel it. The loud sound of his snores was the only thing which made it up the stairs that night, not for the first time.

Anne gazed at the tiny child suckling at her breast. She felt she could stare at him for hours and never wish to look upon anything else. He fed hungrily, as always, and it made her happy to see him take nourishment from her. Pel had suggested a wet nurse, at least for the late-night feedings, but Anne refused. She kept the child's cradle in her bedroom and went to him whenever he cried. She would have felt cheated to have anyone else respond to him.

For the past week since his birth, Anne had recovered quickly from the delivery which, she had to admit, was a blessing for its swiftness and lack of complications. Obviously this child was meant to live, no matter what the impetus had been for its conception. She wouldn't let herself think about that, however; these days were full of happiness and love for her son, and she would not allow her father any part of it, even in her thoughts. During Jarvis's single visit to Highcrest, he had been the perfect gentleman, for he'd been before the audience of Pel, the physician, and Christian as well. He'd behaved like the proud grandfather. Anne saw the look in his eye, the gleam of triumph, the glimmer of greed, and conquest over Christian.

If she let herself dwell on it, she would feel once again all the shame she'd felt at her part in the scheme against Christian. And, even more than that, hatred for her father. But instead, these days, all she felt was love. Love for her son, and love for Christian.

Thoughts of Christian, as always, made Anne's heart dance in her breast. She was in love with Christian; she could face it now. There was, after all, no use denying it. A simple denial wouldn't make it untrue. He made it so easy to love him. He treated her more kindly than she'd ever been treated before. He brought her breakfast like any servant, fussed over her like a mother hen, even cooed at the baby without a bit of embarrassment. And Anne loved it all, and loved him for it.

In these days of her recovery there was no sexual tension between them. When he turned that intense gaze on her, it was with concern, not lust. When he teased her it was with innocent affection, without a trace of the sensual undertones he'd used in the past.

But the way in which he treated her son touched Anne most. Christian visited the child so often. He was not shy around the baby, even though he confessed he'd never held one before. He talked to the tiny infant with ease. Anne loved to watch them together. The baby was perfectly content in Christian's strong arms, hearing his deep, gentle voice.

That, along with Christian's obvious affection for Anne herself, gave her hope for a bright future. As she watched her son suckle so hungrily, she thought of how lucky he would be to have a father like Christian. Surely marriage between Anne and Christian was not so far-fetched. Christian enjoyed her company even now, when the temptations of the flesh were set aside. And he seemed to make a natural, loving father to Anne's little son. She could not help thinking there was very real hope that Christian would see marriage between them as a logical step. Why not, after all?

Anne swallowed hard when she reminded herself of Christian's own words, that he liked women in general far too much to give up the rest for just one. Was that still true? Perhaps he had gone back to his old life-style in France. And now that the title would be turned over to Anne's heir, he may very well behave in any way he saw fit.

Alone in her room but for the child at her breast, Anne came to a decision. Since she had, indeed, faced the love she felt for Christian, there was but one thing to do. She could not, she knew, reveal her father's plot, even though love for

Christian made her want to more than ever. Doing that certainly wouldn't endear Christian to her, and, more importantly, her mother's very life was still at stake. Maybe someday she could tell Christian the truth—after her father no longer had control over her. Perhaps, with Christian as her husband, that day would come sooner than she hoped. After all, Christian and Anne would be the child's guardians and thereby control the fortune, leaving Jarvis with nothing. If Anne could find protection for her mother in Christian, then she could eventually reveal the truth about her child—once she was secure in Christian's love.

Besides, what better way was there to overcome the guilt of her part in this plot? She would make it up to him by loving him—wildly and unselfishly—so thoroughly even she would be able to forget what she'd done against him. Christian already evoked her passion every time he displayed such affection not only for herself but also for the new heir. Obviously Christian cared little for the lost inheritance—otherwise he wouldn't have accepted Anne's son so quickly and effortlessly.

For the first time in her life, Anne schemed. She would do her best to make Christian love her by simply loving him; and after the last few days of his solicitous treatment, she had every reason to believe this plan would succeed.

Christian tapped lightly at Anne's door and a moment later heard her voice calling him to enter. He stepped inside, and for a moment just stared at the picture she made sitting on the chair before the fireplace, holding the baby. His baby. Anne was dressed in gray rather than black, a new gown he guessed, for it wasn't the type she wore while pregnant. It was open at the bodice, and she'd draped a small blanket over her shoulder for modesty's sake as the child suckled her breast. He could hear the smacking noises and wished, not for the first time, that Anne would remove the blanket and let Christian see his son as he fed. The desire wasn't entirely sexual, he admitted, although he did realize it was partially so. But he wanted to watch his son take nourishment, see him feed with the obvious vigor his sounds made Christian expect.

"We're almost finished," Anne said, greeting Christian with a smile. The smile that made Christian feel both drawn to her, as well as wary. Something was different, he'd realized days ago, but he'd attributed it to motherhood. Her smile is maternal, he decided, even toward me. But that conclusion didn't sit well with him, though for what reason he was not yet ready to explore.

He took a seat opposite her, watching the fire crackle in the hearth. It was a cozy scene, one he'd viewed so often of late, one which stirred something inside him, made him wish it were exactly as it appeared: man, woman and the child they had made together. Perhaps the facts were true, but how he hated the reality of it, the truth that their child had been made of deceit instead of love.

Love was a word Christian shied away from, even now when he found it so difficult to stop wishing their son had been born of it. His guilty conscience still raged within for his part in his son's existence. And as each day went by and still Anne made no move to tell him the truth, he realized he had but one option left. He didn't like thinking about it, especially when in her company. But he had no choice. He must tell Mortimer the whole truth, and see to it that the old, loyal barrister set the wheels of justice in motion. He was sure Mortimer would be shocked, but once he heard the whole story, including Guiscard's confession, he would want the truth to be known and the Thornton inheritance to pass to its rightful heir. Mortimer was, Christian knew, a man who wanted the truth above all else. Especially where the Thornton money was concerned.

"Have you decided on a name yet?" he asked at last, once Anne had deftly extracted the child from her breast and fastened her bodice, all modestly done beneath the blanket. Christian's son was snoozing, satiated, upon Anne's shoulder.

Anne smiled. "Yes, in fact, I have. I'd like to call him David."

"David," Christian repeated aloud, as if testing the name. "David Thornton."

"Do you like it?"

He nodded, though he said, "I'm surprised, though."

"Oh? Why?"

"I thought you would name him after Selwyn," Christian said in a low voice. "Or perhaps after your father."

He watched her face harden for barely a moment. Guilt, he wondered? Or something else? But the emotion disappeared quickly and she glanced down at the child. And as always when her eyes fell to him, her face softened measurably. "He hardly looks like a Selwyn or a Jarvis, don't you think? The name David suits him very well."

Christian stood, nearing them until he had a better view of the child's face as if seeing him for the first time. Little David wasn't sleeping soundly, his eyes opened when he heard Christian speak. "It does, indeed, Countess. A name well chosen. May I take him?"

Anne gently transferred David from her soft bosom to Christian's secure arms. As she did so, Christian's eyes caught hers. She was smiling again and, for the barest moment he could have sworn he saw love there. But no, he thought. He must have merely noticed the love she directed to David.

With David in his arms, Christian took a seat. He felt Anne's eyes on him but for some reason did not meet her gaze. Instead, he stared down at the infant and tried not to wonder what Anne was thinking.

"I would like to share supper with you tonight, Christian," Anne said, "if that is all right with you."

Christian looked up, for her words, as well as her tone of voice, piqued his interest. Her gaze held his, and once again he saw something in her eyes that he'd not seen before. And it didn't look maternal, no matter what he told himself.

"That would be fine," he said still holding her gaze. David squirmed just then, and Christian was almost grateful to avert his attention from Anne. David let out one brief wail, but Christian shifted the baby's position, patted his back, and, a moment later, the tiny boy was once again resting peacefully.

"He'll sleep for a while now," Anne said.

"I'll put him in his bed, then."

Christian did just that, then went to the door. He'd planned to make his visit a lengthy one, but with the way Anne was looking at him he had all he could do not to stare right back at her and take her in his arms. But he knew that would be the wrong thing to do. She'd made it perfectly clear she didn't want him to make love to her. And that was all he wanted. He assured himself of that.

But by late that evening, well after dinner, Christian was no longer sure what he wanted. Her company at the supper table had been so enjoyable, so warm and happy, that Christian realized more than once he would be glad to spend the rest of his suppers in just such a way.

Now, however, alone in his room and away from her gaze, her smile, and her warmth, other thoughts returned. He wanted her in more ways than physical, he knew, but he remembered that she had never once revealed her true spirit to him. The treacherous spirit which had gotten her with child for one purpose.

Yet while that might be a fair observation, it was nonetheless incomplete. For whatever reason she'd conceived David, Christian knew Anne loved her son. Their son. Christian had only to look at Anne's face when she gazed upon the child at her breast to see that. It would be hard for her to give him up, for it was more than just the money the child represented to her. That should have surprised him. Wasn't she the cold-blooded schemer? Could such a woman who plotted to conceive solely for an inheritance really love the product of her deceit? Hadn't she wanted the child only for the money it could steal for her?

He pushed the questions away. He'd done nothing but ask himself such things for days now. Certainly Christian could find no insight into Anne Thornton's wily mind. He kept telling himself it was best this way, that in a few days time he would announce to her that Mortimer would be presenting Christian's case against her in the House of Lords, to be judged by the peers of their class. He had little doubt they would assign the inheritance to him with a swift enactment of justice. As for the child, anyone would see he would be better off with Christian. It was a simple matter, really. And something which must be done. He could not change his mind simply because Anne was more than capable of charming her way into his heart.

25

Lord Newell Franklin called on Anne a very proper three weeks after her son's birth. They sat in the parlor with a roaring fire and the heavy drapes drawn across the window to keep out drafts. Still, Anne wore a shawl, and she'd bundled David up in a soft cloth wrap and heaped him with blankets. He was sound asleep in the cradle beside her.

Newell brought with him an array of gifts for the child, toys and games and clothing which David would surely have to grow into in order to fit. But Anne, despite being happy to see Newell, insisted he return all but one of the gifts.

"I can't take them back, silly," Newell chided her affectionately. "A woman in town made the clothes especially for the little lord-to-be, and the toys were made by the innkeeper's father. To be honest, Anne, they practically gave them to me once they found out who the gifts were for. If I took them back, it would be a great insult."

"Are you sure they didn't overcharge you?" Anne asked skeptically. "I love the villagers, it's true, but they're not wealthy people. And when nobility comes through wanting to spend—"

"I was not taken advantage of, I assure you," Newell said as if taking an oath of honesty. Then he grinned. "You know, Anne, you really shouldn't worry so about my finances. My family is rather well off."

"And that is why you had to flee that bet back in London?" She spoke without thinking, but after all,

Mortimer's spies had not told her anything Newell himself hadn't already mentioned.

"I fled the bet because it was a socially unpopular wager—over a woman, you see, and my father thought it best that I disappear for the time being." That seemed to explain it well enough for Newell. He smiled anew and then with a glance to the sleeping baby he switched the subject entirely. "Let's go upstairs, Anne, and finish the painting. It's been a long time since I've seen it."

Anne glanced at David and then at the clock on the mantel. She frowned. "I don't know . . . it's almost time for his feeding."

"He's sound asleep!" Newell said coaxingly. "And heaven knows Highcrest has enough servants to take care of him."

"But no one else can feed him," she reminded Newell.

Newell blushed at the reference to how the child was nourished. "You mean you . . . don't you have a nurse to do that sort of thing?"

Anne shook her head, amused at his discomfiture. How different he was from Christian, who was so comfortable around David, and so obviously approving of the way Anne cared for her son.

"Then we'll just stay long enough for me to have a look at the painting and decide how close I am to finishing it. I'd like to see the other paintings I left up there, too."

"All right," Anne said, seeing no harm in it. They would not be gone long, and Anne would return before David even stirred. She stood, going first to the kitchen to summon Mistress Lindall to stay with the child for the few minutes Anne would be gone.

The large, almost empty room Newell had used as a studio was on the second floor at the opposite end from the rest of the bedrooms. This wing of Highcrest was rarely used and so when they entered the room Anne shivered. The tall windows were curtainless, letting brilliant but wintery sunlight spill into the room. In the center of the room was the portrait, still propped up before the small round dias on

which Anne had stood. Against two walls were a variety of
other paintings, some sketches of Anne, and other finished
paintings Newell had completed while staying in Wynchly.
He'd long ago outgrown his room at the inn, and Anne had
suggested he store some of the canvases here.

Newell went to the portrait and threw back the
protective cloth covering. Anne went to his side.

Seeing the portrait never failed to make Anne stare in
wonder. It truly was lovely, a full, life-size portrait that she
thought was far more beautiful than she had ever really
looked. How tiny he'd made her waist! Was it ever that
small? Though she had regained her shapes and curves since
delivering David, she knew the curves were just a trifle fuller,
and she would never again have the figure Newell recorded in
the portrait—if she ever had! He had a way of making something exquisite out of what was just passably pretty.

"I'm so close to finishing it, Anne," he said, his voice
barely a whisper. "Won't you let me?"

"Of course, Newell," she told him. She wanted it
finished to, even if it was out of pure vanity. Then she
frowned. "But not today."

He smiled. "Then I shall just have to return, Countess.
Perhaps . . . tomorrow?"

She laughed at his eagerness. "Is there some hurry?"
Then she asked, as an afterthought, "Are you returning to
London soon?"

When Newell spoke, he placed his hands on her
shoulders. "I do intend to return soon, Anne. But there is
something I'd like to ask you regarding that." He looked
very earnest, very young. Anne knew he was at least five
years older than herself, yet at the moment she felt far more
mature. Newell looked like a little boy intent on asking a
great favor of an adult. "I—that is, my family, I'm sure,
would be most happy to have you as a guest at Franklin
House, our home in London. You and David, if you like."

She tilted her head and looked at him, surprised. "If I
like?"

"Well, motherhood is a strain on some."

She stiffened. "Not on me."

He smiled charmingly. "The invitation is extended to David as well, Anne."

She squirmed free of his firm hold and turned away from him as well as his portrait. "It's very kind of you, Newell, and I'm sure when I do come to London I shall visit you and your family often. But Selwyn has a town home where I shall be more than comfortable whenever I wish to visit London."

"But it hasn't been used in years!" he exclaimed. "I assure you, Anne, the place is barely livable. The servants who inhabit his house keep only a portion of it presentable. Besides, you'd be terribly lonely there. It's a big, rambling estate that's not as centrally located as Franklin House."

"It sounds like I will like the Thornton town home," she assured him, "after a lifetime of quiet Sussex life."

"Anne," Newell said slowly, coming up behind her and standing so close she could feel the warmth from his body. "I don't think you understand what I'm offering. I'd like you to come to Franklin House with me so we could get to know one another better—and, of course, for my family to get to know you as well. Perhaps, if we're lucky, we will both agree our relationship should be put on a permanent basis."

Anne turned around. She was somewhat surprised by his proposal. She'd hoped he'd begun to understand she felt nothing more than friendship for him.

"Newell, I know you think because of Selwyn's wish that I need someone to take care of me—"

"Oh, no, Anne. I'm just glad Selwyn's invitation gave me the opportunity to meet you. Wanting to marry you has nothing at all to do with his last wishes."

She kept her voice brisk. "Nonetheless, I think you might be mixing up some of your emotions. You're far from home and here in Sussex there aren't as many of the ladies you're used to seeing. I may be pale, indeed, once you see me in London and compare me to the women there."

"Anne, that is truly ridiculous—"

"And," she continued, "I can't help but be honest with you, Newell. Entirely honest. I believe your family might be expecting a lucrative marriage settlement from you, a way for you to help their presently unstable finances. I think that might be another issue coloring your infatuation with me."

He looked momentarily surprised, she noticed, but then he took her elbow and directed her back to the painting. "Look at it, Anne. Do you honestly think I could have painted it without really believing I could love you?"

Anne turned from the painting and gently touched his cheek. "Newell, I am flattered that you think love inspired this painting, but you are underestimating your talent. Look at these other paintings—and some of the portraits. The one of the innkeeper's father, the old man with his woodwork. If love inspired those, it's love of the art, not of the subject."

She watched as he studied the paintings around them. "You don't need a lucrative match, Newell," she said slowly. "I know it's not common for an earl to earn a living working, but you could sell your paintings under an assumed name. Hire a lawyer to arrange it all. I'm sure Mortimer could recommend someone. The paintings are sure to sell, they're so lovely."

Newell did not reply, but he clearly considered her suggestion as a possibility. However, a moment later he was grinning at her again. "You have it all figured out, don't you, Anne? Why I'm feeling what I'm feeling, how I can prevent myself from a marriage you're sure would be wrong. But I'm not so easily convinced. I really do love you, Anne."

She shook her head. "Go back to London, Newell. You'll like the ladies there and won't miss me once you've returned to them." She put her hand on his arm and directed him out of the room. "You'll see I'm right, Newell. Now let's go back downstairs. We've been gone much longer than I expected."

Anne heard David's cries before they were halfway downstairs. Immediately her step quickened, and she felt the milk in her breasts begin to flow in anticipation of her son's hunger. When she stepped into the parlor, however, she stopped suddenly. Christian was holding David, obviously trying to soothe him, but when he caught sight of Anne on Newell's arm he glared and visibly stiffened. David's cries heightened.

"Your son is hungry, Countess," Christian said coldly. "And if you think entertaining company more important than caring for him, I suggest that you hire a wet nurse."

Then he placed David into her arms and strode from the room, the scowl never leaving his face.

"I—I'm sorry for that display, Newell," Anne said over David's cries. "But unless you want to see a countess feed her son exactly the way any peasant mother does it, I suggest you be on your way."

She was so eager to satisfy her child's cry, her fingers were already at the laces of her bodice.

"I'll come back tomorrow," he said. His gaze fell to her fingers at the bodice of her gown, fascinated by the fact she was already freeing herself. But then he seemed to listen to his own words and raised his gaze to her eyes. "In the morning. We can finish the painting."

With that, he was gone.

Not long after David was finished, Anne summoned Pel to give the child a bath while Anne herself went in search of Christian. She knew he was angry that she'd left David for what must have seemed like a long time, but she hoped his anger involved more than just concern for the child. She hoped jealousy played a part in Christian's outburst, as he'd seen her return on Newell's arm.

She found him in the solicitor's salon, seated at the desk and perusing various papers scattered before him. When she entered, closing the door behind her, he looked up but paid her scant attention, as if she were a bumble bee which posed just enough threat to evoke a glance as it passed by.

But when she took a seat directly opposite him, staring at him until he looked up again, it was clear that she was not merely passing by for a book or to retrieve a forgotten article. She had come to see him.

"Is there something you wanted?" he asked tersely.

"I came to apologize, actually," she began, although her voice was far too light to be contrite. "For your having to listen to David's crying while I was busy."

"Busy," he repeated irritably, returning his gaze to the papers in front of him.

"Yes," she said calmly, unruffled by his mood. Surely he was jealous! "While you were in France, Newell started a portrait of me. It's upstairs. Would you like to see it?"

"And that's what you were doing?" he asked skeptically. "Having him paint your portrait?"

"No," she admitted. "Not today. There wasn't time. We merely went up to look at it, and some of the other paintings he left upstairs."

"Sounds like he made himself quite at home while I was gone."

"He did come by on a regular basis," Anne said. "But I'm sure you'll be pleased when you see the painting."

"I'll be sure to see it, then," he said coolly. "When I have a moment."

She stood. It wasn't exactly the response she'd hoped for, but then she wasn't sure what she'd expected. If he truly was jealous—and she could not attribute his anger to anything else—then it was probably best to leave the next step to him. She left the room, smiling. Sooner or later, she thought, Christian would realize what Anne already knew. He loved her son, he wanted Anne, and cared for her even if he didn't want to admit it. Enough to be jealous over. It all led so logically to marriage that she was sure he would also come to that conclusion before long.

Christian pushed the papers away. He hadn't been reading them, anyway; they'd only been a ruse to make Anne think his attention was elsewhere. But, alone now, there was no need to continue the farce.

He could still smell the faint perfume of her; lavender and something else, too, a slightly sweet smell, perhaps milk from feeding David. It made him want to follow her, to stay in her company and with their son, too. His jaw clenched. That, however, was exactly what he must *not* do.

He'd put it off long enough. He'd summoned Mortimer that morning. At first he thought he might keep the discussion on unrelated matters. But now he knew, unless he did something and did it soon, he would be lost. He would give in entirely to Anne's schemes, ignoring her deceitful nature. Let her take the fortune, the title. It would all go to his son, anyway, so what was the difference? The difference was, of course, that he *knew*. He knew it all, and that would forever be a wedge between them. It must come out, and if Anne wasn't willing to tell him, then he must force it from her, through Mortimer.

Mortimer arrived on schedule and Christian was noticeably quiet for the first quarter hour of the barrister's visit. Mortimer brought up several matters, to which Christian gave, at best, perfunctory comments.

At last Mortimer was silent for one long moment. Christian barely noticed until Mortimer said, "Is something troubling you? Business other than what I've gotten to so far?"

"How well do you know Anne, Mortimer?" Christian asked suddenly.

"Well enough."

"What does that mean?" He sounded impatient, even to himself. "Do you trust her?"

"Of course."

"Do you think she's honest?"

Mortimer nodded.

"What if I told you that her son is not Selwyn's? That she schemed to get herself pregnant after Selwyn's death just to steal the legacy away from me?"

Mortimer's face did not change; it was as if he were weighing it as solely hypothetical, not even considering the accustation as possibly true. "I would say someone has been spreading some humorless lies about her."

Christian stood, went to the mantel for a glass of wine, then faced Mortimer again. "It's no lie."

Mortimer stood, as well, and came to Christian's side. He, too, poured himself a glass.

"How did you come by this knowledge? Who is the source?"

Christian smiled crookedly. "I'm surprised that you, with all your spies, didn't come upon the plan before me. A man named Guiscard came to me with the news."

"I've not heard of him," Mortimer said. "How do you

know it's true?''

"Because, my friend, I myself played Guiscard's role in the scheme. He was to father Anne's child.''

Mortimer looked intrigued, appalled and confused all at the same time. "How—?''

"He was paid to bed her in a darkened room, so that he would never know the woman he impregnated.'' Christian smirked. "That way there would be no complications later, no demands for gold when the inheritance was secured.''

Mortimer returned his glass to the mantel, his hand was shaking so. "And you went through with it?'' He was plainly aghast.

Christian knew a moment of compunction, certainly not the first, but as of recently he'd talked himself out of the guilt he'd felt for his own part in it. "It . . . got out of hand. I didn't intend to go through with it. But the fact is, I did. And the result is David. My son.''

Mortimer let out a long breath. Then he looked closely at Christian. "What is it you want me to do?''

"Start proceedings to keep the inheritance in my name due to Anne's trickery, and to give me custody of the child. David will indeed inherit, but Anne will have no part of the Thornton fortune.''

Mortimer returned to his seat, his shoulders stooped. He suddenly looked very old. "I cannot believe it.''

Christian finished his wine. "Believe it,'' he said firmly.

"You do know where to find this Guiscard? We'll need him.''

"He's in London already, awaiting word from me. He's been paid enough to wait as long as it takes.''

26

"Have you seen his lordship, Mistress Lindall?"

The servant looked up while clearing away the dishes from the table, obviously surprised to see Anne enter the dining room. Christian must have breakfasted early, for Anne had hoped she would be in time to join him.

"He left only minutes ago, my lady. I think he was off for the stables."

Anne turned on her heel and headed in that direction without delay, despite the fact she was not wearing riding clothes.

She found Christian just emerging from the Highcrest stable, leading his Arabian behind him. When he saw Anne, however, he stopped. But he was not smiling. In fact, Anne noticed, he did not look at all pleased to see her, as he had in previous days.

"Are you going riding, my lord?"

He cocked his head to one side, as if the answer was too obvious to offer a reply.

Anne laughed, a trifle nervously. Was he still angry about Newell's visit? What else could it be?

"If you will wait for me to change, I'd be happy to go with you," she volunteered.

The horse behind him nudged Christian's shoulder, and Christian turned to pat the huge beast. He did not look at Anne as he spoke. "I don't think so."

She frowned. "I assure you, I'm perfectly recovered

from childbirth. It's been almost a month, and I feel fully able to ride again."

He threw the reins back over the horse's head and prepared to mount. That was answer enough; her company was not welcome. Anne watched him, knowing no other way to confront this situation than directly. After all, only a few days ago he'd been bringing her breakfast in bed. The only thing that had happened between now and then was Newell Franklin's visit.

"If you're still jealous over Newell—"

Christian spun around, his face so incredulous Anne would have laughed. Except it wasn't funny; she read total denial to her words.

"Me—jealous? Over that nincompoop?"

"Yes," Anne said, holding her chin high. She had started this; there was no other choice but to see it through. "What other reason is there for you to be so cold to me? Before his visit yesterday you were kind and solicitous. Since then you've been avoiding me. And now when I've offered my company, you refuse. You wouldn't have done that a couple days ago."

"Don't be so sure," he said over his shoulder, facing his horse again. Once again, he prepared to mount.

She gulped hard before speaking, but kept her voice low and as steady as she could. "Then you must still want me."

Her statement achieved the response she'd sought. He turned to her again, this time the astonishment was joined by curiosity. "What makes you think so?"

"For the very simple reason that you avoided me before because you couldn't control your . . . your . . ."

"Lust?" he supplied.

"Desire," she corrected. "You even went to France because of it."

"I also had business to take care of in France."

She shrugged lightly. "So you killed two birds with one stone—only one bird is still alive. Your leaving did nothing to rid you of wanting me." Then she smiled, and she hoped it appeared as confident and yes, seductive, as she planned.

"Perhaps, my lord, if you would stop running from your desires, you might find them fulfilled."

He raised a brow with interest, but looked highly skeptical. "We've had this discussion before, my lady. The next words out of your mouth will no doubt have something to do with marriage. Is that right?"

Anne gave nothing more than a smile. She would offer neither denial nor admission. Let him think about that, she thought to herself. This time it was Anne who turned away first, she heading back to the manor.

Before Anne had reached the manor steps, she heard his horse's hoofbeats race past. She glanced up, but he didn't look her way. Anne smiled again. He may still be running, she thought, but no one can run forever.

Without intention, Christian ended up at the very riverside in which he'd almost shown Anne exactly how deep his desires went. He realized his mistake too late, for once his gaze fell on the spot they'd lain, his frustration only intensified.

Blast the woman! What was this new game of hers? She knew very well he had no intention of marrying her—he would bloody well die a celibate rather than allow himself to marry such a treacherous woman—yet just now she'd all but offered herself to him in no uncertain terms. Without marriage.

He jumped from the back of his horse, suddenly too restless to remain still for very long. Damn if he didn't want the woman, every bit as much as the first moment he'd seen her. But he'd tried, really tried, to build more out of their relationship than mere lust. If she would have only trusted him, come to him with the truth, been honest, he might have considered marriage, he realized with vague surprise. But now it was back to one thing: lust. He couldn't trust her, couldn't possibly love her, yet he still wanted her. And if she truly was offering herself? Regardless of marriage vows, would he take her up on that offer? He let out a long sigh. He knew very well the answer to that. It was indeed why he'd fled to France. He couldn't resist her, and she knew it.

There was but one honest thing to do. Stay clear of her until Mortimer's London spies acquired Guiscard's testimony, sealing their case against her. Then he'd confront her with it. He smirked. If she still wanted him after that, well, no power in heaven or on earth would keep him from her. But he knew the chances of that. She'd hate him sure enough. If not for revealing her treachery, then certainly for taking their child from her and raising it on his own.

When Christian returned to Highcrest, he scowled to discover the Franklin carriage waiting outside the manor. Considering his resolution to stay clear of Anne—for the simple fact that he thought her good enough for only one thing—why did it rankle him so to think she was with Franklin? Hadn't he told himself again and again that it didn't matter who she tried to shackle? He should feel sorry for the poor fool.

He tried to reach his own chambers without seeing either one of them; however, just as he entered he met them both at the foot of the stairs. No doubt they were on their way to his cozy studio on the second floor.

"Oh, Lord Christian," she said sweetly and oh, so politely. "You're in time to accompany us upstairs." Then she spoke to Newell, who stood at her side, looking uncomfortable. "Lord Christian expressed an interest yesterday in seeing your portrait, Newell. Perhaps he may watch you put the finishing touches to it."

"I really work better without an audience," Newell said stiffly.

There was nothing Christian wanted to do less than watch Newell Franklin fawn over Anne. However, the thought of them alone upstairs did not sit at all well with him. And despite his own better judgment, he fell in step beside them before giving it further thought.

"I assure you, Franklin," Christian said pleasantly, "I won't get in the way."

A few moments later they were in the huge hall-like room. It was a bit warmer than it had been the day before, for Anne had ordered fires in the two hearths, one at each end of the room. Cold sunlight still lit the room, for she

knew better than to have draperies added to the drafty
windows and mar the lighting Newell had admired the room
for months ago.

For the occasion of the sitting, Anne no longer wore
mourning black. Christian had barely noticed the difference
until setting foot into the bright room. She looked, as
always, quite lovely, as she took a formal pose on the raised
dias.

God, but she was beautiful. The gown she wore was
midnight blue with a tiny fringe of white lace along the
bodice and sleeves. But it was the bodice his gaze lingered on,
for it was cut quite low and her breasts looked smooth and
creamy white and, he noticed possessively, far too exposed.
He glanced to Franklin, who studied her as he recorded her
image. How long had he stared at Anne, at her face and her
body, under the guise of painting her portrait? It was enough
to make Christian want to order Newell from the room,
painting be damned.

But when Christian saw the portrait, even he could not
deny its worth. Anne was, of course, a lovely subject, and
that was the reason for the beauty of the portrait. But
Newell's talent was evident, and for a moment Christian
forgot his irrational jealousy.

"What do you think?" he heard Anne ask, and her
voice lured his attention away from the painting. He could
have stared at it far longer if he'd let himself.

"I've always said Newell has talent," he replied
evasively. It wasn't necessary to tell her what he really
thought; she'd start thinking of marriage again.

When he saw her disappointment at his answer, he was
tempted to adjust his statement, add to it that he thought it
was the most beautiful painting—the most beautiful
subject—he'd ever seen. But he would not let himself.

He watched in silence as Newell finished the painting,
adding just a touch of color to the background and to the
detail of Anne's gown. Her hair, golden as ever, was tied up
in a knot at the back of her head, and the fairness of her face
was fully revealed. However, the longer Christian stared at
the painting, the more he saw in it. Newell had captured

more than just her loveliness, Christian realized. Newell saw
what Christian had seen that first day of meeting her; her
eyes were as wide and guileless and innocent. Christian's
heart hardened against such thoughts; they had both been
fooled. Lucky for Christian he'd learned the truth about her.

"It is finished," Newell announced after a short while,
stepping back to inspect his work as if seeing it for the first
time.

Anne came around and looked at the portrait again. As
she did, Christian couldn't help but think that as lovely as the
portrait was, it didn't compare with the beauty of its living
counterpart. But when she glanced up at him he quickly
rejected such thoughts; she was far too adept at reading him
well. Better to banish all such ideas from his mind.

"Well done, Franklin," Christian said briskly, not
looking at Anne any longer. His voice sounded oddly jovial,
even to himself. "Is this one you'll be able to part with, or
will you keep it for yourself?"

Newell looked at Christian a long moment before
answering. "It is a gift for the countess, of course."

"Rumor has it you could use a bit of money, Franklin,"
Christian said coarsely. He had no idea why he was even
bothering with the lad; he was little more than a ninny—a
talented ninny, but a ninny just the same. "Why don't you
let us pay you for it?" Now why had he said "us," as if he
and Anne were partners of a sort?

"Lord Thornton," Newell said coldly, for the first time
looking Christian eye to eye. "A gift is a gift, and I have no
intention of taking payment for my work. Now if you'll
excuse me, I came to finish the portrait. With that done, I'll
be on my way."

Newell strode toward the doorway, but paused long
enough to say over his shoulder, "I'll send someone for the
rest of my paintings, Countess. I'm returning to London
tomorrow."

Christian watched as Anne followed after the young
twit. She would no doubt apologize for Christian's behavior
along with her farewells. In spite of himself, Christian

couldn't deny he was inordinately pleased that Franklin would be out of Sussex in only a matter of hours.

Anne caught up with Newell at the head of the stairs. She caught his arm and spoke earnestly.

"I'm sorry he's so rude to you, Newell," Anne said.

But Newell gently, yet firmly, freed himself from her touch and began walking down the stairs. Anne followed.

"I imagine the two of you have had some very funny conversations about the Franklin financial matters."

"Newell! You can't mean that. Of course I never discussed your finances with Christian."

"Christian," he repeated, mocking the way she'd said his name. "Then how else does he know?"

Anne bowed her head. "Mortimer, our barrister. He knows everything about the visitors who come to Highcrest."

Newell stopped even though they were in the middle of the stairway. Finally, he laughed, not a loud laugh, but an amused one. "I should have known it wouldn't be long before everyone knew. I'm sorry, Anne."

They continued walking, and this time Newell took Anne's hand, placing it on his arm once again.

"I've decided to sell my paintings, Anne," he told her quietly. "And talk to my family about hiring someone to oversee our finances. Between the two, I think we'll be solvent again soon."

"I'm glad, Newell," she said as they headed toward the door.

Newell faced her and took both her hands in his. "I hope to see you in London one day, Anne." He grinned. "I'm sure you're wrong about paling in comparison to the city ladies. I hope you'll give me a chance to prove that."

She nodded. "I'm sure I'll come to London, sooner or later."

He seemed ready to leave, but hesitated. He glanced upstairs, then frowned. "He's probably watching you from somewhere up there—or wanting to."

Anne glanced up, startled. But there was no one to be

seen.

He smiled at her. "See, even you think it's a possibility."

She lowered her lids, embarrassed.

"Anne, I know there is something between the two of you. I think that's why it was so easy for you to resist me—that sounds quite cocksure, I know, but let me at least think that's the reason, otherwise my confidence will be sorely tested now that I'm returning to London."

Anne laughed. "If I'm lucky, Newell, when I come to London, I will be at Christian's side."

Newell kissed her cheek. "Good luck then, my lady."

"Thank you, Newell."

Then he was gone.

Anne made her way back upstairs toward her room where Pel was caring for David. Anne had to feed her son soon, but first she wanted to change her clothes back to black. However, she saw Christian heading toward the stairs from the direction of the studio, and she paused when he caught sight of her.

"Finished your farewells already?" he asked tauntingly.

"Yes," she said. Then she added, feeling especially bold, "You know, it was really unnecessary to be rude to Newell. He would have left, anyway."

"Your vanity astounds me, Countess," Christian said. "Do you think I wanted him out of here just to keep him away from you?"

She nodded, her eyes wide and honest.

He looked as though he might speak, but then thought the better of it and walked past her. Anne watched him retreat, sure that jealousy had indeed been the cause for Christian's behavior.

Anne did not see Christian at all for the rest of the day, despite the fact that she looked for him twice. The following day he was every bit as successful at avoiding her. How was she to stir emotion in him when he continued to avoid her? she wondered.

After supper the following day, a lonely meal in the huge dining room during which Anne vainly hoped Christian would return home to join her, she retrieved David from her room and went to the parlor. She would wait for Christian there.

Time passed slowly, despite her son's cheerful company. He cooed and gurgled and smiled and Anne delighted in him, yet she could not help wondering where Christian kept himself in order to avoid her company. With someone else?

Mistress Lindall brought some chocolate, and Anne welcomed the warming drink. She told the servant she could retire for the evening. It was late already, and she needn't concern herself with clearing away the silver chocolate server and china cup until morning. The servant restoked the fire, then left Anne alone with her child.

David fed hungrily that night. The last feeding of the day had become special to both Anne and her son, for Anne let him nestle at her breast as long as he liked. As she was alone, she didn't bother to cover herself modestly. She enjoyed watching the tiny baby at her breast. It was the most tranquil time of day for Anne, and very often she dozed, as well. Tonight was no different as she held David securely in her arms, and she felt herself drift into a warm, dreamy state.

She had no idea what woke her, whether it was the sudden coolness at her breast or the feeling of David being lifted from her arms. Her eyes fluttered open and she saw Christian holding her son, looking down at the sleeping child with such tenderness Anne felt her heart twist with pleasure.

"Good evening," she said sleepily, still watching Christian.

Christian's gaze went from David to Anne, and in a moment slipped from her face to her exposed breast. Anne watched him a moment as he looked at her, and was slow to cover herself. If she had ever doubted he wanted her, she did not doubt it now. Then, carefully, she replaced her bodice.

"I—I'll carry him upstairs if you're still sleepy," Christian said. His voice sounded tight, strained. Was he struggling against his desire?

Anne stood. She was fully awake now, each and every nerve in her body seemed to be alive and alert, awaiting his touch. But she did not want to take David from his secure arms; she felt so atwitter she feared her trembling hands would wake her son, or even drop him.

"Thank you," Anne said at last, then led the way toward her room.

Christian settled David in his cradle without disturbing him. When Christian straightened, he faced Anne again, who was standing not far from him at the foot of her bed. The room was dimly lit by the fireplace and one lamp beside the bed. Even so, Anne could see his face clearly. He looked as nervous as she felt, she realized with surprise.

"He'll sleep through the night, I think," she said. "He has every night this week, and he fed well tonight."

Her voice seemed to compound the strain Christian was under. He didn't move, although he did look once from her toward the door, as if telling himself he should leave.

"You should sleep well, too," Christian said after a moment.

Christian moved stiffly toward the door. With each step taking him farther from her, Anne felt her heart sink deeper and deeper. When he reached the door, she spoke breathlessly.

"Christian." Her voice was barely a whisper. "Don't go."

He stopped, but did not face her immediately. His hand was on the doorknob, and the door was still open. When he looked at her he tried to smile but she could tell any levity was forced. He felt as serious as she did.

"It's a bit late for teatime, Anne."

She took three steps near him, bringing her so close she had merely to reach out to put her arms around him. But she did not do so—not yet.

"I don't want tea," she told him.

"Anne . . ."

It was hardly a protest. When he said her name, it felt like a caress. She wasn't sure who reached for who first, but in a moment they were in each other's arms, her body pressed close to his, his lips coming down on hers.

Anne felt dizzy. Perhaps it was the darkness or that manly smell of leather. Something was achingly familiar in this kiss, the kiss itself, the smell of him, the way his hands felt on her. But she did not dwell on it. Her senses reeled, her knees felt weak. If Christian hadn't been holding her so tight she was sure she would have sunk to the floor.

His lips felt warm on hers, and in a moment when his tongue sought entrance, she reveled in the feel of him. She'd dreamed of this so often, too often, and now the reality of it was even more enticing than any dream. His arms felt strong about her, his lips firm and demanding, and the desire between them inevitably erupted.

"You want me," she whispered when his kiss traveled from her mouth to her cheeks, ears, throat. It was a heady discovery, even if she had known of it all along. Somehow the reality of it was far more than she'd expected. Her voice was breathlessly happy. "You do want me."

"You couldn't have doubted that," he said into her ear.

When his hand came to her breast, loosening her bodice, she knew a moment's caution. "Wait," she said. "Not here. The baby."

Instead of being impatient, as Anne had feared, Christian glanced over to the cradle. "Will you hear him from my room if he cries?"

She nodded, her eyes sparkling with desire. "I—I think so."

Leaving the door open behind him, he swept her up into his arms and carried her to his room down the hall. Once there, he gently deposited her on his bed. Before joining her he kicked off his shoes, removed his coat, cravat and waistcoat, then laid at her side.

Waites had obviously been expecting his master, for the room was brightly lit. Christian didn't bother to extinguish any lights; he'd waited far too long to bed her in full light.

Anne was as eager as Christian. When he lay beside her she turned to him and slid against his long length. His mouth was on hers in a moment, his tongue teasing hers. His hands, too, went to work, freeing her laces and removing her garments. Anne was almost as bold as she unbuttoned his shirt and ran her hands over the softly curled hair covering his muscled chest. But he did not remove his shirt, and she did not ask him. Instead, he loosened his breeches and discarded the rest of his clothing.

Christian's kiss skimmed her throat and chest, only briefly touching the peaks of her breasts. Anne did not protest when his kiss didn't linger; even now when her breasts should have been empty, they seeped milk in readiness for feeding. Christian tasted her but, uncertain she was willing to share that part of her which seemed to belong more to her son, his kiss traveled onward, back to her throat, along her jawline, at her ear.

His fingers were more bold. He found that most sensitive part of her and Anne writhed under his touch. She was ready for him immediately, wet and warm and certainly willing. But still Christian held back, drawing out their passion, letting it build slowly. His fingers worked their gentle magic, until she thought she could stand it no longer.

"I—want you, the rest of you," she whispered breathlessly.

He kissed her mouth, and his touch stilled. Then, slowly, he shifted himself above her. But he held back, keeping himself from her.

"I am healed," she whispered, knowing he hesitated only out of concern.

His gaze found hers, and he smiled. Then, still tentative, still watching her for any sign of discomfort, holding his weight on his elbows, he eased himself inside . . . gently.

Too gently, Anne discovered. She was touched by his care, but quickly became frustrated by it. She wanted more.

"Christian," she said, low, into his ear. "It doesn't hurt. Don't worry so."

He looked at her and gave her a smile. "The pain of childbirth doesn't seem that long ago. I watched you, you know."

"I can't remember any pain," she told him, then flashed him a grin and thrust her hips upward. He hadn't been expecting the move, and was deep inside her before even attempting to retreat. "You see? No pain . . . but there is need. Growing more demanding."

She moved again, tightening herself around him, enveloping him, demanding more and proving he would not hurt her. Gradually he followed the increasing rhythm she set beneath him. Anne kissed Christian, wanting him to forget the caution, to forget to hold back and enjoy this as much as she was. And before long his kiss deepened and she sensed the passion growing in him as surely as it grew in her. She felt herself spiraling without weight, without limit to her physical being. She watched Christian and he watched her, and their joining seemed to be as much spiritual as physical, as the passion mounted and mounted. Then, at the very last moment before all senses were consumed, he kissed her, following her over the edge.

Neither moved for what seemed like an eternity. Anne's eyes were closed, reveling in the feeling of Christian still within her.

"Are you . . . did it hurt at all?"

Anne wanted to laugh, but couldn't. She hadn't entirely regained her breath yet. She moved her head to kiss him.

"If you give me a few minutes to breathe, I'll prove to you that it didn't hurt by starting all over again."

Christian did laugh, although it was a short one as he rolled off of her. She realized he still wore his shirt, their passion had demanded fulfillment so quickly.

"Maybe this time we can take time to disrobe." She picked up the sleeve of his shirt and his arm came with it as though without muscle. She laughed at his exhaustion.

"You'll have to give me more than breathing time," he said after a moment, and they laughed.

Just then Anne heard the faint cries of David. She sat up immediately, her maternal instincts lending her renewed energy. But she frowned when she looked at Christian, for she didn't want to leave him.

Christian smiled. "Why don't you bring him back here?" he suggested.

Anne's brows raised. "You—you don't mind?"

He shook his head, but added with a leering smile, "I trust he won't be staying long?"

She was out of bed in an instant. "Only long enough to feed him." Then she stopped as she was about to turn around. "I'll have to get dressed again."

But Christian, too, sat up, taking off his shirt. "Here," he said, "wear this. It's indecent, I suppose, but I've had more than a few indecent visions of you, so you shouldn't be shy."

She laughed as she slipped into it. It was huge on her, reaching her knees, with the sleeves extending to her fingertips. But it was just enough covering to let her steal from the room to retrieve David.

David's cries ceased immediately once Anne picked him up. He was still half asleep and so, hoping she could get him back to sleep without taking him to bed with her, she rocked him and spoke gently to him. In a few moments he was sound asleep.

Anne returned to Christian's room. It was still brightly lit and she was glad for it; she wanted no similarities to her other lover, her first lover. Christian lay on his back upon the bed, his arm over his eyes. He was totally naked and obviously unself-conscious, for he hadn't bothered to cover himself while she'd been gone.

She nestled beside him, and he automatically put his arms around her. Then he opened his eyes, surprised to find her alone.

"Where's David?"

"Sleeping."

Christian's brows lifted, but whether the gesture was more from surprise or pleasure that they would still be alone, she couldn't guess.

He shifted above her, although he kept most of his weight from her.

"Are we going to make love with you wearing the shirt this time?" he asked.

She grinned but didn't move. She was enjoying the position too much, for his entire length was pressed close to her. "It appears so, my lord."

Her hands luxuriated in the feel of his taut skin over his

muscled back. He felt strong, she thought. His back was hard and smooth, widening to meet his broad shoulders. On his shoulders her hands rested and then, at first almost without realizing what she felt, her touch lingered on a scar. It was large for a scar, indicating a wound that had once been serious. And it was crescent-shaped.

"I didn't know you had a scar here," she said musingly.

Then, suddenly, she pulled her fingers away as if they'd been burned. She stiffened. The scar. The crescent-shaped scar. The one part of the stranger, on his right shoulder in the exact same spot, that she would always remember. The only part of him she knew, the only thing which distinguished her secret lover from every other man. It couldn't be!

If she knew a moment's doubt, it was eliminated by Christian's face. He was watching her as if he knew each thought, as if he fully expected her to come to the only conclusion possible. He *knew* her thoughts, he *knew!* And there was only one way he could.

Anne stiffened but still did not move. Her hands fell to her sides and she lay prone, like a victim, and stared up at the ceiling.

Christian pulled away, sitting beside her on the bed. Suddenly he was no longer the smiling, affectionate lover. He looked at her coldly and, when he spoke, his voice held no tenderness.

"I'm surprised it took you so long—or does every lover feel the same inside?"

That made her stare at him, and for a moment she felt tears sting her eyes. But she would be damned before she'd shed a tear in front of him.

She sat up, still clutching the shirt about herself for modesty's sake. Then she stood and picked up her clothes which lay strewn about the floor.

Christian did not move, watching her.

"As always, you play the part of the wounded innocent to perfection," he sneered.

She stopped, holding her clothes in front of her. She knew the shirt had become askew and her heaving breasts were revealed but she didn't care. She knew only hatred at that moment.

"You should know about deception, my lord. You've known, all this time you've known. You practiced as much deception as I."

He shrugged as if it hardly bothered him. "What I did, I did of necessity."

She glared at him. "Necessity. You don't know the first thing about it."

Then she turned, still barefoot, and left the room.

27

Anne found her way back to her room, tears blinding her eyes every step of the way. Once inside she slammed the door behind her, not thinking until afterward that the noise could have awakened the baby. She threw her clothes on the floor and then, as if newly realizing it was *his* shirt she wore, she pulled it viciously from her body, tearing a seam or two.

She felt the tears coursing down her face, but she didn't care. At that moment, standing there entirely naked, staring at the heap of clothing on the floor, she wasn't sure what she felt more deeply: pain or anger.

At last she brushed away her tears and found the lawn nightgown Pel had left out for her to wear. She yanked it over her head but didn't bother to button the two tiny, satin-covered buttons at the throat.

She would not cry another tear, she commanded herself. But when she thought of Christian's deceit, she almost broke down. He'd known all along! Obviously her father had no idea that Christian had somehow fathomed their plan and had taken the place of the man Jarvis had hired.

Anne paced back and forth, her fists clenching and unclenching, kicking the discarded clothing out of her way. Why had he done it? Why hadn't he just confronted them with the knowledge of the plan? Why had he gone through with taking the stranger's place?

The answer was too painful to tolerate. Obviously Christian's objective was to make their plan work for himself instead of profiting Anne and her father. What better way than to claim the bastard as his own?

One low wimper from the cradle sent Anne to David's side. He was sound asleep, but Anne continued to look at him—her son, and Christian's.

It would have been wonderful news if it didn't mean so much. It meant Christian thought her as deceitful as her father; that fact she didn't mind quite so much as the other fact this revealed. That Christian, too, had wanted the money more than anything. Enough to be as deceitful as Jarvis, in a way. Everything for the money. It was enough to make Anne vow never to touch another farthing.

Anne slumped into the chair nearest the cradle and continued watching her son, as if seeing him for the first time. In a way it was as if he had a new identity. He was no longer hers now. He was hers—but he was also Christian's.

Panic assailed her with further thought. What did it mean if Christian intended to recognize the child as his own? It was clear he had never had any intention to marry Anne, and now she knew why. But he wanted her son. A tiny sob escaped her lips. Did that mean he would try to take him from her?

Having such a suspicion and not knowing the answer was too much for Anne to bear. She stood and started back to Christian's room. She would have this out with him, and do it now.

At his door she paused for the briefest moment. Perhaps she should wait until morning, when they could discuss it in the light of day, fully dressed in the parlor or some other less intimate place than his bedroom. After what had just gone on in there, she was hesitant to even enter. But she did not give in to such weakness. Her child was at stake.

She did not knock, in fact gave no warning whatsoever. She burst into the room with such force that the door banged against the wall behind.

But the dramatics were wasted, for the room was surprisingly empty. Where could he have gone at this hour?

Without returning to her own room, Anne made her

way downstairs. She had an idea where to find him.

Sure enough, there was a narrow shaft of light escaping the crack at the solicitor's salon door. This time, Anne was not so hasty in her entrance; she would present a more collected facade, even if she did feel her very world collapsing.

She opened the door and stepped inside, closing it firmly behind her. Christian was seated behind the desk, his feet propped up on the edge of the mahogany furniture, a bottle of wine in one hand, a glass in the other. Although minus a coat and cravat, he was fully dressed, having the advantage over Anne's nightwear. He seemed totally unsurprised to see her, almost as if he'd expected her.

"Only one glass," he said without a trace of apology, holding it up for her to see. He didn't bother to stand when she neared, but merely tilted the glass to his lips and took a long drink.

"I don't care for any," she told him. "I came to discuss your plans."

Leisurely, he pulled his feet from the desk and sat up straight, setting aside the bottle and glass. All the while his face was a mask, a cold unreadable blank.

"My plans should be obvious to one of your cleverness, Anne," he said, adding, "I intend to protect my interests."

"It's David I wish to discuss, not the bloody money."

Suddenly he laughed. "You don't want to talk about the money? When that's what started all of this? Without that, David wouldn't even be here."

She ignored his words. "What do you think you're going to do with him?"

He laughed again, this time eyeing her cruelly. "I don't 'think' anything, Anne. What I intend to do—what I *will* do—is raise him as my own. Since, after all, he is mine."

"And mine," she told him.

He shrugged. "You gave birth to him, of course, but I'm sure the courts will see he will be much better off with his father. Even if they don't, the Thornton money will go a long way to convince anyone who needs convincing."

Anne stared at him, realizing she had never really known him until this moment. He spoke of money and manipulation as if it were all second nature to him, something she never would have guessed he knew the first thing about.

Something in the way she stared at him must have touched him, for he poured himself another glass of wine and for a moment almost looked uncomfortable under her close scrutiny. Then he said briskly, "Don't think I'm the treacherous one in the room, Anne. This was all your own doing."

That made her laugh. "You don't know anything about my reasons for doing what I did."

"It wouldn't matter in any case," he told her, once more perfectly at ease. "You bore a child to inherit the Thornton dynasty. And inherit he will. The only difference is that you won't have access to the fortune. So your plan wasn't a total failure, after all."

She stood and stared down at him. "You won't take him from me. My home is right here under the same roof, no matter if you think you have total control over David or not."

"After trying to steal my inheritance—yes, *steal*," he repeated for emphasis, "you'll be lucky if Newgate isn't your new home."

She glared at him. "You wouldn't dare have me imprisoned."

"Wouldn't I? Or would you just prefer banishment from Highcrest?"

Anger clouded her vision. "None of this will work. You can't have me thrown in prison and you won't have David taken from me."

Still, Christian did not rise from his comfortable seat. He gave her a crooked smile and said, "Your loyalty to him is touching if a bit overdone, Anne. Do you really think I will believe you love him more than you love money? Granted, you've been an attentive mother. But I won't forget why you conceived him in the first place: for the money."

She would have turned away but something kept her rooted in place. She hated him in that moment, how she hated him. "Isn't that why you did it, too, then? To 'protect your interests?' "

He only shrugged.

"Then why do you suppose the House will see it your way to take David from me? If we both acted out of greed, then why should they give him to you rather than me?"

"I already told you, Anne. Whoever needs convincing will be convinced; the great House of Lords is not without its weaknesses."

"You won't succeed," she told him. Then, before any more threats could be exchanged, she left the room.

Her heart was beating every bit as hard once she made it back to her own room. David was still sleeping, thank goodness. She needed all her concentration to work out a plan.

But it was nearly impossible to think about anything except Christian. Was he the same man, this cold, heartless person who threatened to wrench her from her son? The same man she'd loved, the same man she'd held in her arms such a short time ago? It was incredible.

She knew she could not dwell on that, however. She did not love him—could not—for he wasn't the sort of person she'd believed him to be.

There was, of course, only one thing to do. She could not stay here to let Christian take David from her. Nor, for that matter, did she particularly relish being around when her father found out his triumphant plan was an utter failure. She had to flee; it was her only choice.

It would be harder to leave this time, she knew. Not only would Jarvis be after her, but Christian as well—and she had no doubt just how relentless Christian could be. She could not go to the convent, as she'd planned to go before; it would be the first place Jarvis would look, and she wanted to stay just as clear of him as she did of Christian. Perhaps she could find her way to the continent, to a city somewhere. She could get some sort of employment at an inn or even be a barmaid; she didn't care. She would be desperate for work to support herself, her mother, and David.

Her heart sank as she looked at the sleeping child. He

was bundled in soft, rich cloth, and his head rested against the purest silk. What would she be able to give him, except a life of poverty?

But she refused to dwell on that. She simply could not be parted from him. Surely a mother's love was worth silky linens and lace swaddling clothes.

Her escape must be swift, for undoubtedly it wouldn't take Christian long to realize she won't sit meekly back and wait for him to take her child away.

Yes, she decided, a city is the answer. But why go to the continent? She could go to London. It was, after all, much closer to all she knew.

London! Immediately Newell Franklin came to mind. Would he help her get to London? It would mean asking for assistance, possibly revealing all her problems, including her mother's illness, but it was something that must be done. With Newell's help perhaps she could get all the way to London and have neither Jarvis nor Christian suspect her whereabouts.

She must act quickly; there were only a few hours until dawn, and she had to get word to Newell not to leave without her. Escaping Highcrest with her mother and David in tow would be the most difficult, she realized. For that she would need Pel's help, and perhaps Gregory's, as well.

The gate lodge where Gregory lived was a few minutes' walk from the manor house, a few minutes more when coming from the back of the house as Anne did. She stole outside from the kitchen entrance, treading silently in the darkness. Once at the gate house, however, Anne pounded as if her very life were in danger. And, indeed, it was.

Gregory pulled open the door as he shrugged into a knee-length sleeping gown. He was wearing breeches, Anne was relieved to see, but it was obvious that she had awakened him from a deep sleep.

"My lady!" Gregory was plainly astonished to see her.

"I need to speak to you, Gregory, and to Pel, as well. Will you get her?"

"Of course," he said, then stumbled through the small parlor to the bedroom at the back of the four room cottage.

Pel was every bit as groggy as her husband as she followed him to the parlor, still tightening a wrapper around herself. Her feet were bare despite the cold, but once she caught sight of Anne's disheveled appearance, she came to her side in concern.

Anne had hurriedly donned a wrapper, slippers and an overcoat before rushing out the back of the manor house. She supposed she should have dressed fully, but at the moment her attire had seemed too trivial to waste time with. Her appearance, however, immediately alerted Pel.

"What is it? Is it David?"

Anne shook her head, but the gravity did not leave her face; Gregory started rekindling a fire in the hearth nearby as Anne spoke.

"I need your help—both of you, actually. I need to get to London. Quickly and secretly."

"What!" Pel was shocked. Even Gregory, who was a mild-mannered, quiet man, stopped what he was doing and looked at Anne as though she were mad.

"Gregory," Anne said, looking at him, "I need you to find Newell Franklin. He's at the inn at Wynchly. You must tell him I need to accompany him to London—but you must do so immediately, and without anyone overhearing. Tell Newell this is to be a secret, that my very life depends on it."

"Anne!" Pel gasped. "You'd better tell me what's going on."

"I can't tell you everything now, Pel. I've told you too much as it is. Knowing where I'll be might prove dangerous for you."

"Dangerous?" she repeated.

"Well," Anne said, "I don't think Christian would actually hurt anyone—other than me, of course."

"His lordship?" Pel asked in disbelief.

"Oh, Pel, he wants to take David from me!"

Anne was nearly sobbing already, and Pel took her immediately into a sisterly embrace, hushing her. "Nobody's going to take that little tiger from you, Anne. Why ever would his lordship want to, anyway? He's so fond of you, and of David, too."

"David is his son!"

Pel, receiving one shock after another, handled this one with the same flabbergasted expression, putting Anne at arm's length to look at her.

"He's the one?" Pel asked. "But how? How did he—"

Anne shook her head, uncertain. "He must have found out what my father had in mind and taken the stranger's place. 'To protect his interests,' he said." She laughed bitterly. "He could have at least said it was lust, even that would have been better."

Pel hugged her again and patted her head as if she were as young and helpless as David. For a moment it felt good to share her fear and grief. But then she sat straight, knowing that to give in to such emotion was to lose the battle entirely.

"He intends to raise David as his own, as the heir to Highcrest. And banish me at best, imprison me at worst. I'm sure he's hoping for the latter. That's why I must get to London—before he has Mortimer plead the case in the House of Lords. Who knows what they'll decide. Christian may very well succeed in having me imprisoned for trying to swindle him. If I can get to London, I can hide there, I'm sure of it. Newell will take me there without asking a thing—I think."

"From what I've seen of him around you, Anne, he'll be more than willing to let you stay with him. He'd protect you from all of this if you'd let him."

Anne shook her head. "He can't protect me from the House of Lords," she said grimly. "And Christian will look for me there, I'm sure. I must make it on my own."

Gregory, who by then had finished stoking the fire and was silently listening, spoke up at last. "I have a brother in London," he said quietly. "He'll take you in."

Pel gave a whoop of happiness and went to her husband, hugging him close. "There, Anne! You've a place to go already."

But Anne was not quite so eager to take advantage of Gregory's kindness. "I really couldn't, Gregory. I'll have my mother with me, and, of course, David."

"Oh, you'd rather sleep in the street with all of them?" Pel asked mockingly.

"Of course not. But taking in three people is a lot to ask of anyone."

"He's got a tavern, my lady," Gregory said. "Nothing fancy, of course, but he'll be willing to take you in if you agree to work for him maybe. Although I can't see a countess working at—"

Anne's brows lifted in interest. Now here was a definite possibility. "Tell me your brother's name and where his tavern is, and I'll check into it once I get to London."

Gregory did so, and Anne committed it to memory. It very well may be the way to gaining her freedom from her father, keeping David to love and raise, and escaping Christian's wrath.

A few minutes later Gregory left, speeding off to the inn where Newell was staying. Anne returned to the manor with Pel at her side; they would have to pack a few belongings and then do the same for Elsbeth.

When Gregory returned from Wynchly, he found Pel and Anne waiting for him at the gate lodge. It was still an hour or more before dawn.

"He's mystified, my lady," Gregory announced as he shut the door behind him. "But he'll do it. 'Anything for Anne,' he said, those were his exact words."

"When is he leaving?"

"He said if it's such a secret that you should meet him outside the village, where the road forks between Highcrest and London. As early as possible. He said he'd be waiting there for you by eight in the morning."

"Eight," she said, considering it. "The sun will be high in the sky by then."

"He didn't think you'd be able to make it any sooner than that."

"He's probably right. It's near five already, and that fork is almost an hour from here."

"How are you going to leave Highcrest without his lordship spotting you?"

Gregory spoke up. "Leave that to me," he said.

Both women eyed him in surprise; Gregory was always so quiet and withdrawn, it was a shock to have him so involved.

Anne and Pel walked back to the manor once again, still being careful to use the kitchen entrance. Anne had dressed in a gray gown of sensible cloth. She'd packed her most somber clothing, not all black, but whatever plain clothing she could find. She would no longer be a countess once she left Highcrest.

They had packed for her mother without even disturbing Elsbeth's sleep. The bags were hidden in Anne's room, beneath her bed.

As they made their way upstairs, Anne's mind went over everything. She would take the time she had now to feed David and then retrieve her mother. They would have to ride by horse to the fork in the road, with David in Anne's arms. She couldn't risk taking a Thornton carriage; it required too much help. Anne could handle a couple horses herself.

Just as they made their way up the stairs, Anne heard David's cries. Her pace increased automatically, and the familiar rush came to her breasts. When she opened her door, however, she stopped suddenly as she caught sight of Christian bending over the cradle. The sight sent a fearful wave of anxiety washing over her. Seeing him there, about to pick up their son, was too close to her greatest fear. Was he taking him away already?

But when he saw her, he stood, leaving David in the cradle.

Anne glanced at Pel for a moment before stepping closer to David. Thank goodness Pel was adept at hiding her thoughts. Her loyal friend looked a bit cold, but nothing too out of the ordinary to give Christian warning.

Anne took David in her arms, going to the nearest chair to prepare herself for feeding him.

"Thank you for coming to his cry, my lord," she said coldly. "But I assure you, all he needs is me."

Christian ignored the double meaning to her words. He was in no hurry to leave, eyeing her suspiciously. "You're up uncommonly early. I take it you didn't sleep well?"

She glared at him, but continued to unlace her bodice nonetheless. She didn't care if he watched; it hardly mattered anymore. A moment later David was suckling contentedly.

Christian remained standing in front of her. "Mortimer will be visiting your father to inform him of the charges being levied against the two of you. In the meantime, Anne, I suggest you stick close to Highcrest."

"It sounds more like a warning than a suggestion, my lord," she said, her voice as cold as ever.

"Take it as you wish. Just remember, if it's a prison I need to keep you here, then consider Highcrest your prison. I'm sure it's more accommodating than Newgate."

With that he left the room, passing Pel as if he didn't even see her.

Once he was gone, Pel neared Anne and patted her shoulder, seeing a frown wrinkling her friend's brow. "Don't worry, Anne, you'll be out of here before he even knows you're gone."

Anne nodded, knowing she must cling to that hope. Perhaps she would indeed succeed if she could get through the day.

Pel sat on the edge of the bed, watching Anne.

"I've been thinking," she said slowly. "I just can't stay here at Highcrest and work for a man who would do such a thing to you."

Anne gazed at her son and spoke. "It's not really that beastly of him, I suppose."

"What!"

Anne looked at Pel. She should be surprised at herself, she realized, but she wasn't. She had loved Christian, truly loved him. If she thought there was any hope, she would still love him.

"I've been doing some thinking myself, Pel," Anne said at length. "If it's true that he went through with this plan just to keep control over the money, then I admit I never really knew him. But part of his anger at me I can understand. He thinks I'm treacherous; he thinks I'm not good enough to be the mother of his child. To be honest, if I didn't know all the facts about this myself, I would agree with him.''

Pel smiled crookedly. ''It sounds as though you're defending him, and that amazes me.'' Then she said, ''You could tell him why you did it. He might understand. At least it would keep him from trying to take David from you. If he believed you, he could still have your father put away, and all your troubles would be solved.''

She shrugged. ''Christian said last night my reasons wouldn't matter; maybe they wouldn't. In any case, I doubt he'd believe me. I don't know what to think anymore. But it wouldn't matter to me, anyway.'' She frowned deeply. ''I know it sounded like I was just defending him, and maybe the part of me that loved him wants to. But I know his part in this is as ignoble as Jarvis's, if he bedded me simply to keep his hands on the fortune. I could never excuse him for that—and I'm only using the very same standard he's using against me. Neither one of us believe the other is a fitting parent.''

''Nonetheless,'' Pel said brusquely, switching back to the subject she'd started, ''I won't want to stay here at Highcrest while worrying about you off in London. And I haven't spoken to Gregory yet, but I'm sure he won't want to work for Lord Thornton after this. We could come to London with you—''

Anne gazed at Pel, her eyes wide with interest and happiness. But then she frowned and before she could speak against the idea, Pel anticipated the reason for her protest.

''We wouldn't come right away, of course,'' Pel assured her. ''We wouldn't want to draw attention to you and lead either his lordship or your father straight to your doorway. But soon, Anne, I'm sure it wouldn't be dangerous.''

Anne smiled, feeling tears of gratitude swimming to her eyes. ''I would welcome you there, Pel. To be honest, I'm scared to death.''

''Now, now,'' Pel said soothingly. ''If Gregory's brother is anything at all like Gregory, you've nothing to worry about. He'll be a fine friend for you until we get there.''

All too soon, it was time to be on their way. Pel went downstairs first as if on an errand, and returned minutes later with a frown.

"His lordship is in the parlor."

Anne frowned as well. "With the front door and the kitchen entrance within sight. We can't act with him just waiting for us to bolt."

"Well, don't worry yet," Pel said hopefully. "Lord Franklin will wait, I'm sure, and before long Gregory will show up to divert his lordship's attention."

It seemed an eternity. Anne visited her mother, told her they would be taking a trip together to London and not to worry because they would all be together. Then she returned to her room. Anne didn't bother to tell Marta, Elsbeth's maid, fearing the servant might announce their trip before Anne was ready to have the news revealed. She doubted the servant would miss the few belongings Anne had taken and so for the time being they were safe.

Pel went at regular intervals to the top of the stairs; she didn't venture below, knowing too many trips would create suspicion. But she listened intently, catching sight of Christian as he made his way from the parlor to the solicitor's salon. He left the door open, however, no doubt to spot any passersby.

On her fourth such visit, Pel heard a commotion below, and she lingered furtively to hear what it was about. Pel recognized the man who entered, demanding Waites take him to Christian; he was a friend of Gregory's who worked in the Highcrest groves about a league to the north of the manor house.

Keeping out of sight, Pel listened. She heard Christian demand what the trouble was.

"A fire in the north grove, my lord. With the wind hitting the way it is, it may set off the entire row of tenants living nearby."

She heard an array of expletives from Christian as he

followed the earnest servant away, leaving Highcrest
blissfully free of his hawklike presence. Pel was back at
Anne's side in a moment.

"Gregory got him out of here in the best of wild goose
chases," Pel said with a smile, explaining what she'd heard.
"It'll take him a good hour to get back and forth from the
north grove."

Anne's brow puckered. "You don't suppose there really
is a fire, do you?"

"Of course not," Pel said, then eyed Anne closely.
"And if there is, so what? None of this is yours to worry
about any more."

Anne nodded in agreement, though her frown did not
disappear altogether. A moment later Anne retrieved her
baggage from beneath the bed.

"Here, give those to me," Pel said. Then she took one
of the linens off the bed. "It'll look like laundry to anyone
who happens to see me," she said as she bundled the sacks
inside the huge sheet. "I'll meet you by the gate, Anne. Go
get your mother, and I'll see you in a few minutes."

Anne nodded, grateful to have someone else helping her
to think; she was so concerned over escaping she feared she
might be getting careless.

With David in her arms and Elsbeth at her side, Anne
made her way downstairs. No sign of movement below, for
which she was grateful. Nonetheless, she walked as quietly as
she could, praying all the while David kept silent.

But at the foot of the stairs, David let out a squeal. It
was almost a laugh, a delightful little sound that would have
made Anne smile at any other time. Instead, she held him
tightly against her and hurried their pace.

Just as she was about to open the door, Waites's voice
reached her from behind.

"My lady," he called. "Is there something you need?"

Anne turned to the servant slowly, forcing an easy smile
to her lips.

"Of course not, Waites. You have enough duties with
his lordship without worrying about my needs as well. I was
just going to take the baby out for some fresh air. I thought

my mother could use some, as well. It's been quite some time since she was out, you know." She knew she was rambling, but didn't seem able to stop herself. "This will be the first time little David will get some outside air."

"It's a bit chilly," Waites said slowly. "Even with the sun shining."

"I think it's very important for him to have some fresh air," she said firmly. "And we won't be gone long."

"Then I'll accompany you."

"Waites," Anne said slowly, "is there some reason for this sudden attentiveness?"

Waites looked momentarily abashed. "His lordship did ask me to keep my eye on you, my lady."

"And did he give you any reason for that extraordinary order?"

"No, he did not."

Anne smiled, feeling a victory already. "He really is a silly man. A little like you, I'm afraid, being so concerned about taking David outside for a little walk. He thinks the winter air will be bad for us all, when in fact my own mother used to take me out frequently when I was a child. The air is the most healthy in the winter, didn't you know?"

"No, actually I didn't—"

"And you'll agree it's been quite some time since my mother has been out. She needs the exercise."

"Surely it's all right if I accompany you, then?"

Anne shook her head slowly, apologetically. She glanced at Elsbeth, who stood clinging to Anne's arm, standing in her daughter's shadow. "You know better than his lordship that my mother doesn't welcome unfamiliar company, most especially male. Really, between you and his lordship it's like living with a pair of mother hens, worrying about nothing at all." She turned toward the door and smiled once more toward Waites. "Give us ten minutes, Waites. If you're still worried by then, you'll find us in the garden and can join us there."

With that, she left the house, closing the door firmly behind her. That was easy enough. In ten minutes' time Waites might very well look for her in the garden. Finding her gone, he'd no doubt find it odd and maybe even send for Christian immediately, rather than waiting for him to return. But by then, going all the way back and forth from the north grove, Anne would be long gone.

It was almost too easy.

28

There had indeed been a fire in the north grove, but by the time Christian arrived it had been entirely extinguished. They'd lost four trees—nominal damage, although Christian did concede it could have turned into a disaster had the wind blown any harder toward the nearby tenant houses. The fire had obviously been caused by human negligence, for the groves during winter were always empty. There had been reports of children playing in the area; perhaps they had started a fire to keep warm and the dry, wintering trees caught ablaze easily.

Christian made his way back to the manor house at a slower pace than the one used on the way out. He was alone. The servant who had summoned him stayed behind to clean up the mess left by the small fire. His presence, Christian realized once he'd gotten there, was hardly necessary. There'd been so many men there already, that Christian wouldn't have been much help, anyway.

Christian did not dwell on the near crisis; instead, his thoughts went back to Anne. Anne who had filled his mind for months now, and who for the last few hours had been almost like an obsession to him.

He'd treated her cruelly, he knew. Anne may indeed be as treacherous as he thought—and he had no reason to believe otherwise—but she was also a loving mother. Threatening to take David from her had made him feel like nothing short of a rat.

Still, he thought stubbornly, David was *his* son as well as hers. True, Anne thought Christian himself as treacherous as he believed of her. But he knew the truth; it had been a mistake to give in to his desire for her on those two nights they'd come together. He hadn't intended to go through with it at all. So his crime, at least, had not been premeditated. He'd acted out of desire, pure and simple. How many babes came into this world outside the union of matrimony because of lust? That was forgiveable. What Anne had done was not.

Mortimer would probably be at Jarvis's by now. Remembering Mortimer's delayed reaction to the news of being told Anne was a swindler, Christian smiled even now. The old barrister had returned the day after being told about Anne's lies; he'd wanted to confront Anne with the case, ask her why she had gone through with it. Mortimer was convinced she was somehow innocent. Innocent! But Christian knew better.

Perhaps it was Mortimer's stubborn refusal to believe ill of Anne, but for a moment Christian had considered what Mortimer had asked. Give Anne a chance to explain herself, if she could. Even this morning, as he recalled the night before—not just the lovemaking, but the pain he'd seen in her eyes when she found out he was David's father—he had wanted to know if there was any possible redemption for her. But she had said nothing. Oh, she'd inferred there was some reason for doing what she'd done, but she hadn't revealed it. Obviously the reason was money, and that was hardly a saving grace.

Yet he could not cast from his mind the look of wounded innocence upon her face. Hadn't he been fooled by it before? Even Newell Franklin's portrait had shown a look of innocence, a look that was a lie.

Was it all a lie, he wondered? Everything? Why had she let him bed her last night? Why, indeed, the coquettish behavior of the past few days? Surely now that she had the Thornton fortune through David she had no use for Christian himself. That part made no sense to him.

Nor did the tightening in his loins make sense to him, as he recalled each and every kiss from last night. He actually still desired her, after all this.

At last he reached the manor house and turned his horse over to one of the grooms. As he made his way inside the house, his thoughts were jumbled. He knew his desire for Anne was a weakness he must overcome, if he was to go through with his case against her.

Once inside, he went upstairs immediately. It was early still, the time of day David usually had a bath. He would just look in on them and—blast if he didn't want to talk to Anne. Ask her forthright why she'd done it, if indeed it had all been for the money.

The first thing he noticed was that her door was ajar and no noise came from within. She and David were obviously elsewhere, and for the moment his heart picked up pace.

"Waites!" he yelled as he stepped back out to the hall and headed toward Elsbeth's wing of the house. He knew Waites would have a hard time finding him if he continued toward Elsbeth's room, but Christian couldn't wait.

Elsbeth's room was as empty as Anne's, although when Christian burst into the room a servant did scurry in from an adjoining chamber.

"Where is Mistress Melbourne?" Christian demanded.

The servant looked almost terrified, but Christian didn't try to hide the fury upon his face which was obviously frightening the young servant.

"I—I don't know, my lord. When I came in to wake her this morning, she was already gone."

Christian swore, then left the room.

"Waites!" he called again, this time more savagely. When Christian reached the stairs, the harried servant was coming from Christian's room, obviously in search of Christian from his previous call.

"Yes, my lord?" he asked worriedly.

"I told you to watch the countess. Where is she?"

"She—she is gone, my lord." His eyes did not meet his master's.

Christian stood perfectly still at the top of the stairs, waiting for the manservant to reach him.

"Gone?" he said with false calm.

"I—I sent someone to fetch you but, you must have crossed paths. Her ladyship told me she was going out to the garden—"

"In the dead of winter?" Christian's voice was still deceptively friendly. "And you didn't think that odd?"

"I—I wanted to accompany her, but she was with her mother, and Mistress Melbourne does not welcome my company—any company, it seems, except that of her ladyship. Her ladyship said the winter air would be good for all three of them—the Countess, her mother, and the child. I didn't realize until nearly a half-hour later that they'd left entirely. On horseback."

For a moment Christian eyed Waites with a menacing look of pure wrath, and the servant looked almost ill, obviously fearing he would be lucky if he escaped his lordship's anger with only his employment lost. Then, without a word, Christian headed down the stairs toward the door. As he'd never removed his greatcoat, he lost little time. He paused just long enough to issue further orders.

"Let's see if you can carry this out, Waites," he said coldly to the servant, who had followed. "I want you to get word to Mortimer that Anne is gone. I'm going now to look for her. I'll start at that cottage she sometimes visits. Tell Mortimer he should send men around as well, in every direction. She is to be brought back immediately. And Waites," he added, "don't delay. And don't fail me again."

"Yes, my lord. I won't fail you." Then he was off to find his own greatcoat.

Christian hastily chose a different horse from the Thornton stables, wanting the optimum speed and knowing his own horse wasn't fresh enough after the long ride from the north grove. He sped from Highcrest, all the while cursing Waites and himself for trusting the servant at all. But most of all, he cursed Anne. She was gone, and all Christian felt was panic for her safety—for her and their son. And guilt that he'd pushed her into this foolishness.

He turned up the collar of his greatcoat as the wind

whipped against his face and neck, getting under his clothes and chilling him to the bone. God, but it was cold! Please let them be at the cottage, safe and warm before a hearty fire. But even as he prayed the desperate prayer he knew they wouldn't be there. The coldness surrounding him penetrated his heart with the grim premonition that Anne had left Sussex entirely.

"His lordship is showing great forbearance by giving you warning, Melbourne. You'll have enough time to build your defense before the case is heard in the House of Lords."

Mortimer stood before Jarvis Melbourne, who had nearly collapsed into a tattered wing chair when Mortimer had announced the case of fraud being levied against him—against him and his daughter. His gaze hadn't met Mortimer's since; he stared ahead, as if blind.

Mortimer knew his job was finished, that he had delivered the news, and that was all that had been required. He could leave that very moment and not set eyes on Jarvis Melbourne again until they all met in the House. But he was maliciously hesitant to go; he liked seeing Jarvis Melbourne in such a sickeningly broken state. He'd hated the man since the very first meeting, and had hated him more since he'd sold his daughter into marriage.

"I don't know how you coerced Anne into playing any part of this, Melbourne," Mortimer said evenly. "But I intend to find out. Don't count on her as a cellmate at Newgate."

Mortimer started to turn away but his words penetrated Jarvis's stupor. He laughed, quietly at first, but slowly it built to a loud, mirth filled guffaw. Mortimer faced him again, and watched as he rose from the chair. Jarvis was nearly a head taller than Mortimer, and quite a bit wider. But Mortimer stood still, unshakable.

"How do you know this wasn't all her idea? That I wasn't just a pawn in her scheme? She's the one with the immediate gain or loss, after all."

Mortimer glared at Jarvis. "You'll have a hard time

proving that with your reputation for greed."

"The way I see it, Anne will be the one with difficulties. She was the one who bore the bastard."

Mortimer narrowed his eyes. "And I intend to find out why. I'm sure the case will be found laying the blame at your feet."

Jarvis laid one heavy hand on Mortimer's shoulder, very close to his neck. "You make it difficult for me to like you, Mortimer. If you show too much persistence against me, old man, you may find yourself in worse straights than me—or dead."

Mortimer only smiled. "I'm an old man, true enough. And if you kill me there will be someone else to take my place against you. Besides," he added, "if you murder me, it'll only strengthen the case against you. So do it if you must."

Jarvis dropped his hand to his side, losing whatever trace of smile he'd shown.

"Get out," he said quietly.

And Mortimer did so.

Jarvis headed straight for the bottle sitting on a nearby table, not bothering to pour the burning liquid into a glass. He gulped it down, not even tasting it. There wasn't much left, and once it was gone he gripped the bottle tight then threw it against the wall. But the sound of shattering glass did little to appease his anger.

He searched for his overcoat in the disorganized mess cluttering the parlor of his manor house, cursing all the while. He would go to Anne, he decided. And if she needed a bit more coercion to get him out of this mess, then so be it. He had little doubt that if she took the blame for this the House would be far more lenient with her than they would be with him. Better to have her confess it all rather than himself.

How had the bastard Thornton found out? He couldn't believe Anne had spilled it, knowing her own neck would be endangered—as well as her mother's. Vaguely, he remembered hearing that Guiscard had been seen spending a great deal of money in London. And while Jarvis had been generous when paying Guiscard for his services, the extravagant sums being reported would not have covered such spendthrift tales. Jarvis had thought the stories were merely exaggerated tales of Guiscard's new life. Now he wondered. Perhaps it had been Guiscard who'd betrayed him.

He made his way to Highcrest, thinking of various ways he would deal with Guiscard when the time came. But first things first; he would see Anne and make sure she got her story right when presenting her case to the House of Lords. Then he would find Guiscard and handle him.

29

Anne sat beside Newell in the swaying carriage with David snuggled in her arms. The steady movement had put the child to sleep. Anne, however, despite having gone the entire night without rest, could not so much as think of sleep for herself.

Elsbeth stared silently out the window. There was no longer blatant fear in her eyes, just that old empty gaze with perhaps a bit more grimness than before. When first meeting her, Newell had been pleasant enough and extended his hand in greeting. Elsbeth had cowered behind Anne, and since then Newell had not ventured to say another word to her.

He was more solicitous toward Anne. So far, in the hour they'd been together in the carriage heading toward London, Newell had asked no questions. He'd been happy to see Anne, teasing her at first about the romantic way they were running off together, but then noting her dismay, he had followed her lead and been as quiet as Anne herself.

Now, with David asleep and Elsbeth looking more settled than she had since stepping foot beyond Highcrest grounds, Anne was ready to talk.

"I'm sorry for all of this, Newell," she said quietly. "But I'm very grateful to you for your help."

He reached over to pat her hand, the one resting on David, but then held back, obviously cautious not to wake the infant.

He gave her a smile instead. "I don't want gratitude.

I'm more than willing to help you in any way I can. And I'm happy you're coming to London with me.''

"I just need transportation to the city, Newell," she said. "Once there, we'll say good-bye."

"Oh." He frowned. "But you'll want to give the servants at the Thornton town home time to tidy up a bit. You'll stay with me at Franklin House while that's being taken care of."

She shook her head. "I won't be going to the Thornton town house, Newell."

He was plainly shocked. "Then where—"

"I can't say, really. It's better for you if you don't know."

"Anne," he said slowly, patiently. A frown burrowed deep in his youthful brow. "You don't have to tell me everything, but I'm terribly worried about you. It's as if you're running for your life, sending me midnight messages and urging me to take you to London in secret. If you're in some kind of danger, I'd like to give you more help than just a ride to the city."

She gazed at him, warming to his kindness. "You're good to me, Newell. Too good. I really don't want to involve you in all of my troubles."

"Not even if that's precisely where I want to be?"

She shook her head.

Then he spoke up again, this time briskly. "I won't ask any more questions, then, Anne, but you really must promise me you'll stay at Franklin House. I can't let you loose in the city if you've no place to go."

"Oh, I have somewhere to go. A friend of mine is taking us in. We'll be very comfortable, I assure you of that." She spoke confidently, wishing she could convince herself as well. As much as she trusted Gregory, she did wonder exactly how warmly his brother would welcome two women and a child—only one of the three of them able to earn their keep.

"Then you'll let me visit you, and see after your welfare?"

"Newell . . ." she began, but he spoke again, his worry

more apparent than ever in the desperate tone of his voice.

"It sounds as if you want to simply disappear once you get to London, Anne!"

"That's precisely what I must do."

"Then someone is after you," he concluded. He looked straight into her eyes. "Lord Thornton?"

She smiled. "I thought you weren't going to ask any questions?"

The worry lines on his forehead did not ease. "Anne, I know my family isn't as well off as Thornton is at the moment, but the Franklin name isn't without power. If he's threatened you in some way, why won't you let me protect you?"

"It isn't quite that way, Newell," she said, pausing to choose her words carefully. "I'm afraid I got myself into this mess. And Christian may very well use the House of Lords itself against me; I don't think anyone is powerful enough to help me out of this. That's why I must disappear."

Newell looked more confused by the moment. "I can't imagine how Thornton could use the House of Lords against you."

"I really don't want to explain all of this, Newell. Maybe one day, after things have settled for me, I'll contact you in London. And tell you everything."

He did not show much hope that she would ever do just that. They settled once again into silence, though this one was a bit more uneasy.

The seaside cottage was empty of Anne's presence, not surprisingly so. Mistress Markay was there, and had not seen the countess for months. Christian left the cottage more worried than angry. A moment later, with a vision of pure inspiration Christian had sped out to the cabin by the coast, the very one he'd hidden in on those nights waiting to go to Anne. It was a likely hiding place, one she would assume he knew nothing about. But it, too, was empty. Desolately so.

He rode back toward Highcrest, all the while searching his brain for any possible notion of where she could be. He thought of conversations they'd had, old and recent, hoping he would remember something to give him a clue to where she would go. He was hardly paying attention to where he headed, trusting the horse to know the way back toward Highcrest.

Then he saw the road to Wynchly and his pulse raced with another guess. Newell Franklin. Who else could she have gone to? Who else could have helped her get away from the quiet isolation of Sussex? Newell Franklin, if Christian had read him at all correctly, would do anything for Anne. Including taking her to London with him.

He kicked his horse and though this mount wasn't nearly as fast as his Arabian would have been, they raced toward Wynchly at breakneck speed.

Jarvis pulled his horse to a slower gait; he wasn't used to dashing down the pitted road leading out of Sussex. Twice he'd nearly been thrown from his horse and had kept astride by the sheer grace of God. But now he was exhausted, and needed a drink to bolster his energy. He reached inside his coat and pulled out a flask.

He didn't halt his mount entirely, though. He couldn't allow that. Time was against him now. That morning, upon finding Anne gone, he knew his hope lie in finding Guiscard. He was sure it had been Anne who'd somehow let the truth slip, and that's why she'd fled. He would find her, with the help of the men he'd commissioned to go after her once again. Probably on her way back to that convent, with her mad mother and infant bastard in tow. Little chance of any convent giving them shelter, unless she'd been clever to steal enough gold from Highcrest to bribe her way in. His men would find her, Jarvis was sure, and he could deal with her later. It was Guiscard he needed now, and he could not have trusted any one of his men to confront that wily Frenchman. It was a delicate situation, and Jarvis didn't want Guiscard fleeing if one of his men blundered when contacting him. Jarvis didn't want to scare Guiscard away. He needed him too much—not just his physical presence, but his cooperation. Thus the harried ride on the road to London.

With Guiscard's testimony he could build a strong case

against Anne. Once Jarvis convinced her to confess, it would
put the final seal on Jarvis's own redemption. He was sure it
would work; Anne had always done as he commanded
before. She would do so again. He knew she'd rather rot in
prison herself than see her mother locked in chains. Anne
could be easily convinced, especially since Jarvis fully
believed the courts would be lenient with her, a young,
beautiful woman. He knew they wouldn't be so kind to
Jarvis himself.

And Guiscard, Jarvis knew, could be bribed into doing
just about anything. He could even embellish the story and
say he'd bedded the girl because he'd wanted her, not even
reveal the fact that he'd done it for money. It would depend,
of course, on how much the stupid chit had told the
Thornton bastard. All Mortimer had let known was the fact
that Thornton knew the child wasn't Selwyn's, that the child
had been conceived for the sole purpose of stealing the
Thornton fortune. But if all worked the way Jarvis had in
mind, he could see to it that no one took the blame for this
except Anne. Guiscard had acted out of lust, been seduced
by a woman of wiles—surely the House of Lords would
understand that—and Jarvis himself had had nothing at all
to do with it, despite what Thornton believed. How could
anyone prove otherwise? Most especially once he had Anne's
confession?

After a long drink Jarvis replaced the cap to the liquor
and returned the flask to his waistcoat pocket. Then, pulling
closed his overcoat, he kicked his horse back into a faster
pace. He had no time to lose.

Newell reached under the carriage seat and pulled out a
basket, opening it to reveal bread, cheese, wine and cake.
Until seeing the food, Anne hadn't realized she was
famished. He took a sharp, silver handled knife to cut several
slices of bread.

"When did you have time to pack this?" Anne asked as
she accepted a hefty portion of bread and cheese.

"The innkeeper didn't mind the early departure, once
he saw the gold I left for him." Then he smiled sheepishly,

waving the knife in the air as he added, "The final bit of extravagant spending, I promise you."

Then he offered Elsbeth some food, but Elsbeth did not accept it. She did not even look at the bread in his hand. She stared, as if transfixed, at the knife Newell held in his other hand.

Anne set aside her own bread, still holding David in the crook of one arm, and offered Elsbeth the food herself. Anne smiled and tried to speak coaxingly.

"Here, Mother, take some cheese. It's very good, I've tasted it myself."

Still, Elsbeth showed no interest in the food. She did, however, stop staring at the silver knife in Newell's hand. She stared out the window again.

"My mother eats very little," Anne said quietly, handing the portion back to Newell. "She—she is ill, you see."

Anne did not meet his gaze, not wanting to discuss the cause of her mother's illness. The moment was awkward, for Anne already felt uncomfortable accepting so much help from Newell and giving him so little explanation.

Just then, however, she heard the hoofbeats of an approaching horse and she banished every thought. Terror crept up her spine, fearing Christian had found them.

Holding David steady, she leaned toward the window but at the sight of her father she thrust herself back into her seat. She realized her mistake too late. How foolish! Her father had caught sight of her in the single instant she'd stuck her head out, and she saw him just long enough to catch the surprise at discovering her.

"Pull over!" she heard him command, then again when the driver refused to do so.

She spoke above his loud voice. "Newell, it's my father! It's him I've been running from. Tell your driver to keep going!"

Newell's full mouth dropped open for one ignoble second. Then, thrusting aside the basket of food and letting it tumble to the floor, he rapped firmly on the ceiling of the coach.

"Keep going, driver. And hurry!"

The pace quickly increased, and the ride became so bumpy over the rutted roads that Anne could not ease every jolt. David awakened with a cry. Anne tried to calm him but despite her efforts, which she knew were hardly convincing since she felt pure horror herself, David's cries did not cease.

A moment later her father caught up to the carriage and raced alongside, flintlock in hand. The weapon was long-barreled and deadly, and aimed upward toward the back of the driver. Before Anne could cry out a warning, the flintlock exploded.

The carriage at first sped along at a greater speed, the horses obviously skittish after the gunshot. But after a few minutes of frenzied running, they must have felt a lack of direction from the driver and slowed, eventually halting entirely some distance off the road on an open field.

Newell's face was white, but he pulled Anne back when she moved to disembark.

"Stay inside. I'll face him."

"Newell—"

"I want to see to my driver as well," he said. Then he stepped outside, closing the door behind him.

It took Jarvis a few minutes to catch up to them, and by that time Newell had already called to Anne that his driver was indeed dead by a fatal wound to the head. When Jarvis reached them a moment later, holding a second flintlock in his hand this time aimed at Newell, Anne knew a moment of pure helplessness. She wanted to protect them all, Newell with his courage, Elsbeth with her blank stare, and most especially David, whom she held tight. Anne hugged her child to her and eventually his cries ceased. And though she dreaded every word, she could hear the exchange between Newell and her father. She watched, powerlessly, with increasing dread.

"I have no idea what it is you're after, sir," Newell said firmly, standing tall and stiff, "but you've committed murder and will be hanged."

Jarvis laughed, dismounting and stepping closer.

"These roads are full of highwaymen," he said. "I'm sure you can be persuaded to say it was one of those dastardly fellows who took your driver's life."

Newell gazed at him in amazement. "Now why should I want to do such a thing for you?"

"If you want to live, you'll do it. So actually, my friend, you'll be doing it for your own good. Now if you'll step aside to let my daughter out of the carriage—"

Newell squared his shoulders. "She isn't going anywhere."

Jarvis frowned. "You really shouldn't stand in the way, young fellow. It would be very easy to kill you and leave your bodies and your carriage, looted of course to look like a robbery."

Newell whitened, but his voice remained steady. "Perhaps you don't know who I am, sir. I am Lord Newell Franklin. If you so much as touch me, I have it in my power to hunt you down and kill you."

Jarvis laughed. "Won't that be difficult, considering you'll be dead?"

"You wouldn't dare."

Anne saw her father and knew that was the wrong choice of words for Newell to issue. Quickly, she settled David into the half-empty basket resting on the carriage floor and prepared to move.

Jarvis raised the weapon in his hand as if to shoot and Anne, from inside, saw Newell shut his eyes tightly. Then, at the very moment the gun sounded, she thrust open the door, hitting Newell with the door soundly on the shoulder and shoving him down.

Not quickly enough, however. She cried out when she saw Newell fall, unconscious. She leapt to his side and pulled open his greatcoat, seeing blood soaking his chest.

Blind anger filled Anne. She stood, with one furious lurch reaching her father and pounding her tiny, ineffectual fists against his hard bulk. All she saw before her was her friend, the one man she'd known who hadn't tried to use her, dead. At her father's doing.

"I hate you!" she screamed, so loudly she felt her throat ache instantly from the strain. "And you'll pay—for once, Jarvis Melbourne—you'll pay for murdering!"

He had dropped the now empty weapon upon Anne's vicious attack, and used both hands to pry her away. Holding her at arm's length, he shook her hard.

"Stop it, Annie, girl! Nobody will pay for either of these murders. Someone will find them and attribute it to another highway robbery, pure and simple. Now stop this fussing."

With that said, he let her go and went toward the carriage. "Is there anything in there worth stealing? We'd better make this look as it should."

He saw Elsbeth then, and laughed upon sight of her. "I should've known you'd burden yourself with her, Annie." He glanced back at Anne and shook his head. "But what's the use?"

All the while David was screaming, the gun shot having frightened him, and Jarvis picked up the basket with surprising care. Anne was there in an instant, snatching her son away.

Jarvis once again shook his head. "I was going to give him to you, girl."

"Why don't you just murder us all, now that we're no good to you?"

Jarvis walked around the back of the carriage as he spoke, obviously looking for loot to make the robbery a convincing explanation for the two deaths. "But you are of use to me, Annie. After all, we have a trial in London to attend."

"You can't mean to actually defend yourself in this," she said, incredulous.

"Well, not myself exactly. I'm the innocent one." He rummaged through the baggage stacked on the back runner of the carriage, conversing as calmly as if they'd been speaking of last night's supper. "It was you who actually did the crime."

He pulled out several cases, in so doing loosening a stack of canvases which had been neatly leaning against the back of the compartment. They fell to the ground in a cloud of dust.

Anne stepped closer as if to catch some of the artwork. Allowing such treatment seemed a desecration to Newell's memory. But with David in her arms she could do nothing. Nor did she want to step any closer to her father.

"If you think I'm going to lie for you before God and man, you're mistaken," Anne said coldly.

Jarvis was busy looking through the satchels and cases and seemed to be barely paying attention to what Anne said.

"You'll do it, Annie. The same way you married Selwyn, the same way you went through with having your little bastard there."

Jarvis emptied a sack of the clothing it contained and used it to fill with goods worth stealing. Once finished, he retrieved the unloaded gun he'd dropped and faced Anne.

"You'll have to walk until we reach someplace I can buy some horses or a carriage," he said. "We can't stay here any longer or someone might see us. We'll have to stay off the road for a while, too. Get your mother."

Anne stayed perfectly still.

Jarvis had started to turn away toward his horse with the booty and begin the long journey back to Wynchly. But when he didn't hear Anne moving to join him, he faced her again.

"Get going," he ordered, his mouth tightening.

With outward calm, Anne turned toward the carriage and placed the basket with David nestled inside on the floor once again. Then she leaned against the open door, folding her arms in front of her.

"We're staying here."

"Annie . . ." he began, warningly.

She shook her head. "No, Father. I'm not going to let you manipulate me any further. This is the end of it."

He let the sack in his hand drop and took two swift steps closer, hitting her soundly across the face. The carriage caught her so she did not fall back, but the impact of the slap sent her head spinning for a moment.

Then Jarvis pulled her arm.

"You can bloody well leave the two of them here for anyone to find; they won't be telling any tales." He laughed harshly. "Let your mad mother care for your infant until help comes along."

Anne struggled against her father, but could not free herself from his iron grip. She fell to her knees but he continued dragging her until, irate, he turned on her and pulled her back on her feet.

Anne used all her weight to try knocking her father down, throwing herself against him. But it was as effective as hitting a stone wall, and his bruising grip on her never eased. Still she fought, kicking, even biting where she could find his flesh—first on his hand where he grasped her shoulder, then when he shook her free she went for him again, this time on the wrist. She tasted blood but she didn't care.

Part of her brain registered sight of her mother, steathily climbing from the carriage. Anne knew she had no choice but to keep up her fight, even though the sight of it must be terrifying Elsbeth. But to give in was to lose her mother altogether.

Just then a huge shadow loomed from the direction of the road. Anne heard the hoofbeats before her father did, for his attention was still solely on her even as she looked behind her father and saw Christian's swift approach. Whatever fear she might have thought she would feel upon him finding her never materalized; she had never been happier to see him. On his face was a mixture of emotion: dread at the carnage around them, terror that Jarvis was in the process of killing her as well.

"Melbourne! Free her or you're a dead man."

Jarvis heard Christian from behind and, holding Anne's neck in a suffocating grip, he backed up toward the carriage. He saw Christian and looked him over as if searching for sign of a weapon, then, confidently, he spoke.

"Hold back Thornton," Jarvis said menacingly. He was heaving for breath from the struggle with Anne, but still his grip was too powerful to break.

Christian slid from his horse, seeing the murder in Jarvis's eyes. He approached slowly, as if dealing with a mad dog.

Jarvis managed a laugh through his deep gasps. "You look almost as afraid as she does, Thornton. What is this, can it be you don't want her dead? When you planned to send her to Newgate before long?"

"No one's going to Newgate," Christian said softly. But then his glance took in the two bodies, the driver still perched on the high seat of the carriage and Newell upon the ground. "At least not Anne."

Jarvis laughed through the wheezing sound of his heavy breathing. "Oh, this is humorous, this is, indeed." He yanked at Anne and she coughed under the momentarily increased pressure. "It looks to me as though the bastard will believe anything you say, Annie, girl. Did she tell you some insane story about protecting that mad mother of hers? You really shouldn't trust her, Thornton. If she betrayed her own father, she can betray you, too."

"No one betrayed you—except Guiscard," Christian said, still staying cautiously back. "He told me the whole plot."

"So my dear little daughter was loyal to the end, was she?" Jarvis wheezed again. "Anything to save that mad mother of hers."

"Why don't you let her go, Melbourne?" Christian suggested in a tone that might even be called friendly, soothing.

Jarvis's eyes widened. "You shouldn't care one way or the other, after what she did to you."

"The way it looks right now, Melbourne, it wasn't her doing."

"Ha," he said tauntingly. "Are your loins doing your thinking or your brain? How will you ever know why she did it?"

"Let her go, Melbourne," Christian said, more firmly. He began an approach, slowly, steadily.

Jarvis backed up. "Stay back, Thornton or I'll kill her

right now.''

"You can't kill her.''

"Oh? With Anne dead and unable to defend herself, the blame can still rest easily at her feet.''

His grip on her throat tightened again and Anne gasped in pain. She was no longer standing on her own power; Jarvis held her so tight he was dragging her like some child's toy as he backed ever nearer the carriage.

And nearer to Elsbeth as well. Step by step, Jarvis backed up to Elsbeth. Anne saw her mother's silhouette getting closer. All at once her mother's shadow moved to meet Jarvis. A bare moment later Anne heard her father grunt, and at that same moment the piercing hold on her throat loosened. Regaining her footing, Anne raised her eyes up to Jarvis, seeing a look of surprised pain covering his dark features. Suddenly his grasp was more for support than suppression and Anne turned to him. Then she saw her mother, the blank stare still there as she gazed at the knife, the very knife Newell had used to cut bread and cheese earlier, glistening with blood in Elsbeth's hand.

Jarvis looked shocked but not overcome; he thrust Anne from him and she fell to the ground with all the force of her father's pain-ridden fury. Anne's head spun and she gasped for air once again, for the solid impact of the hard ground had forced the air from her lungs. But she spared no thought to her own pain; she knew her mother still held the knife.

Christian moved the instant Anne was free. He was upon Jarvis before Anne had even regained her breath, and Jarvis tried to force the younger man away with a well aimed punch. But Christian ducked and the blow hit air. From behind, Elsbeth did not retreat. Instead, her attack resumed.

"Mother!" But Anne's throat was still constricted from the pain of her father's attack. She barely heard her own voice.

Elsbeth's aim found Jarvis's back once again, then a third time before Christian caught the falling man and pulled him just beyond Elsbeth's reach. But by then it was too late; he slipped from Christian's arm in an unmoving heap.

Elsbeth stepped back, collapsing against the side of the

carriage. Anne struggled to her feet, and in a moment Christian stepped away from Jarvis and came to her side, helping her. She went to her mother, taking her in her arms.

"Mother, mother," she whispered. But Elsbeth did not reply. She did not cry, she did not laugh. She simply let the bloody knife slip from her fingers. It landed with a dull thud on the ground.

Her father lay, lifeless, a look of angry pain forever etched in his face. Anne had seen that anger so many times before, but not the pain. She saw the look, then turned away, feeling nothing at all. She pulled her mother's face to her chest.

When Anne looked at Christian, his face was grim.

"Let me get your mother away from here," he said. "You'd better see to David."

David had stopped crying for a while but was wimpering once again. Automatically, Anne reached for him.

Christian swept away some of the debris from the floor of the carriage, gently commanding Elsbeth to go back inside. She did so, even allowing him to help her up the step. Anne moved to follow at her mother's side, but Christian held her steady before helping her aboard.

For one long moment he gazed at her, then at the child still in her arms. He said nothing, nor did Anne. But there was something there in those golden, suddenly moist eyes, which spoke for him. Anne felt her own eyes moisten, but the moment did not linger; neither had any wish to remain where they were.

A moment later Christian pulled the body of the dead driver from the high seat and placed him alongside of Newell. From inside the carriage Anne watched through the window, although she felt as though she were already farther, much farther, away. She felt devoid of feeling, even as she looked at Newell's body once again. Christian stood, as if to take the driver's place, but before doing so he bent beside Newell and listened for a sign of life.

He raised astonished eyes to Anne. "He's alive!" Christian exclaimed.

That was enough to stir Anne to life. She placed David

back into the basket and jumped from the carriage, her heart pounding with hope. She helped Christian put Newell's unconscious body inside the carriage, and once he was laying across the seat opposite her, Anne knelt at his side, holding him to secure his balance on the seat.

Christian climbed onto the driver's seat and minutes later they were back on the road. The nearest village was nearly a half-hour back, and the ride seemed interminable with every bang and bump of the poor roads. Between keeping Newell on the seat and trying to ease her crying son, Anne heartily wished an end to the ride. Her mother sat perfectly still, as if she saw nothing, heard nothing.

At the inn Christian went inside first for help. Anne was almost as dazed as her mother, watching Christian giving orders for Newell to be helped and for local authorities to see to the bodies just outside of town. He was vague when giving explanations, saying the man who had attacked the carriage was one of the men who had died. Anne knew they would all think the attacker had been a highwayman, and she said nothing to dissuade that line of thought.

She had no idea of time. Christian had given her something to drink when they first stepped inside the inn. It was strong and burned its way to her stomach. He gave the same thing to Elsbeth who took it from him trustingly. Vaguely, she thought how odd it was that Elsbeth had so easily accepted Christian.

A while later they were in another carriage on their way back to Highcrest. Christian was with them, and told them Newell was being cared for by a physician he'd summoned from Wynchly. He said the physician was hopeful for Newell's swift recovery. The small, lead ball from the flintlock was easily removed from the shoulder. There would, understandably, be pain for some time, but Christian said Newell had even regained consciousness before leaving his side. Anne had wanted to see him but the physician had not allowed it—and Anne did not have the strength to argue. She stayed at her mother's side, all the while holding her hand.

Silently, Anne watched as Highcrest came into view. She

had left only hours ago, expecting never to see this place again. But now, no matter what, she was glad to be back.

She ventured a glance to Christian with their child asleep in his arms. Christian didn't look her way; he was gazing out the window. Was Christian her enemy? Was she free of her father only to be faced with someone else who threatened her happiness?

Her heart twisted inside. She could not give up David, she knew that. But Christian loved the child, too. And Anne, despite everything, still loved Christian. She couldn't deny that, even knowing he had deliberately deceived her.

Whatever happened, she would not let herself be parted from either one of them.

30

Anne settled David into his cradle. He was well fed and warm and no doubt happy to be back in his familiar little bed. She stared down at him for a long moment, feeling grateful for the thousandth time that the day's horror had not touched him. Not yet, in any case.

She frowned, pulling closed her velvet wrapper. He would have to one day learn of the violence in his family's past, but Anne hoped he would be secure enough in his own parent's love not to let the past effect him. She sighed; she only hoped Christian would let David know his mother's love.

Just then a tap sounded at the door. She answered, thinking it might be Pel again. She was no doubt still worried over Anne's welfare, despite the fact Anne had told her she was sure Christian would be fair when dealing with David's future.

But it was not Pel at her door. Her heart lurched about crazily; Christian stood there, and the mere sight of him sent Anne's insides into disarray—with as much trepidation as pleasure, for he held her future in his hands. For her future was inexorably tied to him as well as David.

He stood there still dressed in the clothes he'd worn earlier. He didn't say anything at first; he merely looked at her, taking in her nightwear despite the relatively early hour. For a moment he looked uncomfortable.

"I wondered if you could join me . . . downstairs. But if you would rather retire for the night—"

"No," she said. She wanted to have this out; there were too many unanswered questions for her to even consider sleep.

"Then come with me to the salon."

He led and she followed, her heart racing all the way. The hallway was cold and she hugged her arms to her; it only added to the chill already growing inside her.

The salon was the warmest room in the house; it was small and the large fireplace spewed forth great heat, and the size of the room contained it well. Once Christian closed the door behind them, however, Anne still felt a chill. It was in her heart, and could not be dispersed.

"Would you like something to drink?" he asked cordially, stepping toward the mantel.

Anne shook her head.

"Have you eaten?"

She nodded. Pel had brought her something soon after Christian had brought her back.

They stood facing each other, Anne on one side of the small room, Christian on the other. They could have been strangers, the formality was so heavy between them.

"Anne," Christian said at last. His voice was quiet; she could barely read any emotion. He seemed weary, perhaps a little sad. But she did not find any anger, and that gave her some small hope. "I want you to tell me the truth."

She looked at him, holding steady his gaze. "I thought you already knew the truth; that's what you said."

He looked impatient. "I want to hear it from you."

"You said you wouldn't care what my explanations—"

"I don't care what I said before, Anne. Tell me now."

She sighed, not looking at him. "You know enough to condemn me."

With three long strides he was standing directly in front of her. He placed his hands firmly on her shoulders and stared straight into her eyes. "Don't play a martyr, Anne, or you may lose it all. Don't you know what is at stake here?"

She stiffened. "David."

He nodded. "David. And more."

She lifted her brows, wondering what he meant. But he

did not enlighten her and she did not want to ask. She was afraid to.

At last he dropped his hands back to his side. He turned from her and took one of the two seats near the desk without even inviting her to do so as well. He looked even more exhausted than before, but as if the battles he'd waged were inward rather than outward. Then he pushed toward her a box which was laying on the center of the desk.

"Your ever faithful lawyer, young Gallen, was here while you were upstairs. He left this for you."

For a moment Anne stared at the box; it was plain, made of rough wood. Then, knowing what it was, she stepped closer and cast aside any trepidation at the extent of her father's evidence, throwing open the lid. Inside was a knife strikingly similar to the one which Elsbeth had used against Jarvis. No wonder she'd been so fascinated by it when Newell had offered cheese upon its blade during lunch. Along with the knife was an old stained and blood-spattered gown belonging to her mother.

"Gallen told me the whole story—or what he knew of it. I knew enough about your father to ask the right questions, and Gallen told me the rest. That Jarvis had buried this in a man's grave—supposedly enough evidence to have your mother put away."

Anne didn't touch the evidence; she replaced the cover of the box and never once let her gaze meet Christian's.

"I didn't want to ask, you know," Christian said at last. He looked straight ahead and from her vantage all she could see was his profile. "I've waited and waited, trying every kind of persuasion I know to get you to trust me, to tell me the truth. If only you would have come to me, Anne. I wanted you to tell me. I wanted you to trust me. Instead you went to Gallen, paid him to help you."

There was something terribly sad in his words, almost as if he'd been asking for love instead of the truth. Anne watched, the chill around her heart just beginning to diminish.

She sat across from him so their faces were even. She watched him closely. "I didn't know you then—I went to

Gallen long before I knew enough to want to trust you."
Then, remembering her own grievances against Christian, she
said, "But *you* were as guilty as I. You purposely came to me
those nights, to give me the heir you thought I wanted, only
to take him away."

He smiled wearily. "I came to you to confront you, to
see if you would really go through with it. I wouldn't have
believed it otherwise."

She stiffened. "You certainly played your part to the
fullest in building the evidence against me."

He leaned forward, earnest now. "I didn't mean to—I
had no intention of going through with it. But Anne, I knew
it was you. I knew it was your embrace, I knew I was kissing
your mouth, holding your body. And I . . . I couldn't stop.
That, I admit, was my mistake. I wanted you too much—and
I let desire rule instead of honor."

She, too, leaned forward. Her pulse was racing again,
and she watched his face intently. "But I thought you
decided to make the plan work for yourself, against me. So
you could keep the inheritance."

He shook his head. "In the beginning all I wanted was
to know if you were capable of going through with it. I was
going to pull back, once I was sure. But I couldn't. After that
first touch, I was doomed. And once having gone that far, I
thought I had to carry on with it. I hoped you wouldn't get
pregnant, and that eventually the truth would come out."

"But I did get pregnant, and you plotted all along to
take David from me." Her words were bitter with
accusation.

He shook his head. "I never plotted, not from the
beginning. I admit I've been more and more angry the longer
you've let this go on. I even convinced myself that someone
so devious couldn't be a fitting mother." He leaned back
again. "I was wrong about that. No matter what, you're a
good mother."

"No matter what?" she said, stiff again.

He continued looking at her. "Don't you think it's time
I heard it from you, Anne? Can you trust me now, with the
whole truth?"

"Don't you know it all now?" Her gaze fell briefly to the box on the desk at their side.

"Yes, I know what's important—why you did what you did. But I also know you've never once trusted me enough to come to me with the truth. But no matter what, I'm in love with you and I hope somehow you'll start to trust me with the truth from now on."

Anne's eyes slowly widened. "You . . . love me?"

"Unconditionally," he affirmed.

Her heart pounded so erratically her body trembled. But, forcing steadiness to her voice, she said, "And if I told you I do trust you? That I wanted to, long ago, but wouldn't let myself?"

"Then I would say we're off to a very good start."

She cleared her throat. There was one way she could demonstrate this trust of hers. There was one thing about her which he didn't know; telling him the truth now may indeed prove the best possible time.

"Do you want to know why I married your father?"

"I have an idea, but I would welcome hearing it from you." His gaze held hers, he was smiling.

"Perhaps you'll be able to prove you trust me, too. By believing I was never a fortune hunter—one who married your father for his money."

"I'm not sure I ever believed that of you—truly believed it."

She smiled crookedly. "You certainly convinced me that's what you believed."

"That was anger, really. I wasn't sure what to believe, not knowing all the facts."

She held his gaze steadily, and the crooked smile faded. "That will never happen again." Then, slowly, she told him about her relationship with his father. "I was coerced into marrying Selwyn. My father reveled in the idea of having access to all the Thornton money, and gave me little choice when Selwyn asked for me. Oh, I was fond of Selwyn," she added, "but I had no wish to marry him. Jarvis told me he would have my mother put in an asylum; I thought I had no choice. In fact, I didn't. The villagers are afraid to come near my mother. They don't understand what's happened to her. They think she's mad. Of course, my father started the stories, and my mother's silence and withdrawal did nothing to counteract the tales. But they would see her locked up out of pure fear of her." She glanced away from Christian for the first time, staring instead at her hands, folded in her lap. "Perhaps they have reason to fear her, in a way. I did not know my mother was capable of doing what she did today."

"She acted only out of desperation, Anne," Christian said. "She was protecting you. If she hadn't killed him, I would have. Are we both mad?"

She raised watery eyes, grateful for the encouragement. She went on with her tale. "It's true that I participated in the plot to steal your inheritance through David. I didn't want to; I hated every part of it. But I had to protect my mother; it was more important to me than whether or not you kept the money."

He leaned closer again, this time so that their knees almost touched. He took her hands in his.

"You did the right thing." Then, when she looked up at him again, he said with a growing smile, "But I don't think you hated every part of it."

"I did, Christian," she assured him. "I felt so guilty—"

He shook his head. "There was one part of this whole thing that you'll never convince me you didn't enjoy. Just as much as I enjoyed it." He kissed her lips briefly, adding, "Conceiving David."

Slowly, her arms crept up about his neck. She was smiling at him, feeling his love cast away every last chill from around her heart. "I thought I could have loved that tender stranger," she told him. "Even when I was falling in love with you."

He pulled her to her feet for a full embrace and pressed her close. "Hmm," he said as he kissed her again. "Perhaps I should have lit a lamp one of those nights so long ago. Maybe we could have worked out all of this way back then. And we'd be married by now."

He would have continued kissing her, but Anne put her hands on his chest, holding him back in surprise.

"Married?"

He looked as surprised as she did. "Don't you want to?"

"Of course, I do! But do you?"

"I thought if I even so much as *mentioned* the word love you would have us walking down the aisle. It's what you expected when I told you I wanted you."

She grimaced. "Then you'll agree to marry me, but only because that's what I want?"

He laughed. "I never thought asking you to marry me would be so much trouble after our previous discussions about it." Then, his tone grew more serious and his gaze bore into hers. "I love you, Anne. And I want to marry you. Will you marry me?"

Her arms tightened and she held him close. She laughed with pure happiness. "Yes!" she exclaimed.

He kissed her again, this time letting his lips linger on hers as all their previous worries quickly gave way to passion.

Still with an arm about her, he led her from the room. He laughed when he saw her initials embroidered on the cuff of her wrapper. He raised her hand to his lips, sliding his fingers over the initials. "You won't even have to change your name, Anne Thornton. Convenient, isn't it?"

She gazed at him, laughing. "Why else would I agree to marry you?"

At her tease, he turned on her, facing her with dark passion blazing in his eyes. "I can think of a few other reasons, Countess. We'll start with the most obvious."

Then he swept her up into his arms and carried her to his room, where Christian proceeded to show her one of those very reasons.